Venge

Hovering like a nurse over Rich Nockleby's barely conscious body, it sings a lullaby as if to comfort him, though nothing could be further from its mind:

> *Nunca tengas miedo de la luna,*
> *mi niño, porque ella te cantará un arrullo . . .*

Vengeance checks its tools one more time to make certain that everything is ready: Sunbeam electric carving knife (battery powered), barbecue tongs, pruning shears, X-Acto knife. A clubby hammer leans against a nearby tree, having served its purpose in driving the spikes. Close at hand stands a five-gallon can of gasoline, fuel for the grand finale. And because this will be hot, thirsty work, Vengeance has brought a bottle of Gatorade and two granola bars.

A gurgling comes from Rich Nockleby's mouth, then a groan. Not much longer now. A few hundred more heartbeats and Rich will be sober enough to appreciate fully what's in store for him over the next several hours. Vengeance plans to savor that first whiff of terror like a sip of good wine . . .

TAINTED BLOOD

A SPINE-TINGLING JOURNEY INTO THE
NATURE OF EVIL

by Andrew Billings

TAINTED
BLOOD

Andrew Billings

JOVE BOOKS, NEW YORK

TAINTED BLOOD

A Jove Book / published by arrangement with
the author

PRINTING HISTORY
Jove edition / April 1997

The Putnam Berkley World Wide Web site address is
http://www.berkley.com/berkley

ISBN: 0-515-12046-4

A JOVE BOOK®
Jove Books are published by The Berkley Publishing Group,
200 Madison Avenue, New York, New York 10016.
JOVE and the "J" design are trademarks
belonging to Jove Publications, Inc.

PRINTED IN THE UNITED STATES OF AMERICA

10 9 8 7 6 5 4 3 2 1

For Leif,
if he's watching

ACKNOWLEDGMENTS

The following people have contributed inestimably to the telling of this story:

Larry McGillivray provided escorted tours of western Oregon's sawmills and a patient explanation of how they work.

Officer Kelly Jennings and the detectives of the Tigard Police Department supplied valuable background on criminal investigations.

Angela Cedillo corrected and beautified my Spanish.

Dan Armstrong helped in the exploration of Pacific Northwest microbrews, an endeavor that continues.

As always, Paula Walker supplied expert editing, inspiration and an elbow in the ribs whenever I needed it.

AB

Prologue

VENGEANCE IS IN NO HURRY. HOVERING LIKE A NURSE over Rich Nockleby's barely conscious body, it sings a lullaby as if to comfort him, though nothing could be further from its mind:

> *Nunca tengas miedo de la luna,*
> *mi niño, porque ella te cantará un arrullo . . .*

The penlight causes the young man's eyelids to flutter, a sign that the methamphetamine has begun to counteract the earlier dosage of sodium pentobarbital. Soon he will thrill to the pain of the punctures in his wrists and feet. The odor of his agony will hang in the air like the perfume of lilacs.

> *Nunca tengas miedo de las estrellas,*
> *mi niño, porque ellas te enviarán un sueño . . .*

Vengeance checks its tools one more time to make certain that everything is ready: Sunbeam electric carving knife (battery powered), barbecue tongs, pruning shears, X-Acto knife. A clubby hammer leans against a nearby tree, having served its purpose in driving the spikes. Close at hand stands a five-gallon can of gasoline, fuel for the grand finale. And because this will be hot, thirsty work, Vengeance has brought a bottle of Gatorade and two granola bars.

A gurgling comes from Rich Nockleby's mouth, then a groan. Not much longer now. A few hundred more heartbeats and Rich will be sober enough to appreciate fully what's in store for him over the next several hours. Vengeance plans to savor that first whiff of terror like a sip of good wine.

A breeze stirs the October night, causing the surrounding Douglas firs to sway and sigh. Vengeance stops singing. A cone drops to a picnic table with a *snick!* and Vengeance flinches, but a glance around confirms that Royal Chinook Park is deserted of anything human except Rich Nockleby. Vengeance doesn't think of itself as human, not anymore, for humans have no sense of justice, no respect for natural checks and balances. They defile everything they touch. Humanity isn't something that Vengeance wants to be part of.

"Wh-what's happening?" the young man moans, coming awake. "Where am I?"

"Royal Chinook Park, next to the creek. If you'd shut up, you could hear the water."

"I-I hurt, man. My arms, my feet—*God!* What the hell has happened to me? *Oh God . . .* !"

Vengeance grins, leans close. "I've drugged you and nailed you to the ground, Richie. Struggle if you want—it won't do any good. You've lost a lot of blood, and you're weak. Even if you manage to pull the spikes up, you won't be able to stand on those punctured feet, much less run away. As for your hands—" A chuckle. "—well, you couldn't make a fist, let alone put up a fight."

Rich Nockleby struggles uselessly against the spikes, then gives up with a whimper. A shiver rattles his naked body. He asks if he's dreaming, and Vengeance assures him that he is not. And like the others before him, he asks why. What has he ever done to deserve this? Who has he ever harmed?

For a moment Vengeance considers telling him the reasons but then decides against it. The kid's only nineteen, a green-chain puller at the Buckthorn sawmill, the simple son of an even simpler filling station operator. This low specimen could never comprehend the fact that he and his kind are a plague, the pliable servants of a demon.

Vengeance sings its death song again:

> *Nunca tengas miedo de la noche,*
> *mi niño, porque la oscuridad es tu amiga.*
> *Recuerda siempre que la Señora está cerca de ti.*
> *La Dama está cerca.*

Vengeance assures itself that Rich Nockleby will be no great loss to the world. Like most of his kindred, Rich Nockleby has never thought deeply about anything in his life. His chief concerns have been getting laid and saving enough to buy new bass speakers for the CD player in his '86 Ranger pickup. He seldom reads, and he accepts at face value most of what he sees on his big-screen TV (for which he's missed three consecutive payments). He hates Bill Clinton, queers and environmentalists, not necessarily in that order. He tolerates only those whom he perceives as being exactly like himself.

"What're you going to do to me?" he croaks, his tears glittering.

"What I've done to all the others. Feel free to scream—sometimes it helps. No one in town can hear you from this distance."

Royal Chinook Park lies across the creek from the tumbledown town of Buckthorn, Oregon, a good half-mile from the Head Rig Bar on Front Street. At this moment most of Rich's buddies are there, hunched over cans of Bud or Oly or Miller Lite, their eyes bleary, voices thick. Someone among them may have wondered where ol' Richie is, why he hadn't shown up at the mill today. Someone else may have joked that maybe the Buckthorn killer got him, which will have provoked laughter all around. Laughter that's just a mite too loud.

"You can't do this," sobs Rich Nockleby. "It's sick. It's not . . . *human*."

"You're right—it's not even remotely human, and that's what makes it great. Hey, you should consider yourself lucky, dude. Most of your breed eventually get cancer or heart disease, or maybe a stroke. You lie around in hospitals for months, maybe even years, while your families wring their hands and wonder how they're going to pay all the medical bills. By the time it's finally over, they're begging God to take you off their hands so they can get on with their own shitty little lives. That's the *human* way, Richie."

Vengeance picks up the carving knife and flicks the switch on the handle. The small motor buzzes like a squadron of angry wasps. Patiently Vengeance explains to Rich Nockleby precisely what it intends to do with each of the arrayed utensils, which spurs the kid to twist and wail. The breeze kicks up again, rustling the Douglas firs, and Vengeance goes to work.

> *Nunca tengas miedo de la luna,*
> *mi niño, porque ella te cantará un arrullo . . .*

Nearly two hours pass before a pair of Rich's drunken buddies stagger out to the parking lot of the Head Rig and—while pissing against the side of the building because the indoor john is full—notice a glimmer of flames in the trees over in the park.

[A]nd yet these ill weeds grow.

—ALDOUS HUXLEY
The Devils of Loudun

PART ONE

1

I

SITTING NEXT TO HIS WIFE'S DEATHBED, PETER COCH-
ran relived a nightmare that took him back more than
fourteen years to the second night of their honeymoon,
when he'd bolted awake, lathered in sweat, gulping air.
He'd dreamed that Sally had found a tumor in her breast,
or in her neck or armpit (the dream wasn't specific on
this point), that she'd fallen sick and wasted away to a
skeleton. She'd died in a hospital room exactly like this
one, lying beneath a MediLogic patient monitor that
beeped relentless doom with her every heartbeat, green
and blue lines spiking across the screen to signal her
failing respiration, weakening blood pressure, dysfunc-
tioning renal system. She'd slipped away from him like
a handful of melting snow, as she was slipping away
from him now.

Pete studied her once-beautiful face, crooked with
death throes, so orange with jaundice that she looked as
if she'd bathed in Merthiolate. Her hands were bony and
clawlike, her eyes huge and unnervingly shiny.

He studied the floral pattern in the bedspread, the Pan-
asonic television set bolted to the ceiling, the texture of
the muted carpet and a dozen other details in the room,
needing to remember them all. He promised himself that
he would call up this scene in his mind often as his own
lonely life wore on, in order to relive the full blast of
desolation and pain—penance for having been so self-
absorbed as to discount the little danger signs that had

popped up repeatedly at the beginning of Sally's sickness. He damned himself for not forcing her to see a doctor before it was too late.

He'd *dreamed* all this, for the love of God. But he hadn't *believed* it.

Sally gripped his hand, a feat of will. Moved her lips, struggled to speak. As Pete leaned close, a tear shot down his nose into the corner of his mouth. "It's okay, Ace," he said. "You don't have to say anything."

"I-I want . . ." She opened her eyes, another feat. "Sarah, Carter. Don't let them see. . . ." She couldn't speak above a whisper, so intense was the pain. She'd adamantly refused to let the doctors increase the dosage of morphine, because she wanted to remain lucid as long as possible. She'd told Pete that she'd wanted to look at his face in her last moment of waking life. "Sarah, Carter . . ."

Pete groped toward the bed table and found the items that their children had brought to the hospital a week ago, the last time they'd seen their mother, the last time they ever would. Sarah, who was twelve, had written a long free-verse poem about what her mother meant to her, recalling past joys and trials, telling how the memory of Sally would inspire her all her life. Sarah wanted to be a writer someday, a poet and a novelist.

Carter, who was ten, had presented an original watercolor of a sailboat on rowdy water, a family of four in the cockpit. The boat was recognizable as the one that the Cochrans had owned but had been forced to sell two years earlier, after Pete lost his high-paying job. Carter had loved that boat, loved the family's sailing trips on Long Island Sound, as had his mother.

Sally clutched the painting and the poem to her chest, the paper crinkling. "Don't let them see me this way," she whispered. "I want them to remember me better than this. Tell them—tell them I'm not really leaving them. And that I'll always love them."

Pete bit his lip, choked back a sob. Nodded.

Her grip tightened on his hand, yet another little miracle. "Promise me, Pete, that you won't let them . . ." She winced with pain, and Pete cursed the cancer-demon silently for the ten thousandth time. ". . . that you'll keep them away from my parents. Promise me, Peter."

"I've given you my word, Ace. We'll be fine, the three of us, so don't worry, okay? We won't need your parents, or anyone . . ."

"Again—*now*! Swear that you'll never let Sarah or Carter even meet them. I need to hear it, Pete. I need . . ." Her voice splintered, and her grip on his hand loosened as she spent her last calorie of strength.

"I swear it. And I promise never to stop loving you. You'll always be my girl, my wife, you hear? You won't ever—" Pete's voice strangled on a sob as Sally's hand went limp, as her face relaxed. She exhaled and didn't draw another breath.

II

THREE DAYS LATER, ON A BRIGHT SATURDAY AFTERnoon in the heat of Indian summer, Peter Cochran and his children hosted a "remembrance" of their beloved wife and mother at their home in the dignified suburb of Rye, New York. Not a lugubrious funeral or a memorial service, for Sally had hated such nonsense, but a simple coming together of friends who needed each other's company right now. No eulogies, no mournful prayers, no superstitious talk about meeting again in the afterlife.

Everyone who attended, it seemed, brought food, and the house smelled thickly of it. Casseroles and pasta dishes, cakes and pies and three-bean-something-or-other, several turkeys, a smoked ham, fruit baskets.

"What're we going to do with all this?" Sarah worried, surveying the crowded countertops of the kitchen. A new arrival had just presented her a Pyrex dish of ravioli. "We'll never be able to eat this much, Dad. It's all going to spoil. Why is everybody bringing food, anyway? Do they think we're poor and can't afford to buy groceries now that Mom's dead?"

In the short eternity since Sally's death Pete had tried to reassure her that the Cochran family would survive, maybe even thrive again, but how credible is a dad who hasn't worked for two years? A dad who can't get anyone to hire him, not even when his breadwinner wife is dying?

"It's okay, Sluggo," he said, using the nickname he'd given her when she was an infant. "Put it on the pool table downstairs. Don't worry about it spoiling. We'll give it away, if we have to."

"Dad, please don't call me that anymore."

"What—you mean Sluggo?" He started to explain that when she was an infant, he'd called her this because she'd fisted her cute little hands and punched him in the nose whenever he picked her up. There'd been a time when she loved the nickname. On her first day of kindergarten she'd even printed Sluggo on her name tag . . .

"Dad, I've heard this a million times. I don't want to be called that name anymore, all right?" Sarah stood there in her grown-up clothes, a deep purple sweater of flouncy cotton and a matching long skirt, the last outfit that Sally had helped her pick out. Within six months she would outgrow it, Pete knew. All too soon she would outgrow her father, too, as twelve-year-old girls have a tendency to do, unless . . .

"Okay," he heard himself say. "I won't call you that anymore."

She nodded her thanks and gave him a bleak smile that barely showed her braces. Her movements and gestures were so full of Sally that he wanted both to laugh and cry—the way she bit her lower lip and folded her arms in front of her, the way she fingered her necklace. She had Sally's barley-colored hair, cropped boyishly short, Sally's blue eyes and wide mouth. And lately she'd begun to carry herself in her mother's tall, self-assured way.

Pete left the kitchen and gave himself over to the mourners who'd thronged the house, suffering a gush of condolences, tearful hugs, squeezes of the hand, pats on the arm. The crowd was mostly Sally's acquaintances at Walker, Schwinden and Cohea, the Madison Avenue advertising firm where she'd started as a copywriter almost ten long years ago. She'd shown an instinctive flair for the ad game and had risen through ever bigger jobs until becoming a senior associate. One of the "big dogs," she'd often joked to her close friends.

The living room was shoulder to shoulder with people she'd worked with, a cross section of the company—lowly clerks, middle-echelon account executives, artists and the three principals themselves, mingling and munching catered food, schmoozing in low tones. Mixed among them were neighbors, acquaintances from PTA, former sailing buddies and a smattering of friends whom Pete and Sally had known at the country club (back in the glory days when the Cochrans could afford the dues).

Pete swam through the crowd like a man adrift in an alien sea, right here in his own house. Though he was on a first-name basis with most of these folks, they seemed like doppelgangers—they had familiar faces, but in their chests beat the hearts of strangers. Then it dawned on him that *he* was the one who had become strange. He'd lost Sally. He'd become a *widower*, for

Christ's sake. Peter Cochran, widower. New guy on the block.

He caught sight of his son in a far corner of the room, sitting alone in a blond leather chair, looking small. Pete went to him, sank to his haunches, leaned close. "So how's it goin', bud? Holding up okay?"

"I guess. When's this going to be over?"

"Another hour, maybe—hour and a half, tops. Why don't you get something to eat, have some punch? I'll save your seat."

"Mom doesn't like it when I eat in the living room."

"Carter, if Mom were with us now . . . if she were still alive . . ." Pete swallowed, took a breath. ". . . she'd make an exception. She'd want you to have something to eat, I know she would. She wouldn't want you to go hungry."

"Rules are rules. That's what she always says." The boy gave his dad a reproachful look that declared, *Mom lays down the law in this house, not you.*

"Well, she was right. Rules are rules." He touched his son's cheek, needing to say so much to him, but not trusting his own voice. When he started to rise, Carter caught his sleeve.

"Dad, are you going to get married again?"

The question was a Sunday punch. The hospice counselor at the hospital had warned that grieving children often ask this question of the surviving parent, but Pete could remember none of her advice. He stared open-mouthed into Carter's deep eyes, and saw another kid who'd lived a long time ago in a western suburb of Chicago. Same narrow face and stick-out ears, same thatch of unruly, chestnut-colored hair. A kid with frightful questions buzzing in his head. He saw himself twenty-six years ago, trying to fathom how his own father could have worked up the gall to die.

He said, "Nobody knows what's in the future, bud.

Right now I miss your Mom so much that I'm almost paralyzed. I can't imagine ever loving another woman. I'm just glad I have you and Slug—'' He caught himself. ''I'm just glad I have you and Sarah. For now, I don't need anyone else.''

''You're going to do it, aren't you? You're going to get married again. You said, 'For now.' That means you're gonna do it later, right?''

''Carter, I didn't mean . . . I don't even know any women who . . .''

''It's okay.'' The boy slid out of the chair and stood. ''Do whatever you want. Mom'll understand, I think. Is it okay if I go upstairs? There's nobody here but old people.''

''Yeah, sure. I'll bring a plate up to you in a little while.''

Pete watched his son twine through the crowd and disappear around a corner. Then someone touched his elbow, and he turned to face a short, middle-aged woman who wore arty-looking earrings and Vuarnet sunglasses. Her hair was a mass of dark, squiggly curls, her dress a drapery of black silk embossed with gold symbols of the zodiac. This was Lara Dischmann, one of Sally's closest friends and a peer at the office. A major creative force in the agency, Sally had often said of her. Lara had visited Sally often during the final, month-long ordeal in the hospital.

''Peter, if there's anything that Eliot and I can do, all you have to do is call. Maybe you'd like to get away for awhile and need someone to take care of the kids. We've got tons of room, you know, and we'd love to have them.''

''Thanks, Lara, I appreciate that. I think I'll stick close to home for a while. The three of us could use some quiet time together.''

''I understand. But if you ever need anything, anything at all . . .'' She pawed through a canvas shoulder bag and pulled out a business card, scribbled a number on the back and handed it to him. "This is our home phone. We're only over in Scarsdale, a hop and a skip from here. You need anything, you call us first. I mean that, Peter.'' She took a tissue from the handbag and dabbed the corners of both eyes without taking off the Vuarnets. "Bless you,'' she said, her voice pinching, and she moved away.

Pete's attention went to the staircase in the foyer, caught by movement in gray flannel. A tall woman alighted and cast a glance in his direction, then turned abruptly away from him and moved behind a knot of guests. She wore mirrored aviation-style sunglasses and a gray flannel business suit that looked too warm for this weather. She had straight platinum hair that seemed artificial, the kind found on mannequins in high-fashion boutiques. Pete tried to remember whether he'd ever met her, then decided he hadn't. Something about her made him uneasy. Why had she gone upstairs—to snoop, to steal?

He started toward her, but she slipped around a corner into the dining room as if to evade him. Dodging guests, he rounded the corner after her, but found only a clutch of innocent doppelgangers picking at the array of food on the dining table. He pushed through a swinging door to the kitchen, where a startled caterer gave him a stare.

"Excuse me," Peter said, "but did you see a woman come in here just now? She's wearing a gray suit, and she has white hair. She looks . . .'' How did she look— suspicious? Dangerous? Pete wondered if his imagination was running amuck.

The caterer answered that he'd seen no one, but then he'd been deeply occupied with the smoked salmon canapés, he confessed. A gorilla could have ambled through the kitchen, and the caterer wouldn't have noticed.

From the backyard came the barking of Gerard, the Cochran family's beloved Bernese mountain dog, whom Pete had relegated to the kennel for the day. Pete went out through the rear door to find the sun deck empty except for wicker furniture and a brightly colored umbrella. The dog continued to bark as Pete descended the outer stairs into the backyard, which was likewise empty of people.

"Gerard, shut up!"

Back up the stairs to the deck and inside again. Across the living room to the foyer, out the front door. Bright sunshine blinded him, but he blinked the world into focus—green lawn, spreading elms at the front of the property, cars parked at the curbs.

A bland Chevy Lumina stood near the mouth of the driveway, and the gray-flannel woman was climbing into it, fastening her safety belt, pulling the door closed. Pete bolted forward as the starter wound, meaning to stop her and find out who she was, what she was doing here. But by the time he reached the brick-paved drive, she was gunning the engine. The Chevy lurched away from the curb, causing an oncoming driver to swerve and hit his brakes hard. The gray-flannel woman rounded the corner to the right and disappeared in a squeal of rubber.

III

ON THE FOLLOWING TUESDAY, LARA DISCHMANN phoned and suggested that Pete come to collect Sally's personal effects from her office at Walker, Schwinden and Cohea. She didn't want to rush him, she emphasized, but Sally's office had been assigned to someone else, and Lara felt that Pete should be the one to pack his wife's things, rather than someone outside the family. So, Pete arranged for a neighbor to drop Sarah and

Carter at school the next morning, which dawned bright and clear and golden with autumn. After the kids left the house, he caught an early commuter train into the city.

Lara met him in the reception area on the forty-eighth floor of the building on Madison Avenue where the firm had its offices. After treating him to a Danish and a cup of coffee in the executive lounge, she led him through a silent corridor to the corner office that had been Sally's. Most of WSC's hourly workers hadn't yet arrived, so the place seemed hushed, almost funereal.

Lara unlocked the door of Sally's office and motioned him through. In the center of the spacious room was a stack of empty cardboard boxes, and on the desk were several rolls of shipping tape, a pair of scissors and a package of stick-on labels. Lara told him to take as much time as he wanted with the packing. If he needed a break for some friendly conversation, she would be in her own office just two doors away.

"Oh, I almost forgot," she said, pulling a slip of paper from her pocket. "This is the combination to the file safe behind those bookshelves. Feel free to go through it and take anything that looks personal. You'll probably find some out-of-date information on various clients— nothing that would mean anything to a civilian, I'm sure. If you see any company secrets, keep them to yourself, okay?"

"Don't worry. WSC's secrets are safe with me."

"Oh, and Peter, we'll ship this stuff anywhere you want. We'll pay the freight, of course. So don't worry about lugging anything out. That includes the furniture, by the way. Everything here belonged to Sally, except the carpet and the paint on the walls."

"Thanks, Lara. This is really decent of you."

After she'd gone he stood a long moment behind Sally's desk and fought an onslaught of new grief. On all sides were things his wife had touched and used, the tools of her profession, mementos, the space she'd filled with her voice. Her presence was damn near palpable, but at the same time chimerical, just beyond his reach.

He heard something, the scrape of a shoe over the carpet or the movement of an arm inside a sleeve, the drawing of a breath—he couldn't be sure. He whirled around and found nothing out of the ordinary. His gaze wandered to a framed print of Georges Seurat's *Bathers*, which he'd given Sally on Valentine's Day seven years ago. Something moved in the glass that covered the picture, the reflection of a bird flying past the window, or the sweep of a cloud's shadow. *Something.* He turned to the window and glanced down at Madison Avenue, where pedestrians swarmed like ants and taxis flowed in a yellow river.

From here he could see grand old hotels like Helmsley Place and Omni Berkshire Place, their upper façades gilded with morning sunlight. Off to his right the Chrysler Building reared proudly into the blue (it was Sally's favorite skyscraper). Beyond it lay the swoopy metalwork of the Queensboro Bridge, spanning the East River into Queens.

These were Sally's sights, he thought. This was *her* perch. She'd worked for it, fought for it, earned it. That death had snatched her away in her prime seemed cruel beyond comprehension.

On her desk were photographs of her family, showing Sarah and Carter garbed for tae kwon do. Pete at the helm of the sailboat they'd once owned, looking stupid in a pith helmet. Even Gerard, soaking wet and skinny-looking after a bath. On the opposite corner of the desk stood reproductions of Henry Moore's *Two Forms*, reduced to figurine size.

What could he do with all these things? he asked himself, sweeping his gaze around the office—display them at home so he could suffer a fresh heartbreak whenever

he happened to glance at one of them? Selling them was
unthinkable. The only alternative was to store everything
in the attic or the basement until . . .

He heard the sound again, or *almost* did. His neck
prickled. Someone was here in this room with him, no
doubt about that now. For a wild moment he let himself
believe that it was Sally, reaching to him from Beyond.
He half-expected the icy touch of her finger on his
cheek. Had she come to comfort him, he wondered, or
to torment him for his occasional resentment of her success?

"Ace? Is that . . . ?"

The room blurred with guilty tears. He'd resented her,
yes, especially after losing his job with Patriot Mutual.
No use denying it. Sally's income had supported the
Cochrans in good stead, letting them keep their presentable house in Rye, their pair of Volvos, the housecleaning service. The kids could still attend a private school,
take tae kwon do lessons and dress in up-to-the-minute
gear. And thanks to Sally's career, Pete could afford to
be choosy in his quest for a new job, which spared him
the humiliation of accepting a lower rung than the one
he'd vacated. Though the Cochrans had given up their
sailboat and a handful of other niceties, they were far
from poor. Ninety percent of American families would
have envied the hell out of them, Pete knew.

Even so, he couldn't help feeling bested by his wife.
She'd risen to a position of importance with a major ad
firm while he'd devolved to the office of househusband.
She'd become the provider, he the dependent, a reality
that hadn't escaped the children. At times, wallowing in
frustration, Pete had become irascible and snappish, but
Sally, bless her heart, had endured with the patience of
a saint. Someday soon the Patriot Mutual debacle would
be forgotten, she'd assured him countless times. Peter

would land a job befitting his enormous talent and energy. Someday soon.

But two years after his firing Peter Cochran still had found no job, befitting or otherwise. He was sure that Patriot Mutual Assurance Corporation had put his name on the industry blacklist, labeling him a loose cannon, a guy with a private agenda who couldn't be a team player. His old company had made him a leper.

The noise came again, a muffled breath or the sliding of fabric over skin. Pete picked up one of the Henry Moore figurines, tested its hardness and heft with a slap into an empty palm. He walked toward the closet opposite the Seurat painting. Someone was inside that closet, an intruder who hadn't counted on anyone being here this morning. Pete's heartbeat hammered in his temples. With his fist tightening on the figurine, he halted and drew breath to demand that the trespasser show himself.

Before he could speak, the closet door blasted open and the gray-flannel woman flew at him, her platinum hair wagging crazily and her skirt riding high on her thighs. She hit Pete like a linebacker, her forearm slamming into his jaw and knocking him headlong into a pile of empty boxes. As he scrambled to get up again, he caught a glimpse of her sneakers—Nikes, judging from the bright swoops on the sides—and she carried a bulky satchel with a shoulder strap, possibly full of things she'd stolen. She plunged through the door into the corridor and pounded away, her footfalls booming through the near-empty office like kettledrums. By the time Pete reached the door, she was gone, whether by elevators or stairs, he never knew.

IV

"WHAT I DON'T UNDERSTAND IS HOW SHE GOT IN," Lara Dischmann griped to one of the beer-gutted cops who'd come to poke around the late Sally Cochran's office. A uniformed security guard stood to one side, looking appropriately sheepish and sipping coffee from a foam cup.

"We pay big money for security in this building," Lara went on. "We've got closed-circuit TV cameras, motion detectors, on-site guards and I don't know what-the-hell else. You'd think we could open a closet without some maniac jumping out at us."

One of the cops shook his head wearily and wet his ball-point pen with his tongue. His name plate identified him as F. McElwain, and he seemed to be the one in charge. He explained that many such intruders were pros who tagged along with maintenance people in order to get past security. Or they phonied up ID cards in order to trick their way in. Or they hid inside a janitor's cart. Experts at blending in, he called them, at looking innocent.

After examining the scratches on the dead-bolt lock on the office door, McElwain added, "In this case, you got someone who's also an expert at picking locks." He jotted something on his pad, then turned his attention to Pete. "Okay, tell me again what this intruder looked like."

Pete described the gray-flannel woman in detail. He explained that four days earlier he'd seen her at his home during the remembrance gathering for his newly deceased wife. Yes, he was certain she was the same woman—same platinum hair with straight-razor bangs, same gray-flannel outfit and mirrored sunglasses. She was tall. Today she wore Nike sneakers, Air Jordans, he thought. After seeing her at the house, Pete had conducted a quick but thorough inspection and had found nothing missing. He'd put the matter out of his mind, having weightier things to worry about—until now.

McElwain grimaced sympathetically, and said, "Look,

pal, I can't tell you we're going to mobilize the whole precinct to collar this lady, especially since nobody got seriously hurt and nothing seems to be missing. But I can tell you there are jerks out there who prey on people who've just had a death in the family. They read about a funeral or a wake in the paper, and they play like grieving friends and go right into somebody's house and steal 'em blind. Happens all the time. My advice to you and your family is to be extra careful for a while. Keep your doors locked, and make sure you know everyone who comes into your house. In this day and age you can't be too careful . . .''

V

AFTER THE COPS HAD GONE, PETE SIPPED COFFEE IN THE executive lounge and gazed through panoramic windows at the skyline of Manhattan. He mulled Officer Mc-Elwain's warning about lowlifes who preyed on bereaved families and decided that the gray-flannel woman didn't fit the category. She hadn't merely intruded into the Cochrans' home, but she'd come *here* to Sally's office, braving organized security, closed-circuit TV and stoutly locked doors. She must have been after something specific, Pete thought, which perhaps explained why she'd passed over silverware and jewelry at the house, as well as notebook computers and artwork here in the office, stuff you'd expect a common lowlife to boost.

Pete wondered whether she was someone Sally had known. A former rival, perhaps, a disgruntled ex-employee of Walker, Schwinden and Cohea. Someone who'd felt entitled to a promotion that had gone to Sally. Maybe the woman craved recompense for an imagined wrong. And maybe she would come back to take another crack at getting it, a thought that gave Pete a chill.

He spent the next hour cleaning out the desk and placing the contents into boxes, which he sealed with tape and labeled. Next he tackled the bookshelves, which held Sally's first-edition collection (mostly by authors Pete had never heard of, the notable exceptions being Theodore Dreiser and Henry James) and recent works on sociology, marketing, psychology and other disciplines that figured into the ad game. Then he dealt with the vases and lamps, the pictures and awards on the wall, the Macintosh PowerBook computer, the organizers, the high-tech digital clock on the desk. He stuck shipping labels on anything that wouldn't fit into a box and stacked the boxes neatly against one wall.

Two hours of packing effectively obliterated Sally's mark on the office. Pete glanced around and felt a pang, as if he'd just killed another part of her. He wondered if this was how it would be from now on, if Sally would die another small death every day as her survivors packed away more material evidence of her life.

He remembered the "file safe" for which Lara had given him the combination. It was where she'd said it would be, behind a swing-away bookshelf, a heavy steel door with a dial next to its handle. He applied the combination and the door swung open, giving him access to two metal drawers, one of which was an ordinary file rack. The other looked like a safe-deposit box similar to those that banks rent out.

A quick perusal of the file rack produced nothing of interest. The folders contained notes on various accounts that Sally had handled, as well as some polling data that evaluated an ad campaign she'd run for a soap maker more than two years earlier. The other drawer was tightly packed with letter-size envelopes, addressed with a strong feminine hand to Sally at various post-office boxes. The most recent had come to a P.O. box in Manhattan, sent only last spring.

Strange, Pete thought. He'd never known that his wife kept post-office boxes.

The drawer contained at least a hundred such envelopes. Shuffling through the first dozen, he noted that the same person had sent them all, someone named Rosa J. Sandoval out in Oregon, from cities like Portland, Eugene, Hillsboro and Buckthorn. They were in chronological order, the earliest postmarked in July of 1978. He opened it, took out three sheets of yellowed stationery and scanned the opening lines, but halted abruptly.

El 9 de julio de 1978
Querida Sally,

Estoy agradecida a tí por tu llamada telefónica de la semana pasada. Verdaderamente necesitaba oírte, y de algún modo tu lo supiste. Tú y yo hemos pasado tiempo juntas . . .

What was this—Spanish? Sally had minored in Spanish at the University of Illinois, while majoring in communications, and she'd spoken it like a native. Pete had majored in economics, minored in English lit. The only Spanish he'd ever learned was *Quiero una cerveza, por favor*, which Sally had taught him a decade ago when they'd vacationed in Mexico—*I would like a beer, please*, ensuring that he wouldn't go thirsty while she was off shopping. He remembered, too, that she'd often sung a lullaby to the kids when they were small, a song with rolling lyrics in Spanish and a haunting melody in a minor key. He closed his eyes and heard that melody in his head, felt a new stab of grief.

He pawed through the stack of envelopes, selecting half a dozen at random and opening them, pulling out the letters in the hope of finding one written in English.

No such luck. Sally and Rosa Sandoval had written to
each other only in Spanish, apparently. And Sally had
squirreled the letters away for more than fifteen years,
keeping them locked up against questioning eyes, including those of her own husband.

Why? Peter asked himself.

He glanced again at the top letter and saw the date—
El 9 de julio de 1978, or July 9, 1978 (that much he
could decipher). And the address, a post office box in a
dormitory at the University of Illinois in Champaign. At
the time she received this letter, Sally had just started
her freshman year in college, having enrolled for the
summer term in order to get a jump on the other incom-
ing freshmen. She and Pete hadn't yet met. The fact that
she'd saved this letter for so many years, together with
the scores of others, could only mean that Rosa Sandoval
had been an important part of her life, a part that she'd
kept hidden from Pete. Another stab.

He'd long ago come to grips with the reality that he
would never know certain fundamental facts about his
wife, for this was how Sally had wanted it. *Insisted* on
it, in fact. She'd never told him anything about her parents or immediate family, except to say that they lived
somewhere in Oregon and that she wanted nothing to do
with them, not ever.

In the early years of their relationship Pete had burned
with curiosity about her childhood, and more than once
Sally's secrecy on the subject had sparked an argument.
He'd felt entitled to know certain things about the
woman he'd fallen in love with, such as where she'd
come from and who her people were. And he'd felt entitled to know why she was so damnably tight-lipped
about them. After all, he'd told her everything about *his*
own past, *his* family.

No matter how much he'd argued, cajoled or even
threatened, Sally had refused to breathe a word about

her parents, her hometown or her siblings (if she even had any). The day she'd arrived at the University of Illinois marked the end of her old life, she'd told him, and the beginning of a new one. Thanks to the availability of academic loans and scholarships she was able to disown her past and sever all ties with it, neither needing nor wanting money from her family. Her past life had ended, and any man who intended to love her had no choice but to accept that fact.

So Peter had accepted it, though he'd occasionally tried to trick her into letting slip some tidbit about her early years. Sally, of course, had stood against such ventures like the Rock of Gibraltar. Despite Pete's frustration, he'd found himself unable to live without her. A week after graduation, they'd gotten married in a quiet civil ceremony with no relatives present, neither his nor hers.

Not once during their married life had they received any kind of communication from Sally's family out in Oregon. No letters, no Christmas cards, no phone calls. Their children had come into the world having only one grandparent that they knew of—Pete's widowed mother who now lived in a nursing home in a western suburb of Chicago. And they had only one aunt—Pete's younger sister, a chemical engineer in Dallas. Sally had exacted Pete's promise never to let Sarah and Carter know their maternal grandparents, and she'd forced him to renew it occasionally, most recently with her final breath on her deathbed.

Pete had grown accustomed to living with the mystery of his wife's past, though his curiosity still itched sometimes. Thankfully, whatever may have alienated Sally from her parents and relatives hadn't affected her basic goodness. She'd been the most decent person he'd ever known, strong and loyal, honest to a fault. She'd loved her kids wholly and selflessly.

Pete packed the letters into several empty portfolios that he'd found in a drawer of Sally's desk. Maybe he would buy a book of Spanish lessons and a dictionary, he thought, take a shot at translating the letters. Or he might find somebody to do it for him, a high-school Spanish teacher who could use a few extra bucks.

Pushing the final handful of envelopes into a portfolio, he noticed that one of them was thicker than the rest, that a fragment of newsprint poked out from under the flap. Pete opened it and took out a bundle of folded newspaper clippings, several of them old and brown. He spread them side by side on the desk, his eyes widening upon discovering that they were in English.

There were six of them, long, comprehensive news stories with handwritten notations in the margins that gave the date and the publication in which they had appeared, the *Portland Oregonian*. The headlines raised the hair on the back of Pete's neck, for each told of the discovery of a young man's hideously tortured body—six murdered men in all. The kickers under the headlines speculated about serial killings, of cults or copycats. And all the datelines were the same: BUCKTHORN.

2

I

BUCKTHORN HAD SEEN BETTER DAYS.

Time was, when a visitor could walk down Main Street and see no vacant buildings with dark, yawning windows, no potholed pavement, no rusted-out pickups hunkering in beds of tall weeds. Time was, when Buckthorn seemed like a rambunctious youth with the bright glint of hope in his eyes. But those days were long gone. Towns, like people, get old and sick. Like people, they eventually wither and die.

This town, what was left of it, lay in northwest Oregon, twenty miles from where the Columbia River flowed into the Pacific Ocean. Though metropolitan Portland lay only thirty-some miles in the opposite direction, Buckthorn's atmosphere was that of an outpost, isolated and rustic. The northern outskirts rose to a high knob known as Mount Olivet, which wore an old-growth forest proudly like a well tailored coat. This was an oddity here, for every other hill within view of Buckthorn looked ragged in comparison, having suffered the savaging of chain saws, bulldozers, skidders and log trucks.

A visitor from the city might have expected the locals to take pride in their unblemished Mount Olivet, but this wasn't so. Buckthorn was a timber town. The vast majority of its three hundred souls drew their livelihoods from the Buckthorn sawmill, which, as its owner proudly declared to anyone who would listen, was the oldest operating sawmill in the state of Oregon. For nearly fifty years the mill had run three eight-hour work shifts every day, but in recent years had cut back to one shift, owing to the fact that the U.S. Forest Service had severely restricted logging on federal land in order to protect the northern spotted owl, an endangered species. Thus, the Buckthorn mill was slowly strangling for lack of precious sawlogs, like scores of other sawmills throughout the Northwest.

When the people of Buckthorn raised their eyes to Mount Olivet, they beheld not the majesty of untouched nature, but fifteen thousand acres of merchantable timber that might sustain their mill and their town for a short while longer, if the powers that be would only get their heads out of their asses.

II

THE MAN WHO OWNED BOTH THE SAWMILL AND THE mountain, Tucker Bannon, lived with his family at the base of Mount Olivet in a fine old Colonial Revival house that seemed out of place amid the rural poverty of this region. These days, his family consisted of his wife, a seventeen-year-old boy whom he called his son, and his Mexican housekeeper of thirty-four years, Esmerelda Sandoval.

Standing on a rise that occupied the equivalent of two full city blocks, Bannon House had Georgian columns, tall brick chimneys and dormers that jutted out from the third story. Rearing above the rude clutter of Buckthorn, guarded on all sides by swaying hemlocks, the house presided over the town like a rich old aunt at a gathering of poor relations.

At sixty-seven, Tucker Bannon was as solid as a tree trunk, sturdy and raw-boned. He'd lived clean, he was fond of saying, having never tasted tobacco, alcohol or a woman other than his wife. He had a determined jaw, bristly white hair that gave way to a bald spot on his crown, and anemic-looking lips over neat dentures. Magnified by rimless bifocals, his eyes were flinty and intensely appraising, while his silver eyebrows made him seem sly even when he laughed. Above his left eyebrow was a reddish mole that bounced and bobbed with every change of expression.

Tucker Bannon wore plaid Pendleton shirts, khaki trousers and polished work boots with steel toes—the simple clothes of a working man—except on Sundays when he put on a plain dark suit for church. He considered himself a godly man, and he preferred the company of other godly men.

On the rainy evening of February 3, 1994, three months after a young mill worker named Rich Nockleby died an unthinkable death, Tucker stood in the bay window of his first-floor study and stared across an expanse of lawn to the front gate, where a black Pontiac Trans Am waited with its headlights on. Having just spoken with the driver via the intercom, he pushed a button on his remote-command device, and the gate swung open. The car proceeded up the drive to the house, the cones of its headlights scooping swarms of raindrops. Another push of the button caused the gate to swing closed again and lock itself. Minutes later the voice of Esmerelda Sandoval came over the intercom.

"El Señor Verduin acaba de llegar, Señor Bannon."

Tucker ground his teeth, for he didn't like dealing with people like Todd Verduin, who would do absolutely anything on God's green earth for money. Sadly, such men were indispensable to a man like himself, who needed certain things done but couldn't afford to soil his own hands. *"Gracias, Esmerelda. Hagalo pasar a mi estudio, por favor."*

He turned from the window and waited while the antique clock on the mantel tick-tocked the seconds away, while the fire hissed and popped in the stone fireplace opposite his desk. Esmerelda knocked twice before showing in Todd Verduin, a slender man of thirty-five who wore a bulky sport coat over a dark T-shirt and badly faded Levis. He carried an expensive-looking leather briefcase spotted with raindrops. Tucker waved him to one of the armchairs near the fire, then asked Esmerelda to bring coffee. The woman nodded and pulled the door closed after her.

"Nice to see you, Todd," Tucker said, offering his hand. "Have a nice flight?"

Verduin shook hands, said the flight had been bumpy out of New York but smooth the rest of the way, and thank God for unlimited beverage service in first class. He was glad to be back in Oregon. New York always made him crazy, all the congestion and noise, the high prices. Absently he reached for the pack of Merits in his breast pocket before remembering that Tucker Bannon abhorred smoking. He apologized and put the pack away.

"Like I said on the phone," Verduin went on, "I figured you'd want to hear what I found out right away. I hope this hasn't inconvenienced you."

"Not at all. I appreciate your driving all the way out here from Portland. Telecommunications being what they are, I've become a firm believer in face-to-face conversation."

Verduin grinned, as if to ask who knew this better than he. One didn't talk about certain things over the telephone these days. Though he billed himself a private investigator, his forte was electronic surveillance and eavesdropping, so he knew well the dangers of unguarded conversation.

In his ten years of service to Tucker Bannon, Verduin had installed hidden cameras at the Buckthorn sawmill in order to catch pilferers and lollygaggers. He'd bugged every phone in the mill office and several in the homes of mill executives, just to keep them honest. He'd even installed an ''infinity transmitter'' in a television set that sat in the office of a rival mill operator, affording Tucker an inside look at a competitor's business strategy. Verduin possessed other skills that Tucker had found useful, but what made him especially valuable was his total lack of ethics.

Verduin placed the briefcase on his knees, opened it, and took out a plastic packet that contained twenty miniature cassettes. He placed a small Grundig recorder on the desk, inserted a cassette into the machine and pressed the fast-forward button to find the desired spot on the tape.

With a slender finger poised on the play button, he looked up and said, ''The first voice you hear will be that of your grandson. There's more of him later, and your granddaughter, too. I'll leave the tapes with you, of course, and you can listen to them at your leisure.'' Tucker nodded, and Verduin pushed the button.

A telephone ringing, a click. A little boy's voice, sounding thick and raspy, as if he has a cold.

''Hello.''

''Hello, I'm calling for Mr. Peter Cochran. Is he in, please?''

''Just a minute.''

Background sounds, muffled voices, footsteps . . .

The reddish mole above Tucker's left eyebrow leapt upward as his face registered surprise. ''You actually bugged their home phone. How on earth did you manage that?''

''You don't want to know, Mr. Bannon. Let's just say I have—ah—an associate who can be very helpful with these things.''

''This is Peter Cochran.''

*"Mr. Cochran, this is Troy Baldwin, associate vice
president for human resources at Telesonix Incorporated
in Boston. I wanted to talk with you personally before
our letter arrives, to tell you that we're very sorry we
can't offer you a position with our firm at this time. We
certainly appreciate the interest you've shown, however..."*

*"I don't understand. Our interviews went so well.
Your vice president for industrial relations said flat-out
that Telesonix needs someone like me. I got the distinct
impression that..."*

*"I'm sorry, Mr. Cochran, but I'm really not at liberty
to discuss this any further with you. I can tell you that
we'll keep your vitae on file, and that we'll..."*

*"It's Patriot Mutual, isn't it? Somebody at Patriot
Mutual got to you and bent your ear about me. Don't
you think I deserve a chance to respond to whatever they
told you? There are two sides to every story, Mr. Baldwin, and I think I'm entitled to tell..."*

*"As I said, I can't discuss this matter. You have my
regrets and best wishes, Mr. Cochran. Good-bye."*

Verduin switched off the recorder and explained that
the call had occurred on November 18, mere weeks after
Sally Cochran had died. Another had come ten days
later, a rejection from a major international grain bro-
kerage in Minneapolis. Verduin played the opening of
that conversation, but Tucker motioned him to turn it
off.

"Patriot Mutual is blackballing him," the old man
said dismally.

"No doubt about it," Verduin said, changing the tape.
"They're doing their best to make sure your son-in-law
never again sees the inside of an executive washroom.
It gets worse."

They listened to three tense conversations between
Peter Cochran and an insurance agent named Raymond

Schorr. The subject was a letter that Pete had received from Patriot Mutual Assurance Company, his former employer, concerning the late Sally Cochran's life insurance policy. The company had declined to pay the two-million-dollar death benefit, citing a "falsehood" that Sally had placed on the policy application—she'd answered no to a question about whether she'd ever had cancer. Her medical records, however, showed that she'd suffered from a common skin cancer at the age of twenty-one. Patriot Mutual had graciously offered to refund the amount of premiums paid over the years, minus "administrative" expenses, but it could not overlook the fact that Mrs. Cochran had "lied" in order to obtain coverage.

"But it wasn't heavy-duty cancer!" thunders Peter Cochran. *"It was just a basal cell carcinoma on her hand, the size of a pinhead! The doctor cured it with a squirt of liquid nitrogen, for Christ's sake. She was a blond and she'd gotten too much sun. You can't deny the death benefit on the basis of a common skin cancer that she had when she was a sophomore in college."*

The underwriting department of Patriot Mutual begs to differ, Raymond Schorr replies. Pete can contest the decision, of course, but this could take up to three years, maybe longer. Plus, he'll need a lawyer, and lawyers need to be paid even if they lose. See you in court.

In the next conversation Pete talked to a man named Philip Julian, the family lawyer. He poured his heart out, telling how he and his kids had counted on Sally's life insurance. He hadn't worked for more than two years, and as yet he'd found no good leads on a job. The mortgage insurance had paid off the house upon Sally's death, but the property taxes were high in Rye, and the maintenance expenses on a house of this size were considerable. Absent Sally's death benefit or a high-paying job, Pete would need to sell the house, pull his kids out of private school and move to a cheaper neighborhood. Too, he would need to hit the bricks and find a menial job in order to keep the wolf away from their door— *any* job, never mind a corporate position appropriate to his MBA. The lawyer promised to do some research and call back.

Click.

The phone rings again, and Pete picks it up.

"Sorry to be the bearer of bad tidings," Julian says, *"but I don't think you've got much of a case against Patriot Mutual. Maybe Sally didn't mean to mislead them concerning her bout with skin cancer—hell, she'd probably forgotten about it, since it happened more than seven years before she filled out the application. But the fact remains that she submitted a falsehood in a statement about her medical history. The company is within its rights to deny payment of the death benefit on that basis. You've got to remember, Pete, that God didn't put insurance companies on earth to lose money. If I were you I'd cut my losses and accept the refunded premiums."*

"Some Christmas present. Thanks for your time, Phil."

"No problem, my friend. I'll knock fifteen percent off your bill."

Esmerelda brought coffee on a tray and administered it wordlessly. Tucker waited until she'd left the study. "What else?"

Verduin inhaled steam from his coffee cup. "If you'd like, we can listen to two more conversations with lawyers, both of whom advised your son-in-law not to take the insurance company to the mat over your daughter's policy. Then we've got calls to realtors concerning the house . . ."

"He's got it up for sale?"

"Right. Trouble is, they're having a ball-buster of a

winter back East. I'm talking snow up to your butt, power outages, the whole nine yards. The real-estate market is in the toilet, and no one expects it to get better until spring.''

"Mmm. Has Peter found work?"

"He's accepted a job with a delivery service in Long Island, driving a truck. I can't remember exactly where. He's supposed to start a training program at the end of March." Verduin consulted a small notebook in which he'd jotted references to the contents of the tapes, meaning to locate and play the relevant conversation. "Farmingdale. The job is in Farmingdale. Care to hear the tape?"

"Never mind."

Tucker wandered over to a glassed-in cabinet that contained his prized collection of guns, some of them old and quaintly venerable, others new and lethal-looking. Pistols, rifles, shotguns, even an ancient blunderbuss that looked like it came to the New World with the conquistadors. He turned back to Verduin, and the reddish mole above his left eye crawled toward the creases between his eyebrows. "How are Sarah and Carter holding up?"

"Okay for now, but it's anybody's guess how they'll handle moving to a new neighborhood, leaving their pals, going to a new school. Kids suffer when they're uprooted." Verduin spoke as if he had experience in such matters. "They've had nasty colds, like everybody else in New York, but they seem to be recuperating. We've got recordings of them talking to friends and their grandmother in Illinois, which I'd be happy to play for you."

"I'll listen to them later."

Tucker sat down at his desk, opened a checkbook and started writing. "You've done yeoman work, Todd, as always. Here's a little well-deserved bonus." He tore out the check, handed it over, his teeth grinding. Five thousand dollars. Verduin nodded his gratitude and folded the check away.

"There's more where that came from if you find Rosa Sandoval," Tucker went on. "For that matter, I'm still interested in obtaining any correspondence between her and my daughter. Bring me those letters, and you'll get a bonus that makes this one look like pin money."

Todd Verduin seemed uncomfortable. "There's no way she can stay hidden forever, Mr. Bannon. Actually I'm quite close to finding her—I'm developing some very promising leads. As for the correspondence, that's a tough nut to crack. You get into somebody's house or office and you're on thin ice. It can be quite dangerous." He glanced at the gun cabinet, and Tucker took his meaning. People were keeping loaded firearms in their houses and offices these days. "Besides, we can't be sure that the letters even exist. They might be in a safe-deposit box, or . . ."

"The letters exist, Todd," Tucker said flatly, and let it go at that. He'd never told Verduin that Rosa Sandoval had sent him photocopies of every letter she'd written to his daughter over the past fifteen years. Letters that could wreck his life if they ever saw the light of day. She'd done this to torment him, to notify him that his fate lay in hands other than his own. No need for Verduin to know this.

"Yeah. Well, I guess I'd better get going," the investigator said, standing. Tucker thought he looked pale, a little frail. A drug user, probably. "I've taken up enough of your time tonight. When should we get together again?"

"Soon. I have another matter that needs your attention, something closer to home. It may require you to put your other cases on the back burner for a while. Are you willing to do that?"

"Ready, willing and able, Mr. Bannon. You're my top-priority client, as always."

As well I should be for what I pay you, thought Tucker, smiling coldly. He pushed a button on his desk, which summoned Esmerelda to show the man out.

III

THEODORE BANNON, TOPPER TO HIS FAMILY AND CLASS-mates, watched from an upstairs window as the taillights of Todd Verduin's Trans Am moved down the hill and disappeared amid the scatter of lights on the main drag of Buckthorn. He tiptoed down the rear stairs, halted at the landing and listened. The faint strains of an electric organ lilted out from the music room in the front of the house—"Just a Closer Walk with Thee," his mother's favorite hymn, played lovingly with her own hands and sprinkled with sour notes. She'd waited until his father's visitor left the house before starting to play, in order not to distract the men from their business. A godly and considerate woman, his mother.

Topper crept through the dining room into the hall and stood stone-still before the oaken doors of his father's study. He pressed his ear to the wood.

Hey, the Verminator hears something in there, ladies and gentlemen, but what is it? Voices, I think—kids' voices, talking on the phone. A tape recording, maybe. Doesn't sound like the radio or the TV. We'll check this out later . . .

Topper turned away from the door and retraced his steps through the dining room, glad that both his parents were occupied. He could safely sneak out now, for they wouldn't check on him until ten o'clock or later, when they were ready to retire for the night. This gave him better than two hours. He was supposed to be doing homework, boning up for a quiz in tomorrow's civics class, but . . .

But the Verminator has more pressing matters tonight, folks.

He stole past the laundry room into the mudroom, which opened onto the rear porch. His hand had just closed on the doorknob when he glanced through the doorway on his left, into the kitchen. Esmerelda stared at him across an island counter, her hands busy with the dismemberment of a chicken for tomorrow's soup. She was dark against the white tiles on the walls, a squat woman with oily eyes and short gray hair. She gave him a look he couldn't read.

Through all his seventeen years Topper had never been more sure of anyone's love than this old woman's. She'd loved him as if he'd been her own. She'd often sung him to sleep at night with an old lullaby in Spanish that her own mother had taught her long ago in her native Mexico, one he sometimes sang to himself when he lay sleepless in his bed, which was often.

He stared back at her and worried for a moment that she sensed what he was up to. Then . . .

Not a problem, ladies and gentlemen. No way would old Esmerelda ever rat on the Verminator. His secrets are safe with her.

He smiled a good-bye to her and darted out onto the porch, where the damp night stung his face. He trotted across the rear lawn to the outbuildings. The rain had stopped, but low-hanging clouds blanketed the moon and stars. The night smelled tartly of moldering bark and fresh green needles, of moss and soil and rain.

He knew the trail so well that he could have followed it with his eyes closed. It rose from the manicured grounds of Bannon House into the virgin forest of Mount Olivet, more a path than an actual trail, until petering out a half-mile later in a thicket of Scotch broom and buckthorn. Reaching the thicket, Topper took out his trusty Coleman flashlight and snapped it on, causing some roosting bird to flap away in panic. Stepping over a fallen log, he waded through a riot of sword fern toward a structure built of smooth river stone, a cabin so choked with moss and holly and vines that it would have looked like a pile of natural forest debris to anyone who didn't know it was here.

Here we are in Rat City, ladies and gentlemen, the Verminator's own private hunting ground, the first stop on tonight's adventure. You can get ordinary rats just about anywhere, of course, but the rats that live here are the smartest and the biggest and the meanest you've ever seen. These are the Verminator's own special rats— accept no substitutes, hear what I'm sayin'? I'm here to tell you that these babies can sing . . .

Topper made the rounds to the wire traps he'd set along the foundation of Rat City and found rats in three of the six—big, active specimens with twitching whiskers, scaly whips for tails and eyes that shone like lasers in the cone of the flashlight. Taking care not to let his fingers poke through the wire mesh, he transferred them all into one cage for ease of transport.

Before heading back to the trail, he swept the light across the front wall of Rat City, playing the beam over the maws of the windows. He half-expected a human face to pop up in a window frame, deathly pale and stonelike. A face that the town of Buckthorn had whispered about for nearly sixty years.

The Mad Witch of Olivet, they called her.

According to legend, she'd lived most of her years alone on this mountainside, having gone mad. She'd met her death in 1934, during a violent confrontation with a logging crew, after which her vengeful ghost had harassed the logging camp and driven the loggers off the mountain, thereby preventing the plunder of her beloved forest. A few oldsters in town whispered that she still returned occasionally to haunt the descendants of the man who'd held the deed to the land back in those days, Noah Bannon, the father of Topper's father—just to remind them who *really* owned the land. The Mad Witch was the reason, some insisted, that no one had yet logged Mount Olivet.

Topper doubted that many in town believed the legend, but then few had actually seen the Mad Witch, unlike himself. He'd seen her up close and personal, in fact.

Once, when he was very small, he'd woken in the dead of night to find her standing at the foot of his bed, staring at him with ice-blue eyes. Before he could take a breath to scream, she'd plunged out his window and escaped like a moth on the wind. Years later he'd seen her on the grounds of Bannon House, prowling among the juniper hedges in her pale, flowing dress, watching. Still later he'd caught glimpses of her face at the dining room window, and again in the parlor, and yet again in the upstairs playroom. Just two years ago, on a hot summer night, he'd even managed to follow her up this very trail to the low stone cabin that he'd later named Rat City.

That's right, ladies and gentlemen, Rat City is where the Mad Witch of Olivet lives, and that makes the place kind of sacred, don't you think? Is it any wonder the rats get so big and fat here, or that they sing so well? They're sacred rats, friends and neighbors, raised by the Mad Witch herself. You may recall that the Verminator actually went into the cabin one time not too long ago, and that he found . . .

Topper shook off that particular memory. It was too ugly.

He hurried down the trail to the grounds of Bannon House and let himself into the gardener's shed, where he picked up a two-quart plastic gasoline can. He had a key, naturally, for the shed was his private domain, his "office." Several years earlier his father had placed him in charge of mowing the vast expanse of grass that surrounded the house, as well as pruning the trees and shrubs, fighting the weeds, and—most important—keeping the grounds free of *vermin*. The old man hated all animals, but he especially hated *vermin*, which he defined as rats, moles, squirrels, raccoons, crows, any kind of wildlife that might poach or leave a mess. So Topper had come to think of himself as the *Verminator*. In the gardener's shed he kept every kind of rodent trap known to the Western world, as well as a .410 gauge shotgun and an array of chemical agents that would have made many a Third-World dictator drool.

He left the estate through the rear gate, which opened onto a brick stairway that led down to Bannon Avenue. At the base of the stairs he turned west and walked briskly past dark bungalows once owned by doctors, bank officers, merchants and other pillars of the community.

This had been an upscale neighborhood in its day, back when Buckthorn was an actual town and not a dump. A derelict school bus, mounded over with thorny blackberries, now stood in the front yard of a home that had belonged to a dentist. The house next to it, once the home of the town druggist, boasted a collection of rusty household appliances in its front porch. Further on was a house so afflicted with rot that it had begun to lean.

He turned south on Second Street, where the Mount of Olives Gospel Church stood on the corner, a white clapboard building with a lighted marquee that displayed in plastic letters the title of the Reverend Randy Roysden's next sermon, "Rebuilding Your Faith." This was the church where the Bannons worshipped every Sunday, where they mingled with the common herd of

Buckthorn over coffee and doughnuts after each service. This was the church in which Topper had attended Sunday school, vacation Bible school, choir practice, confirmation classes, Teen Discipleship, weekly Bible studies and prophecy sessions—not because his soul hungered and thirsted for the Gospel, but because his parents had forced him. These were the activities of good Christians. And that's what his parents had always expected him to be. A good Christian.

Topper cringed when he thought about the countless precious hours he'd lost in that place.

Someday, ladies and gentlemen, the Verminator's going to burn the Mount of Olives Gospel Church to the ground. Maybe he'll do it on a Sunday morning when the service is in full swing, when they're all whooping to high heaven and moaning, "Yes, Jesus!" Maybe he'll chain the doors first, and lock 'em with good strong padlocks, then douse the walls with gasoline and set the whole shebang off with a Molotov cocktail. Should be a good show, so stay tuned . . .

He crossed Columbia Avenue, where the old Allegro Theater had stood empty for nearly a decade. He turned right on Nehalem Avenue, jogging now, the wire cage bouncing against his thigh, gasoline sloshing in the can. The rats squealed occasionally, and Topper thought, *Good voices.*

He moved past Bertinello's Antiques and Tom Sawyer's Saloon, both of which had survived to this day, but who could say how much longer? He went left on Main Street, where Chubby Chuck's Old-Fashioned Cafe stood on the corner, closed until tomorrow. Next to it loomed a ruin that had once housed an International Harvester dealership, surrounded by rust-bucket log trucks that the owner had accepted as trade-ins twenty years ago but had failed to move before the business went belly-up.

Not fifty feet from where Main Street became Highway 49 lay the access road to the Buckthorn sawmill,
which was a cluster of ragged buildings on a hillside
above Royal Chinook Creek. Lumber stood in neat
stacks in the yard, lit by floodlights and attended by a
pair of eighteen-wheel semis that would soon whisk their
loads to a retail lumberyard in Portland or some other
point east of here. Higher on the hill stood the boiler
plant, where two large boilers generated steam to run the
saws.

Topper skirted the chain-link fence that enclosed the
mill and moved quickly up the hillside. When he reached
a plateau behind the boiler plant, he heard the growl of
boilers and smelled the sharp aroma of wood smoke. A
mist always hovered here, even in dry weather, thanks
to three powerful sprinklers atop the roof of the boiler
plant. These kept the roof wet as a precaution against
the sparks and embers that leapt from the smoke stacks
in yellow swarms.

The beam of a flashlight found Topper's face, blinding him.

"What took you so long?" Topper recognized the
voice of Kyle Matzko, a boy two years younger than he.
Like himself, Matzko attended Nehalem County High
School in the town of Paulsen, just nine miles from
Buckthorn. His father worked in the machine shop of
the mill. "We've been waiting here for like forty-five
minutes, man," Matzko griped. "Think we ain't got
anything better to do?"

Three figures stepped forward—Matzko, a second boy
and a girl. Each carried a forty-ounce bottle of Olympia
beer. All smoked cigarettes that glowed like little amber
eyes in the dark.

"Lose the light," Topper ordered, and the beam vanished with a click. "Is everyone here who's coming?"

"We're all here," answered Bunny Coglin. She took

a nip from her forty and a quick drag from her cig. "Can we like get this over with? It's cold, man." She was a tall, painfully thin girl with limp blond hair.

"Chill out," said the second boy, Cory Dunwoody, a sophomore. His father drove a straddle buggy at the mill, as Cory himself would likely do someday, assuming the mill stayed in business that long. "We're paying good money to see a show, and I don't want to rush it."

Several days ago the three had approached Topper at school, having heard the rumor that he had a certain way with rodents and that he could put on a hell of a show when the spirit moved him. Topper was a living legend of sorts, the kind whom the other kids whispered and snickered about behind his back. But this had never bothered him. He existed on a plane above these mere *peones*. He was the Verminator, for Christ's sake. And he was Tucker Bannon's son.

"So when does it start?" Kyle Matzko wanted to know.

"It'll start," answered Topper, setting the cage on the ground, "when I see your money."

The others dug into their baggy jeans for ten-dollar bills, which Topper accepted and folded away. Getting money from sources other than his father always made him feel good.

"What you're about to see and hear, ladies and gentlemen, is a sacred ritual—something only a privileged few ever get to experience . . ."

"As long as they can come up with the cost of admission," Bunny put in.

"Money changing hands enhances the meaning of the ritual," Topper said with solemnity, "a small sacrifice that serves to show your good faith and make you worthy. Besides, you'll take away something tonight that's far more valuable than the pittance you've paid me."

"This is like so *weird*," Bunny said, rolling her eyes.

"I can't believe we're actually doing this."

"And what about *you*?" demanded Cory Dunwoody of Topper. "What makes *you* so worthy, Mr. Verminator?"

Topper shook his head. "People, I'm the high priest. I'm the Son of the Most High . . ."

"Tucker Bannon's kid, you mean," Bunny said, sniggering.

"People, I'm talking about the mill itself." Topper gestured toward the buildings that cluttered the hillside below them. "Tucker Bannon *is* the mill, and the mill is our god, is it not? The mill feeds us, clothes us, gives us useful work to do. It provides order and regularity. The mill is our *life*, say Amen."

"So you're the son of a sawmill," jeered Dunwoody, sipping from his forty.

"That's exactly what I am. What you're about to hear, people, is a hymn of praise to the god who sustains us all, say Amen." He indicated the cage at his feet. "So, without further chitchat, won't you welcome, please, the Rat Choir from Rat City, high on beautiful Mount Olivet overlooking fabulous Buckthorn, Oregon."

The three spectators clapped noncommittally and said Amen, snickering. They fell silent abruptly, though, when Topper unscrewed the spout of the can and started to douse the caged rats with regular lead-free.

"That smells like gasoline," said Bunny Coglin. "You're not actually going to—" The rats squealed as if they sensed the pending atrocity. "Topper, are you *serious*? I mean like you're not actually going to—"

"Ladies and gentlemen, we must have quiet from this moment on, and I must ask you to extinguish all smoking materials. The Rat Choir is very sensitive to distractions from the audience. If you'll all stand back, please . . ."

Topper loved this part. He could damn-near smell the

apprehension steaming off their bodies as the truth
dawned on them. Suddenly he had a gigantic hard-on.
He pulled a box of farmer matches from the pocket of
his jacket and struck one against the rough strip on the
side of the box. Fire balled on the tip of the match,
bathing his broad face with light. The audience shrank
back.

"I give you Shadrach, Meshach and Abednego, the
Rat Choir, directed by yours truly, the Verminator himself. Uh-one and uh-two and uh . . ."

He tossed the match into the cage. A mass of flame
blossomed, and instantly the rats wore fiery robes of
orange and yellow. They started to dance like herky-
jerky puppets. They threw themselves frantically against
the wire walls of the cage, blinded by fire. As if cued
by a conductor, they started "singing" almost in unison,
their screams slicing through the growl of the boilers.

As the three sophomores from Nehalem County High
watched wide-eyed, the Verminator turned toward the
rats and waved, his arms in grand gestures, as though
conducting a choir, a black silhouette against the jittering
firelight. He opened his pants and let his cock spring
free, let it bounce and wave, a third arm for conducting.

" '. . . and they were cast into the midst of the burning fiery furnace,' " he intoned, quoting the book of
Daniel, " '. . . and the fire had no power.' "

This fire did indeed have power, however. The rats'
hideous song rose to a crescendo and died abruptly as
the flames seared their lungs. They stopped writhing as
the fire itself withered, leaving only glowing embers and
three twisted clots in the bottom of the cage. Topper
ejaculated, sending jets of semen into the embers, again
and again and again until he thought his heart would
burst. Within thirty seconds the spectacle was over. The
air stank of charred flesh and fur.

With his hard-on flagging, Topper turned to his audience, who stood mute, their faces sober in the fading glow. Barely able to hold back his laughter, he said, ''On behalf of the late great Rat Choir, the Verminator thanks you and wishes you a pleasant evening. Be careful on your way home, won't you?—especially if you've been drinking.''

He zipped himself up, then picked up the gas can and the cage, which by now had cooled just enough to touch. He headed back down the hill, quietly humming an old Mexican lullaby. He dumped the remains of his Rat Choir in the weedy yard of a once-presentable bungalow on Bannon Avenue, then climbed the brick stairs to the rear gate of the family estate. After reaching the safety of his room, he pulled off his clothes, which smelled vaguely of gasoline fumes, and threw them into a hamper. He switched off the light and lay down on his bed. Alone in the dark, hissing the song of the Rat Choir between his teeth and visualizing their bodies clothed in fire, he masturbated.

3

I

ON THE MORNING OF FRIDAY, FEBRUARY 11, 1994, much of the East Coast lay under a two-foot blanket of fresh snow. The Cochrans' neighborhood in Rye, New York, looked like a Currier and Ives painting, with snowmen standing in the yards of cozy-looking houses, icicles drooping from the eaves and smoke ribboning upward from chimneys. Many suburban schools had closed, and the police were warning citizens to stay off the icy streets except in emergencies.

Around midmorning the phone rang in Peter Cochran's study, and he answered it eagerly, hoping to hear the voice of some corporate headhunter who'd read his résumé and had called to set up a job interview. But it was only the realtor. Undaunted by the weather, she'd hooked a pair of prospective buyers and wanted to bring them by in an hour. Pete gave his blessing even though a house tour was the last thing he needed right now. A severe cold had laid him low. He wanted nothing so much as to knock back a dose of NyQuil and drowse the day away.

The storm had provided a school holiday, so Sarah and Carter were available to help with some quick dusting and vacuuming. Pete tackled a sinkful of dirty dishes in the kitchen, then bundled himself into a parka and cleared the drive and walks with the snow blower. This done, he banished Gerard to his kennel and sequestered the kids in their rooms with orders to stay put until the realtor and her prospects had left (this had become standard operating procedure for showings). By now Pete was coughing badly, the cold winter air having tortured his inflamed bronchial passages.

The realtor appeared promptly at eleven with her prospects in tow, a well-attired couple in their late twenties, she with a cellular telephone, he with an electronic organizer. Pete sized them up and thought, Bright young executroids—good schools, good salaries, Republicans. An hour later the tour was complete, and the realtor shepherded the couple out through the foyer. She winked optimistically at Pete as she pulled the door closed after her, and Pete dared to hope that yes, these were the ones, the destined buyers. Soon they would call with an offer that was ten grand less than the asking price, and Pete would snap it up fast enough to make their heads spin.

Still, the thought of leaving this place gave him a pit in his stomach, for Sally had loved this house. She'd wanted it to be the last one that she and Pete would ever buy, the one in which they grew old and gray together. She'd wanted it to be the house their kids forever thought of as home. Though she was nearly four months dead, Pete often found himself expecting her to walk through a door from the next room, laden with laundry or groceries or gardening tools, wearing a smart-ass smirk as if to say, *Here's a flash for you, big guy—that jugful of ashes on the dresser upstairs isn't me. This whole dying thing has been an elaborate and extraordinarily tasteless gag . . . !*

Selling the place and leaving Rye wasn't an option, of course: it was a cast-in-concrete necessity. He'd accepted a job as a delivery truck driver in Farmingdale out on Long Island, and he was due to start his training in six weeks. He had exactly that long to buy and occupy a house within reasonable commuting distance to his new job, so time was of the essence.

His savings had dwindled alarmingly, thanks in part to hefty COBRA payments that kept the family's health insurance alive, since Sally's employer had stopped paying the premiums upon her death. Too, there were car payments, car insurance, utilities, house insurance and property taxes, the kids' tuition and Sarah's orthodontia, groceries and clothes and fees for this or that activity at school. Because Pete's old employer, Patriot Mutual, had weaseled out of paying the death benefit in Sally's life insurance policy, he needed the money from a sale just to keep the household running, never mind a down payment for a lesser home.

And then there was his top priority: He wanted to transfuse substantial amounts into the kids' college funds, making certain once and for all that lack of money would never again stand between them and first-rate schools.

He meant to say good-bye to his old life—a life in which he'd once been a "quality person" with big hopes and bright prospects. He'd already jettisoned the dreams he'd fashioned for himself, because the main feature of those dreams, Sally, was gone. He meant to live for Sarah and Carter now. He would work to fulfill *their* dreams. The money from the sale of the house in Rye, wisely invested, would serve as their grubstake.

II

SHORTLY BEFORE ONE O'CLOCK THE DOORBELL CHIMED. Gerard trotted into the foyer and started barking as he did whenever a visitor came. Pete had taken some NyQuil and had fallen asleep on the couch in his study, but he came instantly awake when the racket started. He pulled on a pair of slippers and padded to the door, his legs feeling like rubber.

"Gerard, relax," he rasped, patting the dog's head. Gerard sat obediently, panting and grinning. Pete squinted through the peep hole and saw a prosperous-looking couple in their late sixties or early seventies standing in the entryway. Terrific, he thought. More prospective buyers. The realtor must have told them to meet her here. But why hadn't she called to warn him?

He opened the door and gasped, for he knew in an instant who this old couple was, though he'd never before laid eyes on them. The woman was tall and lightly complected, blue-eyed. She wore a forest-green coat of expensive wool. She could have been Sally with another quarter-century under her belt, same straight nose, expressive mouth, blond hair turned silver. The family resemblance was unmistakable. This woman was Sally's mother.

The man spoke, and when Pete looked into his face, he saw Sally there, too, in the high brow and the strong jaw. "Are you Peter Cochran?"

Pete swallowed and grimaced from the burning in his throat. "Yes. And you're . . . you're . . ."

"I'm Tucker Bannon, Sally's father. This is my wife."

"Call me Dolly." The woman offered her hand and a warm smile. As he took her hand, Pete noticed a silver pin on her coat, the outline of a fish, the badge of a born-again Christian.

"And you can call me Tuck. All my friends do. Sorry to show up with no warning. We really hadn't planned it this way. We're in New York on business, in Manhattan actually, and we thought that as long as we were this close, we should see where our daughter lived. So we rented a car . . ."

"You drove all the way up here from the city? In this weather?" Pete thought they must be out of their minds, but he didn't say so.

Dolly recounted with pride how they'd bought a map at the hotel and set out for Rye, she herself navigating. They'd taken the Washington Bridge into the Bronx and gotten on the Major Deegan Expressway, heading north. They'd taken the New York State Thruway up to Yonkers and cut over to I-95 on the Cross County Parkway . . .

"The important thing," Tucker said, shushing his wife good-naturedly, "is that we're here in one piece, praise God. Like I said, we just stopped on impulse. Saw smoke coming out of your chimney, figured you must be home."

Feeling queasy, Pete asked himself, What now? Do I invite them in . . . ? He heard Sally's strangling voice in his head. *"Promise me, Pete, that you'll keep them away . . ."*

"I realize this is awfully sudden," Dolly Bannon said. "We could come back later."

"Or we could go and not bother you again," Tucker put in. "I wouldn't blame you if that's what you wanted. I mean, you certainly don't owe us anything."

The old man stood ramrod-straight in his sensible anorak and overshoes, his rimless glasses fogging in the cold. A strong and steady man, Pete thought, the kind who looks you in the eye and says what's on his mind. The woman, too, had a look of square-jawed honesty about her. Pete felt certain that if he told them to go away, that's exactly what they would do, and they wouldn't hold it against him.

"We wanted to tell you how sorry we are about Sally's passing," said Dolly, laying a hand on Pete's arm. "As you know, we haven't seen her in many years, but we still loved her very much. She was a wonderful girl, and . . .'' Tears welled in her eyes.

"How are the kids?" Tucker asked. "Sarah must be—
what? Thirteen? And Carter's probably about ten,
right?"

"Sarah will be thirteen in May, and Carter will be
eleven in August," Pete confirmed. "They're doing—
fine."

"Good. Good." Tucker studied his overshoes, his
cheeks reddening from the cold. "I suppose they're in
school today."

"Actually the schools are closed because of the
weather. The kids are home with me."

"Son, we don't have any right to ask this, but . . ."
The old man took off his foggy glasses and stared level
at Pete. Above his left eyebrow he had a large, reddish
mole that twitched as he talked. "Do you think we could
meet them?"

"It would mean so very much to us," Dolly said,
wiping a tear with a pink Kleenex. "I wish I could tell
you how many nights I've lain awake in the dark, trying
to imagine what Sarah and Carter looked like, wondering how they're doing in school, praying that the Lord
will walk with them and keep them safe from all the
craziness in this world. You'd be doing us a tremendous
kindness, Mr. Cochran, if you'd let us . . ."

Suddenly Pete started coughing. The fire in his throat
became a blowtorch, and his headache pounded like a
howitzer. He feared for a moment that he would faint.

"I'm sorry, but I really don't feel very well," he managed. "I think I've got the flu, and I . . ." He coughed
again, almost gagged. His eyes watered and his head
swam.

"You poor thing," Dolly said. She pulled off a glove
and pressed a palm to his forehead. "Why, you're burning up. You should be down in bed, not standing here

in this cold doorway.'' She steered him back into the
foyer, snaking her arm around him.

"Please don't worry about me. It's really not that bad,
and I'm . . .''

"Nonsense. You don't want this to turn into pneu-
monia, which is exactly what it'll do if we don't take
care of it.''

Pete heard Tucker Bannon push the front door
closed and felt the old man's arm on his shoulders.
Gerard whined excitedly and danced around the foyer,
his toenails clicking on the tiles, but the newcomers
ignored him, their attention focused on Pete. Something screamed in Pete's head—*"No! You gave your
word . . . !"*

The Bannons guided him into the living room to a
sofa, where he reluctantly lay down as ordered. Dolly
took off her coat and spread it over him, then pulled off
his slippers. She asked where the kitchen was, whether
there were any lemons and honey. She meant to brew
some tea.

"Seriously, I don't need to be taken care of," Pete
insisted, sitting up despite his aching back. "I need to
tell you something . . . you have no way of knowing this,
but Sally—your daughter—made me promise that I
would never let you . . .''

"Dad, is everything okay?" Sarah stood at the foot
of the stairs in a shaft of light from a window in the
stairwell, her eyes round with concern. "I heard the
doorbell, and then I heard you coughing. Are these people here to check out the house . . . ?"

She wore shapeless jeans and an oversized Harvard
sweatshirt. Her blond hair shone like a halo in the shaft
of light, so much like Sally's that Pete felt a pang.

He thought, *Here it goes—I'm going to break the
promise I made to my wife on her deathbed and a hundred times before that . . .*

But he had little choice, he told himself, with the old couple standing here in the living room. He couldn't simply order them out. They'd driven all the way from Manhattan, for God's sake, braving icy roads and snow. Besides, they didn't seem evil. They seemed like good people. Dolly wanted to make tea for him, and Tucker had called him *son*.

"Sarah, these are your—" He tried to smile. "—your grandmother and grandfather from out West, your mother's parents. Their names are Mr. and Mrs. Bannon."

"You can call me Gramps, if you want," Tucker said, stepping toward the girl, his hand extended, a grin consuming his face. "Or you can call me Grampa Tuck."

"And I'd be pleased if you'd call me Gramma," said Dolly. "We've waited so long for this moment—you have no idea. I must say, you're even more beautiful than I'd dreamed you'd be."

Cringing under the weight of the broken promise, Peter half-hoped that Sarah would bound away up the stairs, lock herself in her room and refuse to come out until the invaders had left. But that's not what she did. Smiling through tears, mindless of her braces, Sarah went straight to Tucker and Dolly Bannon and allowed them to wrap her in their arms, as if she'd waited all her life for this moment.

III

TUCKER CALLED THE HOTEL IN MANHATTAN AND ORdered their baggage sent, after which he and Dolly settled into temporary residence in the Cochrans' guest room. For the next five days the old couple waited on Pete hand and foot while he suffered in bed with the flu. They fed him enough orange juice and herbal tea to float

an aircraft carrier. They kept him thoroughly dosed with
cough syrup, hot chicken soup and ascorbic acid tablets.
At least three times a day Dolly coerced him into drap-
ing a towel over his head and hunkering over a steaming
bowl of apple cider vinegar to inhale the fumes, a remedy given her by a naturopath back home in Oregon.
Skeptical of folk medicine though Pete was, he couldn't
deny that the treatment made him feel better.

Dolly and Tucker also took over administration of the
household, for which Pete supposed he should have been
grateful. Dolly prepared passable meals, did the shopping and kept the house tidy. On Sunday Tucker took
the kids to a movie and later treated them to a pizza. On
Monday he became their chauffeur, driving them to and
from school, Sarah to and from her music lessons, Carter
to and from basketball practice. He repeated the routine
the following day, clearly loving it. Both kids gave every
indication of accepting their newly found grandparents
enthusiastically.

Tuck turned out to be a first-rate storyteller. Every
evening at dinner he regaled Sarah and Carter with yarns
about the rip-roaring old days in his hometown of Buckthorn. He talked about lumberjacks and sawyers, trav-
eling gamblers and swindlers and sideshow preachers,
while the kids listened transfixed. Dolly played the part
of a one-woman truth squad, tsk-tsking in the appropriate places, jumping in with something like, ''Tucker,
that's nonsense—he didn't weigh anything near four
hundred pounds, and you know it!''

Pete couldn't remember when he'd last heard his kids
laugh so loudly—

He allowed all this to happen without really making
a conscious decision to do so, feeling like a bug being
swept along in a gutter after a hard rain. Sick with the
flu, he simply lacked both the strength and the will to

turn back the Bannons' "invasion." They simply overwhelmed his household with kindness.

In the small hours of Wednesday morning Pete sat up
in bed, damp with fever, having heard a whisper that
sounded unthinkably familiar. The burnished urn that
held Sally's ashes stood on a dresser opposite the bed,
spotlighted by a moonbeam slanting through a skylight.
The whisper came again, silken and barely understand-
able, but he knew whose voice it was. He'd heard it
countless times in the night, in another age, when the
Cochran family was whole. When he himself was whole.

Peter, you promised . . .

The urn moved, he was sure of it. Or had it *throbbed*?
Squinting now, he saw the stopper fall slowly away. A
column of silvery grains ascended through the neck and
undulated in the moonlight like a living thing. Quickly
the cloud coalesced into a shape that was unmistakable,
Sally's head, taking on mass, acquiring flesh and bone
and skin and hair, casting a reflection in the mirror behind it. Her eyes were closed. Her lips moved as she
whispered his name. Laserlike needles of light escaped
between her teeth, as if she had an embryonic sun in her
throat. *You broke your promise, Pete. How could you do
it . . . ?*

Pete's scalp prickled as the head floated toward the
bed, whispering. Sweat stung his eyes. *Why, Pete? Have
you stopped loving me? Is that it*?

He tried to back away, but he encountered the head-
board. The bedroom had become a deep freeze. His body
shivered, his teeth chattered. His breathing produced
clouds of steam. He nearly pissed himself when he saw
that Sally's head, too, issued steam from its nostrils,
which meant that the thing was no apparition—it had
substance. It gave off heat.

After all we've been through together, Pete, how

*could you do it? Are you that weak? Is your love for me
that small . . . ?*

The head floated to within two feet of his face and
halted. Pete got the hellish notion that it meant to kiss
him, which caused his stomach to do a flop. And Sally
opened her eyes—blazing red eyes with slitted pupils of
gold. A lizard's dreadful eyes, full of killing anger. She
began to sing the lullaby that she'd often sung to Sarah
and Carter when they were babies:

> *Nunca tengas miedo de la luna,
> mi niño, porque ella te cantará un arrullo . . .*

Pete would have screamed, except that he'd never
been able to scream in dreams. He could only croak and
gasp and flail himself awake. Blessed darkness greeted
him. No pale moonlight, no floating head over his bed.

He groped for the lamp on the bed table and snapped
it on. The urn stood in its spot on the dresser, an innocent jug full of lifeless ashes—a "suitable receptacle,"
the funeral director had called it. His eyes bled tears as
he gazed at the thing, and guilt washed over him. Eventually he got back to sleep, but not before stowing the
urn on a shelf in the closet.

The next morning he knew that the flu had broken,
because he woke up feeling like a new man. The dream
was a mere shadow on the cusp of his unconscious. He
showered, dressed and drove the kids to school, reclaim-
ing from his father-in-law the chauffeur's duties.

When he arrived home again, he went straight to the
kitchen, drawn by the aromas of frying eggs and strong
coffee. Tucker sat in the breakfast nook, wearing a plaid
wool shirt with a bolo tie, the *New York Times* spread
before him. Dolly puttered over the range, wearing an
apron of Sally's, on which was stitched, *It's okay to kiss
the cook!*

The old man looked up from the newspaper. "Better hurry up with those eggs and flapjacks, Mother. This guy looks hungry enough to eat a yearling mule."

Dolly set before Pete a breakfast that was heavy on fat and cholesterol—delicious, in other words—and he ate it greedily, spurring Dolly to pronounce him cured of the flu. After clearing away the dishes, she said, "I guess you'll want to have some men's talk, so I'll leave you two alone. If you need anything, I'll be in the living room, reading my Bible and having my prayer time."

Old-fashioned woman, Pete said to himself, watching her go. Thinks of herself as a servant of the menfolk.

Pete and Tucker sat in the winter sunlight that shone through the latticed window of the breakfast nook, each sipping his coffee. The time had come, Pete decided, to ask the questions that had itched in his mind since his in-laws had shown up on his doorstep. No need to pussy-foot around the issues with a man like Tucker Bannon, no need for preliminary small talk.

"How did you find us, Tuck?" Pete asked.

"Oh, we've always known your whereabouts," the old man answered with a faint smile. "In fact, we've kept fairly close tabs on you. We knew when you got married, naturally. We knew about the little house you bought in White Plains after you landed your job with Patriot Mutual. And we knew when you moved to the condominium up in Stamford. I don't mind saying we were tickled pink when you bought this place, which must've been about six years ago, if memory serves." He glanced around the room, indicating his approval of the house that Pete now meant to sell. "We respected Sally's wishes, of course, and kept our distance, but we couldn't let our own daughter just disappear from our lives. I'm sure you can appreciate that."

"You knew about Sarah and Carter, their names and ages. How . . . ?"

"Let's not get into all that, Pete. Suffice it to say that a father keeps track of his child, even if she doesn't want him to."

"Are you saying that you spied on us?" Pete felt a nibble of anger. "What gave you the right, for Christ's sake?"

"Now-now, there's no reason to feel violated. I merely needed to know where you were in case it ever became necessary to contact you." Tucker looked into his son-in-law's face, his gray eyes steady as granite. "You see, I'm a rich man, praise God. I inherited a sawmill and some timberland when my father died, and I've held on to them, kept the mill going all these years. I make and sell studs, pulp and bark dust, like my old man did before me. For the last few years, though, I've been in semiretirement—I let somebody else do the work, for a change."

He went on to explain that the mill employed close to a hundred people, which made Buckthorn a company town, he supposed. Sally had grown up in the house that Tucker's own father had built. She had been his primary heir, and now that she was gone, he'd named Sarah and Carter his heirs. Having legitimate heirs with Bannon blood in their veins was very important to him.

Here he paused and ran a hand over his brushy scalp. "Oh, Dolly and I have another son, Theodore—we call him Topper—but he's . . ." Pete could have sworn that the old man's eyes darkened a shade. "Well, let's say that Topper isn't the ideal heir and let it go at that. You'll understand when you meet him. If you ever come to Buckthorn, that is."

Mention of Buckthorn caused Pete to think about the letters he'd found in Sally's office safe, all written in Spanish. And the newspaper clippings about a string of serial killings—the "Buckthorn killings." He'd stowed the envelopes and the news clippings in a small wall safe in his study. Briefly he considered broaching the subject of the murders to Tucker, but decided that this wasn't the right time. He pressed on. "What happened between you and Sally?"

"She never told you?"

"Refused to talk about it. Said it was part of her old life and that she wanted to keep it behind her."

Tucker's face softened. He admitted that he didn't know exactly what had happened between his daughter and himself, but he guessed that it was the kind of thing that happened between kids and their parents back in the sixties and seventies, maybe even earlier. More than youthful rebellion, he ventured. More like total rejection of everything their parents stood for.

As God-fearing, born-again Christians, Tucker and Dolly had taken their kids to church every Sunday, read the Bible to them, taught them to pray. They'd instilled godly values in their children, raised them to be jewels in Christ's crown. Then one day, out of a clear blue sky, came a lightning bolt. Sally had informed her dad that he was an oppressor, a "member of the illegitimate ruling capitalist class." She declared herself on the side of the poor, the disadvantaged, an advocate for working men and women. Where she'd picked up such inclinations, Tucker couldn't guess. Buckthorn wasn't exactly a hotbed of radicalism.

Looking back, he knew that he'd overreacted to Sally's godless political ideas, that his anger had driven a wedge between them. He'd become a humbler man since then, and he'd asked Christ's forgiveness for having become so angry with his daughter. And Tucker had long since forgiven Sally her heresy, but . . .

"But it's too late now, isn't it?" Pete put in. "She's gone. And she'll never be able to forgive you."

Tucker nodded sadly and sat quiet a long moment. "It's not too late for *us*, though—you, Dolly and me,

the kids," he said. "I've been doing a lot of thinking
and praying about this, Pete, and I've decided that it's
time for the healing to start. God didn't mean for families to split up and wall themselves off from each other.
He meant for them to love one another and help each
other, even if they can't agree about some things. That's
what I propose we do, the Bannons and the Cochrans. I
propose that we become the family we should've been
years ago."

Pete stared into his coffee cup. All this talk about
Sally's alienation didn't quite ring true. She'd never
shown any hostility to capitalism while he'd known her,
not even during her college days when campuses teemed
with hippies and revolutionaries, when radicalism was
as fashionable as bell-bottom jeans. She'd made a career
in advertising, for crying out loud. *Advertising*, the
mouthpiece of capitalism.

"Why now?" Pete demanded. "Why didn't you
make this overture before Sally died? I can't believe you
didn't know she was sick."

Tucker admitted that he'd known about Sally's illness
and its dire prognosis, but he and Dolly had decided to
respect her wishes. The last thing his daughter had said
to him left no doubt about her feelings—and he remembered it as though it had happened only yesterday, the
day she'd left Buckthorn for the University of Illinois:
*If ever you've felt any love for me, don't let me see your
faces for the rest of my life. Don't write, don't call.
Pretend I'm dead, because that's how I'll be thinking of
you.*

Tucker looked away, as if steeling himself. His eyes
stayed dry. "Those were the last words I ever heard my
daughter speak, Pete, and I resolved then and there that
I would respect her wishes, no matter how much pain it
caused us. Naturally I'd hoped that she would someday

change her mind and contact us, but she never did, as you well know.''

Pete felt the temptation to tell him about Sally's dying words, about how she'd forced him to renew his promise never to let the kids meet their grandparents. But he decided that it would only sharpen an old man's pain over something that had happened long ago. Plainly, Tucker and Dolly had never stopped loving their daughter, and this counted for something.

Tucker then changed the subject so abruptly that Pete stared for a moment in surprise. ''I should probably tell you that your realtor has called several times while you've been sick. She's got folks who want to see this place, but I've put her off. Figured there wasn't much good in bringing people in when you were flat on your back with the flu.''

Pete felt his sphincter tighten. He glanced at his watch and noted the date, February 16. Five precious days had slipped away while he'd been in bed, days he needed not only to sell this house but also to find another one, a lesser house.

''Hope you don't mind that I borrowed your study while you were laid up,'' Tucker went on. ''I needed to catch up on some work I brought along from home, letters to write and some reports to read, accountant's recommendations, that kind of stuff.''

He got up from the table and went to the coffeemaker to top off his cup, then stood for a moment next to the table. He took a long, slow sip of coffee, staring at Pete through the steam.

''I couldn't help but notice all the degrees and awards hanging on your wall next to your desk,'' he said. ''Bachelor's degree *cum laude* in economics, master's in business administration from Illinois, memberships in honorary societies. Very impressive, I don't mind saying.''

Oh yeah, very impressive, Pete allowed. The owner of those degrees and the certificates was about to take a job as a truck driver. A commercial chauffeur's license was more useful to him than the hard-won sheepskins hanging on his wall.

Tucker nodded like a sympathetic uncle, unfazed, then asked simply how things had come to this.

IV

PETE CHUCKLED AND KEPT SILENT A LONG WHILE, STAR-ing through the window at a snowy hedge. He'd lost his job, he admitted finally, because he couldn't control his mouth. This had always been a problem for him, even when he was a kid. He would get to talking, and he would say things that should have stayed unsaid.

He told the story about how he'd risen meteorically to associate vice president for underwriting and pricing in one of the nation's largest insurance companies, Patriot Mutual Assurance Corporation. As a young executive he'd manifested all the earmarks of a genuine wunderkind, the stuff of a future CEO, or so many of his co-workers had whispered.

He'd been an idealist in those early days. He'd believed in the fundamental goodness of human beings and the inclination of most to do the decent thing. He'd believed that the insurance industry played a positive role in the economy, that its leaders were good, honest people.

In time his idealism took a pounding, however. He'd discovered that Patriot Mutual's practices in underwriting and pricing were wholly mercenary, that the company cared nothing for those it insured. The size of insurance premiums had little to do with actual risk and everything to do with how much the company could get away with. He'd come to the conclusion that the industry was a parasite, that it sucked capital out of the economy while providing a product that in most cases proved illusory.

Despite the warm and fuzzy ads that Patriot Mutual ran on television—ads that sold the company as a "member of the family" or a "partner you can count on"—Patriot Mutual maintained a huge staff of lawyers whose mission was to find ways to avoid paying claims and obligations whenever possible. The fact that people's lives stood to be ruined wasn't a concern among the company's leadership. Unlike Peter Cochran, Patriot Mutual didn't care about lives. It cared only about money.

In June of 1992, Pete had attended a conference on pricing and underwriting in Minneapolis, as part of a team representing Patriot Mutual. He'd met a writer from the *Wall Street Journal*, who'd come to cover the conference, a winsome young woman whose name he saw no reason to mention to his father-in-law. Pete and this writer, together with several other attendees of the conference, had dined on Greek food one night in a quiet little restaurant in Columbia Heights. Primed by ouzo, Pete had waxed eloquent on the challenge facing the American insurance industry.

In order to avoid causing an "economic train wreck," he'd pronounced with sacerdotal authority, the industry needed to undertake major changes, particularly in the arena of health care. Unless insurance companies acted voluntarily to amend their mercenary business policies, the government would step in and begin regulating them, he'd predicted. For that matter, insurance companies— like banks and S & Ls and other bearers of substantial fiduciary responsibility—should be willing to accept some federal regulation in order to cure the abusive profiteering that had become a matter of business policy within their ranks. He'd elaborated ad nauseam, of course, needing to impress the winsome reporter, who had legs all the way up to her neck.

Pete hadn't expected to read this heresy in the next day's *Wall Street Journal*, which he'd ordered to his hotel room in Minneapolis so he could peruse it over a room-service breakfast. The winsome young reporter had apparently pounded out a story on her notebook computer and sent it by modem to her editors overnight. When he saw the headline and the kicker, Pete had dropped a glass of orange juice into his lap. His stomach had tried to climb into his throat.

EXECUTIVE URGES OVERHAUL OF INSURANCE INDUSTRY'S PRACTICES AND GOALS:

PROFITEERING MAY CAUSE "ECONOMIC TRAIN WRECK," PATRIOT MUTUAL'S PETER COCHRAN WARNS

The phone had rung just as he finished reading. He'd known before he picked it up that he was about to hear the voice of Patriot Mutual's CEO, calling from New York:

"*Peter, I've just read this morning's* Journal, *and I must say you're either a man who's risen to a high position despite incredible stupidity, or you're a disloyal son of a bitch. In any event, you're fired. Use your return ticket to fly back here now. Have your office cleaned out by the close of business tonight.*"

Firing alone was too good for Pete Cochran, the mandarins of Patriot Mutual must have decided, for they'd gone a step further. They'd circulated within the corporate community a black ball with his name on it. They had faxed the *Journal* story to a long list of CEOs, to contacts in a dozen top head-hunting firms and maybe

twenty human resource directors in major companies.
They'd passed the word in steam rooms after tennis or
squash, over drinks at the nineteenth hole.

This guy's a liberal in a Brooks Brothers suit . . .

. . . a loose cannon . . .

. . . a solo bird . . .

. . . advocates government regulation . . .

. . . pops off to reporters . . .

In a twinkling, Peter Cochran's name had become poi-
son on the corporate circuit, and it couldn't have happened at a worse time, the lean-mean nineties, when an
article of faith was doing more with less. Practically
every company in America was seeking ways to down-
size, ways to dump executives over the side. Finding a
corporate job in this environment was tough even for
someone with sterling references, let alone some poor
wretch whose former bosses were taking pains to ensure
that no corporation ever gave him the time of day.

And that was where the story ended, at least for the
old Pete Cochran, the "quality person." Enter the *new*
Pete Cochran, the househusband, the dependent, the guy
with scaled-down dreams.

"So you're selling this house in order to take a job
as a delivery boy out in Farmingdale," Tucker said, his
face betraying neither sympathy nor scorn.

Pete explained that Patriot Mutual had found a way
to avoid paying the death benefit in Sally's life insurance
policy, probably in further retaliation for his indiscre-
tion. The bottom line was that he would soon be flat
broke. Selling the house was his only means of providing for Sarah and Carter, the only way to ensure a decent
future with a good college education for his kids. He
meant to drive a truck in order to make ends meet, but
at least the ends *would* meet. He would become a provider again.

"Who knows?" he added, forcing a grin. "Maybe I'll

take a correspondence course and get into the exciting
world of refrigerator repair.'' The remark fell flat, but
Tucker smiled anyway, causing the mole above his left
eyebrow to move sideways.

V

LATER THAT MORNING PETE CALLED THE REALTOR AND
lifted the quarantine, notifying her that the house was
again available for showing. He was glad to learn that
the young couple who'd seen the place last Friday were
close to tendering an offer and that they wanted to see
the house again. Time to start looking seriously for a
home in proximity to Farmingdale, the realtor suggested,
and Pete agreed, wincing.

Farmingdale.

*So you're selling this house in order to take a job as
a delivery boy out in Farmingdale,* Tucker had said.

Pete was certain that he'd never mentioned the name
Farmingdale to Tucker or Dolly Bannon, or even to the
kids. Yet the old man had let slip that he'd known where
Pete's new job was. Out in *Farmingdale.*

Was this important?

He sat down at the desk in his study and tapped the
blotter with a Mont Blanc fountain pen that Sally had
bought for him years ago while attending an international advertising confab in Geneva. He replayed this
morning's talk in his head, recalling that Tucker had
listened to his hard-luck story as if hearing it for the first
time, even though he was obviously aware of Pete's dire
circumstances.

Why had Tucker listened to the story of woe as if
he'd known nothing about it—merely to hear Pete tell
it in his own words? Or to endear himself by playing
the role of a sympathetic father-in-law?

Pete left the study and drifted into the living room, which had tall windows that looked out on a faultless expanse of snow that stretched to the street. As he stared at a frost-encrusted willow, he endured a chill of loneliness, the kind for which no cure exists short of bringing a wife back from the dead. And for a sinking moment he was unable to visualize Sally's face.

Have you stopped loving me, Pete . . . ?

A moment later her face came back to him, mercifully, her eyes clear and her smile forgiving. That he could have forgotten what she'd looked like, if only for a few seconds, frightened him. He feared that he was coming unhinged.

4

I

WADE BESWICK STARTED THE MEETING AT PRECISELY 7:00 P.M., not waiting for stragglers to show up as he normally did. He pounded his gavel on the pulpit, producing a crack that reverberated like a pistol shot through the nearly empty sanctuary of the Mount of Olives Gospel Church. The turnout was disappointingly small. A grand total of seven people sat in the first pew, and one of those was the pastor, the Reverend Randy Roysden, who didn't count because he was tonight's speaker.

"The February meeting of the Buckthorn Chapter of the Oregon Citizens Alliance will come to order," Beswick intoned, trying to sound enthusiastic. His heart wasn't in it tonight, for he had more important things on his mind than saving the world from creeping homosexuality. "All stand for the Pledge of Allegiance."

At forty, Beswick was soft and pudgy, double-chinned and thick around the gut. He grew his sandy hair long on one side in order to comb it over a bald spot. The bridge of his nose wrinkled slightly, as if he smelled something rancid.

"The secretary will now read the minutes of the last meeting," he declared after the Pledge concluded. He yielded the pulpit to the chapter secretary, Candy Bertinello, a rail-thin woman of fifty whose jet-black page boy didn't look real, whose thick eyelashes looked even less so. She owned and operated Bertinello's Antiques on Nehalem Avenue.

The minutes recounted how the chapter had decided at last month's meeting to gather signatures toward putting a new anti-gay measure on the local ballot, one that prohibited any mention of homosexuality in schools and removed job protection for any teacher found to be gay. Beswick himself had proposed the measure and had pushed it hard, even though the Nehalem county attorney had issued a legal opinion that pronounced it unconstitutional.

Beswick barely listened to the reading of the minutes. He wanted the meeting to end so he could get on with other things, more important things. He was tired of putting on appearances, tired of going through the motions of leadership. More than anything in the world, he wanted to get away from these losers, these jughead sawmill workers and their frowzy wives.

As general manager of the Buckthorn mill, Wade Beswick was one of Buckthorn's leading citizens. He and his family were members in good standing of this very church. For the past eighteen years he'd done exactly what everyone had expected of him, ever the stalwart family man and pillar of the community—good Christian (by outward appearances, at least), devoted father of two boys, crusader against abortion, homosexuals and environmentalists. Whenever he needed to drink and blow off steam, he drove into Portland to an obscure little bar on Barbur Boulevard, where he could loosen up without scandalizing anyone.

Wade Beswick meant to change his life dramatically within the next few months. He meant to put Buckthorn behind him forever, along with his stinking job and his subservience to Tucker Bannon. In fact, he meant to bring down the old tyrant and make himself a millionaire in the process.

Candy Bertinello finished reading the minutes, and no one offered any additions or corrections. Next came the treasurer's report by Marvin Dirkey, owner of Dirkey's Saw Shop on Main Street, a report that took fully thirty seconds. Beswick moved on to committee reports, but none of the committee chairmen had showed for tonight's meeting, which was a good break.

He called for old business. He called for new business. The chapter membership sat silent as wooden Indians in the pew, their eyes following his every move as though they expected him to drop his pants at any moment and wave his pecker at them. If they only knew what he was *really* up to, he thought, holding back a smile.

He introduced the Reverend Randy Roysden, a sinewy man of fifty with a brush haircut and a bushy red mustache. The pastor needed no introduction, since nearly all the local OCA members attended this church. Roysden filled in as a featured speaker whenever Wade couldn't get one, which was often.

Tonight's topic was the Buckthorn murders. After reminding his small audience of the sexual nature of the crimes (as if anyone in town needed reminding), Roysden questioned whether any thinking Christian could doubt that the killer was a homosexual. He suggested that God had allowed this demon to run rampant in Buckthorn, as He'd let AIDS loose upon the world, in order to send a sweet and simple message to normal people everywhere: Stamp out the plague of homosexuality! Stop the recruitment of young kids to the gay lifestyle! Make the world safe for God's natural children!

With his voice pounding in the rafters of the small church, Roysden suggested that God was actually using the Buckthorn killer to illustrate just how low the homosexual could sink—so low as to nail young men to the ground, mutilate them and burn them to death. How much more incentive did the people of Oregon need? he thundered. After eighteen years and eight young lives lost, how long before the people rose up and threw off the yoke of the "homosexualists," of liberals and intellectuals and secular humanists?

The tiny audience applauded enthusiastically.

Beswick had heard this speech before, and not so long ago it would have stirred his blood and fired him up for action. Though he still hated queers and liberals, he'd reached a point in his life at which material concerns superseded political and religious commitments. Fate had given him an opportunity, a once-in-a-lifetime chance to haul himself out of the muck, and he wasn't about to pass it up, even if he needed to turn his back on those he'd called his friends and neighbors for almost two decades.

Roysden's speech finally ended with a short prayer. Beswick took the pulpit, thanked the pastor and thanked the faithful for coming out on a rainy winter night. Then he adjourned the meeting, upon which he glanced at his watch—8:05. Roysden had blathered on for almost an hour.

II

BESWICK GOT INTO HIS FORD EXPLORER AND PUNCHED his home number on the cellular phone.

"Hi, precious—it's me. Listen, something's come up, and I need to go to a meeting. Shouldn't take more than a couple hours, but you never know . . ."

Sorry to miss dinner again. Make sure the boys do their homework, and don't wait up. Love ya. Nancy Beswick had heard it all before, and because she valued

her dental work, she never asked questions. Not anymore.

Beswick drove out of the church parking lot onto Bannon Avenue and went half a block to Main, where he
turned left. He headed south out of town on Highway
49, bound for a Chinese restaurant in the Portland suburb
of Hillsboro, where he would confer with one of the men
who was about to make him rich.

How ridiculously simple all this had turned out to be,
he thought, staring through the swishing wipers at the
rain-soaked highway. Illegal, to be sure, underhanded
and cold-hearted—yes, all those things. But simple and
easy, too. And *necessary*, no question of that.

Eighteen years ago, when he was a shavetail graduate
of Oregon State, Beswick had accepted Tucker Bannon's
offer of the job of safety officer in the sawmill, along
with the old man's promise to groom him for upper
management. Tucker had kept that promise, elevating
Beswick quickly through the ranks, sometimes at the
expense of older, more experienced officers. Tucker had
even financed construction of a presentable four-
bedroom ranch-style for him on the outskirts of Buckthorn, a token of his faith in the bright young college
grad.

Within five years, Beswick had learned everything
he'd needed to know in order to run Buckthorn Wood
Products, and Tucker had promoted him to mill manager. Tucker himself had then started his own slow fade
into retirement, gradually divorcing himself from the
day-to-day operations. Wade Beswick became the sole
authority at the sawmill, except in major financial matters that involved the Bannon family's credit, a rein that
Tucker still held firmly.

Wade had been happy for a time, and he'd performed
up to and beyond Tucker's expectations. He'd married,
fathered two sons, participated in community affairs and

the local church. Next to Tucker Bannon himself, he became the most important man in Nehalem County, a man everyone smiled at on the street.

Over the years, though, he'd watched the town waste away. He'd watched the timber industry change profoundly, seen the mill's profits dwindle. Federal timber became ever harder to obtain, thanks to environmentalists who persuaded the government to tighten restrictions on federal sales of large-diameter, old-growth trees. The firms that best weathered the change were those that upgraded their operations to handle small-diameter logs and produce "value-added" products—not merely lumber, but also furniture, finished products, specialized construction materials. Such upgrades were costly, however, and Tucker Bannon wasn't the sort who spent money on new equipment and technology when the old gear still chugged along.

Beswick had chafed under the weight of old Tucker's obstinacy, and he'd grown frustrated, restless. He'd eventually concluded that he'd hitched his wagon to the wrong star. At conferences and conventions of wood products managers, he'd met classmates who made far more money than he, guys who owned vacation houses on the beaches, drove Mercedes Benzes and sent their kids to prestigious private schools. His former roommate at Oregon State, for example, had become deputy human resources manager for the western region of Weyerhaeuser, a job that paid four times what Beswick made. Even though Beswick had become a sawmill manager at an impressively young age, the mill he managed was the *Buckthorn* mill, which industry insiders deemed an anachronism, a dinosaur. People in the business knew Tucker Bannon as someone who belonged in the 1800s, a stubborn holdout against progress.

Over the years, Beswick had floated his résumé to wood products manufacturers in Oregon and Washing-

ton, and had quietly put out the word that he was looking
for a change. No one in the industry had taken him seriously. Despite his more than a decade of experience in
production management, he'd become known as the cu-
rator of Tucker Bannon's museum. Real manufacturers
wanted real managers, not curators.

One winter morning in 1992, Beswick read a story in
the business section of the *Oregonian* about a group of
investors who'd bought a failing sawmill in central
Oregon with the sole intent of liquidating it. Their profits
came mainly from the sale of private timberlands that
went with the mill. The investors cared nothing for the
mill workers who lost their jobs, nothing about the tiny
community that suffered the devastation of losing its
source of economic life. The investors cared only about
money, as investors always do.

A plan had formed in his mind so quickly that it almost scared him. It required breaking the law, stabbing
his mentor in the back and throwing more than a hundred good people out of work. Unholy though the plan
was, not once did Wade Beswick seriously consider *not*
doing it.

This was what the world had come to, he knew—the
ruthless pursuit of money. Either you joined the hunt, or
you sat on the sidelines with your thumb up your butt.
This was the world of Ivan Boesky and Michael Milken,
a world in which "respectable" giants like General
Electric could be convicted of fraud three times in eight
years. As Dow Chemical, A.H. Robbins and BCCI had
shown, scandal was no big deal anymore, as long as you
took steps either to avoid detection or beat the rap. Betraying a trust was nothing, as long as you insulated
yourself against the backlash.

This was business in America, he told himself, so get
used to it.

III

HILLSBORO. STREETS SHINY WITH RAIN, REFLECTING RIB-
bons of neon light. Beswick parked behind a BMW that
he was certain belonged to the man he'd come to meet.

The lounge of the Chinese restaurant was nearly deserted, this being a Wednesday evening. Beswick stood
a moment in the entrance, his briefcase at his side, scan-
ning the room. He blotted moisture from his forehead
with a handkerchief and tried not to displace the hair
combed over his bald spot. He spotted Paul Garson, who
sat alone at a booth in the rear, nursing a glass of white
wine.

Garson stood as Beswick approached, offered his
hand. Beswick peeled off his raincoat and slid into the
opposite side of the booth. The two traded pleasantries,
talked briefly about the weather, politics. A young Asian
woman with raven-black hair came to the table and
asked Beswick what he wanted to drink. He ordered a
Jack Daniels with a short beer on the side. He watched
the waitress walk back toward the bar, her hips swinging, and a leer spread across his face.

"Look at the pooper on that, would you?" he said.
"I'd eat a mile of her shit just to see where it came
from."

"Pretty girl," Garson allowed with a pained smile.
He coughed. "Did you bring the memos?"

"Of course I brought the memos—what do I look
like, an idiot? Let's relax awhile, okay? I need a drink
to get my head on straight, if you don't mind."

"I don't mind," Garson replied. "By all means, have
your drink. Relax."

Garson looked younger than his thirty-two years,
blond and trim, handsome. He wore an expensive Nau-

tica sweatshirt with sailboats embroidered on it. Probably keeps a sailing yacht at Tomahawk Bay, Beswick thought, or maybe at the Portland Yacht Club. The Garson family had prospered in the timber business since the turn of the century, and young Paul had the smooth, uncalloused hands of a man who'd chosen his ancestors wisely. He was a principal partner in the Conifer Group, a consortium of Portland investors who bought and sold sawmills, log-trucking companies and timberlands. He'd used a portion of his inheritance as up-front money. Nice work if you can get it, Beswick thought.

The waitress brought Beswick's beer and whiskey, then asked if either man wanted anything else. Beswick grinned up at her.

"How about sitting down and having a drink with us, Snuggle Bunny? You could sure brighten up our lives if you wanted to, make us forget about our troubles. How 'bout it?"

The girl backed away from the table, blushing hotly. Sitting with the customers was against the rules, she replied. Then she turned and hurried away.

Beswick sipped his whiskey, chuckled. "Boy, I'd love to get into an Oriental chick some day, wouldn't you?"

"She's just a girl, Wade. You embarrassed the hell out of her."

"She's old enough to serve booze in the state of Oregon, which means she's old enough to do most anything else. Besides, I like 'em young. The younger, the better, as far as I'm concerned."

"I think we ought to get down to business. It's a long drive back to—"

"Hey, you're not queer, are you Paul?" Beswick habitually interrupted people. "Sweet young thing like her should get the old trouser mouse's attention, seems to me." He winked to show that he was joking, but Garson missed it.

"I've been married for six years, Wade. I've got a son who's four and a new baby girl. If you think—"

"I'm *bullshitting*, Paul." He opened his briefcase and took out a stack of manila envelopes, which he handed over. "I know you're an upstanding member of the business community, same as me. Guys like us do things by the book, don't we?"

"These are the memos?"

"These are the memos."

Garson opened one of the envelopes, took out a type-written sheet and squinted at it in the feeble light of the potted candle. A moment later he pronounced it authentic looking.

"It looks authentic because it *is* authentic," Beswick said.

"You actually got the old man to initial them?" Garson pawed through the envelopes, pulled out more sheets and squinted at them.

"It was no problem. Tuck signs or initials anything I put in front of him these days. I've earned his trust, you see, after only eighteen years of working my butt off for next to nothing. He knows I'd never screw him. *Ha!*"

Garson shook his head and stared across the table at Beswick, his young face betraying a grudging admiration. "But these are directives to you that blatantly contravene the loan contract."

"You know that, and I know that. But Tucker doesn't know that. In fact, I'm fairly certain that he doesn't even know about the performance clause. He relied on me to negotiate the loan, and he's relying on me to make sure that Buckthorn Wood Products abides by the agreement. I'd be surprised if he's even read the fucking thing."

"Does he understand that the Mount Olivet timber-lands are the collateral for the loan?"

"Oh, yeah. He's not quite stupid enough to think that the Conifer Group would fork over an unsecured loan of two-point-five million. But he doesn't know that we need to buy the new equipment and get it all up and running by April Fool's Day.'' Beswick took a long pull of bourbon and a quick sip of beer. ''I guess I sort of neglected to point that out to him.''

Garson chuckled softly. ''So he doesn't realize that we're within our rights to foreclose and take possession of the mountain anytime after the first of April?''

''Where have you been, boy? That's the whole point of this exercise, remember? These memos are from Tucker to me, just like you guys wanted. They specifically reject all my carefully formulated plans to spend the money you lent us to upgrade our plant, even though the result could be foreclosure. There are twenty-two such memos, roughly two a month for the past year. So you see, my ass is covered—I was only following the orders of the mill owner.''

''Yes, I see.''

Beswick tossed down the remainder of his bourbon and grimaced. ''I've done everything I told you I would. I got Tuck to buy off on the loan, and I've delayed making the improvements so you can foreclose. You'll get your fifty million dollars' worth of timberland, and I'll get my measly five million. There's no misunderstanding about any of this, right?''

Garson thrummed his fingers on the table. ''No misunderstanding. Everything is just as you say, and as we've stated to you face-to-face more than once, we intend to fulfill our obligation to you in its entirety. You understand, though, that after we foreclose, we can't simply write you a check for five million dollars.''

Beswick didn't understand this at all, and said so— through grinding teeth. Garson explained that a quick, lump-sum payment would attract the attention of the lawyers Tucker Bannon would surely hire to challenge the Conifer Group's foreclosure. They would suspect that Beswick was exactly what he was, a confederate.

Rather than pay Beswick a lump sum, the Conifer Group proposed to set up a dummy corporation that would retain him as a "consultant." His retainer would be a hefty $250,000, and the dummy corporation would pay him the remainder of the agreed-upon five million in installments over three years.

Beswick's face looked as if he'd just suffered an acute gas attack. He protested that his cut of the take was due immediately upon foreclosure, that the Conifer Group had never said anything about spreading his payments over three years. He reminded young Mr. Garson that he could take what he knew to the attorney general's office and probably send all the principal partners of the Conifer Group to prison. By cooperating with the authorities, he was certain that he himself could avoid jail time.

"You'll get your money, Wade—every penny of it," Garson assured him, scowling. "If you let us handle this our way, it'll look like you're merely landing on your feet after Buckthorn Wood Products goes under. You'll be a highly paid consultant to a new company that speculates in wood products assets. You'll pay your taxes like any other good citizen, probably buy yourself a nice house in Lake Oswego or maybe over on the beach somewhere, maybe become a member of a big-time country club."

Beswick backed off. The talk of a house on the beach and the country club membership made him feel warm inside.

"Yeah, well—you've convinced me for now." He waved to the waitress and made a circle in the air with his finger, telling her he wanted another round. "But I need more than a quarter of a million up front. I want at least five hundred thousand."

Garson slumped a little and wiped sweat from his upper lip. "Very well. I'll take this back to the partners, and we'll call you. In the meantime, I'll review these memos with our lawyer to make sure they really indicate that Bannon willfully reneged on the loan contract. If we can't prove that, then we're—"

"Don't worry," Beswick interrupted. "I drafted them very carefully. I'm no idiot, you know."

Garson sipped his white wine and said, "That's for sure. Whatever you are, you're no idiot."

5

I

HOUSE HUNTING PROVED AN EVEN WORSE DRAG THAN Pete Cochran had feared, thanks to a mean cold front that swept through the New York City metro area. With fresh snow flurries and temperatures in the teens, traffic became a Gordian knot. He spent the next three days chasing down leads on Long Island, braving icy streets and stressed-out drivers.

This part of Long Island had none of Rye's Currier-and-Ives quaintness. Utility lines ran overhead in ugly tangles and rusty cars lined the streets. Houses in his price range were drab, cramped structures with tiny yards surrounded by chain-link fences.

Can I stand to live in a place like this? he'd asked himself again and again.

Truth was, he felt qualms over the prospect of moving into a racially mixed neighborhood. Pete had grown up in the lily-white Chicago suburb of Glen Ellyn and had lived in affluent bedroom communities virtually all his adult life. He'd always believed in equality and supported civil rights, but the only blacks or Hispanics he'd known were orthodontists or lawyers who spoke in perfected WASPian English and dressed like bankers. Now he was about to move into a neighborhood where whites were just another minority, where kids passed through metal detectors when entering the schools and armed cops patrolled the playgrounds.

He tried not to be afraid, told himself that this was a

far cry from Bedford-Stuyvesant. These were respectable
middle-class neighborhoods peopled with folks who
loved their kids and worked hard for their living. Black,
white, yellow or brown, they were decent people who
wanted essentially the same things from life that Peter
Cochran wanted. He told himself that growing up in
such a neighborhood would be good for Sarah and Carter. Here they could experience diversity and learn firsthand that the good life isn't a matter of birthright, but
something to be worked for, sacrificed for.

This is what he told himself. At times he almost believed it.

II

ON SUNDAY MORNING TUCKER BANNON ANNOUNCED
over breakfast that he and Dolly would return home tomorrow on an early flight out of Kennedy Airport, news
that visibly saddened Sarah and Carter. Their grandparents had clearly won their hearts.

Pete made a show of urging Tuck and Dolly to stay
a little longer (a show strictly for the kids' benefit), but
he was glad they were leaving. He couldn't look at either
of them without remembering that he'd broken a solemn
promise to his wife.

Tucker stood up from the breakfast table and assured
the kids they wouldn't stay away long. He even proposed that the Cochran family visit Buckthorn within the
near future, maybe as early as this coming summer.
Plenty of things to do in and around Buckthorn, he
added. Hiking, biking, fishing, flying kites on the nearby
Oregon shore.

Sarah and Carter looked excitedly to their father for
his approval, but before Pete could open his mouth,

Tucker leaned over and whispered, "Pete, can I have a minute of your time—in your study?"

They went to the study. Tucker pulled the door closed and fixed Pete with his gray stare. "I don't know whether you've accepted an offer on this house, or whether you've made one on a house out on Long Island, but before you do anything final, I want you to think about the one I'm about to make."

"Don't tell me you're interested in buying this place."

"No, no. I'm proposing that you keep it, rent it out, if need be. Hire a management company to collect the payments and take care of the maintenance. Your mortgage insurance paid the place off when Sally died, right?—so you don't owe the bank anything. The rental income would cover the insurance, taxes and upkeep, and still give you something on the side."

"I couldn't do that even if I wanted to. I need a down payment for another place, and I need a chunk of money to invest for Sarah and Carter. Selling this house is the only . . ."

Tucker held up a hand. "You haven't heard my offer yet. My business needs a chief financial officer and a personnel guy. Human resources manager, I guess it's called now. All the regulations these days—equal opportunity, affirmative action, safety, sexual harassment, all the rest—they're more than I can handle with a mill manager and a low-level accountant. I need somebody who's up to speed on all the latest management thinking, somebody who's been in the trenches. I need somebody like you, Pete. You've got the education and the background, plus you've got the grit—I can see that. You're not too proud to take a job driving a truck in order to provide for your kids, and that shows me something."

Pete's jaw went slack, and he gazed senselessly at

Tuck for a long moment. "You're offering me a job? In your sawmill?"

"A combination of jobs, actually. CFO and human resources manager. You'd be the number-two man, right under the mill manager, who's a heck of a nice guy named Wade Beswick. I can vouch for him, because I hired him right out of college and taught him everything he knows. I'll pay what you were making when Patriot Mutual canned you, plus retirement and comprehensive health coverage for you and the kids."

Pete gripped the edges of the desk, wondered whether he was dreaming. He heard his own voice protest that he knew nothing about sawmills or the wood products business, nothing about state regulations out in Oregon. His background was insurance, not manufacturing. What he knew about manufacturing you could stuff into a shoelace.

But Tucker Bannon insisted that Pete was up to the job, that he would quickly learn everything he needed to know. The University of Illinois didn't hand out MBAs to nitwits, he put in with a wink that made the red mole on his forehead bounce.

"You and the kids can live with Dolly and me for a while," the old man went on, "at least until you're settled and have a chance to look around for a place of your own. We've got more room in that old house than we can use. You and the kids can each have a bedroom. Then, if things don't work out and you decide you want out, you won't be saddled with another house that needs selling."

"Tucker, I don't know what to say. Moving the kids out West, to the country—I'm not sure how they'd handle it. They're basically city kids. They're accustomed to a certain way of life . . ."

They were accustomed to life in Rye, the *good* life. When it came right down to it, though, he couldn't log-

ically conclude that moving to Buckthorn would be less
traumatic for them than moving to a marginal neighborhood on Long Island.

Buckthorn wasn't much of a town, Tucker confessed.
In fact, Buckthorn was pretty decrepit, even by rural
Oregon's standards. Fortunately, Portland's western suburbs were only half an hour away. As for schools, Sarah
and Carter could transfer into the Nehalem County
school system and attend classes in nearby Paulsen. Next
fall, if things went well and Peter felt the need to do so,
he could enroll them in one of Portland's many fine
private schools. For that matter, Pete might decide that
he wanted to live in Portland or one of its suburbs, and
that was okay, too. Commuting to and from Buckthorn
would pose no problem.

Pete took a deep breath and forced himself to think
slowly, carefully. Several days earlier Tucker had revealed that he'd made Sarah and Carter his heirs, but
the revelation had made little impact on him. If anything,
Pete had felt a heightened need to become his kids' provider. He hadn't seen Tucker Bannon's statement of net
worth or a balance sheet or an income statement from
the family business, so he had no way of knowing just
how rich Tucker was. He certainly couldn't assume that
his kids' futures were secure merely on the strength of
Tucker's oral statements. Besides, both Tucker and
Dolly looked hale and hearty enough to live another
thirty years, so the fact that Sarah and Carter had become
heirs was probably irrelevant until they were well into
adulthood.

The offer of a job was another thing entirely. It had
immediate relevance.

"Listen to me, Pete," Tucker said, laying a hand on
his shoulder. "You and your kids deserve better than
what's available to you here. You're an executive and a
businessman, not a truck driver. What I'm offering you

is no sinecure, be assured of that. It's real work, hard
work. Our financial practices and personnel policies are
probably four or five decades behind the times, and it
won't be easy to bring them up to snuff. You'll earn
every penny I pay you, believe me.''

"Tucker, I . . .''

"Think of your kids, Pete. Do you really want to put
them in some drab New York public school where
maybe a third of their classmates carry guns? What'll
they learn in a place like that? What kind of outlook will
they have by the time they graduate from high school?
Do you seriously think they'll be ready for Harvard or
Stanford or . . .''

"I'll tutor them. They're smart kids, and they'll be
ready. Some of the best scholars in this country are coming out of public schools.''

"So we're told, and it may even be true. But do you
really want to take Sarah and Carter out to some third-
rate neighborhood on Long Island? *Your* kids, *Sally's*
kids. They'll grow up coarse in a place like that, full of
attitude. Isn't that what it's called these days?—thinking
it's cool to be overbearing and self-consumed and rude.
We don't have *attitude* out in Buckthorn, Pete. What we
have are decent schools, where the kids respect the
teachers and each other. We have clean air and water
and trees. We have space to move around in, and we
have room for you.''

Pete went to the window, stared out. He couldn't deny
that Tucker's offer had some appeal. It was a graceless
world out there, where fashion emulated the savage culture of the inner city, where even girls strove to look
street-tough and grade-schoolers practiced a primitive
"in-your-face'' etiquette. Tucker Bannon had offered
him the means to ensure a comfortable life for his children and maybe even revive his hopes for his career.
This was a chance for Peter to become an *executive*

again, not for a major corporation but for a successful
family business out in rural Oregon. No great shakes,
but a hell of a lot more appealing than driving a delivery
truck. The job would be a slow pitch for a man with his
talent, certainly. And it could lead to bigger and better
things, if he played his cards right.

"I—I'll have to think about it, Tuck. I'll need . . ."

Tucker shushed him, grinning in his wrinkled, avun-
cular way. "Don't say anything yet. Take as long as you
need to think and pray about it." He tossed a business
card onto the desk. "You'll want to check me out, look
me up in Dun and Bradstreet, make sure our business is
all I've said it is. Do your research and your soul-
searching, and call me when you've made your decision.
I know you'll make the right one, whatever it is."

He turned to leave, but before he'd even reached the
door, Pete knew what his decision would be.

6

I

GAZING DOWN FROM ITS PERCH ON MOUNT OLIVET, VEN-
geance sniffs the wind and smells *change*. Over the past
few days a rumor has rumbled through Buckthorn—a
rumor of new blood and brains coming to town, a hotshot executive-type who'll run the financial side of the
sawmill, pull old man Bannon's bacon out of the fire.
The mill might yet be revived and made into a going
concern, a few have even dared to suggest. Things might
finally be looking up in this tired old town.

Vengeance has laughed silently at such talk.

For decades these grimy yokels have sat in their
smoky taverns and cried in their beer about how badly
the outside world has fucked them. Between mouthfuls
of Polish sausage and pickled egg they've groused about
crooked politicians and liberals, unions, environmentalists, fags and international Jewish bankers. They've
blamed everyone but themselves for the darkness that
has nested in Buckthorn, the hard times and lost jobs,
the crumbling pavement and ramshackle houses—not to
mention the killer who moves silently among them.

But lo, suddenly they're ready to embrace a rescuer
from the same world that has supposedly fucked them
over, a messiah who will make everything right. Salvation is at hand, they tell each other with their beery
eyes. And the funny thing is, they believe their own
dreck.

Vengeance knows the truth: The demon has corrupted

their brains, made them blind, enslaved them. And because the people of Buckthorn have allowed the corruption to happen, even welcomed it, they richly deserve all that Vengeance has laid on them, not to mention all that Vengeance will yet do. They've made their bed, and Vengeance intends to see that they lie in it.

"So, they want *change*, do they?" the dark angel whispers to itself, grinning with perfect teeth. "Then that's what I'll give them. *Change*."

And for the next hour it mulls a list of soon-to-be victims.

II

ON THURSDAY MORNING, FEBRUARY 24, 1994, A DAY OF rare winter sunshine, a Ford van rolled into Buckthorn on Highway 49 and turned left off Main Street onto Columbia Avenue. It jounced past a hulk that had once housed the Buckthorn City Bank, long ago the commercial heart of a thriving wood products community, now a caricature of its former self. Directly across the street loomed a derelict once known as the Hotel St. Helens, its Victorian filigree having wasted to tatters, its windows gaping like empty eye sockets. The lettering on the side of the van said *KATU-TV, Channel 2, Portland*.

The van swung into a U-turn at the Head Rig Bar and pulled over to the curb next to a sturdy-looking, two-story structure built of tan brick, an island of solidity in a sea of decrepitude. The building had terra-cotta facing and marble insets shaped like Doric columns on either side of the main entrance. Above the door was a slab of polished granite, upon which was engraved *Komack's Mercantile Emporium, Est. 1908*. A neatly lettered sign

on a display window superseded the message engraved
in stone: *The Nehalem County Renegade*.

Inside, Nita Vale glanced down from her second-floor
apartment window and saw the van, saw three people
climbing out. *Christ, I'm not ready for this,* she whispered to herself. She was behind schedule this morning,
thanks to suffering a foot injury during her morning run
on Mount Olivet. The injury had forced her to limp
slowly on the homeward leg of the run, a distance of
more than three miles.

She wore a gray sweat suit with perspiration spots at
the neck and armpits. A peek in the bathroom mirror
confirmed that her short, blond hair lay plastered to her
forehead like a wet bathing cap.

"I look like a gargoyle," she said aloud, though she
knew this wasn't true. She'd planned to shower and eat
half a cantaloupe before the TV people arrived, but that
plan was clearly in the toilet. She thumped down the
stairs, wincing with every step from a bolt of pain in her
left ankle. Nita doubted that the injury was serious, since
she hadn't actually turned the ankle, but she'd strained
it badly enough to cause pain whenever she placed her
full weight on the foot. To avoid aggravating it, she
would probably need to knock off running for at least a
week, maybe longer.

This thought rankled her. Nita Vale needed her wake-
up run like most people needed their morning coffee.
Exercise was a huge part of her life—running, workouts
with her weights in the afternoon, bicycling whenever
possible. Revving up her metabolism on a regular basis
made her feel younger than her thirty-three years, kept
her taut and trim.

She unlocked the front door and opened it. "Hi, I'm
Nita," she said to the TV folks. "Welcome to the *Renegade*. Throw your stuff anywhere and make yourselves
comfortable. As you can see, I'm a little damp."

"Hope you had a nice workout," said Keena Martin, first through the door. She was the producer whom Nita had gotten to know over the phone during the past week, a thirtyish black woman in bulky painter's pants and a bomber jacket. "Morning is the best time, don't you think? I'm always out on the track by six, no matter what the weather."

She introduced "Casey-the-camera guy," a dour young slacker type who wore a baseball cap backwards and a warm-up jacket with the Portland Trail Blazers' logo on it. Next was Brink Erdmann, the "talent," an on-camera reporter whose face Nita recognized from Channel 2's nightly news show. Tanned, dark-haired and under forty, he wore an Armani sport coat over a casual sport shirt.

"Keena tells me you run this paper all by yourself," he said. "You must be hiding another pair of hands somewhere in that sweat suit."

Nita confirmed that she was indeed the paper's only actual employee—publisher, editor, sales manager, typesetter, layout artist and janitor all rolled into one, thanks to the miracle of computerized desktop publishing.

"I've got stringers who keep track of the local gossip," she added, "and some amateur columnists who send in stuff about gardening, fishing—that kind of thing. I also write a weekly column, but otherwise the *Renegade* is mostly advertising and classifieds."

"So you don't need to reinvent the wheel with every issue," Keena said.

"Exactly."

"Looks like you're doing okay for yourself," Erdmann said, inspecting the reception area. "I like what you've done with the place. It's very—warm."

Ficus trees and ferns grew in hand-thrown pots in the corners of the room, and photos of driftwood and stream-beds hung on the bare-brick walls. The floor was refinished hardwood beneath a colorful Persian carpet. Nita had salvaged a long cocktail bar from the Hotel St. Helens on Main Street, given it a new coat of varnish and installed it to serve as a reception counter.

"This was a dry goods store back when the Komack family had the place," she said, leading the crew toward a doorway at the end of the bar. She tried not to limp on her damaged foot. "It was floor-to-ceiling with antiques when I bought it, and I made enough selling them to pay for the remodeling—almost. I turned the second floor into an apartment."

"You live here alone, then?" Erdmann's tone suggested more than a passing interest.

"For the time being," Nita answered ambiguously. She didn't want to encourage this asshole.

Keena suggested that Nita might want to "freshen up" before they started the on-camera interview, to which Nita chuckled. She needed more than freshening, she told them. At minimum she required a shower, a bite of breakfast and at least one cup of coffee before the tape started rolling.

She led the crew up a narrow stairway to her apartment where the smell of coffee was already strong, seated them in the living room and brought them mugs from the kitchen. She tried to interest them in bagels and homemade blackberry preserves, but Casey-the-camera-guy was the only taker. He took enough for three.

Nita disappeared into the rear rooms of the apartment, leaving the TV crew to peruse her back issues of *Bicycling, Runner's World* and *The Smithsonian*. Twenty minutes later she emerged, scrubbed and blow-dried, wearing a freshly pressed work shirt and jeans. After a quick bite of cantaloupe she poured herself a mug of coffee and led the crew back downstairs.

"I call this the newsroom," she said, ushering them into an open area with a rear wall that was mostly window. Computer equipment sat on a large oak desk, along with a hand-carved plaque that said *Live simply, that others might simply live.* An array of framed newspaper pages hung on one wall, columns that Nita had written about environmental abuses at the Buckthorn sawmill. Nearby hung several citations and letters of recognition from groups like the Sierra Club and National Wildlife Federation.

Beyond the window a field of blackberries fell away to a creek, from which a mist rose into a bright morning sky, a scene almost too idyllic to be real.

"Not exactly a throbbing nerve center, is it?" Nita said.

"If I had a view like this, I'd never get any work done," commented Keena Martin.

"A few years ago that field was full of abandoned houses. It was a residential neighborhood, mostly logging families and mill people, but then the sawmill cut back from three shifts to just one. When the jobs disappeared the people moved out—like dead leaves falling off a tree, I guess you could say."

A developer from Portland had torn down all the houses and laid plans to build vacation homes along Royal Chinook Creek, she went on. A last-minute marketing study, however, had shown that developing property anywhere near Buckthorn was a swift and certain way to lose money. The project had gone belly-up, and the blackberries had taken over.

Nita grinned sardonically. "Can you imagine anyone in his right mind buying property in this town, after what's been happening here for the past eighteen years?"

"*You* did," Brink Erdmann put in, winking. "You bought this building, moved in and started a newspaper."

"Actually, I didn't start the *Renegade*. It was a going

concern long before anyone in this room was even born, a real newspaper in its heyday."

Erdmann studied a poster that depicted an evergreen tree emitting oxygen molecules into a bright blue sky. The caption said, *Save your breath . . . Save a tree.* In the lower margin was the logo of the Earth Insurrection, reputed to be the most militant environmentalist group in North America. Over the past decade, spokesmen for the timber industry had accused Earth Insurrectionists of sneaking into forests and hammering steel spikes into the trunks of merchantable trees. Sawing into a spike with a powered tool could mean serious injury or even death to a logger or mill worker, which meant that the Earth Insurrection was no better than a band of terrorists, the industry spokesmen had proclaimed.

"This town is the last place I would've expected to find an Earth Insurrectionist at the helm of a newspaper," Erdmann remarked. "I mean, the timber folks around here must take a pretty dim view of anyone who pounds spikes into trees. Ever worry about being tarred and feathered and ridden out on a rail?"

"Not really. I'll admit that hardly anyone around here likes my editorials, but the *Renegade's* the only show in town. There's no other source of local news and ads. So everybody reads my paper and puts up with me."

"A voice crying in the wilderness," Erdmann said.

"Hardly. I've found a niche, that's all."

"And that's the secret to succeeding in business these days," Keena put in. "Find yourself a niche. By the way, Brink, *your* niche is here." She waved him to a chair in front of the desk, then asked Casey-the-camera-guy whether he could shoot Nita against the window. Through a mouthful of bagel and blackberry jam Casey said yes, he could do anything she wanted.

"Nita, I'd like you sitting behind your desk with your back to the window," Keena went on. "With a little luck we can pick up that view of the creek in the background.''

Casey busied himself with the equipment, stringing cords to outlets, setting up lights, clipping microphones to Brink's tie and the collar of Nita's blue work shirt.

Nita suddenly felt nervous without really knowing why. She'd endured TV interviews before, as had nearly every other prominent citizen of Buckthorn at one time or another. Hell, she'd even been a daily newspaper reporter herself before moving to town, so she knew the drill. But now she had the irrational feeling that her skin had turned to cellophane, that the camera could look right through her. Crazy though the notion was, she couldn't shrug it off.

Keena sensed her discomfort. "Hey, listen. Brink won't ask any questions that you and I didn't cover when we talked on the phone, so all you need to do is say exactly what you said to me before. No surprises, I promise. It'll be a cakewalk.''

"I'm okay.'' Nita took a long moment to sip her coffee. "It's just that I've said the same thing to every reporter who's ever come to town. I've said it so many times that it's started to sound phony even to me. I feel like a flack for the Chamber of Commerce—if we *had* a Chamber of Commerce.''

"Don't sweat it. You'll be great.''

"I just wish I could give you something new, something hopeful. I get so tired of saying the same old things, time after time.''

The previous October, immediately after the murder of young Rich Nockleby, CBS News had sent a veteran reporter to tape a segment on the Buckthorn killer for the "Eye On America'' series, to be shown on the *Evening News* with Dan Rather and Connie Chung—not the first time CBS had dealt with the matter, and possibly not the last. Tabloid reporters and other network news teams had followed in quick succession, and they'd all sought out Nita Vale, the local news hen, whose take on the eighteen-year-old mystery they'd deemed worth reporting, no matter how many times they'd interviewed her before. As usual, she'd performed with aplomb, and they'd all given her prominent play.

Nobody in Buckthorn believes that the killer lives here, she'd told them smoothly, as she'd told so many others in years past. *Nobody thinks the killer could be a friend or a neighbor . . .*

And that was the truth, as far as it went.

Now it was KATU's turn. An in-depth, hour-long special, Keena Martin had called it, to be shown in prime time. A cut above the razor-thin pieces that the networks and tabloids had done.

"Well, don't worry," Keena said to Nita with a reassuring wink. "We're not expecting any earth-shaking revelations today. These murders have been happening since, what—'seventy-six? If the answers were easy to find, someone would've found them by now, and eight young men wouldn't be dead. So you don't need to beat yourself up over anything."

"You're right, I know. But every time someone gets himself butchered, the news crews come out of the woodwork, and everyone in town gets a mike stuck in his face, and suddenly we're all experts on serial murder. Do you have any idea what it's like to live in the serial murder capital of America?"

She looked away for a moment and told herself to get a grip. When she spoke again it was barely above a whisper. "Want to know something weird? We're not so much afraid anymore as *ashamed*. I moved here just seven years ago from Portland, so I wasn't even around when the first five murders happened. But I've been around for three of them, and now *I've* even started to feel it. It's been happening for so long that we've all started to feel guilty somehow, like we're being punished for something. This isn't making any sense, is it? I'm sorry . . .''

"Nita, it makes perfect sense." Keena settled onto the edge of the desk and scribbled something in her notebook. She looked up again, her dark eyes earnest. "I don't want to seem insensitive, but can we get into this on camera—what it's like to live in Buckthorn, the feelings of shame? You people must feel as if your town has become a fish bowl, like your lives aren't your own anymore. What do you think? Are you following this, Brink?''

"Of course I'm following it, Keena.''

"So, how about it, Nita? People need to hear this— a side of the tragedy that gets ignored too often. We need to know how you cope, what you tell each other when you meet on the street. We need to know where you get the strength to stay on and face each new day. Do you think you could tell us about that on camera?''

Nita thought a moment, nodded.

Keena eased off the desk and retreated behind the camera, gave a happy-face hand sign to Nita. "Okay, let's do this thing, people. No sense putting it off any longer.''

The lights came on, and a red dot lit up on the front of the camera. Casey-the-camera-guy gave a go signal. Using his broadcast baritone, Brink Erdmann asked the questions that Keena had given him, then asked a few of his own. Nita answered them—the same predictable questions she'd answered for CBS News back in October after a young mill worker named Rich Nockleby met his death. And in October of 1991 after Keith McCurdy was found butchered. And in October of 1989 after Travis Langdon's murder. The same predictable questions she'd heard whenever some freelance crime writer hit town to research a book.

And finally, she tried to describe to Brink Erdmann what it was like to live in a town where some faceless maniac had murdered eight young employees of the Buckthorn sawmill over eighteen long years. But today her aplomb deserted her, and she found herself stammering, groping for words. Her eyes filled with tears, despite her efforts to hold them back.

After the interview ended, Keena Martin gave her another happy-face hand sign and declared that all had gone swimmingly. TV news producers, it seemed, found nothing more compelling than close-ups of people in anguish, people crying real tears.

For Nita Vale, however, the taping had been no triumph. The camera had seen more of her than she'd wanted it to. It had peered into her soul. *I lost control,* she said to herself, and she'd let herself *feel.* That was bad.

Very bad.

III

DETECTIVE LIEUTENANT DANIEL KANTOR OF THE OREgon State Police leaned against the front fender of his unmarked car and lit a Marlboro, his fifth this morning. Only recently he'd conceded to himself the ugly possibility that he would never kick the filthy habit, which ran parallel in his mind to the even uglier possibility that the Buckthorn killer would never be caught.

He was a ropey, olive-skinned man of thirty-eight who wore his prematurely graying hair clipped close to the scalp. He had a hawkish nose and deeply set eyes that his ex-wife had once described as "compassionate brown." He would have looked comfortable in the blue uniform and Smokey hat of the Oregon State Police, but these days he dressed in corduroy sport coats over khaki

Dockers and penny loafers. He carried a Sig Sauer nine-millimeter pistol in a shoulder holster under his sport coat.

A low winter sun peered through the Douglas firs of Royal Chinook Park, casting blades of light into the surrounding thicket. A mist rose off the creek. Scrub jays and crows patrolled the area around the garbage racks for edible morsels, though the park was closed for the season and the ground was bare of anything but needles and cones.

Nothing in the peaceful scene hinted of the atrocity that had occurred here only four months earlier, when a psychopath had nailed young Rich Nockleby to the ground, sliced off his penis, snipped his fingers off below the second knuckle and gouged out his eyes. The animal had then doused him with gasoline, except for his head and face, and burned him to death.

The elements had erased all traces of the blood and the fire. Within a few weeks the park would open to picnickers and campers again, and little kids would romp over the spot where Rich Nockleby had spent his final hellish hours. This thought made Kantor's flesh crawl.

He glanced at his watch and noted that the KATU-TV news team was ten minutes late. He didn't mind. His schedule wasn't exactly crowded now that the furor over the latest Buckthorn killing had begun to subside.

Since the first week of November, Lieutenant Daniel Kantor had served as the supervisor of the Buckthorn Task Force, which was an alliance of federal, state and local law enforcement agencies that had come together after the third Buckthorn killing back in 1981, when authorities concluded that they had a serial killer on their hands. The stated mission of the Task Force was simple: Catch and convict the Buckthorn killer. Kantor was the ninth man to hold the job, and he was grimly determined to be the last. But then all his predecessors had shared that determination—testimony to the fact that carrying out the stated mission was anything but simple. The Buckthorn killer had outlasted them all.

Immediately after the Nockleby killing, the supervisor slot became vacant, a surprise to no one in law enforcement, given the emotional hell that its most recent holder had endured. Kantor had seen what he'd figured was a once-in-a-career opportunity. As a homicide cop with thirteen years of experience under his belt, he'd known that in eighty percent of all solved murders, the cops get the break they need within a week of commission. He'd concluded that the Buckthorn killer, despite being a cagey guy who'd killed eight and had eluded capture for eighteen years, was only human. The maniac was bound to make a mistake. Kantor's gut told him that the mistake could very well have happened with the Nockleby killing.

So why not take a turn at the roulette wheel? he'd asked himself. If the marble landed on the right number, the Buckthorn case would break on his watch and the world would open to him like a roasting oyster shell. He'd envisioned interviews with Ted Koppel, a book contract with a fat advance, a lecture tour of law enforcement academies, maybe even a movie deal. He'd fantasized about lazing in the warm sand of an island in the Aegean, watching topless nymphs from Italy frolicking in the sun.

He'd literally begged the chief of the Oregon State Police for the job, even calling in some past favors in order to get the nod. Fortunately the competition wasn't fierce, inasmuch as the wisest among Kantor's peers considered it a likely dead end, a career-killer.

Kantor's hunch about the odds being with him had turned out to be wrong. The Buckthorn killer had made no mistakes in the butchering and burning of Rich Nockleby, just as he'd made no mistakes in the burning and butchering of seven other young men in similarly lonely settings around Buckthorn. Time, which Kantor had deemed an ally upon taking this job, had become an enemy. Any clues that the killer had left were eroding under assaults by wind, rain and rot. Thus it was with the vast majority of homicides: you either cleared them within the first ten days or you never cleared them at all.

A Ford van pulled into the entrance of the park and halted behind his car. The doors opened and four people clambered out, three of whom he assumed were the KATU news team. The fourth was someone he was to-tally unprepared to see—Nita Vale, whose eyes caught his briefly. She looked away.

Kantor dropped his cigarette to the ground and stepped on it as a young black woman strode toward him with her hand outstretched. She introduced herself as Keena Martin, the producer with whom he'd talked several times on the telephone over the past week. She had a handshake like a blacksmith's. Close on her heels was a man Kantor recognized as Brink Erdmann, one of KATU's ace reporters. Kantor shook hands with him, too.

Keena Martin thanked him for agreeing to do this in-terview and expressed hope that the TV special might help catch the Buckthorn killer, maybe jog the memory of someone who'd seen something suspicious. The hour-long special would cover not only the local people who've lived with the tragedy year in and year out, but also the technical aspects of the investigation—the fo-rensic evidence, the psychological profiling, that kind of thing. That was where Kantor came in.

"You'll have my enthusiastic cooperation," Kantor assured her, flashing his practiced PR grin. "We're al-ways happy to get help from the news media in cases like this." He had a knack for dealing with newsies.

"In addition to yourself, we'll be interviewing some outside experts in murder investigation just to give our viewers a balanced view. Of course you'll get a chance to comment on whatever they tell us," Keena Martin added.

A balanced view, Kantor thought, smiling. What they really wanted were grisly bits and pieces, stuff they weren't likely to get from the cops. As a rule cops don't say much about blood and gore for publication, but an "outside consultant"—well, that was another matter. In describing what had happened to young Rich Nockleby, a cop would use terms like "sexual mutilation" and let it go at that. But an outside consultant would lay everything out in gut-twisting detail: *Even though the body was heavily charred, the medical examiners were able to conclude that the victim's penis had been cut off when he was alive, probably with a very sharp cutting instrument . . .*

Such was the stuff of good ratings.

Keena asked Kantor to point out exactly where Nockleby's body had lain, which he did. She wanted to know where the spikes had been driven, where the head and feet had lain, and Kantor showed her these spots, to the best of his recollection.

"No marks on the ground," she said, sounding disappointed.

"No marks. We've had a lot of rain and wind in the last four months, even a fair amount of snow. Sorry."

Keena made a face, excused herself and led the camera man off toward the creek bank, gesticulating to indicate what video shots she wanted. Kantor took this opportunity to approach Nita, who leaned against the van with her arms crossed. She wore a bulky Scandinavian sweater to keep the chill off. Her cheeks had already become rosy. She looked beautiful in her own uneasy way, lithe and fit. Her eyes were green with a bluish cast, the effect of heavily tinted contact lenses. Her lashes were long and dark. Her broad Latin cheekbones, high on an oval face, gave her an exotic look that Kantor admired.

"Let me guess," he said, pocketing his hands. "You've given up the weekly newspaper game and entered the exciting world of TV news. A year from now you and Brink Erdmann will be co-anchors."

"Hello, Daniel." She didn't smile. "No, it's just me, the same old slice of stale cheese. Keena had just finished interviewing me, and I made the mistake of showing her the Death Room. She took one look at all the stuff I've collected and begged me to come along on her set-ups. I guess she figured I'm an expert on the Buckthorn killings, and—"

"And a good source of free consultation. Can't say I blame her."

"I couldn't say no. As you know, that's been a problem of mine."

"The Death Room *is* impressive," Kantor replied. "You've probably got more material on the Buckthorn killings than anyone in the world outside the Nehalem County Sheriff's Department."

Nita Vale had converted a rear room of her building into a repository of information on the Buckthorn killings. The "Death Room," she called it. She'd tacked up pictures of all the victims, photos of the various crime scenes and poop sheets that summarized the victims' short lives. There were maps of the town and diagrams of the killer's probable movements before and after the killings, boxes full of news clippings, bundles of Xeroxed pages from books on serial murder and homicide investigation, as well as other general source material—

all categorized by subject and labeled for quick reference.

She'd set up the Death Room with the goal of collecting everything known about the Buckthorn killings and someday writing the definitive book on the subject. As the years wore on, however, she'd lost her enthusiasm for the project. She still dutifully collected facts about the murders and placed them in the appropriate box or stuck them on the appropriate wall, but she did it because she felt somehow obliged, as if she'd been drafted for the duty and couldn't get out of it.

She'd confessed this to Dan Kantor only two weeks ago, toward the end of their short love affair, which had started soon after Kantor had moved to Paulsen from the state police headquarters in Salem to assume the reins of the Buckthorn Task Force. He'd urged her to do away with the Death Room, throw all the stuff in the Dumpster and get on with her crusade against Tucker Bannon and the timber industry. Why trouble herself with the grisly arcana of the killings, now that she'd all but given up the idea of writing a book?

Kantor hadn't known whether she'd taken his advice, because a few days later their affair had come to an abrupt halt. The breakup had come as no great shock to him, since he'd gotten clear danger signals from the outset. For starters, Nita was a health freak and Kantor was a smoker, not an ideal match. Their lovemaking had rarely been good, as Nita had mostly lain on her back and impersonated a corpse whenever Kantor acted randy. Though she was beautiful, smart and passionately committed to saving the world from industrial rape, something about her had troubled Kantor—something artificial. An androidal quality. He'd wondered if she wore her feelings like a costume, if she could peel them off and put on new ones to suit the occasion. When she told him that she couldn't see him anymore, that her decision wasn't open to discussion, she'd done it without venom or tears. She'd been downright civil, in fact. Even sympathetic. But yet—androidal.

"I hope everything's okay for you," Kantor ventured, trying to meet her gaze. "I thought I saw you limping a minute ago."

"I hurt my foot on my run this morning, nothing major. Things are fine."

"Good. Me too."

"Good."

And that was that, Kantor supposed.

Keena Martin walked back from the bank of the creek and drew him into a huddle with Brink Erdmann. Flipping through her notes, she went over some background material, confirmed Kantor's rank and title, the spelling of his name, and the fact that he'd taken charge of the Buckthorn Task Force only three months earlier.

"So tell me about the Task Force," she said. "How many people do you have, and who are they?"

Kantor explained that the Task Force consisted of fourteen investigators, all on loan from nearby local law enforcement agencies, the Oregon State Police and the FBI office in Portland. Of these, Kantor himself was the only one who devoted all his time to the case, since each of the others had full-time duties with his or her home agency. He did *not* reveal that home-agency duties often superseded those assigned by the Task Force supervisor, which made his job interesting, to say the least. Getting anything done often required groveling at the feet of some sheriff or police chief for permission to use an investigator that the sheriff or chief himself had assigned to the Task Force. Neither did he reveal that this was a major source of stress for the supervisor.

IV

FIRST ON THE AGENDA WAS A "WALK-AND-TALK," IN which Kantor and Brink Erdmann strolled through Royal Chinook Park and chatted like two old college buddies. Erdmann, with his costly sport coat slung over his shoulder and his tie loose, looked like a refugee from a menswear ad in *Rolling Stone*.

"Lieutenant Kantor, we in the Pacific Northwest sometimes feel as if we're under siege by serial killers. Ted Bundy got started in Seattle, and for years the Green River killer has operated along the I-5 corridor, never having been caught, as we all know. Here in the Portland area we've been terrorized by Dayton Leroy Rogers, who beat and strangled young women. We've had Westly Allen Dodd, who tortured and killed little boys, Cesar Barone, who raped and killed older women. And, of course, the Buckthorn killer, who's still at large. Are there more serial killers here in the Northwest than in other parts of the country, and if so, why?"

Kantor took a deep breath, shook his head. "We've had some high-profile cases in this region, but I doubt that we have more serial killers than other parts of the world. Fact is, these animals have been around since day one, in every society, every country. The Russians just recently arrested Andrei Chikatilo, who killed and mutilated something like fifty-five women, girls and boys in and around the city of Rostov over a period of twelve years. Serial killers are at least as common in Russia as they are here, and the same's true for the rest of the world. I guess it's only natural that we hear the most about those closet to our own homes and communities."

"More than one investigator has said that the Buckthorn killer is a very strange case, one that defies all the common assumptions about serial killers. Is this true in your estimation?''

Kantor thought a long moment before opening his mouth, feeling no need to hurry. He knew that Keena Martin would edit out any dead air.

The Buckthorn killer *did* present an unusual case, he allowed. Seldom if ever had a serial killer operated so long without getting caught. Neither John Wayne Gacy of Chicago nor Jeffrey Dahmer of Milwaukee, both butchers of young men and boys, had lasted as long. Even the bestial Chikatilo of Rostov had lasted only twelve years. The Buckthorn killer's career, however, had gone on and on—for eighteen years and still counting. Gacy, Dahmer and Chikatilo had all made mistakes that led to their capture, as was typical of psychosexual killers. Overcome with a sexual lust to kill, they'd lost their discipline and had become careless. But the Buckthorn killer hadn't become careless—not yet.

''Our killer's unusual in another way, too,'' Kantor added. ''He's obviously very patient. He can wait two or maybe even three years between killings. Most psychosexual killers need to do their thing more often than he does. Once they get started, they crave the gratification that killing brings. They need it like an addict needs his drug.''

By now Kantor and Erdmann had walked nearly to the creek bed. They halted and faced each other, while Casey shot them against the heavily foliated backdrop of the opposite bank.

''Is it safe to say that the unusual nature of this case makes it hard to develop a profile of the killer?'' Erdmann asked.

Kantor acknowledged that several forensic psychiatrists and psychologists had tried to develop profiles of the killer, including a handful from the FBI's well-known Violent Criminal Apprehension Program in

Quantico, Virginia, or VICAP, as cops called it. The problem was that no expert could build a serviceable profile with the paucity of evidence left at the scenes of the crimes. No forensic shrink had been able to say, *This is how your killer lives*, or *This is the kind of work he does*, or *This is what he's done in the past*.

"We do feel some general assumptions are possible, however," Kantor added, trying to sound hopeful. "We have a body of research showing that the great majority of psychosexual killers come from dysfunctional childhood homes and that they're often intelligent people. Based on the meticulous, disciplined way that the Buckthorn killer operates, we think he probably has a very high IQ, maybe one-twenty or more. We also know that half of all serial killers have a history of mental illness and that seven out of ten have a family history of substance abuse. The research says that *all* serial killers have a history of emotional abuse and that all become sexually dysfunctional in adulthood."

"But none of this really helps you narrow the field, does it? There's a lot of people walking around who are smart, have a history of mental illness of some kind, and have families who've done drugs or alcohol to excess. But none of them are serial killers, are they?"

Kantor gave a thin smile. "At least one of them is."

Erdmann turned his attention to the crime scene and the physical evidence, what there was of it. He asked whether the killer had taken Rich Nockleby's severed body parts with him, as had been leaked to the press after some earlier killings. The eyes, the fingers, the penis. Kantor answered yes, which led to the next question: Could this mean that the killer was a Jeffrey Dahmer–type, somebody who keeps gruesome artifacts of his crimes in the refrigerator and brings them out occasionally to fantasize over them, maybe even eat them? On this Kantor wouldn't speculate.

"Can we assume that you haven't mentioned some feature of the crime that only the killer could know about, in order to screen out false confessions and leads?"

"Yes, you can assume that." Kantor let a silence endure. More work for Keena in the editing room.

What he didn't say was that starting with the third Buckthorn murder on October 26, 1981, the killer had used a strong anesthetic, sodium pentobarbital, to render his victims pliable before nailing them to the ground. Then, apparently to bring the victim around again and thus ensure his full appreciation of the pain, the killer had administered methamphetamine, orally, in all likelihood. The Task Force had withheld this tidbit from the news media. Sodium pentobarbital was a controlled pharmaceutical that was available only to certified health professionals, a fact that one day could generate a valuable lead. A hospital, a doctor's office or pharmacy might report a theft or diversion, the investigation of which might lead to the Buckthorn killer. Kantor doubted that the maniac was stupid enough to get caught in this way, but what the hell? Kantor wasn't above grasping at straws. Not anymore.

Keena called a break, and Kantor wandered toward Nita, who'd followed along and listened to the interview up to this point. She gave him a hard look, notifying him that she didn't want to talk. So Kantor smoked a cigarette and chatted with Casey-the-camera-guy about the Portland Trail Blazers' disastrous season. When the break was over, Keena directed him to sit opposite Erdmann at a picnic table. The camera rolled.

"There are several experts who've suggested that these killings are the work of a satanic cult," Erdmann said. "The positioning of the victims like crucifixes, the taking of body parts, the burning—all these suggest some sort of ritualistic sacrifice, do they not?"

Kantor declared that the people who perpetrated satanic-murder theories were not experts, but charlatans and scam artists who profited by preying on a gullible public. No one had ever found actual evidence to suggest that satanist cults had abducted or kidnapped anyone. Even so, certain fundamentalist churches, evangelists and unscrupulous psychologists had reaped millions in the sale of books, tracts and videos that purported to expose a vast cultist conspiracy to kidnap and kill people in the name of Satan. Sally Jesse Raphael, Geraldo and other talk-show hosts had feasted on "eyewitness" accounts from various misfits, wackos and frauds who claimed that their satanist parents had abused them as kids, that they'd witnessed the torture and sacrificial killing of animals and humans. Some misguided sheriffs and police chiefs around the country had even contracted with "experts" on the satanist conspiracy to provide specialized "training" to their investigators, showing that not even cops were immune to this drivel.

"This isn't to say," Kantor continued, "that our killer doesn't have some warped religious belief that motivates him to kill. Back in the early seventies there was a man in Northern California named Herbert Mullin, who executed thirteen people as human sacrifices. He thought he needed to kill people in order to placate Mother Nature and stave off earthquakes."

"Would a serial killer be capable of living a life that appears outwardly normal?"

Kantor took a deep breath and tried to disguise his unease. This was the crux of the matter, wasn't it?—the fact that the killer had obviously gone on with his life while letting slip no clue to family and friends as to his hidden side, his dark and deadly nature.

The guy could be anyone, anywhere. A member of the PTA, maybe. A church deacon or a volunteer fireman. A scoutmaster or a soccer coach. A workaday monster who patiently schemed his next kill while mowing his yard or cleaning his rain gutters.

He's probably watching this program and cackling up his sleeve.

"I'm not a psychologist or a psychiatrist, Mr. Erdmann," Kantor said finally, "but it would seem that he is, in fact, living like a normal human being. If this is the case, then . . ."

Kantor's pager went off, and he flinched. He found that he had goose bumps.

"Sorry, duty calls," he said after glancing at the coded message on the LED display. He chuckled awkwardly, got up from the picnic table and slipped the cordless microphone off his shirt. "We'll have to finish this later, if you don't mind. You have my number." He headed toward his car, meaning to use the radio.

V

TUCKER BANNON PARKED HIS BIG SUBURBAN ON MAIN Street in Paulsen, the seat of Nehalem County, and sat a moment, his huge fists gripping the steering wheel tightly enough to whiten his knuckles.

"Give me strength, Lord," he prayed silently. "Don't let me be consumed by my anger."

A minute passed, and his hands gradually loosened on the wheel. Blood flowed again into his fingers.

"Let Thy anger be mine, Lord, Thy serenity my own." The muscles in his jaw relaxed, and he opened his eyes. He breathed deeply. "Thank you, Lord. I'm ready now."

He got out of the Suburban and walked across the street to a neat storefront that housed the offices of the Nehalem County School District, which served the towns of Buckthorn and Paulsen together with the unincorporated population of the county. From here a small staff managed one facility that housed a grade school and a middle school, another that housed the high school. The buildings stood at opposite ends of this very block, local landmarks. Nehalem County was among the least populated in Oregon, and the population was shrinking, thanks to the spotted owl and its human allies.

Glancing at his watch, Tucker saw that it was exactly 10:30 A.M., the appointed time. He walked into the reception room and told the receptionist who he was, though this was hardly necessary. Nearly everyone in Paulsen knew Tucker Bannon on sight, and he was on nodding terms with at least half the adults in the county, if not a first-name basis—even with the Latinos, many of whom worked in his mill.

The receptionist smiled sweetly and buzzed her boss, the superintendent of schools. "Dr. Dorn says to go right in, Mr. Bannon."

Andrea Dorn was a comely middle-aged woman with brown hair in a French braid and half-lensed reading glasses that lay on the tip of her nose. She carried herself with a commanding bearing that Tucker found unbecoming in women. She thanked him for coming and introduced him to a balding man in a double-breasted suit, a clinical psychologist from Portland named Dennis Feldon.

"Dr. Feldon performs counseling and psychological services for the school district on a contract basis," Dorn explained. "It was he who administered the test to your son and evaluated the results."

"I see," Tucker said, shedding his sheepskin jacket and setting aside his Stetson. He smiled tightly, trying to hide his annoyance over the fact that a woman had the authority to summon him like this. He lowered himself into the armchair that Dorn had indicated. "Forgive me if I seem a little bewildered, but my wife and I only got back from New York three days ago. We'd been away on business for about two weeks, and I knew nothing about any of this until you called this morning. I'm still unclear as to exactly what's happened.''

"Yes, I'm sorry I couldn't be more specific when we spoke on the phone,'' Dorn said, leaning against her desk. "I thought it would be better if we discussed the matter face-to-face.''

"I understand.'' Actually, Tucker didn't understand at all. He knew only that his son was in trouble. Again. *Help me, Lord* . . . "So you've given Topper—Theodore—some sort of psychological test, is that it?''

"Perhaps I should start at the beginning, Mr. Bannon.'' Dorn picked up a manila file folder and consulted its contents. "About two weeks ago, on the eighth of February to be exact, a female student at Nehalem High visited the school counselor and complained of being anxious and afraid. She said she'd been unable to sleep at night and that she'd lost her appetite. She'd lost weight, and whenever she saw your son around the school, she . . .''

"Excuse me—anxious and afraid of what?'' Tucker interrupted. "Who is this girl?''

"Her name is Bunny Coglin, and according to the counselor's notes, the girl did seem agitated and generally symptomatic of depression and anxiety. She complained of having nightmares. She couldn't concentrate on her schoolwork. And she . . .''

"But what was she afraid of, Miss Dorn—I mean *Doctor* Dorn?''

"She was afraid of your son, Mr. Bannon.''

"Topper? The Coglin girl was scared of *Topper*?'' Tucker shook his head. He'd known the Coglin family for years. The father, Ed Coglin, had once worked in the machine shop of the Buckthorn sawmill as a filer before opening his own tool-repair business in Paulsen.

Good man. Tucker had been sad to lose him. "Why on earth would she be scared of Topper?"

The superintendent explained that Bunny Coglin had told the counselor about the rendezvous that she and two male classmates, Kyle Matzko and Cory Dunwoody, had kept with Topper on the previous Thursday night. She described what had happened on the hillside behind the sawmill in Buckthorn, some sort of crass religious rite. The burning of live rats. Topper's sexual display. Kyle and Cory had corroborated the story.

"The girl had clearly been traumatized by all this," Dr. Dorn went on. "What gave us a sense of urgency was the fact that such incidents had happened before and that they've evolved to include overtly sexual acts. Bunny stated that your son, Topper, is well known around the school as someone who tortures mice and rats. He's something of a living legend, it seems. He even calls himself . . ."

"The Verminator, yes. I know all about that. It's his job to control weeds and vermin on our property, and he does it well, praise God. This Verminator business is a little game with him, that's all."

"That may have been true in the beginning," said Dr. Feldon, speaking for the first time. "Your son's behavior has gone far beyond what any rational person would call a game, Mr. Bannon. Our test results clearly show this. In fact, the results have been disturbing, to say the least."

"What tests are we talking about?"

"The Minnesota Multiphasic Personality Inventory, or MMPI, among others," Feldon answered. "The school counselor notified Dr. Dorn of everything she learned about your son's aberrant behavior, and she decided to consult me. I suggested the MMPI because it's often helpful in evaluating people who do the kind of things your son does."

"Dr. Feldon was good enough to drive out from Portland on short notice and conduct an examination of Topper," Dorn added.

Tucker prayed silently a moment, staring at his own huge hands. "An examination?"

"Merely an interview, to start with," Feldon answered. "It was on the basis of that interview that I recommended the MMPI, together with a thorough examination. I thought it best not to wait."

"Why wasn't I notified?"

"Your son consented to the test and exam," Dorn answered. "The school district has taken the position that it can ask students to submit to such investigations with or without their guardians' permission, if they've engaged in any kind of criminal activity. Besides, you were out of town, and your housekeeper wouldn't tell us where you'd gone or when you'd be back."

Esmerelda, Tucker thought. *Esmerelda kept this from me.* "What do you mean by criminal activity?"

"If what Bunny Coglin, Cory Dunwoody and Kyle Matzko say is true, then Topper is guilty of indecent exposure as well as lewd and lascivious behavior. The lawyer for the school district tells me that he's old enough to be tried as an adult on these charges, if someone were to press the issue. He could also be guilty of wanton cruelty to animals."

Tucker leaned back in his chair and let out a long, slow breath. *Why, Lord? Haven't I atoned after all these years . . . ?*

He folded and unfolded his calloused hands, forced himself not to make fists. He told himself to relax. He listened to the rest of what Doctors Dorn and Feldon

had to say without uttering a word himself, except for a
short, silent prayer now and then.

VI

LIEUTENANT DANIEL KANTOR TURNED OFF PAULSEN'S
Main Street into the parking lot of the Nehalem County
Courthouse and nosed his unmarked Caprice into the
space reserved for the supervisor of the Buckthorn Task
Force. The courthouse was a blockish, three-story
brownstone built in 1875, when public buildings looked
the part.

Like his predecessors, Kantor worked out of a
cramped office in the county sheriff's five-man department, which shared the basement of the courthouse with
Paulsen's five-man police force. The place had a damp,
earthworm-kind of smell and always felt chilly. Long-
outdated posters hung on the wall behind the reception
counter—March of Dimes, the United Way, a blood-
hound in a trench coat exhorting people to take a bite
out of crime.

Kantor's office was a windowless cube not much bigger than a janitor's closet. A computer work station and
a gray-metal desk occupied nearly half the space, while
six locked filing cabinets took up the other half. To take
the edge off the chill, Kantor had scrounged an electric
space heater that he kept on the floor near his chair. He
flipped it on as he sat down, then reached for the telephone.

The Sheriff of Nehalem County appeared in the doorway, nearly filling it with his bulk. Nick Graybill was a
round, silver-haired man whose starched brown uniform
fit him like a sausage skin. A gold and silver star glittered above his left pocket, an emphatic symbol of his
office and authority. On his hip hung a Glock .45 in a

patent leather holster, along with ammo pouches, an aerosol can of pepper mace and a set of chromed handcuffs—all the latest cop gear. A huge green cigar protruded from his teeth like a sooty stovepipe (his deputies called him "the Cigar" behind his back).

"I hear the FBI's looking for you," the sheriff said, "and I'm not talking about those goofs in the Portland office—I'm talking about Quantico. As per usual you weren't in, so I routed 'em to Wacka. Have you talked to 'em?"

"Wacka" was shorthand for Washington County Consolidated Communications Agency, located in Beaverton, a suburb of Portland in neighboring Washington County. The agency provided dispatch services for the police and fire departments within its own county's borders and, through an interlocal agreement, for the two law enforcement agencies in tiny, financially strapped Nehalem County.

"And a good morning to you, too, Nick. Great day, isn't it? I've just been over in Royal Chinook Park. We're in for an early spring this year if the buds in the trees are any indication. The air has that certain sweetness, if you know what I mean."

Kantor waited for something that might pass for a pleasantry from the Cigar, but nothing doing. Nick Graybill had little use for the Oregon State Police, so he simply grunted and waited. Yes, Kantor confirmed with a sigh, Wacka had beeped his pager, and he'd checked in on his car radio. The dispatcher had notified him that he'd received an urgent telephone call from someone named Dr. Ariel Sheplov at the FBI's VICAP, to whom Kantor had sent some material earlier in the week. He'd interrupted his interview with KATU News to speed back to his office and return the call on a secure line, rather than use his cellular phone, which wasn't sufficiently secure for this type of business.

"So what's it all about?" Graybill wanted to know. "What kind of material did you send them?"

"I needed their advice about something. Nothing earth-shaking."

The Cigar made a face, waited for more.

"After I talk to them," Kantor added, "you and I can have a sit-down, hash things over. I'll need your advice, too."

Graybill harrumphed and blew a cloud of acrid cigar smoke into Kantor's office, showing that he knew when he was being stroked. He trudged off toward his own office at the far end of the corridor, his cowboy boots clopping on the tile like the hooves of an old dray horse.

Kantor punched a number on his phone and heard the buzz of another telephone on the far edge of the continent, which was answered almost immediately. He identified himself and asked for Dr. Ariel Sheplov.

The next voice sounded too young to belong to a board-certified forensic psychiatrist. "Yes, Lieutenant Kantor? This is Ariel Sheplov at VICAP. Thanks for returning my call."

"My pleasure, Doctor. What can I do for you this fine day?"

"Lieutenant, I've just faxed you some material that details everything I'm about to say. Normally, I wouldn't discuss this sort of thing over the phone, but time may be critical, so I'll risk it. What I'm about to tell you concerns the results of an MMPI that you Fed-Exed to us a few days ago, that of a local high schooler named Theodore Bannon."

"Right. I appreciate your getting back to me so fast."

"Before I say anything more, I need to ask you something. Is it your belief that Theodore Bannon is somehow involved with the Buckthorn murders?"

Kantor took a breath, thought a moment. "To be

frank, Doctor, I don't know what to believe. Like I said in the cover letter, the local school super decided to have Topper Bannon tested after receiving a complaint about him. The psychologist who did the testing got pretty agitated over the results, as I understand it. He called me and suggested that I show the results to a forensic shrink. You people have been involved with the Buckthorn investigation from the beginning, and that's why I sent the results to you. Any weirdo is fair game, as far as I'm concerned, even if I don't have anything that ties him to the killings.''

"I understand. Your letter said that this individual has a reputation for some rather alarming behavior that includes exhibitionism and torturing animals.''

"So I'm told.''

"Then I'm afraid you may have trouble on your hands, Lieutenant. The consensus among my colleagues in VICAP and the Bureau's Behavioral Science Unit is that this Theodore Bannon—this Topper—is a time bomb waiting to go off, if he hasn't done so already. Your school district's psychologist—I think his name was—'' Kantor heard the shuffling of papers on the other end as Sheplov looked up the name. "Feldon. It seems that Dr. Feldon reached the same conclusion. Now, I've skimmed the file on the Buckthorn murders . . .''

While she talked, Kantor picked through the stack of letters and faxes in his in-box until he found the one from VICAP, a lengthy message more than a dozen pages long. It had arrived while he was in Buckthorn giving the interview. He listened and read at the same time.

"... and I realize that he couldn't be the original Buckthorn killer, since he wasn't even alive when the first homicide was committed. Still, his kind of personality inventory is very rare, almost too rare for it to occur coincidentally in a place like Buckthorn, where you've had an eighteen-year string of serial killings.''

Kantor felt a tingling in his gut. ''Are you telling me there's a likelihood that Topper Bannon *is* actually connected somehow to the Buckthorn killer?''

''I'd prefer to say that there's a better-than-even chance that the killer's personality inventory would look similar to Topper's, if we could find the guy and compel him to sit still for an MMPI. In a population pool as small as the one you're in, that's way beyond the realm of coincidence.''

''Tell me something, Doctor. Could this kind of thing run in families—the predilection to commit serial murder?''

''Good question. Heredity can play a role in various types of mental illness, certainly. Schizophrenia, notably. But psychosexual killers are almost never schizophrenic. You could argue persuasively that they're all sick, but rarely are they mentally ill in the sense that they fail to appreciate the wrongness of their crimes. Unlike schizophrenics, they live in the real world, and they're capable of laying elaborate plans to snare their victims and avoid capture. That's why so few have used the insanity defense with any success. They know what they're doing, and they know it's wrong, but they just don't care. They have an extreme form of what we call antisocial personality disorder.''

''So it's not hereditary. Is that what I'm hearing? If I started poking into Topper Bannon's family, I'd be on the wrong track, right?''

''I didn't say that. The evidence we've collected over the years indicates that psychosexual killers become the way they are because of their childhood environment. Broken homes, abuse, addictive parents and so forth. Whether heredity plays a part we don't yet know, but we do know that certain kinds of environment can breed serial killers. That's all I'm telling you, Lieutenant. This young man, this Topper, shows all the earmarks of someone who's about to become extremely dangerous. Even though he couldn't possibly be the one you're looking for, he may very well come from the same environment that bred your Buckthorn killer. If I were you, that's where I'd concentrate my attention. I'd also keep a close eye on Topper for the obvious reasons, maybe contrive some means of restraining him before he moves to the next level. It's not very often that we're able to identify one of this type before he actually starts killing people, and it would be a shame to blow it, don't you think?''

The next level. Kantor's pulse sped up, and the tingle of excitement intensified. ''Thanks, Doctor Sheplov. I appreciate your prompt attention to this matter.''

''Not at all, Lieutenant.''

Seconds later Kantor was knocking on the door of Nick Graybill's personal office, which brought an irritable ''Come!'' Kantor pushed through the door into a large room with cheap laminate paneling and eye-level windows. Filling every available square inch of wall space were plaques and citations from the Lion's Club, Kiwanis and Rotary, and framed photos of Graybill shaking hands with governors of Oregon and members of the congressional delegation, both past and present. On one wall hung a glassed-in display of shoulder patches from sheriff's departments around the nation.

Kantor dropped Dr. Sheplov's fax onto the blotter in front of Graybill, then lit a Marlboro as the sheriff leafed through the papers. Graybill's squinty eyes widened perceptibly as they absorbed the message.

. . . *subject is self-centered, with a limited capacity to form deep interpersonal relationships. He is highly intelligent, but impulsive. He has little patience, and be-*

comes easily bored. He is militantly rebellious toward authority figures, particularly those who represent religion. He rejects traditional social values and standards. There can be no question that even though he has yet to reach the age of eighteen, at which age a definitive diagnosis could be reached, he suffers from a precursor to antisocial personality disorder, which is an incurable behavioral defect . . .

"What the hell is this?" Graybill demanded, holding the paper away from him as if it were a piece of used toilet tissue. "You sent Theodore Bannon's MMPI to Quantico?"

Kantor nodded, blew out smoke.

"Do you have any idea who you're dealing with here?"

"We're dealing with a dangerous kid, someone who shows all the earmarks of antisocial personality disorder. But that's not the point, Nick. The point is . . ."

"Forget the psychiatric booshwah. This is Tucker Bannon's kid we're talking about. Tucker Bannon is the leading citizen of this county. He owns the oldest sawmill in the whole friggin' state and he's a solid, born-again Christian to boot. His family has provided work for half the loggers and millmen in both Paulsen and Buckthorn for the better part of a goddamn century. He also happens to be one of my oldest friends and supporters. You can't come in here and accuse Tuck Bannon's kid of—" He narrowed his eyes again on the paper in front of him. "—of suffering from . . . *an incurable behavioral defect.*"

Kantor ground his teeth, took a deep breath. "What I'm trying to tell you, Nick, is that Topper Bannon is probably a danger to the community, and that his situation might very well have some connection to the Buckthorn killer. It's all there in black and white, if you'd just take the time . . ."

"Now you listen to me," Graybill said, getting to his feet. He snatched the cigar out of his teeth and pointed the bitten end at Kantor. "I've cooperated with you people from the get-go, and I plan to keep on cooperating as long as it takes to catch the Buckthorn killer. But I'm not gonna stand by and watch you tar a decent family with this . . . this *mental-disorder* crap. Topper Bannon hadn't even been born when the first murder went down, and he's been hardly more than a boy when all but the last one went down. That puts him off the playing field, far as I can tell. Your job is to investigate the friggin' Buckthorn killings—am I right? It's not your job to worry about a seventeen-year-old kid who burns a few rats now and then."

Kantor kept his cool. He hadn't risen to his present level by getting into pissing matches with local lawmen. "I appreciate your input, Nick. Nonetheless I'm calling a meeting of the Task Force this afternoon, kick around the idea of changing the basic direction of the investigation."

"Change the direction of the investigation? How in the hell can you do that when you don't have any direction to start with?"

"Point well taken. Still, we've got some good people on this Task Force, and I think it's time we took full advantage of their talents. I hope you'll attend and share your thoughts with us."

"So you're calling a meeting." Graybill's upper lip whitened. "Well that's just dandy." He couldn't say in a meeting what he'd said just now to Kantor, because he would sound as if he was trying to steer a criminal investigation away from a political crony. He had no choice but to back off, which Kantor could see was making him livid.

"I'll schedule it for three o'clock, give you time to

let your lunch settle,'' Kantor said, tucking the VICAP
message under his arm. ''I really hope you can see your
way clear to attend.'' He winked good-naturedly on his
way out.

7

I

...OVER HERE, LADIES AND GENTLEMEN, IS WEED Control Central. This is where the Verminator stores and mixes the various agents that account for the vast, unspoiled expanse of Oregon bluegrass that surrounds the big house. You'll note the array of tightly sealed chemical containers...

Topper had skipped school today after overhearing an early-morning phone call his father had received from the superintendent of schools. Instead of catching the school bus at the corner of Second and Columbia for the ride into Paulsen, he'd hidden in the weedy lot behind the old Allegro Theater, using a broken-down corn popper for cover. He'd waited until the bus had come and gone, then climbed the stone stairway from Bannon Avenue to the woods behind the gardener's shed. He hadn't ventured out of the thicket until his father's Suburban moved down the drive toward the main gate, and even then he hadn't shown himself in the house. He'd come here, to his "office," the gardener's shed. The Verminator's office.

It's never too early to get a jump on the weeds, ladies and gentlemen. Now I realize it's still February, and nobody's thinking about taking care of their grass—except the Verminator, of course. But I'm here to tell you that weeds are insidious enemies who'll cut you no breaks. Even as we speak, they're growing and producing seeds and spores, soaking up precious water needed

*by decorative grasses and flowers, sapping the soil of
critical nutrients . . .*

He'd spent the morning taking inventory of his various poisons and mixtures, mapping out his spring
campaign against a diverse army of weeds. Dichloro-
phenoxyacitic acid and dimethylamine salt. Propionic
acid. Paraquat and diquat. Various inert ingredients. The
labels on the plastic containers warned against exposure
to eyes and skin, ingestion, contamination of feed and
foodstuffs. Topper made notations on a clipboard as he
moved from one stack of containers to the next.

*As you might have guessed, these are serious agents,
babes and dudes. Corrosive, toxic. You wouldn't want
to get any of this stuff on you, believe me. And you sure
as hell wouldn't want to get any IN you, either . . .*

He paused as though waiting for laughter to die down,
one dark eyebrow arched slyly, then addressed a beam
of sunlight slanting through a dusty window. *Before you
start pissin' and moanin' about the effects of this stuff
on the ecology, think about the enemy. We're talking
about black medic here. We're talking about Canada
thistle and carpetweed and sheep sorrel. Ever see what
carpetweed does to a lawn? Ever see a major infestation
of shepherd's purse or beggar weed? How about wild
onion or speedwell or hawkweed? If you're ever unfortunate enough to see a lawn or garden caught in the
clutches of these guys, you won't be persnickety about
using a little propionic acid. In fact you'll . . .*

He heard something—footsteps outside on the walk.
He set aside the clipboard and moved to the door of the
shed, edged it open a crack. *Excuse me, ladies and gentlemen. We're picking up something on the sensors . . .*

Esmerelda stood outside the door, her face tight with
concern, her oily eyes wide and fearful. She apparently

had seen him sneak out of the woods to the gardener's shed, despite his precautions.

"*¡Corre y escondete, mi muchacho!*" she warned, her words hissing. "*¡El Señor Bannon esta llegando!*"

Topper cocked his head and listened. Sure enough, he could hear the engine of his father's big four-by-four in the distance, moving up the drive toward the house. His guts knotted. By now his father would have talked to the school officials and that nerdy head doctor from Portland who'd administered the psychological tests. His father had undoubtedly learned about the rat burning and all the rest, all the Verminator stuff. *Time to pay the piper—right, ladies and gentlemen*?

Esmerelda wrung her hands and bobbed her head in time to some nervous, inner rhythm that only she could hear apparently. She looked very old, he thought. Older than he could ever remember, and this frightened him a little.

"No," Topper answered, steeling himself. "I'm not going to hide. Hiding isn't cool anymore. In fact, it sucks."

"*¡No me desobedezcas! ¡Escucha a tu abuela, si sabes lo que es bueno para ti!*"

He'd always liked the way she referred to herself as his grandmother, his *abuela*. And he'd always obeyed her as if she was in fact his grandmother. But Topper was no longer a little boy, and he could no longer cower behind the skirts of his *abuela* whenever his father came looking to beat sin out of his hide.

"*¡No correré de él!*" Topper declared stoutly. "*Ya él no me asusta.*" He wouldn't run from his father. He was no longer afraid—not quite the truth, but it sounded good.

Esmerelda pushed the door open and grabbed him by a sleeve. "Someday I will tell you what he is capable

of," she said in lightly accented English. "It is not for
the ears of children—"

"I'm not a child, Abuela."

She relaxed her grip on his sleeve, and her eyes
brimmed with tears. "No, perhaps you're not. But neither are you a man."

Not a child, not a man, he thought. *I'm the Verminator. And the Verminator knows no fear, cares only
about killing vermin. Thus was it in the beginning, is
now, and ever shall be—killing without letup. Amen.*

Esmerelda whirled away and scurried on her fat legs
toward the house. Topper had seen in her face that she
meant to intercept his father, and suddenly he was as
afraid for her as he was for himself.

II

DURING THE SHORT DRIVE HOME FROM PAULSEN,
Tucker Bannon had decided on a course of action concerning the boy he'd called his son for seventeen long,
trying years. He'd decided to beat the living tarnation
out of him. Once again he would drag Topper kicking
and screaming back to the path of righteousness before
his unwholesome cravings brought ruination and shame
to the Bannon family.

The decision hadn't come wholly from Tucker's gut.
Withhold not correction from the child, the book of
Proverbs advised, *for if thou beatest him with the rod,
he shall not die.*

So Tucker had convinced himself that it was for the
boy's own good that he would fill a sock with sand and
work him over with it, a method that generated sufficient
pain without leaving blatant cuts or contusions. Tucker's
own father had used the method liberally on both of his
sons, and Tucker had used it on Topper at least a dozen

times. Pain cleanses, Tucker knew. Pain releases the soul from sin.

In his own way he loved Topper despite the boy's obvious afflictions—not as a son, for Topper had precious little Bannon blood in his veins, but as a ward, a responsibility. God had sent him as a flesh-and-blood reminder of a past sin, a burden to be shouldered and looked after. The boy's real mother was the half-Mexican girl, Rosa Juanita Sandoval, the daughter of the Bannons' housekeeper, Esmerelda. Rosa too had been a burden, a reminder of yet another blood-sin committed long ago. Tucker had raised Topper's mother as his own child, as a sister to his real daughter, Sally, whom God had later taken from him.

He'd fed and clothed Rosa, given her a home and taught her the Gospel, just as he'd done for Sally, because this was what God had expected of him. This was how a good Christian man atoned for the killing of a child's father. For some reason God had seen fit to take Rosa from him, too, and make her his mortal enemy. God's ways were beyond human understanding, so Tucker didn't even try.

Within a few weeks Bannon House would again ring with the laughter and roughhousing of children, a thought that brought joy to his heart. Bright and happy children, these—not like poor, twisted Topper. The Cochran kids were Tucker's legitimate grandchildren, the offspring of his daughter, Sally. Their veins surged with rich Bannon blood, which made them suitable heirs to the land and the fortune that God had bestowed upon the Bannons. Having suitable heirs was of surpassing importance to Tucker.

After this morning's meeting with Superintendent Dorn and Dr. Feldon, Tucker had gone to the high school, meaning to fetch Topper and bring him home, which had only seemed appropriate under the circumstances. But Topper hadn't arrived at school today, his teachers had reported. The kid had played hooky. Tucker had no choice but to find him and minister to him in the proper way—with a sock full of sand.

Give me the strength and the courage to do what I need to do, Lord, he'd prayed as he entered the town of Buckthorn. *Guide my hand. Make me merciless, even as Thou art merciless against the forces of darkness.*

III

A STEEL-BARRED GATE GAVE ONTO A DRIVE THAT LED upward toward Bannon House, which stood bright against the wooded face of Mount Olivet. Tucker touched a button on the dash, and the gate opened. He lowered the window as he drove through, needing to hear the satisfying clink of the gate as it locked itself behind him. The sound always reassured him that the iniquity of the outside world hadn't yet penetrated this place.

He parked in the garage and went into the adjoining workshop, where he stored several bags of cement and clean sand. He often mixed his own concrete for the occasional repair of a cracked walk or driveway, and this was why he kept cement and sand on hand.

A pair of hip waders hung on a hook next to the door, holdovers from an era when he spent his spare time knee-deep in trout streams, before arthritis had bored into his knees and ankles like virulent worms. He took the waders down, pulled from one a long sock of heavy red cotton. It stank of mothballs, but this didn't matter.

He went to a sack of sand, opened it and filled the sock, then knotted it securely, creating a pliable truncheon. Several whaps into the palm of his hand confirmed that the thing was hefty and hard, but not *too* hefty, not *too* hard. He didn't want to maim the boy, after all. He would try not to hit the face or neck unless absolutely necessary.

Tucker felt the heat of righteous anger mounting, and it felt good. Heat in his face, his hands, his groin. Pure, God-given heat. He almost didn't hear the door open behind him, and he turned to face Esmerelda.

"Señor Bannon, le ruego no maltratar el muchacho," she pleaded, worrying her apron with her fists. She wore a simple dark housedress, as Tucker had always demanded—never slacks or shorts. And never jewelry or makeup, either. Mexican women looked so slutty when they wore makeup and jewelry, he felt. Even the old ones.

Just now she'd begged him not to hurt the boy. When she saw the red-cloth truncheon in his hand, she started to speak again, but Tucker cut her off.

"Esmerelda, why didn't you tell me about this business with Topper and the school superintendent? And the psychological testing? I've just spent an hour with Dr. Dorn and some namby-pamby psychologist from Portland, hearing about how my son suffers from something called antisocial personality disorder. Did you really think that you could keep all this from me, you stupid woman?"

"Señor Bannon, estoy muy arrepentida . . ."

"Speak English, for God's sake."

She lowered her head, almost bowed before him. "I had hoped nothing would come of it. After all, he is so young, and young boys make mistakes, no?"

"Did they tell you what he *did*, Esmerelda? Did they tell you about the rats, the fire, all the rest?"

"Si, they told me."

Tucker rolled his eyes, shook his head in disbelief. Where was the woman's moral outrage, her God-given common sense? Did she think that such evil would simply go away on its own? He shouted these questions at her, but Esmerelda merely stared at the floor. Tucker stood silent for a long moment, waiting, then shrugged and moved around her toward the door. She grabbed an open flap of his sheepskin jacket and hung on.

"Please, *Señor* Bannon, do not harm him. It is not his fault that he is this way."

"Oh? Then whose fault is it?"

Esmerelda's round face came alive with anger. "Look into your own heart. Perhaps you will find the answer there."

"So it's *my* fault, is it?" Tucker smiled coldly. "Woman, I'm surprised at you. And a little hurt, I don't mind saying. I guess I've overestimated you all these years, given you more credit than you deserve." He walked a slow circle around her, riveting her with his gray eyes. "You forget that I'm the guy who raised his mother as my own daughter, then raised him as my own son and gave him a life most kids only dream about. I've put food in his mouth and clothes on his back, given him useful work to do, a future if he wants it. How can it be *my* fault that he coaxes other kids into the woods so he can burn live rats and abuse himself while they watch? I'm the guy who taught him to pray, remember? I taught him to read Scripture and compelled him to give his heart to the Lord. I didn't teach him to do evil."

"You've beaten him," she answered, spitting the words. "From the time he was just able to walk, you've beaten him like an animal. Look into your heart, *Señor* Bannon, and tell me what kind of man beats a child this way."

Tucker felt tremors of rage in his chest, the kind that could blind him and make him powerless over himself. The kind of rage that could kill, as had happened more than once. But it hadn't conquered him yet, and he fought it. Though his eyelids quivered and the mole above his left eyebrow twitched like a thing with a will of its own, he kept his voice low, his words measured.

"Your own people beat their children, Esmerelda. You know that as well as I do."

"Not the way you have beaten this boy."

"I've only done it for his own good. Scripture commands us, *Thou shalt beat him with the rod, and shalt deliver his soul from hell.* This is the way God means it to be, don't you see? All this modern child-psychology business, all this stuff about *empowerment* and *enabling* and calling time-out instead of spanking, and all the other secular humanist garbage that's fallen down on our heads—it's all deception designed to drive a wedge between the child and his parent. It's the devil's deception, Esmerelda. Its purpose is to make the righteous parent powerless over his child, so that the devil can sink his claws into him and drag him off to hell. It's happening all around us."

Tucker saw disbelief in her eyes and scowled in frustration. How could he expect this simple woman to understand? She'd had little schooling, she was Catholic, and she was Mexican, a most unfortunate combination. The fact that her weak Mexican blood flowed in Topper's veins was probably the chief cause of his mental and spiritual deformities. Explaining things to her was a waste of time.

He turned for the door, but again Esmerelda grabbed his jacket. He shook her off, but she came back at him, her hands fisted.

"Please do not hurt him!"

Tucker heard the bellowing of his own voice, felt the sudden eruption of anger. The woman scrabbled at his face with her nails, but he fended her off, shoved her back. Still she came at him, shrieking now, spraying hot tears and spit.

Tucker scarcely thought about the fact that he was

raising the truncheon, hauling it back to let fly a blow toward the woman who'd cleaned his house and cooked his meals for the past thirty-four years. The blow happened almost before he knew it. The sock full of sand caught her squarely across the mouth, snapping her head back and jarring loose her upper dentures. The teeth skittered across the cement floor of the shop, and Esmerelda went down, her eyes rolling back and her arms flailing.

"Abuela!"

The shout came from the door, and Tucker whirled to see Topper there, shoulder braced against the jamb, his eyes and mouth wide with horror. Not a handsome lad, Topper—swarthy, thick of body and round of face, dressed in those horrible grunge clothes that today's kids thought so cool.

"So there you are," Tucker said, his voice rasping. "You and I have things to discuss. For starters, you can tell me why you aren't in school."

"What have you *done* to her?" The kid flew past Tucker and knelt over Esmerelda, then lifted her head gently off the cement and cradled it. Blood spilled from the old woman's mouth. "How could you do it, Dad? How could you—?"

"Shut your mouth. Get up on your feet and look at me when I'm talking to you." The boy paid him no mind, and Tucker's anger erupted again. He launched a size-eleven boot into Topper's ribs, and the boy doubled up on the floor next to his grandmother. Tucker caught handfuls of Topper's bulky sweatshirt and hauled him to his feet, but the kid couldn't stand.

"Face me like a man," Tucker growled, "or by God I'll rip your arm off and beat you to death with it!"

Topper suddenly vomited, spattering his father's steel-toed work boots. Tucker gaped at the mess and felt his rage take him like fire takes an old barn. He delivered a roundhouse blow to Topper's jaw with the sockful of sand, then caught him with another on the back swing. He caught him twice more about the neck and shoulders before the kid hit the floor, where he cowered and blubbered under the hail of pain.

"Foolishness is bound in the heart of a child," Tucker thundered, quoting Proverbs between blows. *"But the rod of correction shall drive it from him."*

He hit the boy again and again, putting his back into the chore and liking the sounds the blows made, liking the heat in his cheeks. He was hardly aware of his son's screams or the wailing of the old woman who knelt in the middle of the shop floor, her palms pressed to her bloody cheeks. He slowed only when he felt the twang of arthritis in his knees and realized that he wasn't as young as he used to be.

Tell me your secrets; you can trust me.
Come near. Come very near.

—JAMES AGEE
A Death in the Family

8

I

SARAH COCHRAN HAD A WINDOW SEAT, HAVING WON
two out of three rounds of paper-scissors-rock with her
brother, Carter, who now pouted in the aisle seat. Shitty
loser, she thought. But then he was only ten, and Sarah
supposed she should make allowances. After all, she was
so much *older* than he, her thirteenth birthday being little
more than a month away. So even though she'd won the
window seat fair and square, she decided that she would
offer it to Carter on the connecting flight out of Dallas,
if for no other reason than to show him what maturity
was all about.

Their father sat between them, looking cramped and
uncomfortable in his tan sport coat, his face too thin, his
color pallid. These past few weeks had been hell on him,
Sarah knew. As the big jet roared away from the runway,
she pressed her cheek to the cold window in order to
take in a final, meaningful look at New York.

The plane circled southward out of JFK International
Airport and swung west over Jamaica Bay, an expanse
of gray water off the eastern edge of Brooklyn. Spring
had yet to show itself in New York, and the landscape
was muddy brown in the aftermath of winter. Manhattan
sprawled in the north, a hazy vision of towers and
bridges. Further north still, Sarah knew, well out of sight
though still within the reaches of the megalopolis, lay
the town of Rye, where the Cochran family had lived.

Had lived.

In her mind she saw the leafy streets of her neighborhood, the familiar local landmarks and manicured yards, the comfortable house where she'd spent most of her life till now. Her bedroom with its flowery wallpaper and stuffed animals. The shaded deck where her father had grilled chicken breasts or shish kebobs on summer weekends. The English garden where her mother had puttered. She heard the barking of Gerard, the squeals of the neighbor kids on their trampoline, the lullaby her mother sang to her when she was young . . .

> *Nunca tengas miedo de la luna,*
> *mi niño, porque ella te cantará un arrullo. . . .*

Suddenly her throat grew tight, and her eyes stung. She kept her face to the window, not wanting Dad or Carter to see the tears. Her mother would've wanted her to be strong for them, having had no use for "whiners and weepers," male or female, grown or not. *When you need to cry, do it when you're alone*, she'd advised Sarah countless times. *Never give some guy an excuse to call you a blubbering little girl. Getting ahead in this world is tough enough without carrying* that *baggage.*

In her lap lay a notebook in which she'd written poems about the coming of this day, this moment. Little girl's poems, she'd decided after reading them later. Almost babyish. Sarah Cochran was her own harshest critic. Early this morning, while waiting for the cab that would take them to the airport, she'd started a new poem that she'd hoped would convey feelings and observations more appropriate to her imminent status as a teenager. But she'd gotten only as far as the title: "The Land of Good-bye."

She'd meant to write about the pain of leaving friends and favorite teachers, the school she'd loved, the house where she'd lived. But whenever she'd pressed her pencil to the page, her heart had welled up and she'd spent all her energy fighting tears.

She'd meant to write about Gerard, the loving Bernese mountain dog, who could not come with them to Oregon because Grampa Tuck didn't allow animals in his house. She'd meant to question whether leaving New York also meant leaving her mother, whose presence had seemed to linger despite the fact that her body was five months dead.

A part of Sarah wanted to believe that her mother's presence would follow the family out to Oregon, that tonight she could lie down in her new bed on the other side of the continent and feel that Mom was nearby, watching, protecting. But another part of her—the coldly realistic part, the one most like her mother—knew that this wasn't possible.

The past is dead or dying, left behind in the Land of Good-bye, this part of Sarah Cochran whispered.

She turned from the window, opened her notebook and began to write, having found the opening lines of what she was certain would be her first grown-up poem.

II

PETER COCHRAN SET HIS WATCH TO PACIFIC TIME AS THE pilot announced that the descent into Portland International Airport was under way—2:55 P.M., on March 24, 1994, a Thursday. He glanced right and left, saw that both kids were asleep, having endured a long and tiring flight. Sarah sprawled in the aisle seat, wearing baggy bib overalls and a white Everlast T-shirt, a blond angel with braces on her teeth. Carter wore knee-length black-denim shorts, a plaid flannel sport shirt and Sony Diskman headphones over his ears. How he could sleep to the music of Snoop Doggy Dogg, Pete couldn't fathom.

Pete wished that he himself could have slept. Though he'd repeatedly screwed his eyes shut and forced the various muscle groups of his body to relax, his mental machine had continued to grind along in high gear, fueled by misgivings, questions, anxieties.

And *guilt*. Mustn't forget *guilt*.

You broke your promise, Pete. How could you do it . . . ?

Whenever he closed his eyes, he saw Gerard, tail wagging, tongue lolling out of a grinning mouth, and he suffered anew that hellish moment when he told the kids that the dog couldn't come with them to Buckthorn. Grampa Tuck didn't allow animals in his house, he'd learned after accepting the old man's offer of a job and a temporary home for his family. *It's just one of those crazy things*, he'd told them. *Some people don't like animals, that's all. It doesn't make them bad people*.

He'd reluctantly approached Lara Dischmann, who'd been Sally's closest friend at the ad firm, to ask whether the Dischmanns could keep a grown Bernese mountain dog for a year, maybe longer, until the Cochrans found a house of their own out in Oregon. Lara, bless her heart, had said yes without hesitating, though her family already owned two collies. Only yesterday Pete had dropped the dog off at the Dischmanns' house in Scarsdale, and he couldn't forget the look of bewilderment in Gerard's eyes at the moment of parting, a look that said, *You can't be serious about leaving me here. Haven't I been a good dog . . . ?*

During the flight Pete had tried to distract himself with news magazines and paperbacks that he'd bought at the airport, tried to tell himself that his own small worries withered next to the real problems of the world. The Serbs were shelling Sarajevo, for Christ's sake, killing helpless civilians by the hundreds. Bill Clinton and Congress were gearing up to reform the nation's health care system. And Oliver North was a serious candidate for the U.S. Senate in Virginia, which was chilling even to a professed conservative like Peter Cochran.

He still doubted his own motives for accepting Tucker Bannon's offer, which meant that he doubted the pureness of his own heart. Had he really done it for the kids, or had he done it for himself, needing to recapture some fragment of his old dreams?

His daughter's notebook lay open on her meal tray, for she'd dropped off to sleep without closing it. Pete took some comfort in the opening lines of a poem she'd just written.

> The past is dead or dying,
> Left behind in the Land of Good-bye.
> The future rings with loud hellos,
> And promises life . . .

He reached over and flipped the cover over, knowing that Sarah hated for anyone to read her stuff until she'd polished it and deemed it ready.

III

TUCKER, DOLLY AND TOPPER GREETED THEM AT THE airport with open arms and smiles, hugs and kisses all around. Pete had never been the touchy-feely type, and he felt awkward hugging people he hardly knew. Still, they *were* family, he supposed, so he did his damnedest to act overjoyed.

Topper turned out to be a strapping, dark-complected lad with a full face and large, widely spaced eyes. Pete thought he looked nothing at all like a Bannon, that he actually looked Hispanic. An adopted child?

Though the kid seemed genuinely happy to meet the

Cochrans and greeted each of them with a grin and a firm handshake, something about him bothered Pete. His eyes glinted with something wild. Pete remembered that Tucker had termed him *not an ideal heir*, whatever the hell that meant. *You'll understand when you meet him*, the old man had promised.

They piled into the Bannons' Suburban, and Topper took the driver's seat, which didn't exactly ease Pete's discomfort. As if he could read minds, Tucker said, "Don't worry—this young buck is an excellent driver. Taught him myself, didn't I, son?"

Topper twisted around in the driver's seat to face his passengers in the rear. "That's right, Dad. Everything I am, I owe to you." He grinned hugely. "Next stop, Buckthorn, Oregon, population three hundred and twenty-two. Estimated travel time, one hour and forty minutes, depending on the traffic. Please let me know if I can do anything to make your trip more comfortable. Also, note the exits on both sides of the vehicle, and in the rear. In the unlikely event of . . ."

"That will do, dear," Dolly said to Topper with a tight smile, and the kid obediently shut up. Carter giggled, entertained by Topper's antics. Sarah traded a surprised glance with her father, and Pete tried not to let his face betray the bad feeling worming inside him.

Within minutes they were out of the parking garage and speeding eastward from the airport toward the heart of Portland on I-84, which the locals called the Banfield Freeway. Peter thought at first that the city seemed absurdly green. Too much healthy grass, too many evergreen trees and shrubbery. And not enough industrial soot or graffiti or garbage along the highway. Overhead was a crisp blue sky that looked free of smog. The traffic actually moved along briskly, though Pete noticed that the oncoming lanes, those headed out of the city, were considerably more crowded. The late-afternoon rush hour was under way, but even so, it was like a lazy Sunday morning in New York.

Welcome to the City of Roses, Pete said to himself, a city that appeared to be everything he'd read about it. Handsome, clean, green. Gleaming business towers, wooded hillsides and vistas garnished with snow-covered volcanoes. The city of the Trail Blazers and Nike, of Intel and Tektronix, of Tonya Harding and Bob Packwood.

Pete had read that despite the nationwide notoriety garnered by the ultraconservative Oregon Citizens Alliance, which was always pushing some draconian ballot measure against gays and lesbians, metropolitan Portland was among the most tolerant and politically liberal communities in the country. *Fortune* magazine had rated it in the top ten for its business climate. Other publications had given the city high marks for "quality of life." Seeing the place for the first time, Pete felt he could live here.

Tucker entertained the kids with a tall tale or two, then promised a trip to the beach within the next few days, providing their father gave his permission. Pete said a trip to the beach sounded good, so of course they could go. Dolly offered to prepare picnic lunches, and Topper offered to teach Carter and Sarah how to fly his acrobatic kite.

They crossed the wide Willamette River on a multi-tiered bridge that Topper announced was the Marquam. Portland fell behind as they headed west on the Sunset Highway through the suburbs of Beaverton, Aloha and Hillsboro. The scenery gradually became less suburban and more pastoral. Forested hills, open fields and cropland. Vineyards. This was wine country, Topper announced. And nut country, too, (*You're telling me, Pete said to himself*) mainly hazelnuts and walnuts.

As the sights flew by, Pete and his father-in-law

traded small talk. Pete told about renting the house in
Rye to a nice young couple with two professional in-
comes. He assured Tucker that he was getting good rent
and that a property maintenance company would keep
the house in first-rate shape. He'd sold the Volvos and
the household furnishings, except for a few sentimen-
tally valuable items that he'd shipped via van line to
Buckthorn. What he couldn't bring to Bannon House he
would store in a commercial storage facility in Hillsboro.
Everything had gone smoothly, he lied, except for saying good-bye to the dog. The break with Rye had been
remarkably clean. Everything was aces.

Tucker leaned across the wide seat of the Suburban
and put his arm around Pete's shoulder. "You're doing
the right thing, son. I know you have misgivings, and
this is to be expected, but soon you'll know that the Lord
has put you on the right road. Trust me on this, okay?"

IV

ABOUT HALFWAY BETWEEN PORTLAND AND THE PACIFIC
Ocean, Topper turned north off Highway 26 onto
Oregon 202 and plunged into timber country. The two-
lane road twisted through the Clatsop State Forest,
which was an uneven patchwork of clear-cuts and replanted stands of Douglas fir. Logging roads branched
off the highway in every direction.

Pete had expected the region to be more scenic, as he
supposed it had been in bygone times, before a growing
nation found need of the trees for lumber, furniture, paper and packing materials. The landscape seemed tangled, not quite healthy. At frequent intervals vast open
areas swept upward onto the hillsides, pocked with
stumps and strewn with slash, scarred with the tracks of
heavy machinery. Signs along the road announced the

years in which various stands had been replanted, as if to reassure visitors that despite the destruction, forests could be regrown.

"Clear-cuts aren't pretty, that's for sure," Tucker said. "But this is what pays the bills, praise God. You look out here—" He pointed to a freshly decimated field of stumps. "—and what you see is livelihoods for loggers and millmen, builders and architects and real estate people, not to mention all the folks who make and sell things for houses. It's food on the table for a big part of America. It's college tuition for the kids, roofs over their heads and clothes on their backs. Our family has been a part of this great industry since my old man got his first logging job almost seventy-five years ago." He took off his Stetson and scratched the red mole above his left eyebrow. "Like a lot of folks, I regret what clear-cuts do to the land, but then I remember what God said to Adam and his woman: *Be fruitful and multiply, and replenish the earth and subdue it.*"

He winked and smiled at Pete, leaned close.

"*And God said, Behold, I have given you every tree . . .* That's what it says in Genesis, Pete—*every tree.* And we're doing exactly what God has told us to do. We're subduing the earth and we're replenishing it. We cut, we replant, and the forest grows back for the next generation to use. Somehow along the way, we make a little money." He patted Pete's knee.

They passed through the towns of Jewell and Birkenfeld, which were scarcely towns at all, but clusters of sad buildings with flat fronts like those in Western-movie towns, and tiny rundown houses, many of which had signs in the yards:

WE'RE A TIMBER FAMILY AND PROUD OF IT!

Topper took the left fork at the junction of Oregon 49 and Oregon 47 and drove a few miles more into the town of Buckthorn, where Oregon 49 became Main Street. Dusk was thickening into night, but it couldn't hide the dilapidation, the dreariness of the town.

Pete saw an access road off Main Street, barred by a chain-link gate with a sign that identified Buckthorn Wood Products, Tucker Bannon's sawmill. He held his breath. Yard lights shone on tired buildings with walls of corroded metal. Newly cut logs floated in a fetid-looking pond, still wearing their bark. Rusting machinery lay in weedy clumps along a fence. The place had the atmosphere of a junkyard. Pete thought, *My God, this is where I'm going to work.*

They drove down Main Street past Nockleby's Texaco, Tom Sawyer's Saloon, Chubby Chuck's Old-Fashioned Cafe. In the next block stood a once-grand structure that a faded sign identified as the Buckthorn Bank, now a ruin that looked ready for the wrecking ball. Across the street stood a long, low derelict with a weather-ravaged marquee, the Allegro Theater.

They turned right on Bannon Avenue and proceeded up a gentle rise toward a retaining wall built of river stone. Beyond a steel-barred gate stood Bannon House, lit by a perishing sunset, tall and clean against the forested hump of Mount Olivet. Topper pushed a button on the dash, the gate swung open, and he drove through.

"Wow!" breathed Carter, craning to eye the house ahead. "It's like a castle, man. It's like in a movie or something, isn't it, Dad?"

"It's beautiful," Pete heard himself say. He glanced into the rearmost seat, where Sarah sat with her brother, staring in disbelief at the house. She met his gaze, and he winked at her, which brought a smile barely big enough to show her braces.

The gray-brick house was a vision. A half-circular

portico with four white columns guarded the entrance. Chimneys towered above the gabled roof, which was covered with rust-colored tiles. Bay windows reflected shards of light from the sunset, while gently swaying cedars and hemlocks cast graceful shadows across the façade. A vision, a dream.

So this was where Sally grew up, Pete thought—an out-and-out rich kid. She'd never let slip any hint that she'd lived like this as a child.

"My old man built the place in nineteen twenty-five," Tucker said, his pride showing. "Six thousand seven hundred and twenty square feet on three floors. Eleven bedrooms, counting servants' quarters. Eight bathrooms, twelve fireplaces and a couple of outbuildings. The garage and shop went up in nineteen-seventy."

"We have a live-in housekeeper, of course," Dolly put in. "Mexican woman whose name is Esmerelda. She's been with us—what? More than thirty years, I think."

"Thirty-four years come July," Tucker confirmed. "Fine lady, fine cook. Like one of the family." He cleared his throat and changed the subject. "You can imagine that a place this size takes a lot of work. Topper handles the grounds, cuts the grass, kills the weeds and vermin. Frees me up to tackle most of the repairs. We bring in a landscaping service every few months for some pruning and fertilizing. Too much work for two pairs of hands—right, son?"

"You got that right," Topper said.

Esmerelda greeted them at the door with a servant's restrained courtesy. She had dark, liquid eyes that looked as if they'd shed many tears over the course of a hard life. Pete felt drawn to her. She led them across the foyer to a wide staircase, then up the stairs to the second floor. Tucker and Dolly followed along, jabbering about where the Persian runner on the stairs had come from, the long-dead craftsmen who'd made the chandeliers, which of the antiques were genuine and which weren't. Topper muscled along the luggage, muttering things to himself that Pete couldn't quite make out.

The first stop was Pete's bedroom in the northeast corner of the second floor, a large room with two sets of windows and a crackling fireplace. Fine Oriental rug on the floor. Antique writing desk in one corner, comfortable-looking leather armchair in the other. Queen-size bed with four oaken posters.

Sarah's bedroom, which was right next door, boasted a fireplace, a bay window that faced east and a separate bathroom immediately adjacent. Carter's room, somewhat smaller than the others, looked out upon the ascending slope of Mount Olivet.

Tucker pointed out that the master suite and Topper's bedroom were on the same floor but on the opposite side of the house, so in effect the Cochran family had its own wing. The kitchen and pantry lay immediately below Carter's room and were easily accessible via the rear stairs, in the event that someone needed a midnight snack.

"Just don't eat all the ice cream," he warned with phony sternness, looking at Carter. Then he broke a grin and ruffled the boy's hair.

A moment later he pulled Pete aside and spoke in a low voice.

"I thought you might want to know that your room was Sally's. It's the room she grew up in. We've remodeled, of course, repainted, taken out all her old things. I wanted you to have it mainly because it's the biggest vacant bedroom with a fireplace on this floor." He glanced down at his steel-toed boots and pushed his hands into his pockets. "I hope it doesn't bother you, Pete, but if it does, you're welcome to any of the other vacant bedrooms. We can put you up on the third floor—plenty of empty ones up there, or you can have the one next to Carter's, even though it doesn't have a fireplace. It's your call, son.''

Pete felt a tingling on the nape of his neck. He cleared his throat before trusting his voice. ''Tuck, it doesn't bother me that it was Sally's room,'' he lied. ''I can sleep anywhere.''

V

THEY ATE A FINE DINNER OF BAKED SALMON AND steamed mussels over rice, expertly prepared by Esmerelda, who was as good a cook as Tucker had bragged she was. Notable was the absence of wine. The Bannons were teetotalers, apparently, and they expected those who lived under their roof to teetotal along with them. Pete could have used a glass of wine or two with dinner. Hell, he could have used a whole bottle.

After dinner, while Tucker and Pete chatted over coffee in the library, Topper took Sarah and Carter on a tour of the mansion, which—as Carter later reported excitedly to his dad—included a playroom on the third floor that was filled with totally awesome old toys. There were fire trucks and dump trucks and cement trucks, cars and airplanes and guns, bugles and drums . . .

Guns? Pete felt himself tighten. Sally had been adamant about not allowing the kids to play with toy guns. Pete had gone along with her on this, though he'd played with toy guns when he was a kid and doubted that he'd suffered any damage as a result.

By nine o'clock the kids were exhausted and ready for bed. They'd started the day in New York, where it was now midnight, and jet lag had hit them hard. Pete too was beat, but he still hadn't unwound. He escorted Sarah and Carter to their respective rooms and tucked them in, kissed them goodnight and hovered too long over them. Then he dragged himself into the bathroom for a long shower. Afterward he sat in the armchair next to his bed, a magazine splayed in his lap, but he couldn't keep his eyes focused. Feeling ready for sleep at long last, he tossed the magazine aside and crawled under the covers, wearing only his boxers.

Cool sheets, good pillow, nice firm mattress. Big day tomorrow, first visit to the mill, meet the manager and all the workers. Sleep was an absolute necessity. He snapped off the lamp on the bed table and shut his eyes, willing himself to unconsciousness.

And saw Sally's face naturally. After all, this was *her* room. This was where she'd laid her head on thousands of consecutive nights and dreamed whatever little girls dream. But she'd probably never dreamed about getting cancer and dying, Pete thought, feeling a swell of bitterness. And she'd probably never dreamed of marrying a man who couldn't keep the most important promise he'd ever made to her. The man she'd dreamed of would've been steadfast and reliable, his word a rock that you could tie your life to and expect it to hold through any storm.

Very likely Sally had lain in this very bed and hatched her plan to leave Buckthorn forever, never to speak to her parents again, never to let her own children cast their shadows here. And she'd executed the plan with precision. She'd won her scholarships to a faraway school, worked part-time jobs to support herself, won her independence from Tucker and Dolly through toil and honest sweat. She'd fashioned a life of her own design, and she'd never looked back.

She couldn't have known that her trusted husband would betray her soon after she'd slipped from this world, that he would not only introduce her children to their grandparents, but bring them here to live. Her *trusted* husband . . .

He drifted into fitful sleep but bolted awake suddenly, roused by some small sound that he couldn't identify. Chilly moonlight streamed through the window, limning the oaken posts at the foot of the bed. Sitting up, Pete thought of the tall woman in gray flannel who'd crashed the remembrance gathering for Sally, the one who'd broken into Sally's office a few days later and knocked him to the floor during her escape. Had he been dreaming of her? he wondered.

He needed badly to piss, so he swung out of bed and groped for the lamp on the bed table. The sound came again, nearer now. A bolt of pure panic shot through him, and his heartbeat thundered in his ears. He took a slow deep breath to gather himself, forced himself to think rational thoughts. This was an old house, and old houses make noises. Aged wood becomes hard, loses its elasticity and . . .

Something made Pete giggle despite his growing panic, something from his boyhood—a recollection of lying in bed, shivering with terror over the reptilian blood-beast that hunkered in his closet. His dad, a rangy giant of a man, had heard his cries and had rushed into his room, led him to the closet, opened it. Shown him that it was empty of anything but clothes and toys. Monsters existed only in movies and comic books and the minds of little boys, the kindly giant had assured him— not in the real world. *It's okay to be scared*, his dad had said, *but only for the right reasons. A monster isn't the right reason*.

Now Pete wondered whether the gray-flannel woman waited for him in the closet. Incredibly, he found himself standing before the closet door, struggling to make his hand close around the knob, needing every ounce of determination to do it. *This is nuts*, he said almost aloud.

He distinctly remembered switching on the bedside
lamp, but now the room was silvery with moonlight. His
flesh crawling, he pulled the door open. Moonlight
spilled across the face of the woman who waited in am-
bush there—not the gray-flannel woman with the
straight-razor bangs, but Sally, her face punky with rot.
Her teeth bared in a grin of rage, her twiggy hands
spread into claws. Tumors bulging in her neck, her hair
falling out.

She had an alligator's eyes.

How could you do it, Pete . . . ? Her voice stung like
a fistful of ground glass hurled in his face. Her breath
smelled like a sewer.

"Ace, I'm so sorry . . ."

Her hands shot toward his throat, and he felt her nails
sink into his larynx, his windpipe. He tried to scream,
but couldn't. He felt his bladder let go . . .

Sorry just isn't good enough, Pete . . .

He woke up, sweat freezing on his face, his body
shaking. The room was alive with moonlight, but he was
still in bed. And he hadn't wet himself, thanks to a tight
erection. He groped for the lamp, switched it on, sat a
moment in the light as if to verify that he wasn't dreaming. He put on his robe and padded across the hall to
the bathroom, where he took a long pee.

While washing his hands he studied his own face in
the mirror, a bloodless face, too deeply lined and
sunken-eyed for a man only a few months shy of his
thirty-sixth birthday. His brown hair was starting to thin
in front, and his short haircut could no longer obscure
that. He looked *old*, he admitted to himself. Old and
weak. Without thinking, he ran his fingers over the stub-
bly skin under his chin, unconsciously searching for
scratches made by Sally's fingernails.

As he closed the bathroom door behind him, he
glanced at a tall window over the staircase that led up

to the third floor. Through it he could see the dark woods where the rear grounds of the mansion ended and the land began its rise toward Mount Olivet. He caught a glimpse of something against the backdrop of forest, a smear of movement in the aura of powerful yard lights mounted on the rear porch. He went to the staircase and climbed two or three steps to get a better look.

What he saw caused his gut to cramp.

A woman stood on the edge of the lawn, wearing a flowing dress that reached almost to the ground. Though the distance was more than a hundred yards, Pete could see that she had short blond hair, that she was tall and square-shouldered. He couldn't make out the features of her face, but he knew immediately who she was, for the way she carried herself was unmistakable.

He gripped the edges of the window casement, needing the feel of hard wood in his hands to keep him anchored to the real world. The woman turned suddenly and slipped into the trees like a shadow. Pete let his breath out, found his mouth dry. His knees went weak. He braved a final look, saw nothing. He descended the stairs and went to his room, sat a long while on the bed, elbows on his knees, head in his hands.

He could make no sense of it, so he didn't try. Hallucination was the obvious explanation, the one he yearned to hang his hat on. But Pete knew that he hadn't hallucinated. And he hadn't dreamed. In his heart he knew that he'd just seen his wife. He knew that he'd just seen Sally.

9

I

TERRY GRIMES, NINETEEN, LIVES IN A BATTERED FORTY-
foot double-wide on the outskirts of Scappoose, a small
residential community on Highway 30 only twenty
minutes north of Portland. An old logging road runs past
his doorstep and peters out in a clear-cut six miles away,
meaning that Terry is never short of mud—cement-hard
mud during the dry months; gooey, sucking mud when
the weather's wet, mud that crawls down the hillside like
lava.

He has lived here since moving out of his parents'
house in Scappoose two years earlier, about the same
time he quit high school and took a job at the Buckthorn
sawmill. He hopes someday to buy this sorry piece of
property from his landlord and build a real house on it.

It's quiet out here on the old logging road. Virtually
no traffic. Now that his girlfriend, Sassy, has gone back
to her husband and kid in Portland, Terry lives alone.

His routine during the work week seldom varies. He
gets up at 6:15 every morning, brushes his teeth, takes
a crap, eats a banana and drinks a quart of milk. He puts
on work clothes and hard hat. He gets into his shiny
1992 Dodge Dakota pickup and heads up Route 45 to
Buckthorn, passing through the towns of Spitzenberg,
Vernonia, Pittsburg and Mist. In dry weather the drive
to Buckthorn takes about twenty-five minutes.

He works the green chain from eight till five, mus-
cling freshly milled lumber off the conveyer and stack-

ing it for shipment. Hard work, the green chain—not particularly cerebral. Keeps a man's muscles hard, does little for his brain.

When the quitting whistle blows at five o'clock, Terry joins a mob of his buddies at the Head Rig Bar over on Front Street, even though he's too young to drink legally. The Head Rig's bartender and proprietor, old Manny Isaacson, never asks for ID if you're from the Buckthorn mill, and Oregon Liquor Control seldom, if ever, comes around to check. Over the next three hours Terry Grimes demolishes a burger and an order of onion rings, sucks down six or seven Miller Lites, smokes half a pack of Camels. Sometimes he plays darts or video poker. He talks about girls, politics, football or basketball (depending on the season), how the hunting or fishing has been, about life at the mill. Like hard hats everywhere, he considers himself an expert in the affairs of state, economics and sports, never mind that he dropped out of high school and hasn't picked up a book since he can't remember when. He would gladly give helpful advice to any world leader if only he were asked, and the advice would be loud and simple: jail all environmentalists and faggots.

Around 8:00 or 8:30 he heads home, maybe stops at the FoodWay in Vernonia to buy bananas and milk, depending on how drunk he is. He once dated the checker at the FoodWay, and he thinks he might have a shot at fucking her. Her name is Fawn, and she's a fat girl, but not as fat as Sassy. Terry is dying to get laid, and he's no stickler for looks.

Upon arriving home he collapses on his fraying sofa and stares at the tube until midnight. He laments that he can't afford cable. The care and feeding of his Dodge Dakota suck up every cent he can scrounge. He gets tired of watching the same old shit night after night, week after week, of coming home to this rust-bucket

trailer house with its leaky roof and sagging floors. Tired
of his ratty old furniture, his dead-end job. Tired of his
fuckin' *life*.

Terry Grimes craves adventure, new sights and sounds,
but the wages of a green-chain puller don't pay for
much adventure. Chances are good he'll end up like his
dad—arthritic and wheezy from breathing too much
sawdust. A chronic beer guzzler with a red nose. A veteran of a career in a sawmill.

If he's lucky, the Buckthorn mill will hang on despite
assaults on the timber industry by all those big-city butt-
wipes who care more about spotted owls than people. If
he's *real* lucky, the mill will supply him a livelihood for
as long as he's able to work. And if the mill doesn't
hang on—well, tough shit. You play the cards you're
dealt and hope you hit the lottery.

On Saturday nights he dresses in his best jeans and
bowls a few lines at the Evergreen Bowl up in St. Helens, the nearest town of any decent size. He knows most
of the regular crowd at the bowling alley, many of whom
are workers at the nearby Boise Cascade paper mill or
the James River mill across the Columbia. Someone
nearly always sneaks him a beer or two (or three) from
the bar, so the outing doesn't cost much. Afterward he
cruises the main drag of St. Helens in his pickup, and
he nearly always gets wind of a party somewhere.
Nearly always ends up drunk on his ass, stoned on pot
or lit up on crank, depending on what his pals have
managed to score.

Sadly, he almost never gets laid. Terry's a scrawny,
pimply kid and not much good at talking to girls.

Such is life for Terry Grimes, age nineteen, height
five-eight, weight one forty-six.

Vengeance knows all about this loser, having scouted
him thoroughly for more than a year. Learning a victim's
habits—his movements, his weak spots, the windows of

opportunity—is a critical aspect of the crusade. But it takes time, and Vengeance never cuts corners. At any given moment, the dark angel has two or three surveillance projects under way—young men who work at the mill, potential contributors of eyes, cocks and fingers to Vengeance's collection. The dark angel learns their lives inside and out, then formulates contingency plans on how best to take them without leaving clues.

Less than six months have passed since Rich Nockleby met his end in Royal Chinook Park, and no one in town expects the next killing for at least another year, maybe two. But the folks of Buckthorn want *change*, don't they? And they dare to hope for it, pray for it. So *change* is what Vengeance plans to give them, a change in the deadly routine of Buckthorn.

Vengeance plans to give them Terry Grimes well ahead of schedule.

II

ON THE MORNING OF WEDNESDAY, MARCH 30, 1994, NITA Vale finished printing and folding the run of this week's *Renegade* as she normally did, then bundled the newspapers and loaded them into her old VW station wagon. She spent the next four hours delivering the newspapers to her outlets in the surrounding towns, where she stacked them in metal display racks with large red labels that said *Don't Forget Your Renegade! It's Free!*

She always started at Olafson's Market and Post Office here in Buckthorn and ended up at the ThriftyKwik over in Paulsen, more than two dozen stops later. As was her custom, she saved half a dozen papers for delivery to Vonda Reuben, a naturopath and herbalist who lived and worked in a mossy old bungalow on Nehalem Avenue in Buckthorn.

Nita parked her Volkswagen near the crooked picket fence and mounted the porch, where a cedarwood sign hung next to the mailbox:

Dr. Vonda Reuben
Naturopath
(Please Walk In)

She pushed through the front door, jangling a pair of antique sleigh bells tacked to the jamb on a leather thong. Though the waiting room was empty of patients, it felt close, a bit too warm. The air was spicy with herbs and ointments. The doctor appeared in an inner doorway, summoned by the bells.

Vonda Reuben was a tall, muscular woman of fifty-three who pulled her gray hair into a ponytail that hung far down her back. She wore loose Wrangler jeans and a colorful Navajo pullover cinched at the waist with a belt of Mexican silver. Her face was clean of makeup and broad across the cheekbones, her eyes hazel. Half-lenses hung around her neck on a beaded chain.

"Must be publication day," she said, seeing Nita.

"Six copies, same as always," Nita replied, placing the papers on a table strewn with old issues of *Newsweek*. "Got any coffee you can part with?"

"I was about to eat a late lunch, which you're welcome to share if you're hungry. How's your foot, by the way? Did I see you limping just now?"

"Still sore, damn it. It's been more than a month, and I thought it would've cleared up by now."

"Better let me take a look. Come on back to the examination room. You can be my first patient of the day."

Nita sat on the examining table and removed her left sneaker. Vonda sat on a low stool and took Nita's foot carefully in her freckled hands, prodded the ankle here and there, then gently rotated it. Nita eyed the vials, jars and bottles that lined the walls, an array that had always fascinated her—herbs and mixtures of herbs, powders and granules, seeds, stems, leaves, oils, husks. *Senna* and *Slippery Elm, Dong Quai* and *Marshmallow*, the labels said. And *Gentian, Irish Moss* and *Siberian Gensing*. And *Black Cohosh, Golden Seal, Butcher's Broom, Yarrow, Myrrh, Capsicum* and hundreds of others.

A few locals whispered that Vonda Reuben was a witch, though nobody had ever reported seeing a jar labeled *Semen of Wizard* or *Eye of Newt* among her collection. The thought caused Nita to smile.

"Tell me again how you hurt this foot," Vonda said. "You were running, right—twisted it?"

"Stepped on a rock, not even a very big one. Didn't hurt too much at first, but it got steadily worse, then kind of evened out. It doesn't keep me from getting around, you understand. It's really just an annoyance."

Vonda pressed her fingertips to the instep, manipulated the toes and scowled at the underside of the foot through her half-lenses. "You're not still running on this, are you?"

"Hey, I'm tough, but I'm not that tough. I've been doing a lot of cycling, which doesn't seem to bother it. Weights, too. But you know me—nothing stirs up my endorphins like running."

"You and your damn endorphins."

"So what's the verdict? Will I live to see another Bastille Day?"

"Oh, you'll live, I suspect."

Vonda rose from the stool and stood to her full height, which was several inches taller than Nita. Big woman, big hands, stout arms and legs. Her face was as severe as any supreme court judge's.

"I'm going to give you something to take, a preparation of bromelain, yucca and alfalfa for the stiffness, and some slippery elm and fenugreek for the sprain itself. Take them every morning before breakfast with a little apple juice, and stay off the foot as much as you can.''

Vonda collected the appropriate jars and vials from the wall and disappeared into a side room, from which came the sounds of a food processor. Minutes later she reappeared with two large brown envelopes filled with powders, which she handed to Nita. Taped to each were instructions for dosage and mixture. ''Take these for the next two weeks and keep me posted on how your foot feels,'' she instructed.

They ate a light lunch at Vonda's kitchen table—organically grown salad with hazelnuts, homemade granola bars and juice smoothies. Afterward, as Vonda poured coffee, Nita quipped that she couldn't remember when she'd eaten so much healthy stuff in one sitting.

''Stick with me, kid,'' Vonda said. ''You'll live to be a hundred and twenty.''

''It's you or nobody. I've lived here seven years and you're the only real friend I have in this town.''

''What do you expect, with the editorials you write? All that stuff about Tucker Bannon's sawmill polluting Royal Chinook Creek with lubricants, the air pollution from the boilers, the dust raised by his trucks—what else?''

''Safety violations.''

''Oh yeah, how could I forget? Worst safety record of any sawmill in Oregon, right?''

''It's true. That mill is a death trap. You should know—you see enough of the injuries.''

''Of course it's true. Just remember that when you make trouble for Tucker Bannon, you make trouble for the whole town. If he goes belly-up, Buckthorn goes belly-up.''

Nita sipped her coffee and thought a long moment. Rain started to patter against the kitchen window, a muffled drum roll. "Maybe the mill won't go belly-up," she said. "Tucker has brought in some outside talent, a guy from back East to run the financial side of things. Blew into town last week as I understand it, with his two kids in tow."

"So I've heard. People are talking about him like he's some sort of messiah. The Savior of Buckthorn."

"It might be the other way around, actually. He's Bannon's son-in-law, and he's an ex-insurance executive. His name is Peter Cochran, and he left his old job under some kind of cloud. The word is that Tucker threw him a lifeline."

"I'm told he's a decent-looking man. I also hear that he just lost his wife, died of cancer last fall. You ought to put something in the paper about him, introduce him to the community."

"I guess it wouldn't hurt to go over to the mill and meet him, maybe ask him a few questions."

"Wouldn't hurt," Vonda agreed. "You need to cultivate some friendships, girl, especially of the male persuasion. My God, people are starting to whisper that maybe you and *I* have a thing going."

Nita laughed. "Rumors courtesy of Wade Beswick, West Coast distributor of homophobia." For years Beswick had counseled his workers at the Buckthorn mill to boycott Dr. Reuben, who clearly was a lesbian, in his view. She lived without benefit of male companionship, didn't she? And wasn't she built like a Russian discus thrower? Beswick had all the proof he needed.

"Don't get your hopes up for me and this Peter Cochran," Nita went on. "I'm not likely to fall in love with somebody who works in the timber industry."

"Anything is possible. I never expected you to fall in love with that cop, either. A smoker, yet."

"What I had with Dan Kantor sure as hell wasn't love, Vonda. I'm not really sure what it was."

"I'll tell you what it was—opportunism. You got close to him so you could milk him for stuff about the Buckthorn killer investigation, stuff you can put in the book you're writing—like Mata Hari, get him talking pillow talk and pretty soon he's spilling all the inside poop." Vonda scowled at Nita's wounded expression. "Come on, don't be appalled. You've been milking *me* for information about the Bannon family for years. Do you hear me complaining? I don't think there's anything wrong with using your friends and acquaintances to get ahead in this world. Everybody does it—you do it, I do it. There's no such thing as integrity anymore."

Nita *had* milked Vonda Reuben for tidbits about goings-on in the Bannon household. Dolly Bannon and Esmerelda Sandoval, the Bannons' housekeeper, were among Vonda's longtime patients. Both had regularly confided in Vonda on matters involving their personal lives.

Nita had never used any of the information in her newspaper—the *Renegade* wasn't that kind of rag. The stuff she'd gotten from Vonda fell into the category of Know Your Enemy. In return, Nita had knocked a third off the good doctor's advertising bill, one hand washing the other.

"I've decided not to write the book about the Buckthorn killings," Nita said.

"You've *what*? I don't believe it. Why? After all the work you've done, the material you've collected?"

"I'll tell you about it someday, but not now, okay?" A long moment ensued, during which each woman studied her plate. "So what's new in the house up on the hill, as long as we've touched on the subject?" Nita asked.

"I thought you'd never ask. This is juicy." Vonda

reported that Esmerelda Sandoval had recently come into the office with her usual complaint of headaches and indigestion. Naturally she'd talked. She'd revealed that Lieutenant Kantor and several police detectives had visited Bannon House in the previous month and that they'd interviewed everyone who lived there, including Esmerelda herself. Kantor had asked each person to account for his or her whereabouts on October 19, 1993, the night Rich Nockleby died. And then he'd asked questions about several of the earlier Buckthorn killings, whether anyone in the household had known the victims personally. Finally, he'd brought up a matter that Vonda had assumed was long dead, the matter of Clarence Bannon.

Nita's eyes widened. "Tucker's long-lost brother. Disappeared back in nineteen-sixty, as I recall. No one ever heard from him again or found any trace of him. He was just—gone."

And still is, Vonda added.

Lieutenant Kantor hadn't let on to Esmerelda why the sudden interest in a case that was almost thirty-four years old. Vonda wondered whether they'd found some connection between Clarence Bannon's disappearance and the Buckthorn killings, crazy as it sounded.

There was more, though, and it concerned Topper Bannon. The Nehalem County school district and the state children's services division had cut a deal with Tucker that required the boy to undergo psychological counseling at least twice a week until the state agency was satisfied that he posed no threat to others. The school district had received complaints about his behavior, something about burning live rats and indecent exposure. A psychological test had revealed that the boy was likely to become dangerous unless intervention occurred. The doctor who performed the tests had notified Dan Kantor, and Kantor had sought and received verification of the test results from the FBI's shrinks in Washington, D.C.

Tucker had agreed to the counseling if the county agreed not to press criminal charges on the matter of lewd behavior.

"Esmerelda is beside herself, of course," Vonda added. "She loves that boy. After all, he's her own flesh and blood, her grandson. Oh, don't act shocked, Nita. Topper isn't the biological son of Tucker and Dolly Bannon, and the whole town knows it."

"Then whose son is he?" Nita asked, her eyes innocently round.

"Remember the story about Rosa, Esmerelda's daughter, who ran away shortly after Sally left?"

"I've heard it, yeah. The Bannons seem to have a tough time keeping kids at home, don't they? First Sally and then Rosa."

"Think about it. Dolly is now sixty-six and Topper is seventeen. Dolly would've been almost fifty when he was born. As her doctor, I happen to know that she was menopausal at the age of forty-eight. Dolly couldn't have given birth to that boy without making biological history."

Because little Rosa had become pregnant without benefit of marriage, Vonda explained, the Bannons staged a charade to make everyone think that Topper was their child. They pulled Rosa out of school and kept her hidden at home after her tummy started to swell, a virtual prisoner. They put out the word that *Dolly* was pregnant, not Rosa. Dolly too stayed within the walls of Bannon House for the duration of the pregnancy.

When the baby came, the Bannons registered him as their own biological son. Rosa then fled Buckthorn as Sally Bannon had done a year earlier. Over the next several years, various locals reported catching glimpses of Rosa, skulking around town and behaving as if she were spying on her former family. Maybe the girl merely wanted to lay eyes on her son, if only from a distance, Vonda speculated. The last time anyone saw her was more than a decade ago.

"Esmerelda went along with the deception," Vonda concluded, "because she thought it would be nice for her grandchild to be the legitimate heir to the Bannon fortune. Of course, almost nobody was fooled. Topper doesn't even look like a Bannon. If he looks like anyone, it's Esmerelda. But then I can't think of anybody who gives a damn, so what difference does it make?"

"Maybe Rosa gives a damn," Nita said, listening to the rain on the roof.

"Maybe so, but she's in no position to do anything about it. My guess is that Tucker gave her a suitcase full of money and told her never to show her face around here again. She probably went off to start a new life, somewhere far away. At least, I *hope* that's what she did."

"Why would you hope that?"

"Because I like it when people break loose of this town. It's a horrible place, and it does horrible things to people. I ought to know—I've been here twenty years."

"You think it's cool to leave your son, go off and start a new life without him—if that's really what happened?" Nita asked.

"Put yourself in Rosa's shoes. She was only sixteen when she turned up pregnant. Tucker and Dolly Bannon kept her prisoner during the pregnancy and stole the baby from her after she gave birth. Seems to me she had plenty of reason to leave."

"She could have raised a stink to get her kid back, gone to the authorities."

"Oh, right. Look who she was up against—the King of Nehalem County, the guy who signs most everyone's paycheck. The guy who bankrolls political campaigns.

Do you think our vaunted legal system would've come
down on Rosa's side, if she'd taken on Tucker Bannon?
Think again, girl.''

The raindrops got louder, and a breeze stirred the
shrubs outside the kitchen. March was going out like a
wet blanket.

''So who do you suppose the father was?'' Nita asked.
''Topper's father, I mean.''

''No way of knowing, unless Esmerelda spills the
beans someday, assuming she knows. I've got a theory,
if you're interested.''

''I'm interested.''

''This just hit me one day out of the blue. The very
first Buckthorn killing occurred on the night before Hal-
loween, in seventy-six. The victim was Kelly Franklin,
remember? Went to Nehalem High. After graduating he
got a job at the mill, lived with his folks over on Front
Street, just a block down from your building.''

''That's right. His body was found down on Columbia
Avenue behind Olafson's Market. I've got it all on file
in my Death Room.'' Only last month Nita had taken a
TV crew to the spot behind Olafson's Market and had
done a ''stand-up'' with Brink Erdmann, KATU's rov-
ing reporter. She'd pointed out where Kelly Franklin's
body had lain and had remarked that the killer hadn't
yet begun to nail his victims to the ground or burn them.
These niceties had come with the second killing.

''Well,'' Vonda continued, ''Master Theodore Bannon was born on the twenty-eighth of July, in seventy-
seven. Exactly nine months after Kelly Franklin's
death.''

''Which means?''

''Esmerelda told me a long time ago that Kelly Franklin had known both Sally Bannon and Rosa Sandoval at
school, that he'd even asked Rosa to be his date at a
school dance. Rosa had asked her mother for permission

to go, but Esmerelda said no. The kid wasn't Mexican, and he was three years older than Rosa, which made him an unsuitable suitor in Mama's eyes. Even worse, he'd gotten caught boinking Lucy MacKenzie in the backseat of his car—caught by none other than Lucy's husband, Wally.''

''Yeah, I've heard about that. Wally's an accountant in the mill office. It broke up their marriage, I hear.''

''You heard right. Lucy hightailed it out of town, but old Wally stayed on, never having fully recovered. He still keeps her picture on his desk, they say. Anyway, my gut tells me that Kelly Franklin's death and Topper Bannon's conception are related. I think Kelly was Topper's dad.''

''Esmerelda told you that the kids had known each other?''

''Not in so many words, but she sort of let it slip out one day. She was wondering out loud whether things would've turned out better if she'd let her daughter go to the dance with Kelly. Maybe the kids would've fallen in love, eventually gotten married. Kelly might still be alive, and Rosa might still be here in Buckthorn. You know how mothers second-guess themselves.

''Interesting theory, and maybe not so farfetched. Do you also have a theory on who the killer was, or *is*?''

Vonda's face hardened, became grim. She stood up from the table and began to clear away the dishes, her gray ponytail swinging across her shoulders. ''As a matter of fact, I do have one,'' she answered finally, ''but I'm not going to share it with you.''

''Why not? What could it hurt?''

Vonda turned on a faucet and squirted Palmolive dish soap into the sinkful of dishes. ''Because it's too weird. You'd only laugh. On top of that, I'm not sure I believe it myself, so it doesn't really qualify as a theory.''

Nita felt something squirm inside her. ''I promise not

to laugh, Vonda. But I won't push you. You'll tell me
when you're ready."

"Yeah," Vonda said, steam rising from the sink into
her face. "I'll tell you when I'm ready."

III

DAN KANTOR CALLED THEM THE SCOUTS, BECAUSE THEY
were so clean, so diligent and hardworking. Neither
smoked nor cursed. Both were cheerful and respectful
of their elders.

The Boy Scout was Detective Roberto Esparza of the
Portland Police Bureau, that agency's most recent assignee to the Buckthorn Task Force. Fireplug of a kid,
swept-back hair, gold bead in one ear. His friends called
him Bob.

The Girl Scout was Detective Ashley Tching of the
Tigard Police Department in suburban Portland, also a
new assignee to the Task Force. She had large Asian
eyes and black hair that she tied in a knot on top of her
head. Her hobby was drag racing.

So far the meeting had lasted two hours, and Kantor
had chain-smoked half a pack of Marlboros, pacing from
one end of the conference room to the other, sometimes
gazing through a rain-streaked window. He'd gotten
clearance from the Nehalem County Commission to hold
Task Force confabs in a paneled conference room on the
main floor of the courthouse, rather than the chilly squad
room in the Sheriff's Department. A lockable door pre-
vented the Cigar from bursting in occasionally to disrupt
things, as he felt entitled to do when the Task Force
used his squad room for meetings.

Since receiving the FBI's psychiatric report on Topper
Bannon more than five weeks ago, Kantor had pushed
his people hard. He'd ordered yet another thorough can-

vass of Buckthorn and its environs, a "knock-and-talk."
All fourteen Task Force investigators had fanned out
over the area, visiting homes and businesses, farms and
ranches in an information-gathering operation that had
taken nearly a month. They'd asked residents to scour
their memories for any detail concerning the nights and
days that led up to October 19, 1993, Rich Nockleby's
last day on earth. Any recollection of suspicious strangers? Any strange behavior by someone they knew?

They'd re-interviewed the poor kid's father, Merle,
a bony husk of a man who operated Nockleby's Texaco on Highway 49 at the south end of town. Yet again
they'd interviewed everyone who worked at the Buckthorn sawmill, asking each to recall whether Rich
Nockleby had mentioned a change in his life—new acquaintances, a new girlfriend, anything out of the ordinary.

Yet again, the Task Force had drawn a total blank.

His predecessors had walked the same road, Kantor
knew. They'd endured the same frustrations. But Kantor
had one thing going for him that his predecessors had
lacked, and that was the Bannon angle.

On a hill above the town stood a mansion built of
gray brick, and in it lived a seventeen-year-old boy
whose mental landscape was that of a psychosexual
killer. Topper Bannon had shown several of the earmarks—torture of small animals, sexual deviation,
extreme hostility to authority figures. *Antisocial personality disorder*, the forensic shrinks at the FBI's Behavioral Science Unit called it, though Topper was
technically too young to be tagged with that diagnosis.
While the shrinks wouldn't go out on that limb for anyone under eighteen, Kantor had stared into the kid's
eyes, seen the wilderness there, and he'd known that
Topper was old *enough*. He'd known that Topper was a
walking time bomb.

The problem for Kantor, of course, was that Topper
Bannon hadn't killed Rich Nockleby. On the night of
the crime Topper had attended something called Teen
Discipleship at the Mount of Olives Gospel Church, a
fact that the Reverend Randy Roysden and four other
teens had verified. Topper had gone right home after the
meeting and had studied for a biology test, an alibi that
his parents and the housekeeper had substantiated.

Kantor could stretch his imagination to the breaking
point and theorize that even though Topper hadn't killed
Nockleby, he could have committed the murder of two
years earlier, the seventh in the Buckthorn series. The
victim in that crime had been twenty-one-year-old Keith
McCurdy. Topper Bannon would have been fifteen at
the time, a strapping lad even then. School records
showed that he'd weighed 135 pounds when he took his
PE physical that year. Good-sized for his age, but certainly not a large person by adult standards. On the day
after the murder, Keith McCurdy's corpse had tipped the
medical examiner's scales at 136, minus the eyes, the
fingers, the penis and an unspecified amount of flesh that
had burned away.

Topper had no alibi for the night of October 29, 1991,
but then the notion that a fifteen-year-old could have
killed and mutilated a grown man more than six years
his senior, a man physically bigger than he, was laugh-
able. As was the notion that he could've done it and not
slipped up, not left clues while committing a complex
crime that involved abduction and the intravenous administration of sodium pentobarbital and methamphetamine.

So, even if Kantor could have stretched his imagination to the breaking point and allowed that Topper was
a suspect in the murder of Keith McCurdy, he still faced
the question of who killed Travis Langdon on October
27, 1989, when Topper had been a mere slip of a

thirteen-year-old. And the question of who killed Joshua
Rittich on October 30, 1986, when Topper was ten. And
so on, back to the night of Kelly Franklin's murder in
1976, before Topper Bannon had even slid down the
chute from his mother's womb.

Still, the FBI's Violent Criminal Apprehension Program, VICAP, had advised Kantor to concentrate on the
environment that had produced Topper, because the odds
were good that it was the same environment that had
spawned the Buckthorn killer. So Kantor had done precisely that, not knowing exactly what he was looking
for. He and the Scouts had visited Bannon House, talked
to Tucker and Dolly Bannon, to Topper himself and the
family's housekeeper. He'd taken their fingerprints and
logged their alibis, poked around the house, tramped the
grounds—all with Tucker's permission, of course, since
he'd obtained no warrant. No judge in his right mind
would have issued a search warrant for Bannon House
on the basis of some forensic shrink's speculation, and
Kantor knew better than to ask.

Thus far, focusing on Topper's environment had produced but one tidbit, the fact that thirty-four years earlier
Tucker Bannon's brother had disappeared without a
trace. Ironically, Sheriff Nick Graybill had brought the
disappearance to light by grousing about Kantor's intention to shine the light of inquiry on Bannon House.
Hadn't the Bannons suffered enough already, having lost
Sally and Rosa, having lost Clarence way back when,
and now all this psychiatric crap with Topper? Didn't
Kantor possess even a shred of compassion?

Clarence? Kantor had asked. *Who the hell is Clarence*?

A search of the department's investigative archives
produced a thin file that told of Clarence Bannon's
disappearance on July 9, 1960. An investigation by
then–Sheriff Dennis Dunphy revealed that Clarence's

girlfriend, Esmerelda Sandoval, had been the last local
person to see him alive. Miss Sandoval had only two
months earlier given birth to a child that she claimed
Clarence had fathered, a daughter named Rosa Juanita.

Clarence Bannon's body had never turned up. The
Sheriff's Office periodically circulated word among the
nation's law enforcement agencies to be on the lookout
for a tall man in his thirties, blond hair and gray eyes,
slender build. But no word had ever come back, no
sighting of Clarence Bannon anywhere in the country,
dead or alive.

Sheriff Dunphy made no reference in the investigative
record to *suspects*, least of all to Tucker, the older
brother, who in the absence of Clarence became the sole
heir to a substantial timber fortune. Big surprise, thought
Kantor. No dead body, no real evidence of foul play.

When Kantor questioned him about Clarence Bannon,
Tucker had ventured the guess that his brother had simply tired of the wood products business and taken off to
livelier climes. Clarence had always been something of
a libertine, never a nose-to-the-grindstone kind of guy.
Tucker had long suspected him of skimming cash from
the business and squirreling it away to finance just this
kind of breakout from the bleak world of Buckthorn
Wood Products. The birth of a bastard daughter was undoubtedly the last straw. He'd probably gone to Mexico
or Costa Rica, changed his name and pursued the kind
of idle life he'd always wanted.

Kantor thought, But why would Clarence have run
away? Why didn't he simply cash out of the Bannon
fortune, claim his half of the business and liquidate it?
If he'd done this, he could've gone to his tropical par-
adise a rich man. This question apparently hadn't occurred to Sheriff Dunphy or any of his deputies.

In the spirit of brotherly love and Christian charity,
Tucker and Dolly had taken in Clarence's Mexican mis-

tress and her illegitimate daughter, given them a home
and a life of plenty. The Bannons had raised little Rosa
as their own, right alongside their Sally, always hoping
that Rosa's father would one day return to Buckthorn
and claim her as his own. But thirty-four years had gone
by, and Clarence Bannon had never shown his face.

IV

FOR MORE THAN TWO HOURS KANTOR AND THE SCOUTS
had rehashed the official investigative record and pored
over old notes. They'd talked about the physical evidence—twenty-eight steel spikes that the killer had left
at seven of the eight death scenes, one for each hand
and foot of seven victims. Only the first victim had escaped the crucifixion treatment.

All the spikes were identical, eight inches long, three-
eighths of an inch in diameter, three-quarter-inch cap.
Ten years earlier, a Task Force investigator had concluded that the spikes were quite old, probably manu-
factured between 1905 and 1920 in a Portland foundry.
In the early timber days, sawmill operators had used this
type of spike in the construction of water flumes for
transporting sawed lumber. Somewhere in the region an
old flume had fallen into ruin and someone had salvaged
the hardware, including the spikes.

Did this mean that the killer was a collector of old
sawmill paraphernalia?

The crime lab in Portland had found no fingerprints
on the spikes, no tool marks that lent themselves to analysis. Careful death scene processing had produced no
hairs or fibers attributable to the killer. The guy had been
careful not to leave any trace of his home environment
at the death scenes. Neither had he left any body fluids
in or around his victims, no semen or urine or saliva.

Beyond amputation of their penises, the victims had
suffered no other sexual molestation, no anal or oral
rape. Only the first two victims had suffered any detectable head-trauma—blows to their skulls, not hard
enough to kill but certainly hard enough to render them
unconscious for a time. Starting with the third victim,
the killer had used sodium pentobarbital to render them
pliable.

Footprints? Nothing usable.

Tire prints? Zilch again, except for the vehicles of the
victims in some cases.

Kantor sat down at the aged oak conference table and
toyed with a Diet Pepsi can he'd sucked dry an hour
earlier and had since used for an ashtray. He stared at a
flow chart on the table, which represented the team's
best guesses about Rich Nockleby's last living hours.

"Nockleby and the killer arrived at the park together
in Nockleby's Ranger pickup, which we know because
those are the only fresh tire prints we have," he said,
reading the chart. "The killer does what he does to
Nockleby, sets him on fire, then leaves in the kid's
pickup. Drives north through Paulsen, ditches the pickup
on a logging road where we later find it, the same place
he's probably stashed his own car. Except that we don't
have any tire prints for the killer's car."

"Or footprints, for that matter," interjected Detective
Ashley Tching, sipping a bottle of Evián. "It's like the
guy can fly, the way he doesn't leave footprints. More
likely, he's smart enough to select sites where he's not
likely to leave tracks. The park is a good example. Layers and layers of pine needles."

"Douglas fir, actually," said Detective Roberto Esparza. He'd just finished peeling an orange, pulling apart
its sections and laying them in a neat row on a napkin.
He popped a section into his mouth and chewed with a
goofy smile.

"Whatever," Tching said. "The point is, the guy leaves nothing to chance. He covers every detail, right down to the problem of leaving footprints. He takes precautions against leaving trace evidence."

"Probably wears rubber gloves, a wet suit and shower cap," Esparza quipped. "Leaves no hairs or fibers that way."

Tching rolled her eyes. "Or maybe it's a San Diego Chicken suit." She looked back to Kantor. "Do you think it's possible he's worked in the system? It seems like he knows how death scenes are processed, knows what to avoid. He may even be a cop. I doubt that a rank civilian would know enough to avoid slipping up eight straight times."

"Don't kid yourself," Kantor said, getting up and wandering back to the window. "There are no rank civilians anymore. People are smart about these things. They watch cop shows, read books, pick up a lot of good information from crime writers and novelists. And remember that we're not dealing with some dipstick here. It's not like he's killed these guys on the spur of the moment, like he dashed into a convenience store waving a gun and somebody got in his way. Uh-uh. He's planned every move ahead of time. He's studied, done research."

"Disciplined dude," Esparza said, swallowing a mouthful of orange. "Eye for detail. Where does a dude pick up that kind of discipline? Army, Marines? Police academy? Maybe graduate school?"

Dan Kantor stared through the rainy glass at Paulsen's main drag, where an occasional car or truck whispered past on wet asphalt. Rain fell in a curtain from low-hanging clouds, bathing the town in grayness.

"Let's go back to the victimology," he said. "They were all young guys. Oldest was what—twenty-two?"

"Twenty-two," Tching confirmed, consulting her

notes. "Lawrence Dillman, back in '81. None of the others was over twenty."

"And they all worked for the Buckthorn sawmill," Kantor continued. "They were all single, though several had live-in girlfriends, and one was divorced. What else?"

"None have been Latino," Esparza offered, "which seems significant. There's lots of Mexican-Americans in this area—have been for generations."

"Good point," Kantor said. "More than a third of the workers at the Buckthorn mill have Hispanic names. I've checked the current employee list. But our guy apparently isn't an equal opportunity killer. He only likes Anglos."

"And little guys," Tching observed. "All the victims have been small in stature. The biggest was the first one, Kelly Franklin, who weighed in at one fifty-two. None of the others have weighed more than one forty-six."

"So what does all this tell us about our maniac?" Kantor asked.

The Scouts traded glances, each urging the other onward. Tching went first. "Male homosexual, probably still in the closet, who's got a thing for young, slightly built Anglos. Acts out his psychosexual fantasies only after careful planning and preparation. He's disciplined and methodical, possibly as the result of military or police training, or maybe rigorous academic work. Might be an artist, a painter or a sculptor."

"Let's not overlook the possibility," said Esparza, "that he's a small dude himself, and he doesn't figure he could handle a bigger man. Might be a Latino, and he's doing a racial thing against Anglos."

"Or a woman," Tching said, half-joking. "A woman wouldn't want to take on big guys, either."

"A small, Latino woman," Esparza said. "In a San Diego Chicken suit."

"It's not a woman," Kantor declared. "In the long, ugly annals of this sport, only one woman has ever been arrested and convicted of pychosexual serial murder, and that was Aileen Wuornos, down in Florida."

"The one who did male truck drivers," Esparza said. "I remember. Three or four years ago, right?"

Kantor nodded. "Women can be killers—everybody knows that, and there're some real humdingers on the books. But females aren't built to get the sexual thrill that these geeks get from killing people. Their sexuality isn't geared to it. That's right out of a psychology text on the subject, my young friends."

"I've read that book," replied Tching, her eyes narrowed with skepticism. "For the sake of discussion, suppose these crimes aren't totally psychosexual in nature. Suppose there's some other motivation."

"Forget it, Ashley," Esparza said, popping the last section of orange into his mouth. "We're talking ritual killing and torture here, postmortem mutilation, taking away body parts. We're talking about a dude who does all this sick stuff because he gets a sexy tickle out of it. He's probably got a shrine in his basement, where he stores all the eyes and fingers and penises in jars of formaldehyde, so he can take them out every so often and masturbate over them."

"That's precisely what everyone who's investigated these crimes has assumed for the past thirteen years," Tching answered, "and it hasn't gotten us very far, has it? Maybe we ought to examine some new possibilities, throw out the old paradigm. Otherwise we might still be investigating the same string of murders eighteen years from now, except we'll be up to number sixteen or seventeen."

Kantor turned from the window, smiling sadly. *Throw out the old paradigm.* Tching talked like the college professor she would probably be someday. She was right,

he knew. This investigation had mired in old assumptions.

"I like what you just said," he told her. "I'm not
convinced there's a chance our killer's a woman, but
you're right—we need to try out some new theories,
look for new motives. Got anything you care to float by
us?"

"How about all the conventional motives for murder,
things we really haven't paid much attention to? Jeal-
ousy, maybe. Racial hatred, as Bob just suggested a minute ago. Or revenge, greed, politics—I don't know. We
shouldn't rule anything out unless we have good reason
to."

"I still say we're looking for a sex killer," Esparza
said wearily. "Everything we've got says sex killer.
We've got nothing that says different."

Kantor leaned against the windowsill, deep in thought,
rain tapping the other side of the pane. He contemplated
the possibility that the Task Force had been barking up
the wrong tree for the past thirteen years, that it could
have based all its efforts on the wrong assumptions. *We
shouldn't rule anything out . . .*

The thought both troubled and excited him.

10

I

Morning burst over the flank of Mount Olivet and daubed the hilltops with buttery sunlight. From the vantage point of Bannon House, the town of Buckthorn looked like a lake of cloud, its clutter buried in gray silence. Robins squealed their early-morning music in the trees around the mansion and stalked the dewy grass for worms. Somewhere in the distance a rooster crowed.

Peter Cochran kissed Carter and Sarah as they slept, standing a moment over each child in the sparse morning light, staring, hoping, fighting down misgivings. He'd enrolled them in school in the nearby town of Paulsen, and they seemed to have begun adjusting to an academic environment radically different from the one they'd known in the manicured affluence of Rye, New York. Their new schoolmates were mostly poor kids who hadn't seen much of the world outside Nehalem County. Kids who wore the same clothes day after day, whose dads worked in mills. Whose moms waited tables or cleaned houses or drove trucks. None took tae kwon do lessons or attended ballet classes. None went to acting school in the evening or tennis camp during spring break. Carter had found not one fellow Knicks fan—all the kids here were Portland Trail Blazer boosters. Talk about rude awakenings.

Sarah and Carter still spoke longingly and often of Gerard. Last night they'd badgered Pete into calling the

Dischmanns back in Scarsdale so that they could talk to Gerard over the phone. Sarah had managed to make him bark.

Like typical grandparents, Tucker and Dolly had lavished attention on Sarah and Carter from the get-go. They seemed incapable of saying no to any request. They'd taken the kids on a trip to the beach over the weekend, bought them kites and expensive play togs. Already they talked about a shopping spree in Portland next weekend, a movie, a visit to a cycle shop for a look at mountain bikes. A mountain bike was almost a necessity for any kid who lived in Buckthorn, Tucker had declared.

Topper, too, had gotten into the act, having taken the kids hiking on Mount Olivet. Lots of mysterious places to explore around here, he'd promised in his broadcaster's voice, and they'd only touched the tip of the iceberg—hidden, out-of-the-way places in the forest, old logging roads where nobody ever went. For some reason this talk about hidden places had made Pete uneasy.

Today he'd risen before anyone except Esmerelda, who gave him breakfast in the kitchen, a charming woman in her quiet way. He liked her soft Spanish accent, her kind face. She seemed fond of Carter and Sarah, and her eyes warmed whenever one of them came into the room.

Pete drove across town to the sawmill in the new Jeep Grand Cherokee that his father-in-law had bought for him. A little bonus, Tucker had called it. Four-wheel drive, leather seats, big V-8, lots of power. A toy for big boys. He trudged into the mill office, which was a converted clapboard house that stood in the shade of an oak, painted a pointless beige at least a decade ago. Old Noah Bannon, founder of the company, had lived here when the mill was new, before he'd become rich enough to build Bannon House. Inside the front door was a recep-

tion area with a pair of desks for the secretaries and
fifties-era dinette chairs for visitors. Down the hall were
offices that once had been bedrooms or a parlor or a
kitchen. Beswick's office was on the left, Pete's on the
right. At the rear was a common room with desks for
an accountant, a forester and a maintenance supervisor.

The mounted head of a black-tailed deer hung over a
door frame, its antlers festooned with spiderwebs. The
linoleum flooring had worn through in places, and the
floorboards squeaked. Tasteless cartoons littered the walls,
most of them blatantly sexist if not pornographic.

Pete hadn't expected much, but he hadn't expected
this.

To make matters worse, Pete had loathed the mill
manager, Wade Beswick, from the moment Tucker Bannon had introduced them. At forty, Beswick was a horse
of a man with small eyes set closely together into a
doughy face. He had the annoying habit of interrupting
people before they could finish a sentence. He squinted
and scrunched his nose as if the whole world smelled
bad.

Beswick loved slogans and motivational kickers, and
he'd tacked them to the walls throughout the head shed.
Expect to Win! above the communal coffeepots. *Attitude
is Everything* on the door of his own office.

Whatever It Takes!
Do It Right the First Time!
Make It Happen!

Beswick had tossed Pete a battered yellow hard hat,
a pair of scratched eye protectors and a new pair of
earplugs. Time for the ''cook's tour,'' he'd announced.

First stop: the millpond that lay across the parking lot
from the head shed. *Mosquito Valhalla*, Pete thought,
staring at the fetid water. Here the log truckers dumped
their loads onto the ''pole deck,'' after which a self-
loader hoisted the logs into the pond, where they floated

in green scum until herded onto a conveyer by a man who drove a motorized water scooter called a "log bronc." The conveyer snatched a log from the water with steel teeth set into a chain, then fed it to the maw of the sawmill. A mechanized debarker tore the bark off in long chunks with nasty-looking knives. The fragmented bark dropped through a grillwork to an area where workers collected it for sale to pulp processors and landscapers.

A newly naked log next went to the "head rig," the main saw. Its operator was the head sawyer, a skilled worker who maneuvered the log with hydraulically run servos and fed it to the saw in just the right way. Screaming like a banshee with every swipe and spewing clouds of sawdust, the head rig produced a "cant," a length of wood with four unrounded sides that met at right angles. Further down the line, a resaw and edger cut each cant into two-by-fours and two-by-twelves, a process that filled the air with mechanical shrieking and sawdust.

Next came the planer, which gave the lumber a smooth finish. Then came the "green chain," where gloved and helmeted workers pulled the lumber off the conveyers and stacked it in a shed with metal walls that had corroded through in places. Dirty sparrows flitted in the rafters. Mice huddled in the dark corners.

The lumber went next to the yard, hauled by men driving strange-looking contraptions called "straddle buggies," tall vehicles that carried boards longitudinally over the axles, straddling them. Forklift operators then loaded the lumber onto trucks for delivery to retailers throughout northern Oregon and southern Washington.

One hundred eighty thousand board feet of lumber per day, Beswick had crowed, his small eyes gleaming. Nearly nine tons of chips for shipment to a paper mill. Ninety-three full-time jobs, not counting his and Pete's.

The oldest operating sawmill in the state of Oregon, and the only one that still ran on steam.

Isn't she a beauty?

To Pete, the mill was a hellish thing. The walkways were old and rickety, the safety railings twisted and fallen away in places. A misstep could send a man quickly into gears or blades, to dismemberment or death.

"Watch yourself whenever you're in the production area," Wade Beswick had shouted over the din. "You take a bad step or lean wrong, and this mill will eat you. I mean that. You wouldn't be the first."

The workers' faces were blank with inurement to the fact that the mill occasionally chewed up a finger or a hand or foot, that it sometimes maimed someone or devoured a life. They were men of all ages, some with unlined faces and others with squinty eyes and furrows in their brows—whites, Latinos, an occasional black. Most had been born to this work as others had been born to steel mills or shipyards or coal mines, followers of their fathers and brothers.

II

BEFORE PETE ASSUMED THE NEWLY CREATED POST OF chief financial officer and director of human resources at Buckthorn Wood Products, his office had belonged to the company accountant, Wally MacKenzie, a sinewy little man of fifty with thick glasses and a thatch of silver hair that lay on his forehead like the early Beatles'. MacKenzie, an avid collector of antique logging equipment, had decorated the office walls with a pair of ancient two-man whipsaws, which Pete had ordered removed. From the beginning, MacKenzie had treated Pete like a long-lost buddy, seeming not to care that he'd lost his personal office space or that Pete had bumped

him down a rung on the company ladder. Pete had wondered if the little guy had an ego.

Today MacKenzie met him in the reception area and
motioned him into the rear room. The only remaining
trapping of MacKenzie's old office was the picture on
the wall behind his chair, a brass-framed photo of his
ex-wife. Though they'd divorced twenty years ago,
MacKenzie talked about her as if they were still married.

"Thought you might want to know that Wade caught
me this morning and asked me what you and I've been
talking about since you got here," MacKenzie whispered. "Wanted to know what you've got in mind for
accounting, payroll, all that."

"And what did you tell him?"

"The truth. I said you're thinking about working up
a plan to put in new payroll software, maybe set up some
new financial planning procedures, that kind of stuff. I
said you were still only in the thinking stage, 'cause
Christ, you've only been on the job four days. Can't
expect too much right away, I said."

"And how did he react to that?"

"Got madder'n a tarred coyote. Asked me who the
fuck you thought you were. Said there's nothing wrong
with the way we do things, and the last thing we need
is to start laying plans to spend scarce cash. Told me I
was supposed to keep him advised of anything and
everything you say from now on."

"Spy on me, in other words?"

"That's one way of puttin' it. Anyway, I thought you
should know." He gave Pete an I'm-your-pal punch on
the shoulder. "Watch yourself with him, Pete. Wade can
be a son of a bitch when the mood strikes him."

"Thanks. I appreciate your telling me this."

Pete went to the bathroom, where someone—his
guess would have been Beswick—had tacked a sign
over the commode:

NOTICE
DUE TO FEDERAL LOGGING RESTRICTIONS AND
THE SHORTAGE OF PULP, WE'VE RUN LOW ON
TOILET PAPER. KINDLY WIPE YOUR ASS WITH A
SPOTTED OWL.

Pete splashed cold water on his face and stared at himself in the mirror for a long moment. Sleeplessness and extended-wear contact lenses had reddened his eyes. The first inkling of a headache gnawed at the base of his skull. He popped three Excedrins.

So Wade Beswick thinks everything is just copacetic, does he? This meant that the guy was not only an asshole, but an incompetent asshole as well. The firm's payroll and cash handling were a shambles. From what he'd seen so far, Pete thought it miraculous that the outfit was still in business.

He'd already concluded that Buckthorn Wood Products needed a complete overhaul of its financial systems. He meant to propose installing a personal computer network that would link all the business's major decision makers in order to control costs—manager, human resources, financial officers, forester, maintenance supervisor and quality control. Basic stuff, nothing fancy. Myriad details remained to be dealt with, but at least he'd established a direction. He'd gotten his arms around the problem after only four days.

Which had pissed off the mill manager, apparently.

Tucker Bannon had named Pete human resources director as well as chief financial officer, and Pete had seen enough so far to conclude that Buckthorn Wood Products was an employee-relations nightmare. It was only a matter of time, Pete was certain, before one of the female staff filed a complaint of sexual harassment. For starters, nearly every wall in the head shed had at least one picture of a naked woman on it, or a cartoon out of

Hustler or some similar publication, stuff that was offensive to any civilized being, male or female. Worse, Wade Beswick himself made life miserable for the two young women who worked in the front office, Denise Ubaldo and Megan Dunn, the receptionist and the secretary. He cracked crude jokes in their presence, pawed and patted them whenever he got the chance, gave them unsolicited advice on how to lose weight or dress "sexier." The situation was ugly.

Wally MacKenzie had pointed out to him that Megan's husband, Scotty, drove the log bronc at this very sawmill. Scotty was a mountainous twenty-four-old who looked as if he could bench-press a Miata. MacKenzie predicted that Scotty would crumple Wade like a paper cup if Megan ever let slip that he'd laid hands on her. Only Megan's fear of losing her job stood between Wade Beswick and multiple broken bones.

Had this been New York, Pete thought, Beswick would be in the unemployment line, having been fired for exposing the company to colossal liability. But in this stinking backwater Beswick could take full advantage of his minions' powerlessness and get away with it. Then again, why should he care? Pete asked himself. He couldn't imagine staying on in Buckthorn, living with his in-laws, working in this dump. The mill was something out of Kafka, for Christ's sake.

An hour later, Beswick called Pete into his office, waved him into a metal chair.

"I like you, Cocky," Beswick began, having tagged Pete with this execrable nickname. "I think we're going to get along fine, you and me. I just want to make sure we're singing off the same page of the hymnal, though, so we don't get crossways with each other later on. To put it bluntly, you need to understand that I'm the bull elephant of Buckthorn Wood Products, and I call the shots around here. I need to know that you have a firm grip on this little fact of life.''

Pete nodded, said nothing.

Beswick chuckled and made a steeple with his fat fingers. His graduation ring looked as if it wouldn't come off without surgery. ''The fact that you're the owner's son-in-law presents us with an interesting situation, seems to me. You blow in from back East, full of big-time ideas about how things should work, and everybody's talking about how brilliant you are, how you're going to save the mill and restore prosperity to this town. And here I am, groaty old Wade Beswick, the guy who's held it all together for the past twenty years—the guy nobody notices anymore. We're here together, you and me, cheek-by-jowl at the same trough, lappin' up the goodies. Now which one do you suppose is more important—the manager or the owner's son-in-law?'' Beswick's small eyes glittered.

''Is there a point to this, Wade?''

''There is, and I'll make it easy for you. Being the owner's son-in-law doesn't amount to a frozen jar of Eskimo piss, Cocky. I'm the guy with the juice, no matter what they're saying out in the street or down in the lunch shed.''

''Then you've got nothing to worry about.''

''Nothing to worry about, that's right. A life without care. And I want the same for you, Cocky. You're making decent money, you've got your shiny new sport utility vehicle, you live in your daddy-in-law's mansion and eat meals cooked by a nice old Mexican lady. All you really need to do is avoid screwing up, don't you see? Which is to say, relax, enjoy. Look busy, look important, make calls on your cellular phone. Collect your checks and be happy. Leave running the mill to those of us who know our asses from third base.''

''My understanding is that Tucker hired me to . . .''

"Tucker's retired, man. He doesn't run this mill any-more—*I* do. How many ways do I need to say it? *I* run the mill. I pay the bills and the salaries and the wages, and we all go home happy, okay? We don't need to start fuckin' around with new computers and payroll software and planning and networks and all this other garbage you MBAs love so much."

"This business is a disaster area, Wade. It's a miracle you're still . . ."

"What do you say we get back to work?" Beswick stood suddenly, thrust his hand out for Pete to shake. "It's been a good meeting—short, to the point. I like that, Cocky. And I like you. We're going to get along fine, you and me."

Grinding his teeth, Pete forced himself to shake Beswick's hand.

11

I

ON THE FOLLOWING MORNING TUCKER BANNON MET with his private investigator, Todd Verduin, in what he called the "quiet room," a small room on the third floor of the mansion. Tucker always kept the door locked. For the past decade he'd allowed no one in but Verduin, not even Esmerelda to clean. When the quiet room needed tidying, Tucker did it himself.

A bank of twelve closed-circuit television monitors lined one wall, showing scenes caught by TV cameras hidden in a dozen locations throughout the Buckthorn sawmill. From here Tucker could observe virtually everything that happened in the facility, from the pole deck to the head shed.

Over the years he'd caught employees stealing, thanks to the cameras. He'd caught them using drugs, abusing equipment, lollygagging. He'd even caught one masturbating over a filthy picture tacked to the door of a shed. In every instance Tucker had taken the appropriate disciplinary action. Workers in the mill whispered that he must have eyes in the back of his head, that he could see through solid walls.

Along one edge of the quiet room stood a console from which Tucker Bannon could overhear and record conversations in every room of the head shed, thanks to hidden microphones. He could also monitor every telephone in the mill. A sophisticated radio receiver let him

pick up signals from remote bugs planted in the cars of
the executives.

Todd Verduin had designed the quiet room ten years
ago, installed the equipment, brought it on line, serviced
it periodically. Tucker had paid him well for his work,
and though he maintained a cautious civility with the
man, Tucker detested him for having become indispensable.

Verduin took the comfortable armchair that his host
offered, opened his briefcase and withdrew a bound
plastic folder that he handed over. The report concerned
Rosa Sandoval, the young woman Tucker had commissioned Verduin to find. Thus far the search had taken
three years.

"This is a summary of everything I've found out so
far," Verduin explained. "I'm *that* close to finding her,
Mr. Bannon, which you'll see when you read it. If you
like, I can walk you through it."

"Not necessary." Tucker forced a smile. Verduin's
silver earring offended him unspeakably.

The report summarized a decade in Rosa's life, beginning when she fled Buckthorn in November of 1977
and ending in mid-1987, when she seemingly fell
through a crack in the earth. As Tucker read, he saw her
face in his mind, oval-shaped and big-eyed, a face that
glowed with native intelligence. Lord, how he'd missed
that little girl, his brother's only child. He'd missed her
almost as much as he'd missed his own daughter, Sally.
The fact that he needed to kill her made his heart ache.

Lord, if it be Thy will, let this cup pass from me . . .

On November 5, 1977, Rosa Sandoval had left Buckthorn, slinking away like a thief in the night. She'd gone
to northeast Portland and taken a job as a waitress. Two
years later she'd gotten her GED, her general equiva-
lency diploma, since she'd missed her final year of high
school because of pregnancy.

Getting a GED was no small feat for a young girl out on her own. Must've worked like a dog, thought Tucker as he read Verduin's lifeless prose. He visualized her slinging hash and busing tables all day, studying at night. Ambitious, energetic girl, just as he'd raised her to be—though not without some trouble, for she'd been a willful child. She'd needed ample doses of discipline, and Tucker had laid it on, yes sir. Laid it on with a willow switch, right on her little bare bottom. Yes *sir*.

Withhold not correction from the child . . .

In the fall of '79, she'd enrolled in Portland State University, declaring journalism as her major. In 1980, she'd won a scholarship to the University of Oregon in Eugene, a hundred miles downstate. In addition to managing her full-time academic schedule, she'd taken a part-time job in the composing room of the *Register-Guard*, the city's daily newspaper, needing the money to make ends meet.

In 1982, she'd graduated and moved back to Portland, the bearer of a newly minted degree in journalism. She'd landed a job with a weekly newspaper, the widely read and highly regarded *Willamette Week*, working as an environmental reporter. She'd written freelance articles on the side, and her byline had appeared in special-interest publications around the country, mainly those of environmental organizations. Working with several local photographers, she'd turned out a series of "coffee table" books that featured environmentalist propaganda along with artsy color pictures of wildlife. Verduin's notation said that these had sold well, that Rosa had prospered financially.

Since leaving home, she'd turned up occasionally around Buckthorn. Several locals had seen her and had dutifully reported their sightings to Tucker. She'd never talked to anyone and had never made any attempt to contact her family. In 1985 those sightings had ceased.

On February 5, 1985, she'd signed on as a reporter with the *Portland Oregonian*, working a metro beat, covering crime and "neighborhood issues." Two years later she'd moved to Sacramento, California, where she'd gotten a job with the *Sacramento Bee*. Shortly thereafter, she'd dropped out of sight.

Tracking Rosa up to this point had been time-consuming, but not difficult. Verduin had interviewed her friends and acquaintances, classmates at PSU and the U of O, former neighbors, co-workers. But after her disappearance no one who knew her could hazard a guess as to where she'd gone or what had happened to her. Verduin had checked the usual sources—credit bureaus, driver licensing records, court documents—and had found nothing.

He'd bought access to several databases and mailing lists and had conducted computer searches for Rosa in various likely categories. He'd found that she'd purchased no insurance since 1987, no auto insurance, life insurance or health insurance. She'd submitted no claims of any kind for any injury, accident or sickness. She'd been in no traffic accidents in the states of Oregon, Washington or California. She'd committed no crimes that showed up on any criminal justice database and had never served on a jury. She'd bought nothing out of mail-order catalogs, bounced no checks, filed for no bankruptcies and applied for no credit cards. She'd made no long-distance telephone calls that required billing. No telephone directory or address directory anywhere in the nation had listed her after the summer of 1987.

Rosa Sandoval had seemingly stepped into an abyss.

But Todd Verduin knew better. People don't simply disappear, not in the real world. What *does* happen is that people change their names. And this was what Rosa Sandoval had done, Verduin concluded in his report.

Tucker looked up and stared into the man's too-youthful face. "Changed her name?"

"There's little doubt of it, Mr. Bannon. I'd say she went to Sacramento, lived there long enough to establish residency under California law, and petitioned a court for a name change. If the change was granted, it would be public record for ninety days, after which the record would be sealed."

"So we can't find out what she changed her name to?"

"Not unless we convince a California judge that we have a compelling interest in reopening the record. Frankly, I don't think there's much hope of that."

"Where does that leave us?"

Verduin smiled delicately, his lips twitching. Tucker wondered what drug he was on. "As you can see, the report concludes with notes on three separate interviews," Verduin said. "Look on page seven—there." He reached over and pointed to a name, Julie Newman.

Newman had been a reporter at the *Sacramento Bee* at the same time Rosa worked for the paper. Next to her name was that of Ned Bryson, a neighbor in her apartment complex. And last was Morgana Torinello, someone she'd met in a health club.

"All three of these people say that Rosa asked them for references to plastic surgeons," Verduin said. "She wanted to know whether any of them had ever undergone plastic surgery, or if they'd known anyone who had."

"And it was this Miss Morgana Torinello who gave her a recommendation—a doctor down in Carmel, it says here."

"That's right. Dr. Norman Jorganson. I got to know this Morgana fairly well. Told her I was working for an insurance company and that I was trying to find Rosa in order to pay her a death benefit from her aunt's life

insurance. That always makes people want to cooper-
ate—the idea of helping someone collect from an insurance company.''

"Did Miss Torinello say whether Rosa went to see
this doctor?"

"She couldn't say for sure, but she strongly suspected
it. Morgana's sister had been this guy's patient—nose
job and a jaw reduction. I saw pictures of the results,
and it was unreal. He gave this girl a face that could
belong to a model, I swear. Morgana said she showed
the pictures to Rosa and that she seemed very excited
about seeing Jorganson. Unfortunately, it was shortly
thereafter that Rosa disappeared.''

"And you're assuming that she was determined to
change her appearance, is that it?''

"New appearance to go with a new name. She wanted
to become someone else, Mr. Bannon. Not so rare, actually. Lots of people want it, but only a few have the
guts and the cash to make it happen. My guess is that
Rosa had both.''

"What's our next step?''

"It's time to have a talk with Dr. Jorganson, I think.
He still practices in Carmel. If you give me the go-
ahead, I'll come up with a way to convince him to tell
us what he knows about her. We're up against patient
confidentiality here, and the fact that it's been a long
time since he saw her. The good doctor's memory might
be a little rusty. I have an—*associate* who could be very
helpful in this undertaking.''

Tucker stared a long moment at Verduin, expression-
less. *Is it finally happening, Lord? Wilt Thou at last
deliver her into my hands?*

"Do it, Todd. Find her. Remember that we're also
looking for correspondence between Rosa and my
daughter, Sally. Probably written in Spanish. I *need*
those letters, Todd.''

"I'll keep this in mind, Mr. Bannon.''

II

A RED LIGHT FLARED ON THE CONSOLE AND EMITTED A sharp beep. One of the tape decks engaged with a click, and the spools started turning. Tucker turned in his swivel chair and punched a button on the console, which turned on a loudspeaker.

"Buckthorn Wood Products, how may I help you?" Denise Ubaldo's voice in the head shed, edged with a Spanish accent.

"This is Paul Garson at the Conifer Group, calling for Wade Beswick."

"I'll see if he's in."

A click, a beep.

"Paul Garson on line one for you, Wade."

"Thanks, precious."

Another click.

"Yeah, Paul. What's up?"

Verduin gave Tucker a knowing look and winked. Paul Garson was the executive vice president of the Conifer Group, a consortium of six investors who specialized in acquiring and liquidating assets in the wood products industry. Last month, Verduin had bugged their offices in downtown Portland. He'd posed as a janitor with the night crew in the high-rise office building, and had gone into the Conifer Group's suite with skeleton keys. It had been laughably easy.

"How're things with our new boy?" Garson asked.

"You mean the chief financial officer?" Beswick pronounced the title with overdone reverence.

"That's the one—old man Bannon's long-lost son-in-law, the one Patriot Mutual bounced down the backstairs."

Chuckling on both ends.

"No need to worry about this guy. In fact, he and I just finished a sit-down not more than an hour ago. I gave him the unsalted reality, told him to forget all this garbage about financial planning and computerized cost control and so forth. Told him not to do or say anything without checking with me first. He's a pussycat, believe me."

"Isn't he going to get a little suspicious? I mean, tax season's here, and he'll want to meet with your tax accountants downtown, won't he? One of these days he's going to want to see all the books. He is the CFO, after all."

"Don't sweat it, Paul. As long as you guys adhere to your schedule, we'll be all right."

As Tucker listened to the conversation his anger warmed dangerously. He'd heard many such exchanges in recent months, proof of Wade Beswick's disloyalty and treachery, but he'd yet to become hardened to it.

On the night that Todd Verduin returned from New York with tapes of the Cochran family's phone calls, Tucker had told him that he needed help with a matter closer to home—*this* matter. A routine monitoring of Beswick's calls had revealed that he'd cooked up some sort of scheme with the Conifer Group. The previous year, Buckthorn Wood Products had procured a loan of two-point-five million from the Group to finance an upgrade of its production equipment. Beswick had urged the loan on Tucker, arguing persuasively that with a new power plant, new saws and conveyers, the Buckthorn mill could attain a decent level of profitability and maintain it for years to come.

Central to Beswick's plan was the huge stand of old-growth timber on Mount Olivet, which the Bannon family had withheld from harvesting since the 1930s. The timber on Mount Olivet could not only serve as collateral for the loan but also supply the Buckthorn sawmill when the new equipment came on line. The time to harvest Mount Olivet had finally come, Beswick had argued. Environmentalists were wielding the Endangered Species Act to shut down logging on a vast scale. Bill Clinton had become president, and no help was forthcoming from the federal government. If Buckthorn Wood Products didn't act to harvest Mount Olivet soon, the timber could be lost forever as an economic resource.

Tucker could not refute this logic, and he'd agreed to apply for the loan. Having only recently gone into semi-retirement, he'd left the matter in Beswick's "capable" hands. He'd trusted Beswick, having spent nearly two decades grooming him to handle matters such as this. Beswick had never given him a reason to question his honesty or loyalty.

But then Tucker had overheard the phone conversations between Beswick and Paul Garson of the Conifer Group. Needing to know the details of their scheme, Tucker had called upon Todd Verduin.

Verduin had installed simple low-band VHF transmitters in the electrical sockets of the Conifer Group's conference room and the personal offices of its principals. He'd parked a rented car in the parking garage next door and left a multichannel receiver locked safely in the trunk, tuned to the frequencies of the transmitters. A few days later Beswick attended a meeting with the Conifer Group in the conference room, and the resultant recording had told Tucker exactly what he needed to know.

The loan contract contained a paragraph that enabled the Conifer Group to foreclose if installation of upgraded equipment didn't occur by a certain date—April 1, 1994, to be exact. April Fool's Day. Wade Beswick had made no effort to retrofit the Buckthorn sawmill, contrary to the assurances he'd given Tucker. Instead, he'd dummied up memos from Tucker that specifically instructed

him to do nothing toward buying and installing new
equipment. Tucker had initialed the memos without
reading them, not dreaming that Beswick would slip
something by him. Thus, the Conifer Group was entitled
to foreclose on its two-point-five-million-dollar loan and
seize the Mount Olivet property, which consisted of
roughly fifteen thousand acres of old-growth Douglas fir
and mountain hemlock. Harvest of Mount Olivet could
produce a profit of fifty million dollars, give or take.
Beswick's cut was to be a frosty five million.

Verduin glanced at his watch and noted the date.
"April first is tomorrow, Mr. Bannon. Something tells
me you won't get tons of new machinery bought and
installed in that old sawmill within the next twenty-four
hours. Am I right?" He grinned with his delicate mouth.

"I'm not worried about that, Todd. Not anymore.
What I want now is the Lord's justice." He turned from
the console and stared into Verduin's agate eyes. "You
can help me get it. And you can become a rich man
doing it. I think the time has come for that to happen,
Todd—don't you?—time for you to reap your reward
for having labored in the vineyard all these years. Are
you willing to help me get the Lord's justice?"

"I'm not sure I follow you, Mr. Bannon."

"I mean simply that you must be ready to do whatever needs to be done, no matter how distasteful it may
be. No matter how . . . *bloody*. You must be willing to
go wherever the Lord points the way. It won't be an
easy road, and it may even be dangerous. But it'll also
be profitable to you. *Very* profitable. I'm talking about
the kind of profit that the vast majority of men only
dream about."

"Distasteful and bloody. Hmmm."

"And dangerous, in all likelihood. It's the kind of job
that takes guts, Todd. *And* brains. Are you the man for
it?"

"What kind of profit are we talking about here, Mr. Bannon, to do this very bloody, distasteful and dangerous job?"

Tucker cleared his throat, leaned back in this chair, spoke through clenched teeth. "I'd say we're talking about a quarter of a million dollars. A quarter of a million dollars to act as the Lord's instrument."

Verduin studied his manicured nails, picked at a white tooth. He smoothed wrinkles from his pleated trousers and looked up at Tucker. "This is a very interesting proposition, Mr. Bannon. I'll say yes, I'm your man. I've got the guts—in fact, I've got a very strong gut. And I guess you already know about my brains."

"I knew you were right for this job. Never doubted it for a moment."

"But I'd say we're talking about half a million, wouldn't you? When you think about it, that's a small price to pay for the kind of justice the Lord means to dish out in this instance. Yeah, I'd say half a million—five, maybe six hundred thousand."

Tucker removed his rimless glasses and polished them with a white handkerchief. "Very well, Todd. Half a million. And you're absolutely right—this kind of justice is expensive. I'm always willing to pay extra to get the job done right."

"You're a wise man, Mr. Bannon." Verduin stood and buttoned his sport coat. Tucker detected something new about him now, a confident, self-possessed air. Verduin apparently now considered himself Tucker's equal, a business partner.

"We'll shake on the deal when I see half the money in cash," Verduin said. "I'll collect the balance when this bloody, distasteful and dangerous work is done—also in cash. Agreed?"

Tucker nodded, and the meeting in the quiet room was over.

12

I

APRIL FOOL'S DAY, WET AND GRAY, A FEW MINUTES after 9:00 A.M.

Nita Vale rode her Trek mountain bike east on Columbia Avenue and turned right on Main Street, bound for the Buckthorn sawmill, pedaling with an easy fluency that testified to countless miles logged on back roads and trails. The exertion warmed her, comforted her, softened the sting of rain in her face.

She waved to old Margit Olafson through the front window of Olafson's Market and Grocery, and smiled, though she knew the kind of things old Margit said behind her back . . .

Strange girl, that Nita Vale. Riding her bicycle all over God's creation, day and night, rain or shine. Wearing that stretchy, slippery-looking stuff—what do you call it—Lycra? Doesn't leave much to the imagination, whatever it is. . . .

She crossed Nehalem Avenue and continued past Chubby Chuck's Old-Fashioned Cafe. The breakfast crowd was gone. Only one customer at the counter, a man in a red baseball cap and a down vest, hunched over coffee.

It's not natural, I tell you—young woman without a man, in the full flower of her womanhood. It's not natural at all. . . .

Just south of Nockleby's Texaco, the access road to the Buckthorn sawmill branched off Main Street. Nita turned in and slalomed between the chuckholes, staying clear of the ruts gouged out by the trucks. She glanced up at the hillside where the mill stood, its maw open on the shore of the millpond. Scotty Dunn was busy on the log bronc, herding logs into a steel-hooked contraption that snatched them from the pond and dragged them to the awaiting blades. In the lumberyard, a straddle buggy ferried newly planed two-by-fours to a dock where other workers stacked them onto pallets. Nita could see that the driver was Jerry Dragstead, a fifty-year-old ex-convict who'd served fifteen years in Oregon State Prison for manslaughter. He stared at her as he always did whenever she encountered him around town, followed her with his eyes as if memorizing her every move. His gaze made her flesh crawl.

Nita became conscious of the mill's growl, which was as much a feature of Buckthorn as the old water tank atop a tower behind City Hall. She endured a familiar thrill of revulsion. This sawmill had made Buckthorn what it was, she knew, a dependent suckling of a town. She'd railed against it in her newspaper, though with little effect. The people of Buckthorn had long ago accepted their lot. They resented any assault on the system that had relegated them to dependence and near poverty. They didn't have much, but at least they had this.

It's a horrible place, Vonda Reuben had said of Buckthorn, *and it does horrible things to people. I ought to know—I've been here twenty years.*

II

SHE PEDALED THROUGH THE MUD TOWARD THE HEAD shed. She dismounted, carried her bike onto the front porch of the head shed, and locked it to the hand railing. Tried not to limp as she pushed through the door into the reception room, though her foot still hurt. The herbal potions that Vonda Reuben had prescribed had yet to help.

Denise Ubaldo, an immaculate young woman who weighed more than two hundred pounds, greeted her in Spanish. The two had become friends four years earlier, even though Wade Beswick had forbidden his employees to associate with Nita, who he suspected was a lesbian as well as a militant environmentalist. A friend of Vonda Reuben was no friend of Beswick.

"¿No te enseñó tu mamá a cubrirte de la lluvia?" Denise asked. Hadn't Nita's mother taught her to come in from the rain?

Nita laughed. *"Si, pero asimismo me enseño a no montar mi bicicleta dentro la casa."* Sure, but her mother had also taught her not to ride her bike in the house.

Shortly after Easter of 1990, Nita had published a story in the *Renegade* about Denise's aged aunt Theresa, who had lived in a mobile home on the south bank of Royal Chinook Creek. The old woman had told her fellow parishioners in Hillsboro that she'd seen the face of the Holy Virgin materialize in the mirror on the medicine cabinet of her cramped bathroom. When word got out, pilgrims arrived in droves to behold the miracle of *Nuestra Señora del Espejo*, "Our Lady of the Mirror."

Nita had written the story of *Nuestra Señora del Espejo* in a reverent tone that respected both Denise's aunt and Mexican-American culture, and for this Denise had been grateful. She'd offered to treat Nita to lunch one Saturday in a Mexican restaurant in Hillsboro—not a grand gesture, but the best she could afford. And Nita had accepted. Now they met for lunch at least once a month, always on a weekend and never in Buckthorn, where eating lunch with Nita Vale could have damaging consequences for an employee of Buckthorn Wood Products.

Denise was twenty-six and single, and her obesity hadn't spared her unwanted sexual attention from Wade Beswick. She'd confided to Nita that he made her life miserable with crude remarks about the enormity of her "fun bags" and other features of her anatomy. Nita had urged Denise to file a formal complaint of sexual harassment against the bastard, because women didn't need to take his kind of abuse anymore. The law gave them a way to fight back. But Denise's job was precious to her, and she didn't want to make trouble that might jeopardize it.

The Buckthorn mentality, Nita had said to herself.

Megan Dunn, a shapely girl with red hair piled on top of her head, sat in the desk opposite Denise's, typing industriously and pretending not to notice Nita. Megan had no use for lesbians or environmentalists. Her eyebrow arched when Denise buzzed Peter Cochran and told him that Nita Vale was here to see him.

Seconds later the new chief financial officer of Buckthorn Wood Products appeared at the door of his office. When he saw Nita, his mouth dropped open in shock.

Nita moved forward, trying not to limp. "Mr. Cochran, I'm Nita Vale, editor and publisher of the Nehalem County *Renegade*. I appreciate your agreeing to see me without an appointment. I would've called first, but I didn't want to seem too formal."

"Call me Pete," he said, shaking hands. "Come in, come in. It's no trouble at all. What was your first name again?"

She told him and limped into his office. What Vonda Reuben had heard was right—Pete Cochran was a decent-looking man, lean and lanky like a runner, a bit on the thin side. Alert eyes, deep-set and blue. Brown hair chopped short, thinning in front. Stick-out ears that didn't detract from his looks.

His office was a pocket of neatness and civility amid

the clutter of the head shed. The furnishings were taste-
ful, comfortable. Potted ficus tree in the corner, Navajo
rug on the floor, Seurat's *Bathers* on a wall. Nita's eyes
went immediately to a brass-framed portrait of his family that stood on his desk, a window into a happier time.
She felt the breath go out of her. Sarah and Carter looked
younger than Nita knew them to be, perhaps by three
years, while Sally glowed blond and bright-eyed, her
smile a melody.

"I hope you'll forgive me," Pete Cochran said, mo-
tioning her to a chair. "When I first saw you, I
thought—" He stopped, cleared his throat. "Well, you
see, you're about the same height as my wife, and your
hair's the same color." He indicated the photograph on
his desk. "I wasn't expecting—"

"I understand." She shed her rain gear and cycling
helmet, then settled into the chair, crossing her legs.
"No need to apologize. I'm told that your wife was a
wonderful woman, and a beautiful one."

"You're obviously aware that she's passed away."

"This is a small town," Nita replied, "and in a place
like this you hear things. Sally was a local girl, as you
know, and a lot of folks remember her. Miss her, too, I
think, even after all these years."

"Yeah." They sat quiet a moment. "How about a cup
of coffee? You look like you could use something to
warm you up. Cream or sugar?"

Straight up, Nita told him, grateful for the change of
mood. Pete fetched the coffee himself, leaving her alone
briefly. She glanced out the window at the log yard of
the sawmill and noticed that Jerry Dragstead had taken
a smoke break. He leaned against his straddle buggy and
stared toward the head shed, his hard hat shiny in the
rain. He had bullish shoulders and a heavy brow that
gave him a vaguely simian look. Nita hoped he couldn't
see her through the window.

Pete returned with two mugs, handed one to Nita and sat down at his desk. "So. What can I do for you, Ms. Vale?"

"I merely wanted to touch base, say welcome to Buckthorn from your friendly weekly newspaper. I was thinking it might be fun to run a little piece on you and your kids, kind of introduce you to the community."

"You're right. Might be fun."

"Are you familiar with the *Renegade*?"

"I haven't seen a copy yet, but I've heard about it— from Wade Beswick, actually."

Nita laughed. "Did he tell you to stay away from me, my being a lesbian environmentalist, and all?"

"Hey, I choose my own friends. I don't run them by Wade for his approval."

"Can I take that to mean that you don't share his religious and moral convictions?"

"I'm like John Steinbeck. I don't think there's any sin or virtue. There's just stuff people do."

"That's from *The Grapes of Wrath*, right? The ex-preacher said it, if I'm not mistaken."

"You're not mistaken." Pete saluted her with his coffee mug.

"So you don't think that some of the 'stuff' people do can be sinful or virtuous?"

"Depends on your point of view, I guess, and whether or not your ox is getting gored. What's wonderful for you might be horrible for somebody else. I don't believe in absolutes—not anymore."

"Enlightened attitude." Nita sipped her coffee. "For the record, I'm not a lesbian. I have friends who are lesbians, and I respect and admire them, but I'm not one myself."

"It wouldn't have mattered to me if you were."

On to the interview, the "important stuff," Nita said. She fetched a small spiral notebook and a pen from her backpack, then asked if Pete and his family had settled in, how the kids liked their new school, whether they missed New York. He replied that the family had begun to feel at home in Bannon House, that Sarah and Carter seemed happy with school in Paulsen, that they had already begun to make new friends. Missing New York was inevitable, he supposed, but kids are resilient. He expected them to do well.

Nita jotted notes and asked more innocuous questions, and suddenly the interview was done. She tucked away the notebook and pen, picked up her coffee mug. Her eyes went back to the picture of Sally and the kids, and something squirmed inside her.

"Listen, Pete—you said I should call you Pete?"

"I wish you would."

"I hope you don't take this wrong, but I've got to say something. It concerns your kids, Sarah and Carter."

"Yes?"

Nita set aside her coffee. "It's for their sake that I need to say this. It's about Theodore Bannon—Topper. Your brother-in-law."

"Oh yeah, good old Topper. You know him, do you?"

"Pete, stop me if you've heard about this, or feel free to tell me it's none of my business, but Topper . . . Topper's not a wholly normal kid."

"That's putting it mildly."

"The Nehalem school district has ordered him to undergo psychological counseling because of some behavioral problems he's been having. It seems he . . ."

"*Behavioral* problems? What kind of behavioral problems?"

Nita told the story as Vonda Reuben had related it to her, spitting it out word for ugly word. The burning of live rats, the exhibitionism, the psychological testing. The fear that Topper might harm someone. She left out nothing. When she'd finished, they sat quiet a long time, Pete staring at his hands, his face pale with low-grade panic. Elsewhere in the head shed telephones beeped and intercoms buzzed. Wade Beswick screamed for one of the women to bring him coffee.

"Pete, I hadn't really intended to mention all this," Nita said finally, "but when I saw that picture of Sally and the kids, I couldn't keep quiet. The thought of children living under the same roof with Topper—well, it got to me. If I were a parent, I'd want to know about him."

Pete picked up his Mont Blanc pen and put the cap on it, turned it over in his hands. "I understand. I'm glad you told me—really I am."

Nita stood and gathered her rain gear and cycling helmet. "Don't take my word as gospel on all this, Pete. I've only told you what I heard from someone I trust. You might want to get the real lowdown before you decide what to do."

"And where do I go for that? To Tucker, maybe?" He chuckled sarcastically.

"Would he tell you, if you asked?"

"Are you kidding? He and Dolly are totally taken with their grandkids, and he'd never admit anything that might make me take them away."

"You're right. He wouldn't tell you. But I know someone who would. His name is Dan Kantor, and he's a lieutenant in the State Police. He's in charge of the Buckthorn Task Force over in Paulsen, and he was instrumental in getting verification of Topper's test results from the FBI. You can reach him through the sheriff's office."

"What's the Buckthorn Task Force?"

She explained about the Buckthorn killings. Peter Cochran's face went from slightly pale to bloodless white.

"You mean the killer hasn't been caught? After all this time, he's still out there somewhere, walking around free?"

"I'm afraid so. His latest victim was a kid named Rich Nockleby, last October. Only nineteen. The Nocklebys have run the Texaco across the street for years. Their son was number eight."

"God, I can't believe this," Pete said, rubbing his forehead. "I'd heard—*read* something about the killings, the mutilations, all that. But I didn't let myself believe that they were still happening. I suppose I didn't want to believe that any of this could actually touch me or my family."

Nita handed him a business card. "Come over to the *Renegade* sometime, and I'll show you what I've got on the killings. I've also got a video of the latest news special by Channel 2 in Portland—it'll give you the whole story in a nutshell."

"Thanks," Pete replied, swallowing. "I'll call before I come."

He escorted her through the reception area, past Denise Ubaldo and Megan Dunn. He waited in the shelter of the porch as Nita unlocked her bicycle.

"Tell me something," he said as she prepared to ride off into the rain. "All this Buckthorn killer business— should I be afraid for Sarah and Carter? I mean, is this town a dangerous place? I know that other people live here with children, but—" He looked up into a gray, unencouraging sky. "I'm wondering if we dare spend another day here, crazy as it sounds."

"I don't think it's as bad as that, Pete. So far, the killer has only gone after young men, and he's only struck every two or three years. Rich Nockleby's murder happened five months ago, so we don't need to start worrying just yet. At least I don't *think* so."

"Then suppose that Sarah and Carter were your kids.

Would you let them spend another night under the same roof with Topper?"

Nita fastened the strap of her helmet under her chin. "Look, Pete—I thought you should know about him, that's all. To my knowledge, Topper has never harmed a fellow human being. And who knows?—maybe the therapy is having some effect on him, making him more normal. You can always hope."

"Yeah, I can always hope." He grinned, but it was a sad grin. A tired one. "This may seem funny, but you're the first person I've met here that I feel comfortable talking to."

"I'm glad," she said, feeling a strange flicker in her chest. "I've enjoyed meeting you, Pete. If you ever need to talk, you know where I am."

She left him in the entrance of the head shed and pedaled back through the muddy lot to Highway 49. Glancing to her right, she noticed that Jerry Dragstead's straddle buggy was parked along the fence. Dragstead himself was nowhere in sight.

13

I

BEFORE LEAVING HIS APARTMENT IN NORTHWEST PORT-
land, Todd Verduin fired up a dope pipe and took a slam
of "cat," which cleared his head and ignited sparks behind his eyes. The anxieties that had plagued him since
dawn vanished like beads of water on a hot skillet. He
felt radioactive, energized.

The drug, a derivative of the khat plant found in Af-
rica and Asia, was a yellowish white powder that phar-
macologists knew as methcathinone. Verduin liked it
better than speed, because it was nearly twice as strong,
and the high was mellower, more even. His dealer called
it "flying euphoria."

Stepping out of the elevator into the lobby, Verduin
suffered a mild hallucination, thinking that his clothes
were sopping wet, as if he'd just climbed fully dressed
out of a hot tub. But the sensation lasted only a few
seconds, as was typical with cat. A glance into the polished marble wall of the foyer confirmed that he was
bone-dry and looking good. His tweed sport coat fit
perfectly, and his denim jeans were baggy in the right
places. He'd shaved extra-close today, leaving his boy-
ish face as smooth as a baby's ass.

The walk to his car burned off some of the high, but
he still felt razor-sharp as he climbed in and started the
engine. The morning sun burst through a blanket of
cloud, brightening the world and raising a mist from the

damp streets. Robins sang in the trees. Somewhere blocks away a church bell rang.

Trust your instincts, he told himself. *You're doing the right thing*. Taking a chance, yes, bringing someone else into it, but he couldn't afford not to—not when dealing with a man like Tucker Bannon.

The Sunday brunch crowd had yet to materialize in force, so traffic was light. Verduin took the Burnside Bridge across the Willamette River into a drab, worn-down neighborhood a few blocks south of Killingsworth Boulevard, where local homeboys had spray-painted their gangs' tags on nearly every fence and exposed wall. He parked his Trans Am behind a junked-out '74 Plymouth Volare and walked to the side entrance of a nearby boardinghouse, stepping around holes in the sidewalk. He descended the stairs to a door that was flaking six colors of old paint, paused a moment to listen, then knocked.

"Who the fuck is it?"

"Gil, it's me—Todd, your cousin. Let me in, man."

"Who?"

Verduin repeated his name and thumped the door again. Harder this time.

"Okay, okay! Don't kick it down!"

The latch clicked, a hinge squealed, and the door swung open to reveal Gil Monahan in his underwear, rangy and hungry-looking, tattoos covering his arms, chest and legs. The stubble on his jaw looked rough enough to strike a match on. Though he wasn't yet twenty-five, Gil Monahan had the mean eyes of a man much older, a man accustomed to risking everything and losing it. On his head he wore what appeared to be pantyhose, rolled and tied to hug his scalp like a shower cap. The fabric oozed thick, white soap suds.

Verduin stared, unable to speak.

"So, what the fuck do you want, Hot Toddy? You here to torment my ass, or what?"

"What's with the pantyhose?"

"Oh man, don't make me go into it."

Verduin knew that Monahan suffered an obsession with his hair, which was blond and kinky, an amorphous mass that stuck out from his head in twisted fingers. Monahan's fondest wish was for hair like Glen Campbell's, the singer from the sixties. Gil wanted hair that was slick and straight and swoopy, that fell over his eye in graceful sickles. He'd tried a dozen home remedies, consulted a legion of professional stylists, but nothing had worked. Gil Monahan had hair like a Brillo pad.

"Another straightening treatment," Verduin ventured.

"Whoa, you're sharp today, Hot Toddy. Mind like a steel trap. Don't just stand there, man—come in and close the door before the neighbors' cat gets in."

The apartment was a landfill. Hamburger wrappers, beer cans and pizza cartons littered the floor. The air was foul with rancid food and cigarette smoke. A naked teenaged girl sprawled on the sofa, barely awake, paralytically drunk. On the wall hung a poster-size photo portrait of Glen Campbell in his prime, dressed in a white buckskin jacket, leaning on the neck of his guitar.

"Who's your girlfriend?" Verduin asked, waving away the warm can of Miller Lite that Monahan offered.

"Little something I picked up in Old Town last night. I forget her name—Mandi, Randi, I don't know. Not a bad bone job, but Jesus, get a load of her face. Is she a fuckin' shar-pei, or what?"

"Get rid of her. You and I need to talk."

Monahan got rid of her, pushed her out the door, threw her clothes out after her. The girl was too drunk to offer much resistance.

"So, what're you doin' here, Hot Toddy? Got some work for me?" Monahan padded to the bathroom and

leaned close to the mirror on the medicine cabinet. He
sipped his beer, then started unwrapping the pantyhose
from his head.

"That's a possibility," Verduin replied. "First I need
to know if you can handle a certain kind of job." He
watched with fascination from the open door of the bathroom as Monahan carefully peeled back the pantyhose.
The soap had dried and formed a crust. "It's a ticklish
deal," Verduin went on, "and I need somebody who's
healthy and dependable. Could you be that man?"

"You know my work, cousin. I've always done you
a good job at a reasonable rate, haven't I?"

This was true. Verduin had sometimes contracted with
Monahan for what he called "specialty work." Several
months earlier, for example, he'd used a hidden camera
to get footage of a rich client's wife in flagrante delicto
with the pastor of their church. Because the client had
wished to avoid a public scandal and spare the church a
ton of embarrassment, Verduin had commissioned Gil to
"chat" with the pastor and persuade him never to look
at the woman again, much less show her his etchings.
The chat had included a solemn pledge to hammer the
pastor's toes flat if he backslid.

Gil started to brush the crustiness out of his hair, using
short strokes. He grimaced as the brush caught snag after
snag.

"I need some assurance that you're not pipin' dope,"
Verduin went on. "I need to feel that I can count on
you." He watched as Monahan tried to separate strands
of hair and make them lie down. "But first you've got
to tell me what the hell you've done to your hair. What
did you put on it?"

Shaving cream mixed with raw egg and lemon juice,
Gil Monahan explained. The girl he'd brought home last
night—Mandi or Randi or whatever—had described a
sure-fire means of straightening hair. First, you soak

your head for an hour in water as hot as you can stand. Then you apply the mixture liberally, allowing it to foam up. You wrap your head tightly in pantyhose so the hair stays straight, and let the mixture dry overnight. In the morning you brush it out, and—would you believe it?— you've got hair like Glen Campbell's.

But the treatment hadn't given Gil hair like Glen Campbell's. What he had was hair like Don King's. It looked like stuffing that had oozed out of an old armchair.

"If I ever see that bitch again, I'll break her fucking wrists," Monahan muttered. "You think she was putting me on, man? Was this some kind of tasteless fucking joke?"

"Forget it, Gil. Take a shower and shampoo that shit off. We'll go out for breakfast, have ourselves a nice talk."

They breakfasted on *huevos rancheros* at a popular Mexican restaurant on the shore of the Columbia River, across the Interstate Bridge in Vancouver. Sailboats tacked and jibed on the water, and occasionally a huge river barge drifted toward the ocean, loaded with grain bound for Japan or China or Singapore.

Verduin watched his cousin mop egg yolk with tortilla and wondered when he'd last had a decent meal. Gil actually looked semirespectable, having showered and dressed in a clean flannel shirt and khakis that covered his tattoos. He wore a Raiders cap to hide his fright-wig hair.

He wasn't stupid, Verduin knew, but he was still a dangerous nut-bag. Gil had served time in California for armed robbery and assault with a deadly weapon. He'd committed at least one homicide that Verduin was aware of, though he'd never been arrested for it. Having won parole on the robbery and assault beefs, he'd absconded the supervision of the California penal system and had

fled to Portland. A judge in L.A. County had issued a
bench warrant on him that was still active. These days
Gil lived by his wits, slinging dope here and there, doing
an occasional burglary or stealing a car, mooching off
girlfriends. And doing occasional specialty work for
Verduin.

"Tell me something," Verduin said, staring dreamily
at the river. "Have you ever dreamed of walking around
and holding your head up, like all these good citizens
here?" He tossed his head to indicate the surrounding
crowd of brunchers. "I'm talking about respectability,
Gil, and *security*—not needing to look over your shoulder all the time."

Gil stopped chewing and stared back at him, his eyes
hard as marbles. He said nothing.

"Or how about this? Some fat dentist tells you that
he'd be proud to have you as his son-in-law, then throws
you a reception at a posh country club. You and the
daughter sail off to the Gulf of California, spend a month
or two honeymooning in Cabo San Lucas. Let's say you
have a kid of your own someday, and the kid's proud
of who you are and what you do, because you're worth
being proud of. You send him to private school, and he
brings his pals home so they can meet you—that's how
proud he is of his old man. Have you ever indulged
yourself in this kind of madness, Gil?"

"Why are you asking me this? I'm the underclass,
man. Nothing good comes to me unless I steal it. I'm
never gonna get some fat dentist's daughter unless I tie
her up and beat the fight out of her."

"Don't be so sure. Every so often the fates conspire
to elevate one of us common jerks to that great fortress
on the hill—that shiny gated community where life is
full and rich, where you pay people to clean your house
and mow your grass and wash your BMW." Verduin
winked and sipped from his water glass. The cat had

made him eloquent. "You see, it's happening for me. I've got a client—a very *special* client who I've worked for since I first got started in the PI business. I've done good work for him all these years, and he's paid me well . . ."

"Your cash cow, right? The dude who keeps you in shiny Trans Ams? You've mentioned him two or three hundred times."

"The point I'm trying to make, Gil, is that all the hard work has finally paid off. This gentleman and I are partners now, and we've got a major deal going down. The money's not huge up front, but it'll get good real quick. My life's about to change. I'm about to step up from working with my hands to letting money do the work—and that's what it's all about in the final analysis. It's finally happening for me, Gil. I'm getting the break of a lifetime, and I intend to take advantage of it."

Monahan arched a cautious eyebrow. "And there's work for me with this dude—is that where you're going with this?"

Verduin pushed his half-finished plate aside, lit a cigarette. "There's work for you, if you can handle it. I want you to be my backup, the guy who covers my ass. Even though I've got a nice working relationship with this client, I'm not sure I can trust him totally. I need someone on my flank, someone like you. I need *family*, Gil."

"I understand. What do we need to do, and what's in it for the kid?"

Verduin gazed out the window at the wide Columbia. Sailboats lazed on the choppy water amid shards of reflected sunlight. He leaned across the table toward his cousin and spoke in a low voice.

"We need to put somebody's lights out. There's ten grand in it for you up front, and like I said—further down the line, we're both looking at the opportunity of a lifetime, the big change of life. I'm talking about waving a wand, Gil. Gated communities and country clubs. Fat dentists with beautiful daughters. I'm talking about the finest hair clinic in the country.''

Monahan's mouth stretched into a grin. "I'm your man, Hot Toddy. I've popped some guys in my time, you know that. This is nothing new for me. Bring me in and I'm here for you, cousin.'' He reached across the table to grip Todd Verduin's hand. "I'm up for a change of life, that's a pure fuckin' fact. All I need is a chance, and I'll never look back."

"This won't be like anything else we've ever done together, Gil. With this one we've got to be extra careful, do everything according to plan. We need discipline and ultratight security. We slip up, we fry."

"I hear you, amigo. From this moment on, I'm Mister Tight Lips, Mister Clean-and-Sober. You be the brains, I'll be the brawn, like always. I'll make you proud, Hot Toddy."

Verduin smiled at his cousin, thinking, *And I'll make you dead, Gil.* No way did Todd Verduin plan to share his hard-won spoils with this flake.

II

WEARING EARPHONES THAT PIPED HEAVY-METAL ROCK directly into his head, the Verminator worked near the wood line of the estate as the afternoon perished in a muddle of long shadows. Using a long-handled nozzle attached with a hose to a plastic tank, he sprayed the encroaching morning glory and pennywort with a mixture of dimethylamine salt and propionic acid, taking care not to overload any particular area lest the chemicals harm the grass.

Fighting weeds can be ticklish work, ladies and gen-

tlemen. You don't want to kill the good stuff along with the bad, now do you? The tricky part, of course, is knowing the difference . . .

He looked up from his work and saw little Carter Cochran, who stood in the grass with his brand-new Rock Hopper mountain bike not six feet away, wearing his shiny cycling helmet.

"What's happenin', buckaroo?" he said to Carter, taking off the earphones. "I didn't hear you coming. Been covering some miles on those new wheels, I bet."

The boy nodded and patted the handlebars proudly, confirmed that he and his sister had ridden all over Buckthorn today. Grampa Tuck had bought the bikes for the kids on their family excursion to Portland yesterday, replacing the ones they'd sold back in New York. These were real *mountain* bikes.

"What are you listening to?" Carter wanted to know, pointing to the earphones around Topper's neck.

"Slayer. Ever hear 'em?"

"Yeah. Except my dad doesn't like for me to listen to groups like that."

Topper grinned at the boy and pulled several CDs from his fanny pack, held them out. "The old man doesn't know I have these," he whispered. "I get other dudes to buy them for me at the mall over in Hillsboro. If he knew I had 'em, he'd go ballistic—probably tear my fuckin' head off."

Carter's eyes widened upon hearing the F-word. He looked at the CD jackets and saw the wild artwork that indicated heavy metal and death-rock, saw the names of the bands. Skinny Puppy, Slayer, Megadeth, Ghandi's Rolex.

"Anytime you want to listen to any of these, just let me know," Topper added. "But don't say anything to the old man, okay? He's got this thing about rules."

"Okay," Carter whispered, looking guilty. He, too, knew about rules.

Tucker had given his grandkids a short speech about the rules that governed life in Bannon House. He didn't allow swearing, the playing of godless rock music or satanic electronic games. He'd confiscated Carter's Sega Genesis outfit, though he'd promised to give it back if and when the grandkids moved away with their father. He'd declared that Jesus Christ walked in this house and that all who lived here should behave as if Jesus stood right beside them.

Carter eyed the spray gun and the containers of chemicals on the ground. "You like taking care of the weeds and stuff?"

"It's okay. Killing weeds isn't as good as killing vermin, though."

"Vermin? What's vermin?"

Sentient beings, the Verminator explained. They had minds and senses, which meant that they could see and hear and feel. Best of all, they could suffer.

"Plants can't *suffer*," he went on. "Oh sure, they're alive and they can be killed, but they have no awareness. In order to feel anything, you need a backbone, a spinal chord and a brain. That's why it's not as *meaningful* to kill weeds or bugs. They're plants and invertebrates, and they aren't even aware of their own existence. What fun is it to kill something that can't suffer, that doesn't know it's alive to start with?"

Carter looked bewildered. He stared at Topper with his head cocked, like a befuddled little dog. "You get your yah-yahs by making things suffer?" he asked.

The Verminator's getting an idea, ladies and gentlemen, and it's a lollapalooza.

Topper chuckled, let the question go. He scratched his head. "Say, buckaroo. You up for something really cool?"

"Yeah, I guess."

Things have been getting a little dull around here, right, ladies and gentlemen? Seeing that shrink twice a week has really taken the bubbles out of the beer, if you know what I mean. Last week the Verminator gave himself a private performance of the Rat Choir—six of them in one cage—and he couldn't even raise a hard-on. The Verminator thinks it's time to move on to bigger and better things . . .

"Let's take a bike ride, you and me. We'll go up the mountain to a place I know, and I'll show you something that I guarantee will pop your brain."

Carter stared down at his sneakers, hesitating. "My dad told me never to go anywhere alone with you," he confessed. "Told Sluggo—I mean Sarah—the same thing. Said we shouldn't listen to anything you say."

The Verminator felt a surge of excitement right down to his crotch. "Well, your dad is like all dads, loves to put down rules for you to follow. Loves to make you do things you don't want to do, keep you from doing what you really like. What dads don't understand is that their fucking rules don't apply when they're not around to grab you or hit you. But hey, I can't force you to come with me, buckaroo. It's your loss. You're going to miss a chance to hear some rats sing."

"Rats? *Sing*?" Carter looked up, his eyes wide and bright. "How can a rat sing?"

"You won't know until the Verminator shows you, now will you? These are sacred rats, the kind you won't find anywhere else on earth."

"I've never heard of rats that can sing. Our dog tries to sing when he hears me play my CDs, but he can't really do it. He's really just howling."

"I'm not talking about howling, buckaroo. I'm talking about sacred music, hymns in tribute to the divine agony. I'm talking about the world-famous Rat Choir of

Mount Olivet.'' Topper could see that the boy's curiosity was near the flash point. ''Look, your dad doesn't
have to know about this, okay? If we leave now, we'll
be back before dark. It'll be your and my little secret.''

Carter craned toward the house and stared for a moment, then turned back to the Verminator. He screwed
up his face, thinking.

''Okay,'' he said finally. ''But we've *got* to be back
before dark, and it's *got* to be our secret. Nobody finds
out about this, right?''

''Right as rain,'' the Verminator said. ''Nobody will
ever find out. Now let's go over to the Verminator's
office and pick up my bike. We're also going to need
some gasoline and a flashlight . . .''

III

DOLLY BANNON KNOCKED SOFTLY ON THE DOOR OF
Pete's bedroom and got no answer. She put her ear to
the varnished wood of the door, heard soft snoring
within.

Asleep at four in the afternoon, she remarked to herself. Which probably wasn't so remarkable, considering
that he'd just started a new and stressful job, that he'd
put in a trying week. He'd complained about not sleeping well at night. The man needed his rest.

She'd wanted to talk with him about Topper, about
the concerns that Peter had raised with Tucker last night.
She'd wanted to assure him that Topper was basically a
good boy, though an eccentric one. That even though
the school district had insisted he receive psychological
counseling, Topper was incapable of hurting anybody.
The Lord had his hand on Topper, she was sure. The
Lord wouldn't let him do any real evil.

But all this could wait until later. Let Peter sleep for
now.

She turned from the door and walked back toward the opposite end of the house. Passing little Sarah's bedroom, she heard the soft, unmistakable sounds of a child crying. She knocked and pushed through the door, saw Sarah lying on the bed, a notebook open on the bedspread beside her. The girl looked up with reddened, watery eyes.

"Sarah, honey—what's wrong?" Dolly sat next to her, smoothed her blond hair with a loving hand. In the notebook Sarah had written the title of a poem, along with several sets of opening lines, all of which she'd scratched out. Only the title had survived: "Gerard."

Sarah clutched Dolly's hand in her own, which made the old woman feel warm and needed.

"I don't know what's wrong with me, Gramma. It's like I can't write about anyone I love. Every time I try, I just lose it. I can't write about Mom, I can't write about home, I can't write about Gerard."

"Sarah, darling, it won't be like this forever—I know it won't. God will give you the strength to write your poems. Maybe He's merely waiting for something else to happen first."

"Something else? Like what?"

"Maybe He's waiting for you to come to Him in prayer, ask Him for His help. God doesn't want His children to suffer, Sarah. He wants them to be happy and productive people. He yearns to help, really He does, but sometimes He needs to be asked first. Have you thought about doing that?"

The girl shook her head.

"Then let's ask Him now. Let's go to Him in prayer. It's easy."

Dolly showed her granddaughter how to fold her hands, as she'd shown two little girls more than thirty years ago. How to bow her head and close her eyes, as she'd done for her own daughter and Rosa. Told her to repeat her words, a simple prayer.

"Father God, we come to You giving thanks and to say we're sorry for sinning against You. We give You our praise, and our love . . ."

Sarah repeated the words, her voice sounding hollow and uncertain. Dolly couldn't know whether the girl felt the presence of Christ, but then she was sure that Christ would make Himself felt when the time was right.

". . . and we ask You to touch Sarah's heart, to ease the pain she feels . . ."

Sarah stammered over this, but Dolly led her gently on. Soon Sarah was praying on her own.

". . . and please take away the grief I feel over losing Mom and leaving home . . ."

Here she stopped, wouldn't go on. Dolly saw the child's face working with emotion, saw tears flowing again. The *connection* is happening, Dolly thought. The Lord is touching her, speaking to her.

"Go on, honey," Dolly urged, her own heart welling. "Say to Jesus whatever you feel. Don't worry about whether it sounds right. He loves you, and He'll understand."

With her eyes clenched and her hands knotted so tightly that her knuckles were white, Sarah prayed. "Please let Gerard come to live with us. Make Grampa Tuck let us bring him here. Please! I miss him so much. If you bring Gerard here, I'll do anything you want, I promise . . ."

Dolly resolved then and there to speak with her husband about making sure that the Lord answered a little girl's prayer.

IV

TOPPER DISMOUNTED HIS MOUNTAIN BIKE AND WAITED
for Carter Cochran to catch up. The trail that climbed
Mount Olivet was steep in places, and the little kid
wasn't a seasoned rider, not like himself. Even with a
half-gallon of gasoline strapped to his bike, Topper had
scarcely broken a sweat.

"We're almost there," he said, indicating the trail
ahead. "You okay?"

Though breathing hard, Carter was game. "I'm
okay."

"Let's go then."

They pedaled onward and upward through deepening
forest shadow, the gloom thickening as the sun dipped
nearer the horizon. On their left the forest broke occasionally, offering a vista of the town below with its drab
roofs and utility poles, its water tower and church stee-
ples. The Buckthorn sawmill lay on a hillside at the far
end of the valley, its boilers issuing plumes of smoke
that rose to a certain height and flattened into a band of
dirty haze.

Soon the trail narrowed and disappeared altogether.
Here the greenness of the forest seemed to crowd inward, a crush of Scotch broom and buckthorn. Vanilla
leaf grew among the Douglas firs and hemlocks, thrust-
ing their stalks through clefts in the trees. Now and then
a great hemlock creaked or grumbled as the breeze
tugged its crown. Birds warbled and twittered. Bugs
buzzed.

Topper leaned his bike against a hemlock, spat on the
ground and nodded toward a fallen log. "We're going
through there, buckaroo. Follow me, and don't get too
far behind. This isn't a place a little kid wants to be
alone in."

He watched Carter's face tighten and felt a thrill of pleasure. *Oh, this is going to be good, ladies and gentlemen. Something tells me the Verminator is about to move into a new dimension . . .*

He stepped over the log and moved into the thicket, pushing away ferns, eager to get where he was going but still apprehensive over what might wait for him there. Carter stayed close behind, taking two steps for every one of his own. Minutes later Topper halted and pointed to a mass of vines and blackberries that reared twenty feet ahead.

"There it is, buckaroo, Rat City. Home of the best rats in the world. They're big motherfuckers, and they're mean. And do you know what?" He bent down and stared Carter straight in the eye. "They can sing like angels."

Carter's mouth formed an O, and he whispered a *wow!* What was this place? he wanted to know—a cabin? A house? It had a dark look, as if bad things had happened here and might happen again. English ivy had laid siege to the structure, obscuring its lines and angles. The windows yawned black amid the tangle of green, and the door had long ago rusted off its hinges. The roof sagged, and the air smelled of moldering wood.

"What was that?" Carter whispered, edging closer to Topper. "Something moved in there."

Topper stared into the blackness behind the windows, his heart pounding, but he saw nothing. He wondered if . . . No. He put the possibility out of his mind. *She* wouldn't be here now. *Would* she?

"Might've been a bird, maybe a rat," he replied. "Doesn't matter. You and I've got work to do, buckaroo. Stay close to me, okay?"

Something stronger than fear drove Topper now, something that the nerdy shrink from Portland had tried to coax out of him with cleverly chosen words during their twice-weekly therapy sessions. Dr. Feldon had suggested that Topper might need drugs to control the thing, whatever it was—the thing that loved to torture and kill sentient beings. The thing that made his dick hard when he did it.

It'll take more than psychotropics and intensive therapy to silence the Verminator, ladies and gentlemen . . .

Topper set the can of gasoline on the ground, then led Carter to a tunnel in the brush that ran along the foundation of the cabin. Carter whispered *ow!* as a blackberry thorn bit into his skin. Crouching low, Topper dug out his flashlight and inspected the first of the wire cage-traps he'd placed earlier. It was empty. Further on, the second cage, too, was empty. The third, however, held a large male rat, its body easily ten inches long and its tail another ten beyond that. The beast's eyes glowed red in the cone of the flashlight. Its bristly tail whipped from side to side as it chattered in panic.

"This is more like it," Topper breathed. He showed Carter how to carry the cage and warned him not to let his fingers poke through the wires, because a rat like this wouldn't miss a chance to sink its teeth into a boy's tender meat.

The next cage also held a rat, a female, as did the next two—four rats in all. A nice little choir, Topper thought as he transferred the three females into one cage with the male.

"Time to go inside," he said, and Carter's face whitened. "You're not scared, are you? I told you I'd show you something that would pop your little mind, didn't I? Well, I can't do it out here, because what I have to show you is in there."

Carter squared his shoulders. "You said you were going to show me rats that can sing. Why can't they sing out here where it's light?"

"Because the altar's in there, you fuckin' little idiot. I told you they're a choir, and that's their church. In there is where they sing—get it? Now come on."

Carter held back. "No way. I heard something in there. If we go in, it'll get us."

Topper bent low. "Listen, you little rat-fuck. I didn't peddle my bike all the way up here for the exercise. You said you wanted to hear the Rat Choir, and I've been nice enough to make the arrangements. The least you can do is to give them a listen, right?"

"My d-dad said I shouldn't—"

"Fuck your dad! You think he's going to help you now? Forget it, buckaroo, and forget about trying to run. If you do anything stupid, I'll turn the Rat Choir loose, I swear, and they'll chase you down, man. They'll leap onto your legs and back, and they'll sink their little yellow teeth into your skin. And do you know what'll happen then? The germs in their mouths—the toxicity—will get into your bloodstream and paralyze you, like *instantly*. You'll twitch and choke like you've got rabies or something. You'll lie paralyzed on the trail, and the squeals of the rats will bring hundreds of others, maybe thousands of rats from all over Mount Olivet. And they'll start to *eat* you, buckaroo, bit by bit. They'll bite off pieces of your neck and face, and you'll bleed till you croak . . ."

Topper straightened suddenly, having himself heard something inside the cabin. A scraping sound, he thought, like a heavy object moving over a stone floor. He beamed the flashlight into the windows and saw nothing but shadows.

He caught Carter by the forearm, held him tight. "No more fuckin' around. You're going to carry the gas can, okay? I'll take the rats. When we get inside, we'll . . ."

"But there's something *in* there—didn't you hear it?"

Tears flowed down the little boy's face. Topper could see that he was thoroughly terrified.

Is this good, ladies and gents, or what? Who's more scared—the little fuckhead or the Verminator? It doesn't really matter, does it? Fear is fear, and pain is pain. It all goes to the same place and eventually comes out the same hole, doesn't it? And isn't it delicious?

"I'm only going to say this once, so listen up. You and I are going in, and we're taking the gasoline and the Rat Choir. We're going to do it because it needs doing, understand? Your old man or my old man are like totally irrelevant, okay? Their shit-eating rules don't count here."

He stared another long moment at the cabin. He grabbed Carter's hand and wrapped it around the handle of the gasoline can.

"You think I'm not scared?" he asked the kid. "Well, here's a flash for you. I'm *fuckin'* scared. And the rats are, too—scared as hell. But it doesn't matter, because you and I are moving into the next dimension, buckaroo. You and the Verminator and the Rat Choir."

With his free hand he picked up the cage, then moved toward the door of the cabin, pulling Carter along. As the smell of rot and corruption thickened in his nostrils, he relived the one other occasion when he'd found the nerve to venture inside Rat City.

It was a day much like this, ladies and gentlemen, about a year after I followed the Mad Witch up here without her knowing it. Saw her go in through that very door, remember? It took me a year to work up the guts to go in myself, not knowing what the fuck I'd find, not knowing if she'd be home . . .

He'd gone in and seen what he'd seen. It had scared him shitless, yes, but at the same time he'd sensed something sacred about the phenomenon. For a tingling, maniacal moment the old cabin really *had* seemed like a church, and Topper had felt as if he were kneeling at an altar. Staring at the phenomenon, he'd established a connection with whatever had come to this place before him. A feeling for it, an empathy . . .

Flesh of my flesh, blood of my blood. That's what it was, ladies and gentlemen—a connection. For a razor-sharp moment I was part of it. I knew it, and it knew me. The Verminator found his beginnings here, his roots. And now the Verminator has come back, and he's ready to move into the next dimension, say Amen . . .

Carter didn't squeal in panic as Topper urged him over the threshold, which was a surprise. The darkness closed over them, dank and cool. They moved forward cautiously, their sneakers crunching over needles and cones that had blown in through gaps in the roof. Behind them the door was a box of brightness, while shafts of feeble daylight streamed in from jagged openings above. Sunset was near, and the light was dying.

"I'm letting go of your arm, buckaroo," Topper whispered. "But remember—you run from me, and I'll send the rats after you, I swear to God." The boy shuddered, but he didn't turn and run.

Topper snapped his flashlight on, and the beam knifed over the clutter inside the cabin. An ancient wood-burning cooking stove lay overturned directly ahead. On all sides lay pieces of roofing amid recognizable components of furniture—armrests of chairs, legs of tables, handles of drawers, all broken and splintered. Cupboards had collapsed from the walls. Shelves had sagged and fallen, along with pots and pans, books and utensils. Spiders had spun webs in every available cranny. Dust and mold covered every square inch where moss couldn't grow. The air was sharp with the stench of rodents' scat.

In one corner of the cabin, however, was an area of the stone floor that was remarkably free of debris, as if it had seen regular use, a trapdoor built of heavy planks,

mossed over in places but not rotted through. Topper
went to it and wedged a hand along one edge, heaved it
upward. Hinges groaned, and the stink of damp earth
wafted up through the hole. Carter whimpered as the
trapdoor fell to rest.

"That's where we're going, buckaroo," Topper said,
shining the flashlight into the maw. "You, me and the
rats. You first."

Carter sat on the filthy stone floor and dangled his
legs over the edge of the hole, feeling for the first rung
on the wooden stairs. He found it and maneuvered himself to descend backward, holding tightly to the gasoline
can. He asked Topper to shine the flashlight downward
so he could see where to put his feet, and Topper
obliged. Four steps, five steps, six, seven—and Carter
was down. Topper came after him, lugging the caged
rats, who squealed or chirrupped as if to protest these
doings.

The cellar of the cabin was even darker than Topper
remembered it. The walls were featureless dirt, lined
with flat stones to waist level. The roots of trees and
shrubs protruded from the walls like arthritic fingers.

*And this, my good friends, was the Mad Witch's root
cellar, where she undoubtedly stored her roots—what
else? What kind of roots, you ask? The Verminator has
not a clue, though if he were to guess, he would say
maybe she stored potatoes down here, or maybe fruits
and vegetables. Potatoes are roots, right? . . .*

The overhead timbers sagged from the weight of the
stone floor above. A startled rat chittered in a corner of
the cellar, causing the rats in Topper's cage to squeal
and claw the wire, begging for rescue.

"Over there," he said, using the flashlight to motion
the boy to the far wall of the cellar. Carter went slowly
forward, the gasoline sloshing in the can, toward a set
of shelves that held a row of glass jars, the kind moms

and aunts and grandmothers use to put up dill pickles or peaches or homemade jam. Kerr jars with stuck-on labels. Festooned with spiderwebs.

"That's far enough. Now put the can down."

Carter did so and turned back to the flashlight. "Please d-don't hurt me," he begged in a small voice. His eyes were bleary with tears. He still wore his cycling helmet.

Did you hear that, ladies and gentlemen? The little goo-head doesn't want the Verminator to hurt him. Isn't that cute? Don't you just wish you could spoon up all this delicious terror and put it in a jar? Then you could save it and have some whenever you felt like it— maybe pour it on ice cream or waffles, or use it for fondue . . .

Topper grinned and stared at the kid under an arched eyebrow. "Know what this is, buckarooo?" He held up the cage.

"A c-cage with rats in it."

Topper made a harsh sound in his throat, like the wrong-answer buzzer on a TV quiz show. "Wrong! It's the Mount of Olives Gospel Church, believe it or don't. Oh, you thought the Mount of Olives Gospel Church was down on the corner of Bannon Avenue and Second Street in beautiful downtown Buckthorn, didn't you? Not so. This is it, the real deal, right here in the Verminator's hand. This big rat here is the Reverend Mister Randy Roysden, pastor, and these others are the congregation. I won't bore you with their names."

He placed the cage on the ground, picked up the gasoline can and opened it.

"What you're about to see is the miracle of transubstantiation," he said as he splashed gasoline over the panicky rats, "not in the traditional sense, as in bread and wine turning into the flesh and blood of Christ. What you're about to see, my little fuckhead and all you other

fuckheads out there in imagination land, is the conversion
of the Rat Choir into the actual person of the Reverend
Randy Roysden and assorted human members of his congregation—who shall remain anonymous except for their
initials, which are Mr. and Mrs. Tucker Bannon."

The male rat sputtered and coughed as the fumes of
the gasoline stung its lungs. The others huddled together
in a corner of the cage, their eyes clenched tight, their
bodies trembling.

"What are you going to do?" Carter asked. He
backed away until his shoulder blades encountered the
shelf that held the glass jars, the Kerr jars that could
have held canned plums or applesauce or string beans.
Topper thought he looked ready to faint.

"Stay with me now, buckaroo, 'cause this is all for
you. We're going to sing a hymn—me and the Rat Choir
here, who are just this moment partaking of Holy Com-
munion, as you can see."

He stepped back from the cage and dug into his jeans
for his farmer matches. Grinning ferociously, he sparked
a match with his thumbnail, watched the flame ball and
flare, watched it settle into an even tongue of yellow light.

"In honor of Tucker Bannon and his rule against dirty
language, we give you the following hymn."

Topper flipped the match into the cage, and fire bal-
looned against the timbers of the ceiling, nearly blinding
him. The heat blasted his face, and the cage became an
inferno. Waving his arms like the conductor of a chorale,
he sang his hymn to Tucker, using the melody of "A
Mighty Fortress":

> Eat, bite, suck, fuck.
> Gobble, nibble, chew.
> Tit, bosom, hair-pie.
> Finger-fuck, screw! . . .

The rats shrieked as fire ate into their gasoline-soaked hides. Their voices rose against the booming of Topper's hymn, tinny with pain. They hurled themselves against the wire, scrabbled at each other, tore off fiery bits of each other's bodies. They "sang" like banshees, and Topper sang along with them, his voice a screech.

> Rat shit, bat shit.
> Dirty rotten twat.
> Four little rattails
> Tied in a knot . . .

Topper finished his hymn and watched the rats die, their bodies twitching and coiling into blackened messes. Watched the flames subside to orange knots. He looked into Carter Cochran's innocent young face, saw the boy's eyes staring down at the embers, wide and unblinking. Unseeing eyes. Mouth hanging open, sucking air. The heat and stench were brutal against their faces.

And that, ladies and gentlemen, pretty well wraps it up, except . . .

Except what?

Topper discovered that he didn't even have a hard-on. He had no warm tickling in his guts. While conducting the choir he'd felt no craving to wave his cock at the flames, no urgent yearning to fuck fear and suffering in the face.

Ladies and gentlemen, I hope you'll bear with us— I'm not quite sure what's happening here. We seem to be having technical difficulties again . . .

What was happening was nothing. No tingle, no excitement, no orgasm. Having brought Carter and the Rat Choir here to the holy of holies, he'd expected something truly colossal, an over-the-top rush that would usher him into the next dimension. But nothing had happened.

Wilting, Topper saw young Carter Cochran turn away from the dying embers in the cage, saw him raise his eyes to the shelf behind him. The flashlight produced an aura just bright enough to reveal what the jars held.

Eight Kerr jars, full of yellowish, unhealthy-looking fluid. The *phenomenon*.

"H-hey, buckaroo—don't look at those . . ." For the first time in his life, Topper Bannon felt something like shame, maybe even remorse.

Help me out here, ladies and gentlemen. Does anyone here know what this is all about? Hands! Give me a show of hands . . .

Quart jars with labels, neatly inked, some turning brown with age . . .

Kelly Franklin, Oct. 30, 1976, the one on the end, farthest to the left, wearing a thick covering of dust.

And *Nathan O'Grady, Oct. 31, 1979*.

An eyeball here, an eyeball there, easily identifiable in the yellow-tinted liquid, staring out through the glass with unnerving detachment. And fingers neatly sliced off at the bases, crammed into the jars, the flesh having grayed, severed bones protruding. And penises, jammed in among the fingers, vesicles and arteries and veins curling out through the severed ends.

Lawrence Dillman, Oct. 26, 1981.

And so on, the names of young dead men, the latest being Rich Nockleby, whose label was clean and white, compared to the others, inked only months ago. Rich Nockleby's pickled parts still looked almost lifelike.

"Okay, i-it's over, buckaroo. All over for today."

Topper picked up the gasoline can. "This'll be our secret, okay? Just like we said, our little secret. Nobody ever has to know . . ."

The boy seemed unable to walk, so Topper carried him.

14

I

THE NEXT MORNING, MONDAY, APRIL 4, DAWNED COOL and sunny after a long night of drizzle. Peter Cochran arrived at the head shed forty-five minutes before the start of the workday, his eyes red and pouchy. His accountant-underling, Wally MacKenzie, had arrived even earlier than he and had made coffee.

"You look like you could use this," Wally said, handing him a cup. "What'd you do—go on a bender, stay out till dawn?"

Pete explained that his son, Carter, had stumbled in shortly after sunset last night, exhausted and uncommunicative, acting half-sick. He'd refused dinner and had gone straight to his room, which was worrisome, because the boy seldom, if ever, passed up food. A short time later, Topper Bannon had arrived to report that he'd found Carter's new mountain bike on a trail up on Mount Olivet, which meant that Carter had walked home, having left his bike behind in the forest. Carter had refused to answer any questions about where he'd been or what he'd done, refused to confirm or deny that he'd eaten any wild berries or mushrooms that might have made him sick.

This wasn't like his son, Pete told MacKenzie, his face grim. Carter was the kind of kid who took good care of his belongings. He wouldn't have left his new bike up on the mountain unless something was terribly wrong.

Pete had sat next to his son's bed most of the night. Though the boy had seemed somewhat better this morning, Pete had kept him home from school. Esmerelda Sandoval had promised to look after him and to call Pete if she noted any change for the worse.

"Shouldn't you've taken him to a doctor?" MacKenzie asked. "Maybe he's picked up a bug or something, needs a shot of penicillin."

"I wanted to, but he didn't have a fever. I probably would've taken him anyway, but . . ."

"But old Tuck talked you out of it. Said you shouldn't be running to doctors every time somebody gets a sniffle or a headache, something like that. Have faith in your creator to take care of you and your loved ones." MacKenzie grinned. "Did I leave anything out?"

"You're good."

"Hey, I worked with the son of a bitch every day for almost thirty years. I know what he's like. He can be—persuasive."

"I intend to look in on Carter at noon, and if he's not better, I'll take him into Hillsboro to a doctor, no matter what the hell Tucker says."

Pete closeted himself in his office and avoided contact with the other workers in the head shed. Trying not to worry about Carter, he pored over financial files in an effort to absorb as much knowledge as he could about Buckthorn Wood Products' recent financial history. He'd scheduled a meeting in Portland with the company's tax accountants later this week in order to receive a briefing on Buckthorn's tax position, and he needed to prepare.

Shortly after ten, he buzzed Wally MacKenzie and asked him into his office. He handed the little man a thick file folder that he'd dug out of the file cabinet earlier in the morning.

"Maybe you can enlighten me on this loan from

somebody called the Conifer Group," he said, toying
with his Mont Blanc pen. "Beswick has never mentioned it, which I find weird, frankly. Two-point-five
million, concluded last year with performance provisions
in the contract. What does it all mean?"

MacKenzie lowered himself into a chair, his lips moving as he read down the lines of computer printout. "Jesus, *that's* where the money came from," he breathed,
his eyes huge behind his thick glasses. He ran a hand
through his gray, early-Beatles hairdo. "Sometime last
year—must've been around the middle of April—Beswick handed me a cashier's check for that amount and
told me to put it into the operating account. Draw from
it as needed, he said. So that's what I've been doing.
It's come in handy, too, since we're not exactly setting
the world on fire with our profits these days."

"The operating account? I don't understand. There's
a contract there, signed by Tucker Bannon. The money
is supposed to go for upgrades in equipment, saws and
conveyers, related things. You should have set up a ded-
icated account to handle it."

"This is the first I've heard about upgrades, Pete."

"But there's a deadline in the contract—a deadline
that passed three days ago, April first. The upgrades
should've happened by now or . . ."

"Or the Conifer Group can foreclose," MacKenzie
put in, reading the paragraph of the contract that Pete
had highlighted in yellow. "And the collateral for the
loan is Mount Olivet."

The two men sat silent and simply stared at each
other. Finally, Pete asked how much Mount Olivet was
worth, ballpark. MacKenzie wiped sweat from his forehead and guessed forty, fifty million, give or take. He
couldn't say for sure, not being a forester, but he could
confirm that the timberland was worth a lot more than
two-point-five million. A *lot* more.

"This is unreal," Pete said, getting up from his desk. "Do you know of any upgrading that's happened over the past year?"

"You've toured the mill, Pete. You see any new saws or conveyers? We're still running on steam, for Christ's sake. This contract calls for a new power plant. I haven't seen any vouchers for upgrades of any kind. Hell, we've been using the money to make payroll and handle routine expenses."

Pete stared at Seurat's *Bathers* on the wall, the painting that had hung in his wife's office in New York. The scene looked tantalizingly serene. He wished he could will himself into it and be done with this place, this job.

He heard himself talk, felt his mouth and vocal cords form words. Wade Beswick should have undertaken detailed planning for equipment upgrades of this magnitude, he heard himself say. Charts should occupy every square inch of wall space—Gannt charts and PERT charts and critical-path charts showing the means by which Buckthorn Wood Products would identify its needs for new equipment, the stages by which the company would buy that equipment and bring it on line, the ways of handling the borrowed money, and hundreds of other details.

But there were no charts on the walls, no detailed memos on how to spend two-point-five million of borrowed money. Only right-wing political cartoons and dirty pictures and . . .

"Oh my God," Wally MacKenzie said, standing suddenly, and Pete came back to earth. "This doesn't look good."

He stared over Pete's shoulder, out the window, and Pete turned to see what had caught his attention. A large young man with broad shoulders and a narrow waist strode across the parking lot toward the head shed, his legs whipping back and forth, his fists swinging at his side. Another man trotted after him, shouting something. Their hard hats glared orange in the pounding sunlight.

"Now what?" Pete said.

"That's Scotty Dunn, works the log bronc. Megan's husband, as you might recall. Nice kid, if he's not mad at you."

"Who's the guy trying to hold him back?"

"Jerry Dragstead. You might remember his personnel jacket—did fifteen years in the joint for manslaughter. Tucker gave him a job when he got out, and he's still here, drives a straddle buggy. Strange bastard, if you ask me. I've never liked him."

Scotty Dunn walked with forceful determination. Jerry Dragstead scrambled after him, grabbing on to him as if to keep him from doing something crazy. Dragstead himself was a brutish-looking man of fifty, and though he looked fit and strong, he was barely able to slow the young giant.

Wally tossed the file folder on the desk and turned for the door. "I think I know what this is about. It's Beswick and Megan—he's been hittin' on her, tryin' to get her into the broom closet with him, like he's tried to do with every woman who's ever worked here. Now it's caught up with him."

"Megan? You mean—oh, Christ."

"Looks to me like she's finally broken down and told her husband, and now Scotty means to tear Wade a new asshole. I predicted this would happen someday, remember?"

"Maybe we ought to let him do it," Pete said, half serious. "Couldn't happen to a nicer guy than Wade. The way he treats Denise and Megan makes me physically ill."

"I hate to see a young buck lose his job for thumpin' on a certifiable scumbag, much less do time for it. If I know Scotty, he's been festerin' all morning about this, wondering just what the hell to do about it, gettin' madder and madder. Now he's hit the boiling point, and if we don't stop him, he'll put Wade in the hospital, maybe worse.''

From outside came men's shouts, the kind that promises violent trouble. Prison yard shouts, Pete thought, before the outbreak of rioting. Mill workers were gathering in the lot. Some were trying to dissuade Scotty Dunn, but others were egging him on.

''Let's go,'' Wally said, swinging into action. ''Maybe we can head him off, talk some sense to him.''

Pete followed him out the door toward the reception area. Behind them another door opened, and Wade Beswick stuck his head out of his office. ''What's going on out there? What's all the noise about?''

Wally didn't miss a stride. ''Wade, if I were you, I'd go out the back way. Scotty Dunn's coming across the parking lot, and if he catches you, he'll break both your legs and drop-kick you over the front gate.''

At the mention of her husband's name, Megan issued a moan of anguish and covered her face with her hands.

''Denise, call nine-one-one,'' Pete ordered as he strode with MacKenzie toward the front door. ''Tell them there's a fight breaking out, to send someone quick.'' Denise nodded and picked up a phone, already punching buttons.

What happened over the next sixty seconds seemed like a poorly filmed bar fight in an old melodrama. Pete saw Scotty Dunn blast through the front door of the head shed, huffing and snorting like a Cape buffalo, bellowing for Wade Beswick. Behind him came Jerry Dragstead, grappling for a hold of Scotty's shirt. Wally MacKenzie tried to head the big man off, but Scotty simply swatted him aside as if he were a meddlesome puppy, sending him crabbing into a cluster of old furniture in the waiting area. And suddenly Pete found himself standing face-to-face with the Cape buffalo, his guts churning, wondering if he was about to be battered senseless.

"Out of my way, Mr. Cochran," Scotty said evenly. "It's the cocksucker behind you I want a piece of."

"Let him come!" Wade Beswick hollered, retreating into his office. "I'm not scared of that ignorant jughead. If he wants a piece of me, he can have it, by God."

Scotty reached out to press a hand against Pete's chest, but Jerry Dragstead pulled his arm away. From somewhere behind Pete, Megan Dunn screamed her husband's name, her voice edged with panic.

Dragstead pleaded with Scotty to let it be, but Scotty shoved him back toward the door. Suddenly little Wally MacKenzie flew at the big man and tried to tackle him. Scotty peeled him off and pitched him into the arms of Jerry Dragstead, sending both men out through the front door. They landed in a scuffle on the porch.

"Scotty, *please!*" Megan screamed from her desk. "Nothing happened between Wade and me, I swear to God! I've never even let him touch me! He's tried to a million times, but I've never . . ."

But the Cape buffalo wasn't listening. He went through Pete like wind through a chain-link fence. Pete tried to grab him, but Dunn was incredibly big and strong. He caught a fistful of Pete's herringbone sport coat and lifted him high off the floor, turned and heaved him into the paths of Jerry Dragstead and Wally MacKenzie. All three went to the floor, flailing and swearing.

Pete saw Scotty plunge through the door of Wade Beswick's inner office. He heard the *whump!* of metal against bone. Scotty lurched backward through the door, his hard hat spinning to the floor, his nose flattened against his face. Jets of blood spewed from his mouth and nostrils, lacing the wall, the door, the front of his shirt. He struck the doorjamb of Pete's office and careened forward again, his knees buckling, his arms working spastically. He went down hard.

"Oh, God—*Nooooooooo!*" Megan scrambled out of her desk to her husband, who lay twitching in the hallway, a lake of blood spreading under his head. Denise Ubaldo went with her, and the two women knelt beside the fallen man, pawed at him, tried to cradle his head.

Wade Beswick stepped out of his office, an aluminum baseball bat resting jauntily on his shoulder as if he'd just popped a double into left field. A piece of hair had fallen away from his bald spot to dangle over his ear.

"You all saw it," he said. "Clear case of self-defense if ever there was one." He stared down at Megan, his nose wrinkled as if he smelled a gas leak. "Tell that big, stupid hubby of yours to check behind my door the next time he stampedes into my office. I just might be there with a baseball bat—you never know."

Pete felt bile rise in his throat. He approached Beswick, his hand extended.

"Give me the bat, Wade," he said. "You won't need it anymore today."

"Can you believe how stupid these people are?" Beswick asked, looking up from his handiwork. He was still in high color. "Must be a symptom of working in sawmills generation after generation, breathing all that sawdust. I figure it gets into their brains, clogs up their synapses or something. Depresses their IQs, makes them stupid. Still, they don't seem to want anything better, so who am I to criticize?"

"Give me the bat, Wade. The fight's over."

"What kills me is the way they get up on their hind legs and demand raises year after year, better benefits, more vacation, more health insurance, all that crap—when the most complicated thing any of them does is run a head rig or drive a log bronc. What do they expect for this kind of work? It doesn't take any training to speak of, no schooling, no long years of college.'' He swiped a hand over the stray piece of hair in order to get it to lie over his bald spot, but it wouldn't stay.

"Give me the goddamn bat, Wade. Nobody's going to . . ."

"Hey, get the hell off my case, Cocky! I'll keep the bat, if it's all the same to you."

Jerry Dragstead approached the fallen, bleeding form of Scotty Dunn, bent low, and stared between the shoulders of Denise and Megan. The women were doing what they could to stop the bleeding, which wasn't much.

"I'll be go-ta-hell," Dragstead wheezed. "Looks like his whole face is caved-in."

"Ambulance is on the way from Hillsboro," Wally MacKenzie shouted above the confusion, having placed another call to nine-one-one.

"I hope they come soon," Denise said, "because he is having difficulty breathing. Too much blood."

Beswick sniffed and giggled, half out of his head on adrenaline. "Hell, he'll be all right. If he doesn't make it, I guess we'll just advertise for a new log bronker, won't we, sweet Megan? Might be a blessing to get that big old gorilla off your hands, huh, precious?"

Megan Dunn sobbed and buried her face in her husband's bloody shirt. Pete's left hand flew out, closed on the baseball bat that rested on Beswick's shoulder and snatched it away. He drove his right fist hard into Beswick's gut, saw him start to fold up. Taking him by the front of his shirt, Pete hauled him into the reception area and slammed him against a wall hard enough to rattle a window. Beswick gagged and fought for air, his doughy face contorting.

"Listen, you sick fuck," Pete said. "You didn't need to cave that boy's face in. You could've held him off, gone out the back way. You didn't need to hit him with a baseball bat.''

Beswick coughed and heaved in a breath of air. "This is really special, Cocky," he said, his eyes bulging. "You've just bought yourself a pink slip and an assault charge. I may even sue your ass—get me some of the Bannon money at long last."

Pete drew back and drove his fist again into Beswick's gut, causing him nearly to retch this time. Doing violence felt weirdly good, as it had in his boyhood when he'd gotten into fistfights. He liked the warmth in his muscles, the pounding of his heart. He pinned Beswick tight against the wall, surprised at his own strength.

"If you ever insult either of those two women again," he said, spitting the words into Beswick's face "or if you try to put your fat hands on one of them, or ever treat them with anything but the deepest respect, I'll *kill* you. That's not a threat, you barbaric asshole—that's a solemn promise. You hear me?"

Pete hit him one more time for good measure, then let go and watched him crumple to the floor. The buzz of rage subsided, and Pete felt shaky, disconnected from himself. His own outpouring of venom now frightened him. Peter Cochran wasn't the kind of man who punched other men in the stomach or threatened them with death. He was a businessman, for Christ's sake, an MBA, an expert on insurance. He hadn't scuffled seriously with anyone since high school.

What the hell was this place doing to him? he wondered, his eyelids fluttering.

He heard the faraway whoop of sirens, probably the sheriff coming to investigate. He was grateful for that sound, which was one he knew well, having lived in New York. The sound of sanity and social order. Of people cleaning up after accidents and altercations.

It was a sound that gave him hope.

II

A SHERIFF'S DEPUTY TRIED TO ADMINISTER CPR TO Scotty Dunn but was unable to do so because of severe trauma to the nose and mouth. After what seemed an eternity, an ambulance arrived from Hillsboro, upon which a team of paramedics sliced a hole in Scotty's throat and stuck a plastic tube into his windpipe to keep him from drowning in his own blood. He still had not regained consciousness when they whisked him away. His wife crouched next to his gurney in the ambulance, clutching his bloody hand, her face gray with shock.

"And the mill claims another one," Nita Vale said to Pete, watching the ambulance pass through the main gate. She'd arrived on the scene shortly after the Nehalem County Sheriff's deputy, armed with a camera, a notepad and a hand-held tape recorder. She'd heard the dispatch on her police scanner and had rushed over on her bicycle to cover the story for the next issue of the *Renegade*.

"It wasn't the mill," Pete said. "It was Beswick."

"It's all the same, Pete. You'll understand someday."

Sheriff Nick Graybill himself arrived later to question the witnesses. Pete watched him strut around the head shed in his sausage-skin uniform, his gigantic cigar clenched in his teeth. After going through the motions of investigating, Graybill buttonholed Nita Vale and informed her for the record that his department would press no charges in this matter. Wade Beswick had clearly acted in self-defense, according to witnesses, and young Scotty Dunn had surely learned his lesson. No need to make a federal case of this scrap.

"He's learned his lesson, all right," Nita replied, jotting notes. "The paramedics said he has a broken nose, a fractured palate, and probably a severe concussion. May even have brain damage. Seems to me that old Wade is getting off kind of light."

Before leaving, the Cigar drew Pete aside. "I had to talk like hell to keep Wade from slapping you with an assault charge for hitting him in the gut. I finally managed to convince him it wouldn't be worth the time and effort. If I were you, I'd be real nice to him for a while, buy him a beer, kiss his ass a little. He'll get over it— he always does."

Pete thought, *I'll kiss Wade Beswick's ass when Rush Limbaugh farts "God Bless America" on national TV.*

"By the way, tell your old dad-in-law that Sheriff Nick says howdy," the Cigar said in parting.

Somehow Pete got through the rest of the workday. At the stroke of five o'clock he went home to Bannon House, where his children were embroiled in a game of croquet with their grandparents in the backyard. Pete watched from the rear porch, thinking that the scene looked like a Norman Rockwell painting—crinkled old couple and their fresh-faced grandkids, wholesome fun. A heartwarming slice of Americana, right here in Buckthorn, America.

Carter seemed full of piss and vinegar, apparently having recovered fully from whatever mysterious malady had afflicted him yesterday. He and Sarah barely acknowledged their dad when he arrived. No hugs and kisses, no *Hi, Dad! Guess what I did in school today!* This hurt a little. For a jealous moment Pete feared that Tucker and Dolly had already co-opted the leading role in his children's lives, a role that was rightfully his. It had happened to him before, hadn't it?

Stop it! he told himself. Tucker and Dolly were just being grandparents, for God's sake. This is what grandparents *do*. They lavish attention on their grandchildren and spoil them rotten.

Tucker glanced up to the rear porch of the mansion where Pete stood, nodded and winked. After taking a turn with his mallet, he ambled over and assured Pete that everything was okay, notwithstanding the madness that had erupted at the mill today.

"God's in his heaven, the birds are singing, and we've got the music of children's laughter to see us through," the old man said, squeezing Pete's arm. "And don't worry about being fired, Pete. Wade Beswick doesn't have authority to fire a Bannon family relation, not even one who's just punched him in the gut." He winked again and chuckled, apparently finding the whole matter funny.

A Bannon family relation, Pete thought. *Is that what I am?*

"As for young Scotty Dunn," Tucker went on, "Dolly and I will pray for his complete recovery. So prepare yourself to witness the astounding power of prayer, Pete, That kid'll be up and on his feet in no time, you'll see. And he'll have a job in our mill, too—I'll make sure of that. You don't think I'd let Wade fire him after what Wade's been trying to do to Megan?"

So he knows about that, too, Pete thought. "I'm sure the Dunns will be very appreciative," he said. Then he cleared his throat. "I need to talk to you about something else, Tuck. It's about a loan that the company got last year from the Conifer Group. The money was supposed to be—"

Tucker shushed him and assured him that the matter was under control.

"But the contract contains performance provisions. There's a deadline for installation of new equipment, and it's already—"

Tucker held up a hand and shook his head, making

clear that he didn't want to hear any more about the matter. "Your daughter just walloped my ball halfway to Portland, and I need to get my head back in this game. In the meantime, trust me, all right? God will take care of our little company, just like He always has."

III

NOT FEELING HUNGRY, PETE SKIPPED DINNER WITH THE family and hiked down the hill from Bannon House into the center of Buckthorn. Reluctant though he was to leave Sarah and Carter even for a few hours, he needed to be alone. He needed to think, work his arms and legs, fill his lungs with cool air. He needed to be free of Tucker Bannon and his relentless sermonizing, if only for a little while.

He walked a block south on Second Street, turned right on Columbia Avenue and went another block to Main Street, which seemed deserted, a corridor of shadow punctuated by neon signs. One sign identified Chubby Chuck's Old-Fashioned Cafe, another the Kwik-Stop grocery. Olafson's Market had the brightest and newest-looking sign, while that of the Head Rig Bar was so quivery and dim that Pete almost missed it. Even so, the Head Rig's parking lot was crowded with the pick-ups and cars of mill workers.

No neon sign identified the Buckthorn Bank, the Allegro Theater, Armstrong's International Harvester, or any of the score of other businesses that had fallen victim to the sickness afoot in Buckthorn. The buildings they'd occupied were dark, boarded over, crumbling.

He stood still a moment with his hands pocketed, his eyes wandering over the ruination. What was he looking for? he asked himself—ghosts? At this moment he missed his wife desperately, her warm arm around his waist, her strength. He missed the sense of being at the center of her world.

Had Sally's dreams perished here with all the others? he wondered. Had she fled Buckthorn because it had stolen something precious from her?

Pete heard the distant twang of country music, steel guitars and some hick singing about lost love and honky-tonks. Maybe Clint Black or Garth Brooks—he wasn't current on his country stars. Must be a jukebox.

He saw colorful neon ahead, an outline of a muscular Paul Bunyan–type in a hard hat, with letters made of sawed logs—Tom Sawyer's Saloon. He pushed through the door and smelled greasy cooking. Stuffed animal heads gazed down from the walls, and antique logging equipment hung from the rafters. Pool table in the rear, liquor bottles in neat ranks. Display racks with packets of Alka Seltzer, air freshener for the car and disposable Bic lighters. A spectacular Wurlitzer jukebox stood against the far wall, the source of the music he'd heard.

Wally MacKenzie had told Pete that this was the "respectable" place in Buckthorn to have a drink. Tom Sawyer's had been his and Lucille's favorite spot in town, back when they were a couple. You could get a decent burger or even a steak, he'd said, depending on whether the owner, old Vinny Boggio, was up to the job on a given night (Vinny was close to eighty, and he had arthritis).

Pete had barely set foot over the threshold before he heard a woman's voice call his name. At first he thought that he was hearing things, for the place appeared empty but for a pair of middle-aged cowboy-types who sat at the bar. Then he caught sight of Nita Vale at a table in a dim corner. She waved at him, causing his heart to miss a beat.

IV

IF HE SQUINTED, SHE LOOKED JUST LIKE SALLY—SAME blond hair, styled in a wedge cut like the one that Sally had worn several years before her death. Same square-shouldered posture. She wore a blue work shirt and jeans, as Sally often did when puttering around the house.

She sat across from a large, solid-looking woman who wore bracelets of heavy Mexican silver and a long gray ponytail. Both women had pints of beer before them.

Nita beckoned Pete over, and he went. Things stirred inside him that had lain dormant for a long time. *Why?* he wondered. Was it the physical similarity between Nita and Sally or the fact that he'd touched no woman in a sexual way since well before his wife's death?

Nita introduced him to her drinking partner, Dr. Vonda Reuben, the local naturopath, who shook his hand stoutly and pulled out a chair for him. Vonda was over fifty, and she had severe hazel eyes embedded in nests of fine wrinkles.

The bartender, a stooped old man who Pete figured must be Vinny Boggio, shuffled to the table. "What'll ya have, young fella?" Pete ordered a beer, but Vonda held up a large, freckled hand.

"This is Oregon," she said. "Have yourself a pint of real microbrewed ale. It'll be on me. Tell him what you're pouring tonight, Vinny."

Vinny recited a short list, and Pete chose one. A moment later the old man set a pint of dark ale before him. Pete tasted it, pronounced it delicious.

"So—Nita tells me you're a good guy," Vonda said, "which I find remarkable. She doesn't usually say nice things about people in the sawmill business, especially those who work for Tucker Bannon.''

"Well, she's right, I am a good guy," Pete replied, wiping foam from his mouth with a sleeve. "As for Nita, what can I say?—any friend of Wade Beswick is a friend of mine." He held up his glass, and the women clinked theirs against his, both laughing. He saw that Vonda could laugh without actually smiling.

"Drinking with the vampire lesbians of Sodom could soil your image among the local folk," Nita said. "If Wade hasn't warned you about us already, I'm sure he soon will."

"After his performance this morning, Wade should worry about his own damn image," Vonda said. "As for what you did to him, Peter, I salute you. You did what nearly everybody I know has wanted to do for years. My only criticism is that you should've hit him harder, maybe ruptured his spleen."

"But I thought he was one of the city fathers, loved and respected by all," Pete said.

"He's a slug, and everybody knows it," Vonda answered, signaling Vinny Boggio for another pint. "People smile at him and shake his hand because they're scared of him. He runs the mill, and he holds almost everybody's job in the palm of his hand."

"Anybody hear how Scotty's doing?" Pete asked.

"I talked to Denise Ubaldo about an hour ago," Nita answered, "and she'd just gotten off the phone with Megan, who'd called from the hospital in Hillsboro. The doctors have decided to transport him to OHSU—"

"OHSU?"

"Oregon Health Sciences University in Portland. Medical school and teaching hospital—"

"A gaggle of witch doctors and quacks," Vonda Reuben put in.

"Scotty has slipped into a coma," Nita went on. "At

the very least, he'll need reconstructive surgery on his nose and mouth, but the doctors can't do anything until he comes out of the coma. Things don't look too good for him."

Vinny brought three more pints, though Pete had yet to finish half of his first one. "So, tell me," he said to Vonda. "Do all naturopaths endorse beer drinking the way you do?"

"This is healthy beer. No preservatives, good honest ingredients, poured from a tap like God intended. A person shouldn't drink too much of it, obviously. Alcohol in any form can make you ugly and obnoxious, not to mention sick."

"Not me," Pete kidded. "I become witty and urbane when I drink. The drunker I get, the more charming I become." Vonda came close to smiling but didn't quite make it. Pete concluded that the wrinkles around her eyes definitely were not laugh lines.

He asked Nita how things were in the world of militant environmentalism.

"I keep telling her that she needs to hang with a new crowd," Vonda said, jumping in before Nita could answer. "The Earth Insurrection is a bunch of Don Quixotes who don't really accomplish anything except making their opponents as mad and militant as they are."

"And I keep telling *her* that somebody has to make a stand somewhere," Nita countered. "Otherwise we'll wake up some smoggy morning and find that all the forests have been cut down, and there's no serviceable watershed left, no more wildlife, no place where it's quiet and untrammeled."

"To which I say, so what?" Vonda said. "So what if we run out of water? So what if we chop down all the rain forests and run out of oxygen? Humanity suffers, maybe goes extinct—big deal. If Mother Nature wants it to happen, it'll happen.''

Pete ventured the opinion that environmentalists and industry should look for compromises that allow both preservation of nature and sane economic development.

But Vonda scoffed. ''You're missing the point, Peter Cochran. At such time as all you humans overburden the land with your numbers and your factories and machines, Mother Nature will simply rub you out. Maybe she'll open the ozone layer wide enough to scorch you to death. Or maybe she'll unleash some killer virus and wipe you all out in a week or a month or a year. She might dry up the rain clouds and starve you out with drought and famine over the course of a century—time doesn't mean much to her.''

''What Vonda's trying to say in her own endearing way,'' Nita put in, ''is that we'll do it to ourselves. Humanity is capable of annihilating itself by abusing nature.''

''Cow flop,'' Vonda said, having swallowed half of her newly delivered pint in one gulp. ''That's not what I'm saying at all. It staggers me how arrogant you humans are. You think that because you're capable of saturating the upper atmosphere with fluorocarbons, you're also capable of *abusing* nature. What you don't understand is that you yourselves are agents of nature. You're nature's tools. If you actually succeed in destroying the ozone layer or cutting down your own source of oxygen, you'll do it because nature wants you to.''

''And why would nature want that?'' Pete asked.

''In order to usher in the next wave of life. No single life form gets to rule the earth forever—not dinosaurs, not humans, probably not even insects. Every dominant life form ultimately is forced to give way in order to let somebody else have a crack at it.''

''What about all the nonhuman species that are going

down the tubes because of human activity?—and I'm not talking about the spotted owl necessarily. Shouldn't somebody try to prevent innocent casualties?''

''Forgive me if I don't get all misty,'' Vonda retorted. ''The fact is, species have been going extinct since life got started on this planet. Less than one percent of all the species that have lived on earth are alive today—did you know that? They fall prey to disease or changes in the weather, or other species edge them out or eat them up. Nature doesn't care what happens to them, whether they go extinct or survive long enough to evolve into something else. Only humans make value judgments about these things.''

Pete took a slow slip of his ale, his mind working. ''So, you're saying that we shouldn't give a damn about polluting the water or the air, even if it makes people sick, that we shouldn't concern ourselves with the harm we inflict on other human beings or other species? Ruining the earth with pollution is just Mother Nature's way of getting rid of humanity, right?''

Vonda held her palm to her mouth and belched softly. A light sheen of perspiration coated her brow. Pete wondered if she'd violated her own pronouncement against drinking too much.

''Not quite,'' she answered. ''You see, mankind can't *ruin* the earth, no matter how hard he tries. He might succeed in making it ugly for a time, and he might even make it unlivable for himself. But no matter how much harm humanity inflicts on the ecosphere, nature will eventually reclaim it. She'll take mankind's hardest punch and rebound better and stronger than ever. In the end, she'll grind to dust everything humans have ever built. She'll fill in every hole they've ever dug. She'll grow back all the trees, and she'll create new species to replace the ones that . . .''

She stopped talking and stared toward the door. Pete

turned in his chair and saw that someone had entered the bar, a bullish man of fifty with a heavy brow and dark, hooded eyes. A huge yellow cat followed close at his heels, its tail standing nearly straight up and twitching with its every stride.

"That's Jerry Dragstead," Nita said. "He works for you at the mill."

Instead of work clothes and a hard hat, Dragstead wore a navy cable-knit sweater and a pair of new blue jeans with ironed-in creases. Having bathed, shaved and combed his graying hair back from his forehead, he looked radically different from the man who'd tried to prevent Scotty Dunn's assault on the head shed that morning. He also looked depressed, as if he'd just lost his best friend.

"That's the biggest cat I've ever seen outside of a circus," Pete said. "How does he get away with bringing it in here? Aren't there ordinances about animals in bars and restaurants?"

"Vinny doesn't care about things like ordinances anymore," Nita answered.

Vinny Boggio wiped the man's table and set a glass of ice water before him. The cat leaped to the tabletop and made himself comfortable, as if this was part of his daily routine.

Pete said, "I wouldn't have known Jerry, the way he's dressed. He doesn't look too happy, does he?"

"Believe me, you don't want to know him at all," Vonda replied.

"Why? Because he's been in the slam?"

"I guess you haven't heard what he did that landed him there," Nita said.

"Wally MacKenzie says he was in for manslaughter. I didn't get the particulars."

Back in 1961, Vonda explained, seventeen-year-old Jerry Dragstead lived with his parents on their farm southeast of Buckthorn, near the town of Birkenfeld. He was an only child, a quiet kid, and an ardent lover of animals. He loved animals so much, in fact, that he wouldn't hunt or fish, which made him something of an odd duck out here in rural Oregon.

One day he hauled a load of hay in his dad's truck to some folks who pastured horses on the outskirts of Buckthorn. While driving north on Main Street, he spotted two teenage boys in the backyard of an abandoned house near the ruins of Kaplan's Drug. They'd tied the tails of two house cats together with a three-foot length of rope and had thrown the rope over the cross member of an old clothesline post. Hanging by their tails and utterly terrified, the cats had clawed and bitten each other bloody. The boys were leaping around and laughing, hurling rocks and sticks at the two exhausted animals, trying to spur them to fight on.

Jerry parked the truck and pulled a long-handled shovel from its holder behind the cab. He bore down on the pair before either saw him.

"He damn-near decapitated one of them with the shovel, killing him outright," Vonda said. "He beat the other within an inch of his life, and would've killed him, too, if someone hadn't seen what was happening and rushed over to stop him. As it was, he made a cripple of the kid, knocked his IQ down into the range of a domestic goat."

Pete sat silent a long moment, his gut churning. The more he learned about Buckthorn, the uglier it got.

"The DA charged Jerry as an adult, even though he was only seventeen," Vonda continued, "and he drew thirty years in the Oregon State Pen. Served fifteen of it, got himself paroled in the summer of 'seventy-six. Tucker Bannon gave him a job in the mill, and he's been here ever since."

"He lives alone in a house on Nehalem Avenue, not

far from Vonda's place," Nita added. "He keeps maybe a dozen cats, three or four dogs. Doesn't have many two-legged friends that I know of, except for Scotty Dunn. They're both car nuts, and Scotty helped him build a hot rod or something—I'm not sure what it is."

"It's a 'fifty-two Mercury coupe," Vonda said, "with a small-block Chevy engine. It could be a nice car, if Jerry had money to put into it."

They watched as Vinny Boggio delivered a cheeseburger, a basket of fries and a Coke to Jerry Dragstead's table. Before starting to eat, Dragstead pinched off a piece of his burger and fed it to the cat.

"Seems to me the guy paid for his crime," Pete added. "I've seen his personnel file, and he's been a good employee for more than eighteen years, kept his nose clean since leaving the joint. Maybe it's time people stopped being scared of him. After all, he was only a kid when he got into trouble."

Nita folded her paper napkin and placed it next to her empty plate. "Have you ever looked into his eyes?"

"Can't say that I have."

"There's something about the way he looks at you— it's hard to describe. A kind of *hunger*, I think. It scares me."

"Plus, he's a prowler," Vonda said. "Sneaks around at night, peeking into windows. He's good at it, too— real quick and stealthy. Couple years ago I caught him in my yard—must've been one, maybe two in the morning. I had my old double-barrel shotgun trained on him, locked and loaded. He was hunkered down in the shrubbery next to my house, trying to hide, and I damn near shot him, except I couldn't quite bring myself to do it. I'm a physician, and I've taken an oath not to harm people, you know. So I let him run off, fool that I am."

Vonda stood up suddenly from the table, and Pete saw

just how large a woman she was. Nearly as tall as himself and solidly built. Stocky but not fat.

"It's time I got home," she announced, pulling on her raincoat. "I'm filling out my tax returns tonight. Only ten days left till tax day, and I've vowed not to wait until the last minute again." She thrust a hand toward Pete, and he shook it. "Nice to have met you, Pete Cochran. I enjoyed this little talk, and I hope we can do it again sometime."

Pete stood and told her that he too had enjoyed the chat.

"Don't stay out too late, girl," Vonda said to Nita. "You never know what's creeping around the streets of Buckthorn at night." Then she left, striding past Jerry Dragstead's table without glancing at him.

Pete sat down again. Nita grinned.

"She's really something, isn't she?" Nita said. "Underneath all that grimacing and grousing beats a heart of warm oatmeal."

"She's an original, I'll give her that."

"She likes you, which should make you feel good. Vonda doesn't suffer fools."

Pete glanced at his watch, saw that it wasn't yet 7:30 and pulled a menu from its holder next to the potted candle. He was hungry. He suggested that they order dinner, have another couple of beers, talk. He even offered to buy.

Nita answered that Vinny Boggio's cooking was too greasy for her taste. "On the other hand, I've been saving a couple of salmon steaks in my freezer for a special occasion. I can broil them, steam some vegetables, and set dinner before you in half an hour. Talk to me nice, and I might even open a bottle of wine."

The offer was too good to refuse.

V

TOPPER BANNON STOLE NOISELESSLY INTO THE THIRD-
floor servants' bedroom and pulled the door closed behind him. Though it was the largest and most
comfortable of the five servants' bedrooms, no one had
lived in this room since his grandfather's time. His
abuela, Esmerelda Sandoval, preferred one of the rear
bedrooms on this floor because she liked the eastern exposure and the morning sunlight that streamed through
her window on clear days.

Directly under this room, on the second floor, lay the
master suite, where his parents slept. Their room, like
this one, boasted a fireplace, as did the parlor directly
beneath the master suite on the first floor. The same
brick superstructure contained all three fireplaces and
their respective chimneys. Immediately adjacent to the
brick superstructure, hidden by the walls, stood a vertical
ventilation duct that served all three rooms.

*Here's the deal, ladies and germs. I noticed very early
in my life that whenever the old man and the old woman
wanted to have a private chitchat, they snuck off to the
master suite, and they always closed the door behind
them. This was their safe place when they needed to talk
about* ME *and what a nasty little shit I was, when they
needed to discuss whether or not to send me off to some
mental institution for my own good. They sure as hell
couldn't do it in front of Esmerelda, right? Otherwise
the whole town would've known about it within a day
or two.*

*Okay, are you ready for this? They never realized—
and they still don't realize—that a sufficiently curious
lad like the Verminator could hear every word they said
simply by lying on the floor of the overhead bedroom*

with his ear directly over this ventilation grillwork. Right here, like this . . .

At dinner this evening he'd surmised that something major was afoot in the Bannon household, and it wasn't necessarily good. For starters, Pete Cochran had left the mansion on foot and hadn't shown up for dinner. His unexplained absence had made his kids nervous and ruined their appetites. Second, Topper had read tension in his parents' faces, though they'd tried hard to camouflage it. He'd worried that Carter, the little snot bag, had blabbed about what had happened yesterday afternoon at the Mad Witch's cabin. If this was the case, life as Topper knew it might soon be over.

Immediately after dinner, the old man and the old woman had retired to their bedroom on the second floor, just as Topper had expected them to do. Their voices sounded tinny and far away through the grillwork, but Topper could hear their every word.

". . . and you know perfectly well, Dolly, how I feel about having animals under the same roof with us. Dogs are dirty critters. They shed, they bring in ticks, fleas, mites, all manner of vermin. It's one thing, I suppose, to have a family dog who stays outside, but you know very well that Sarah and Carter would never settle for that. They'd want—"

"Tucker, stop this," Dolly said, her voice sharper than Topper could remember hearing it in a long, long time. "What we're talking about is a little girl's faith. She's asked the Lord to bring her dog here, and you have the power to answer that prayer."

"Sometimes children need to learn that they must sacrifice, that not every prayer can be answered. That's the problem with kids these days. They think they're entitled to get anything and everything they want. They have no concept of limits. They don't understand that . . ."

"Tucker, this is *Sarah*, our granddaughter. She's new

to the Lord. She's lived all her life in a home where there was no faith, and she doesn't know the power of prayer. I heard her promise the Lord that if He brought Gerard here, she would do anything He asked of her.''

Topper heard muffled thumps that he interpreted as Tucker stomping across the carpeted bedroom to where his mother stood. He could almost see his father, standing straight as a chess piece, his huge fists planted on his hips.

"Dolly, I can't believe I'm hearing this from you. You're my wife, and you're fighting me on something I believe very deeply. You'd do well to remember Paul's letter to the Ephesians, chapter five, verse twenty-two: *As the church submits to Christ, so also wives should submit to their husbands.*''

"Oh, I remember that passage—I remember it well, because you throw it at me every time we disagree on something. But this time I'm not giving up, because I know I'm right. I pray that you'll soften your heart, Tuck, and see what a golden opportunity you have here.''

"An opportunity to do what?''

"To answer your granddaughter's prayer and show her that the Lord loves her. You have it in your power to win her over, Tuck—don't you see? You can win her for Jesus by demonstrating that Jesus answers prayer. After a childhood of godlessness, she'll become one of *us*. She'll truly belong to *you* and *me*.''

Whoa—she's really pushing his buttons, isn't she, ladies and gentlemen? You've got to hand it to the old bitch. . . .

Silence. An uncertain footfall, the sound of Tucker shuffling around, staring at nothing, thinking. Then:

"You're saying that by bringing Gerard to live with us here, we can win Sarah over, and—''

"And that she'll truly become one with us in Christ.

Isn't that what you want, Tuck? Isn't that what you've been praying for?''

Another long silence.

"Yes, I guess it is." Tucker coughed. "I suppose we all must make sacrifices, huh? I suppose I can learn to endure the presence of a four-legged animal in the house, if it means showing the way, the truth and the light to a little girl."

"Not just any little girl. *Our* little girl."

"Yeah, our little girl."

"Oh, Tuck! . . ."

The Verminator has heard enough, ladies and gentlemen.

Topper quietly stole from the dark bedroom, feeling a deep sense of relief.

VI

DINNER WAS SIMPLE AND DELICIOUS—BROILED SALMON with lemon and dill, steamed broccoli and carrots (lightly buttered), fresh-baked Pillsbury biscuits. They drank a bottle of Oregon pinot noir and ate Tillamook ice cream smothered in blackberries that Nita had picked last summer in the field behind her building.

Conversation was light and airy, the kind people have when they haven't known each other long—*safe* conversation. They talked briefly about their respective childhoods, Pete telling about his parents who were teachers, his spinster sister who was a chemical engineer in Dallas, about growing up in the Chicago suburbs and the vicissitudes of life as a Cubs fan. Nita revealed that she was a small-town girl who'd dreamed of becoming a reporter since the age of twelve, when she'd watched the Watergate crisis unfold on television. She'd envisioned becoming a female Bob Woodward or Carl Bernstein, tracking down Deep Throats, exposing scandals and rooting out corruption from high places.

About their adult lives they remained discreetly vague. Pete said little about his wife's sickness and eventual death, nothing at all about his less-than-stellar history as a high-rung corporate executive. The day might come when he felt comfortable discussing such matters with Nita, but not now. Not so soon.

Neither did he press her for details about her adult history. She gave him a sketchy account of having majored in journalism at the University of Oregon, of having worked for several urban newspapers before deciding to quit the rat race and buy a rural weekly newspaper.

They sat in her living room upstairs from the *Nehalem County Renegade*, Pete in a blue leather recliner and Nita on her mission-style sofa, sipping refills of coffee after dessert. The conversation stalled, but not uncomfortably.

Finally Pete asked the question that had itched inside him since first sitting down to dinner. "So, do you actually *like* it here in Buckthorn?"

Nita thought a moment, then said yes, she liked it here, despite the negatives. Despite having so few real friends. She was doing something in Buckthorn that needed doing, she felt. She was giving people what they desperately needed, whether they appreciated it or not— a dissident view of their community. If not for the *Renegade*, the folks of Nehalem County would never hear or read anything other than the industry line.

"I won't win any friends around here, doing what I do," she went on, "but I might succeed in making just one person think. And that one person may actually make a difference someday. That's my hope. It's what keeps me going."

"Good for you," Pete said, thinking how much like

Sally she sounded. Committed. Altruistic. "I admire your guts."

"Guts or stupidity—sometimes they're interchangeable, aren't they? I guess I feel something for these people, even though they don't feel much for me. I'm basically a small-town girl, like I said, and the people of Buckthorn are very much like the folks I grew up with. They're chained to this place, because they think it's all they have—the mill, their crummy little jobs, their dead-end lives."

"Doesn't it get to you, all the dilapidation, the ghost-town atmosphere? I'd think it would be depressing as hell. Not to mention the serial killer—how do you live with *that*?"

Nita stared at him a moment, her face an unsettling blank. During this short moment Pete realized that the vivid bluish green of her eyes was artificial, the effect of tinted contact lenses. And he perceived that her blond hair didn't quite jibe with the olive undertones of her cheeks. Still, whether a bleached blond or not, Nita was beautiful in her own self-contradictory way. Pete felt a longing that until tonight he thought had burned out months ago.

She rose from the sofa and went to the television set, took a videocassette from a holder and pushed it into the VCR. "Remember the news special I told you about when I saw you at the mill on Friday?" she asked. "Well, here it is. It may answer some of your questions, or it may not. I hope it helps."

She returned to the sofa and pressed a button on the remote control. The TV screen lit up with a commercial for a car dealership in Portland, featuring the owner, a Harvey Milquetoast type who concluded with, "*If you don't come see me today, I can't save you any money.*"

Next came the lead-in for KATU-TV news, with aerial footage of Portland's skyline and bridges, followed by a graphic that said, "*Special Report.*" Black and white photographs materialized in a moving collage, with blood-red dates superimposed and flowing the opposite direction across the screen. The faces of young men stared out from the photos, some from high-school yearbooks, others from snapshots taken on fishing trips or at parties.

October 30, 1976 . . .
October 31, 1979 . . .
October 26, 1981 . . .

"They were all young working men who lived in or around the sleepy little town of Buckthorn, Oregon," intoned a deep baritone with appropriate reverence. *"Each of their eight deaths occurred in the month of October, beginning eighteen years ago, in nineteen seventy-six . . ."*

Each face passed through the screen with a sibilant rushing sound. In the background was the metronomic lub-dubbing of a human heart over suspense music.

"They died violently, horribly, at the hands of a man whose face is a question mark, a man whose grisly leavings have terrified this town and the entire Pacific Northwest. The world has come to know him as the Buckthorn Killer."

The next shot showed a tanned, athletic man in open sport coat, walking toward the camera on Main Street. He introduced himself as Brink Erdmann, then talked about how Buckthorn had suffered over the years. Cutbacks at the local sawmill had eliminated nearly two-thirds of the town's jobs. Businesses had gone belly-up, and most of the people had moved away. Those few hundred who remained lived with the constant knowledge that somewhere, probably very near, lurked a monster who had killed young workers at the Buckthorn mill every two or three years since 1976.

The scene switched to Royal Chinook Park on the

outskirts of Buckthorn, where the latest victim, Rich
Nockleby, had met his end only last October. Erdmann
introduced a tall, intense-looking man in a corduroy
sport coat, Lieutenant Daniel Kantor of the Oregon State
Police, supervisor of the Buckthorn Task Force.

"Wait a minute," Pete said to Nita. "Isn't that the
guy you said I should talk to about Topper?"

Nita confirmed that Kantor was the man.

Erdmann and Kantor were walking through the park,
talking about various "psychosexual killers" like John
Wayne Gacy, Jeffrey Dahmer and some Russian whose
name Pete didn't catch. Kantor pointed out the Buckthorn killer's career had lasted far longer than most other
serial killers', that the Buckthorn killer waited longer
between killings. Then Kantor and Erdmann covered the
gruesome details of Rich Nockleby's murder, the amputation and theft of the victim's penis, his fingers, his
eyes. The burning alive.

Next up, to Pete's surprise, was none other than Nita
Vale, editor of the local weekly newspaper, talking with
Erdmann in her newsroom on the first floor of this very
building. She looked almost as good on TV as she did
in the flesh.

She spoke on camera about how the townspeople had
suffered over the years. She spoke about how people
hated themselves for feeling relief each time the killer
struck, because a new killing meant that their own surviving young men would be safe for another two years,
maybe three. She talked about the widespread feeling
that the killings were punishment for a wrong that someone in Buckthorn must have committed. The camera
pulled in for a tight shot of her face, revealing glim-
mering tears in her eyes.

She looks terrified, Pete thought.

With Nita as a guide, Erdmann led his viewers on a
tour of the murder scenes in and around Buckthorn,

which included a vacant lot, a hayfield, an abandoned barn, a clear-cut south of town. Nita provided short but interesting background on each victim, which allowed Erdmann to segue into on-camera interviews with the surviving mother or father or sister or neighbor. Pictures of the victims flashed on the screen, episodes from their lives, underscoring that these had been real people, not abstractions or statistics. These had been brothers and sons and boyfriends and co-workers.

Occasionally the scene shifted to an urban office, where a bearded forensic expert supplied his expert views on why and how the killer had done what he'd done. The expert talked about ''antisocial personality disorder'' and opined that the killer's gruesome fantasies were far more important to him than any consideration of the anguish he'd inflicted on the victims' families and friends.

Eventually Erdmann ended up back in Royal Chinook Park with Lieutenant Dan Kantor, who discussed the cops' efforts to catch the fiend, none of which had yet succeeded. The killer was clearly an intelligent man, not to mention a very careful one.

''Would a serial killer be capable of living a life that appears outwardly normal?'' Erdmann asked. Kantor, looking pained, answered yes, he believed so, though he reminded the viewers that he was no psychiatrist or psychologist. The unavoidable conclusion, in Kantor's estimation, was that the killer could be anyone.

And suddenly, almost before Pete knew it, the program was over. Erdmann concluded by needlessly reiterating that a forlorn corner of rural Oregon had been under siege for eighteen hellish years, and no one seemed able to do anything about it.

Wasn't *that* just swell? Pete thought. A real-life horror movie was playing out right here in Buckthorn, the town to which Pete had just moved his children. He glanced at Nita, who was studying the remote control in her hands. When she finally glanced up, he saw that a tear glistened in the corner of her left eye.

"I want to show you something," she said, getting to her feet. He followed her out of the living room and down the stairs to the newsroom of the *Renegade*. He noticed that she limped slightly, as she had three days ago when she visited him at the mill. She led him through a hallway to a rear room that she opened with a key. She turned on a light and ushered him through a heavy door.

He found himself in a large room with concrete-block walls painted light blue. Three long tables stood in the center of the room, each crowded with cardboard filing boxes. Cork bulletin boards occupied most of the wall space, each board holding scores of photographs, charts and maps. In a far corner of the room stood a small writing table with a lamp on it, a nook for reading and writing.

Pete moved along the walls and studied the photographs, which showed the Buckthorn killer's victims, their relatives, the investigators assigned to their cases, the crime scenes and various stages of the crime scene processing. Pinned beneath each photo was an explanation card. The maps and charts depicted likely routes that the killer and the victims had used in each of the murders. Nita explained that the boxes on the tables held notes, as well as copies of articles and texts on criminal investigations, monographs written by forensic psychiatrists and psychologists. One box contained a theoretical chronology of each of the eight Buckthorn homicides.

Pete stood a moment in the center of the array, his eyes wandering over the tables and walls, his head buzzing. Despite its utilitarian bareness, the room had the atmosphere of a mortuary, a place reserved for remembrance of the dead.

"Good Lord," he whispered.

Nita told him that this was her "Death Room," her repository of virtually everything known about the Buckthorn killings outside the investigative records of the Task Force and the FBI. She'd meant to write a book someday about the Buckthorn killings, maybe get rich like Ann Rule. This had been her working library. But she'd recently dumped the plan.

She admitted that putting the information into electronic files would probably have made more sense than keeping hard copies, but she'd found that she was better able to *feel* the realities of the killings by assembling the material in a single room. Here she could physically survey the facts and the photographic images. Here she felt close to the victims and their families, tasted their fear, their frustration and loss. She also felt close to the killer for reasons she couldn't quite explain, not even to herself.

"Vonda thinks I've created something strange in this room, something extranormal," Nita said, hugging herself as if she was cold. "She calls it the locus of all the negative energies associated with the killings. Isn't that just what you'd expect from her? I suppose she could be right, but I prefer to believe it's something psychological, something inside my own head. The power of suggestion can make the unreal seem real, and I'm as suggestible as they come."

"Me too," Pete said, pocketing his chilly hands. "Tell me why you abandoned your book idea."

"I've lost faith in my ability to write the story and do it justice. I'm personally caught up in the thing now, as you can plainly see from my goose bumps."

"And that's bad? I've always thought the best writing was deeply personal."

"You forget that I'm a trained journalist. We trained journalists aren't supposed to get involved in the things we write about. We're supposed to be objective, dispassionate. That's the first thing they teach you in J-school."

"Well, you're not in J-school now. You don't have to worry about letting your feelings show."

"Don't I?"

"No. You don't. Not—not in your writing, I mean. Or anywhere else, I guess."

She took a tentative step toward him, and he felt his throat go dry.

"Then neither do you. Whatever you're feeling, you're entitled to let it show."

And just like that she was in his arms, her cheek pressed against his chest. He felt her soft hair on his face, smelled her shampoo. He pulled her in tight and felt the swells of her breasts against his ribs. She clung to him as if he was a life preserver.

She turned her face upward, and he kissed her. She parted her lips, and he tasted the wine she'd drunk at dinner. He wondered how things had come to this, when just hours earlier he'd so desperately missed his dead wife that he doubted whether he would ever feel really alive again. He felt alive *now*, no question of that, his hands urgently running over Nita's shoulders, down her back.

She unbuttoned her jeans, and his hands went in. They pulled at each other's clothing, stroking and groping, until they were naked—naked in the Death Room with the faces of the dead staring down from cork bulletin boards. Pete kissed her small breasts, flicking the nipples with his tongue, then moved downward over the flat expanse of her abdomen. He kissed her navel, kissed the sharp ridges of her hipbones. He nuzzled the mound of her pubic hair, which was black as night, but she urged him upward again, covering his mouth with hers and pushing her breasts into him.

She twisted in his arms, wanting him from behind. She braced her palms against the edge of a table and thrust her buttocks into him, but he held back—this had been one of Sally's favorite ways. For a blind moment he wondered what cosmic force had decreed that he should meet a woman who wore her hair like Sally's, who carried herself in Sally's square-shouldered way, who wanted sex in Sally's favorite position. But the moment passed as he slipped into her, found her tight and warm and wet. They pumped at each other furiously, his hands gripping her hipbones, their skin slapping together, the legs of the table thumping the tiled floor as they mindlessly pushed it toward the wall.

Pete's orgasm exploded. A box of files slipped off the table and landed on the floor with a crash, but neither cared. They leaned over the table for a long while, locked together. They slowly disentangled and started glancing around for their clothing, then noticed where the table was—tight against the wall—and the now-empty file box on the floor, manila folders and the contents splayed over the tiles.

That's when they started laughing.

VII

AFTER ONE LAST, LONG KISS, PETE LEFT THROUGH THE rear door of Nita's building, in order to avoid walking past the Head Rig Bar, which stood directly across the street. The place would still be full of mill workers, Nita had warned, and how would it look?—Tucker Bannon's son-in-law, the number-two guy at Buckthorn Wood Products, seen leaving the *Renegade* building at 10:05 in the evening?

Pete felt better than he'd felt in months, maybe years. "I'll call you tomorrow," he said. "We can drive into Portland, have some dinner, catch a movie or something."

Nita kissed her index finger and pressed it to his lips. "Let's take it slow, Pete, kind of feel our way along with this. We both have a lot to lose if we don't do it right. But yes, call. I'd love to hear from you, even if we don't go to dinner."

He walked north along what had been an alley before some developer tore down most of the buildings on this side of Front Street. Turned east on Bannon Avenue and walked toward Main Street. Mulled what had happened tonight with Nita.

He supposed that they'd simply done what adult males and females do when conditions are right. Sometimes it's love, but more often it's not. Sometimes it's the beginning of something wonderful, but most often it's only a few stolen moments.

He felt no guilt over having been unfaithful to Sally, perhaps because he sensed so much of Sally in Nita. It was more than the color of her hair and eyes, more than the squared posture. It was something fundamental, an attitude, a way of talking—almost as if Sally was actually part of her.

You'll always be my girl, my wife . . .

He kept to the sidewalk on the north side of the street, because here was where the few streetlights were. No shortage of bare, useless utility poles in Buckthorn.

He walked past Buckthorn City Hall, which stood on the corner of Main and Bannon, a white clapboard building that badly needed paint. East of the Mount of Olives Gospel Church, Bannon Avenue was a tunnel of blackness. No need for streetlights here, since all the houses but one stood vacant. Old elms and oaks grew along both sides of the street, their limbs arching overhead in a basketwork of branches and twigs. Pete wished he'd accepted Nita's offer to drive him home or that he'd asked her for a flashlight.

Then it happened. He stepped off a curb into a pot-hole, tripped and pitched forward. Pain exploded in his hands and his left knee as he landed on the grainy asphalt. He drew himself up to a kneeling position, remained still a moment and inventoried himself for serious injury. No broken bones, fortunately. His ankle was sore, but he doubted that he'd sprained it. He got slowly to his feet and tried to ignore the fire that burned on the heels of his hands.

He chided himself, told himself to slow down. What was he afraid of, for Christ's sake? The Buckthorn killer?

He heard something behind him, a small sound that stood out from the soft hiss of foliage in the breeze. The scrape of a shoe over crumbling cement, he thought. The dance of a pebble accidentally kicked by someone walking in the dark.

Someone following.

Pete's stomach tried to climb into his throat. He stood stone still and stared back toward the lights of the Mount of Olives Gospel Church. But his follower had also halted to listen.

He heard another noise, off to his right this time, the thump of feet moving hastily through weeds. His follower had apparently decided to flank him by moving through the yard of an abandoned house, meaning to jump him as he passed by. Pete was about to whirl and run blindly toward Bannon House when a car turned off Main Street and moved toward him, its headlights washing over him. The car cruised slowly past the Mount of Olives Gospel Church and continued across Second Street before drawing even with him and halting. It was a new-looking Pontiac Trans Am. The driver's window lowered with a buzz.

"You're Mr. Cochran, aren't you?" the driver asked. "Peter Cochran of Buckthorn Wood Products?"

Pete could just make out the man's face in the amber light of the instrument panel. A fine-featured face, almost delicate.

"I'm afraid you have me at a disadvantage."

"Yeah, I guess I do at that. Sorry. My name is Todd Verduin. I do consulting work for your father-in-law—background checks on employees, security matters, things like that." Verduin offered a slender hand through the open car window, and Pete shook it.

"Yes, I'm Pete Cochran. I don't think I've heard Tucker mention you."

"That doesn't surprise me. But hey, I'm on my way to meet with him now. Would you like a ride up to the house?"

"You're meeting with Tucker at—" Pete looked at his watch. "—a quarter after ten?"

"I know it seems late, but when Tuck decides he wants to take a meeting, I give him a meeting. He's not the kind of man I say no to."

"I appreciate the offer," Pete said. He crossed in front of the car, walking through the beams of the headlights, and he heard Verduin disengage the door locks. As he pulled the passenger's door open, he glanced back toward the Mount of Olives Gospel Church and saw movement, a red smear in the glare of the taillights—a man running across the street. Pete got quickly into the car, pulled the door closed and fastened his safety belt.

Verduin shifted into drive but immediately stepped on the brake, causing the car's nose to dive and bounce. "Looks like we've got company," he said, staring ahead through the windshield. "I guess we'll have to go around him."

A chill shot down Pete's spine as his eyes focused on the street ahead. A huge yellow cat sat directly in the middle of Bannon Avenue, its green eyes burning like hot coals in the glare of the headlights.

VIII

ESMERELDA SANDOVAL ESCORTED VERDUIN TO THE "quiet room" on the third floor of the mansion, where Tucker Bannon welcomed him and served coffee. Verduin mentioned that he'd encountered Tucker's son-in-law just minutes ago on the street and had given him a lift, but the news generated no reaction on the old man's face.

"I made a delivery to the Conifer Group late this afternoon," the private detective went on, getting down to business. "I imagine that it created quite a stir."

"I assume you're talking about the tape recording," Tucker said, smiling.

"I am. I made a copy for each partner and personally placed it in his hands, making a point to mention that it was a little gift from you. I wish I could've been there when they played them, seen their faces. They've probably been rolling up the carpets and tearing apart their telephones, looking for the bugs."

"Or talking to their lawyers. What about Wade—shouldn't he get a copy of his very own?"

"No need. I don't doubt that he'll receive an urgent phone call from one of the partners at the start of business tomorrow. You'll be able to overhear it, of course, assuming they reach him at his office." Verduin nodded toward Tucker's bank of audio monitoring equipment. "It should be very entertaining."

"You've done yeoman work, as usual," Tucker said, standing. He went to a cabinet and withdrew a small leather satchel. "This isn't your customary bonus—it's the down payment on your other project, the one we spoke of last week." He handed over the satchel.

Verduin placed it on his knees and zippered it open, his agate-hard eyes gleaming as he pawed through the contents—packets of hundred-dollar bills, a hundred to a packet. Twenty-five packets. A quarter of a million dollars.

"It's all there," Tucker assured him, settling into his armchair. "I'll hand you another bag just like that one when the project is complete."

"And that will be very soon," Verduin replied, grinning. "I can move on it as early as tomorrow night. Wade will make it easy, I'm sure—he'll be drinking his brains out. He'll probably slip off to his little hideaway on Barbur Boulevard in Portland, like he always does when he's stressed."

"I'm sure you're right. Handle it any way you see fit. I have a small request, though."

"And what might that be?"

"I know it would be difficult if not impossible to arrange for my son-in-law to get credit for this project . . ."

"You mean frame him for the murder of Wade Beswick?"

Tucker coughed into a fist. "I'm saying that I understand the difficulties that such a notion presents. Nonetheless, I'd like for him to receive some attention from the authorities concerning this matter."

"You'd like for him to be a suspect, right?"

"At least initially, yes. It would serve my purpose for him to be detained and questioned, told not to leave town—you know what I mean. Can you arrange this?"

"I'll do my best. No guarantees, of course."

"Of course. Your best will be good enough. As always."

They stood and shook hands again.

"I'd better head home and get some sleep," Verduin said. "I have an early day tomorrow."

And so do I, thought Tucker as he escorted this hateful man to the front door.

15

I

ON THE FINAL MORNING OF HIS LIFE, WADE BESWICK arrived at the head shed fifteen minutes late, moving more slowly than usual. His midsection was black and blue, thanks to the pounding that Pete Cochran gave him yesterday. Even breathing was painful.

"Morning, precious," he said to Denise Ubaldo, walking stiffly past her desk. "Looks like you're busier than a one-armed wallpaper hanger."

"Megan won't be in today," Denise replied, not looking away from her computer screen. "She's at OHSU with Scotty, waiting for the doctors to tell her whether they can operate yet. I'm covering for her."

"That's good. God knows you're a big enough lady to handle two jobs." He disappeared into his office. His intercom buzzed almost immediately. "Paul Garson of the Conifer Group on line three for you, Wade," Denise said.

"Thanks, precious." Beswick punched a button as he sat down carefully behind his desk, taking care not to twist his midsection. "Yeah, Paul. What can I do for you?"

"Wade, listen—we've got trouble. Something ugly has materialized with respect to our—uh—deal. I'm afraid . . ."

"What do you mean *trouble*? There can't be any *trouble*. This thing is wrapped up tighter than a Chinese whore."

"Wade, we got a visit late yesterday from someone named Todd Verduin—"

Garson mispronounced the name and Beswick interrupted to correct him. Yes, Beswick knew who the man was. Small-time private investigator, nobody important.

"Well, he's important now," Garson said with a shaky voice. "He has a tape of a meeting between you, me and the other partners, a meeting that took place back in February. He gave each of us a copy. Compliments of Tucker Bannon, he said."

"A *tape*—you mean a recording? How the fuck did he get it?"

"Wade, he bugged the place, okay? We've got a security outfit in here now, and they're finding microphones and transmitters in all our personal offices and conference rooms—little things in the electrical sockets. What's important is that Verduin gave the tape to Tucker Bannon, and it spells everything out in great detail— everything we planned."

Beswick felt tightness in his chest. "You mean . . . we're dead in the water? Is that what you're saying?"

"I mean that we don't dare foreclose on the loan now. In fact, we don't even dare try collecting repayment of the principal. Don't you see—sending Verduin over here with the tapes was Tucker's cute way of telling us that he's got us by the short hairs. If we start foreclosure proceedings, he'll send the tapes to the police, and bingo—we're all up on fraud and conspiracy charges. That's you, me, the other partners—*everybody*, Wade."

Beswick felt the room start to twirl around him. His eyes burned. "Paul, this better not be some kind of trick. If you're trying to weasel out of paying me what I . . ."

"Listen, you silly son of a bitch—I'll play the tape for you. You be the judge."

Wade Beswick listened to fifteen minutes of conversation among the Conifer Group partners and himself, in which they virtually confessed to setting up Tucker Bannon in order to steal valuable timberlands from him. Beswick heard himself laugh and brag about how he'd secured Tucker's initials on memos that instructed him to disregard the provisions of the loan agreement. He heard himself fantasize about what he would do with his share of the take—buy a condo in Maui, take a year-long vacation in France, send his kids off to some expensive school.

Having heard all this, Wade Beswick dropped the phone onto his desk and staggered into the toilet, where he ejected his breakfast.

II

PETER COCHRAN SPENT THE MORNING HUDDLED WITH Wally MacKenzie in preparation for a meeting with the company's tax accountants later in the week. At 10:15 the intercom buzzed. "Todd Verduin is here to see you, Pete," Denise Ubaldo announced. "He says it'll only take a minute."

"I'll be right with him."

"I'll leave you two alone," Wally said. "I need a break anyway."

"Wait a minute. Do you know this guy Verduin?"

"Not personally. I've seen him around from time to time. Way I hear it, he's a private detective from Portland, does work for Tuck. Background checks on job applicants, security consulting, I don't know what else. A little spooky."

"Mmm. I wonder what he wants with me."

"Only one way to find out." Wally got up from his chair and headed for the door. "Buzz me when you want me back."

Pete went out to the reception area, shook hands with

Verduin and led him to his office. Here in the light of morning, Pete got a better look at the man than he'd gotten last night. Verduin was fashionably short-haired and slim, almost wispy. He wore a tiny silver earring in one ear, and he dressed as if he worked in show business, not private investigations.

"Thanks again for giving me a lift last night," Pete said, sitting down behind his desk. "I'd gone out for a walk, and before I knew it, the sun was down."

"Glad I could help—no trouble at all." Verduin laced his long fingers over one knee. "I admire anyone with nerve enough to traipse around Buckthorn at night—all alone yet."

"Oh? Why's that?"

"All this Buckthorn killer business. Whenever I'm in town, I feel like I'm being watched."

Pete got the disquieting notion that he'd met this guy in another life. "I don't worry much about the Buckthorn killer," he lied. "I'm not his type. Too old and stringy." He forced a laugh, as did his visitor. "So, what can I do for you, Mr. Verduin?"

"Call me Todd. Your father-in-law does, as do all my friends."

Pete nodded, waited for him to go on.

"I just wanted to stop by and tell you that I'm available anytime you need my services—anytime at all. I do private investigations, which you may already know. My specialty is electronic surveillance, both video and audio, but I'm available for other kinds of work as well."

Pete tapped his Mont Blanc pen on his blotter and said, "I see." He paused, studying Verduin's youthful, almost beardless face. How old was this guy? Late twenties, early thirties? "Just out of curiosity, Todd, what makes you think I would ever need a private investigator?"

"Your father-in-law has used my services for more than a decade. It seemed natural to me that you'd want to continue what has been a mutually beneficial association."

"Have you discussed continuing this association with Wade Beswick? He's the company manager—not me."

Verduin winked. "After the show Mr. Beswick put on yesterday, I'm less than confident about his long-term prospects. I feel much more confident discussing the future with you."

"You do?" Pete wondered what the hell was happening here. Had Tucker sent this guy to intimate that Wade was about to be fired? He tossed his Mont Blanc onto the desktop and planted his hands to push himself out of his chair, signaling that the meeting was over. "It was nice of you to come by, and if I ever need a private detective, you're the one I'll call."

Verduin rose with him. "Excellent. I won't take any more of your time." His eyes went to the Seurat print on the wall, *Bathers*. He walked over to it, squinted at it. "This is an exquisite picture. Where did you get it, may I ask?"

Pete told him—a little gallery near the Metropolitan Museum of Modern Art in New York, one that specialized in French Impressionist prints among other things.

"I can't quite make out the print number. That *is* a print number, isn't it?"

Pete took a deep breath. He went to the wall and looked hard at the lower right margin of the picture, focusing on a lightly penciled scribble. "I'm not sure it's a print number," he said. "I can't read it either. But if you're interested in buying one, I can look up the name of the gallery and—"

"Oh, that's not necessary," Verduin said from behind him. "I was just admiring it—I've always really dug Seurat, you know?" He shook Pete's hand, handed him a business card, and walked to the door. "Thanks again for your time, and don't worry about seeing me out."

After he'd gone, Pete stared a long moment at the business card and chewed on the question of where the hell he'd met Todd Verduin before.

III

ON THE FINAL EVENING OF HIS LIFE, TERRY GRIMES drank only one can of Miller Lite at the Head Rig Bar before announcing that he was heading home. His fellow mill workers razzed him, called him a pussy.

Whatsa matter, Grimes—can't hold your liquor anymore?

He tried to explain that he needed to save money and put his time to better use. He'd read about a scholarship program at Portland Community College, and he thought he might qualify. Thought he might study drafting or computer science. But first he needed to get a handle on his life, kick some bad habits. He needed to save enough to pay the tuition.

Don't give us that shit, Grimes. You've got a little honey waitin' for you somewhere, don't you? Come on, boy, don't hold out on us—who is she? Is she fat like your last one . . . ?

He left the bar without trying to explain further. No way could he have made his pals understand how sick he was of working in the Buckthorn mill for next to nothing. They would only have reminded him that he wasn't anybody special. Working in a mill had been good enough for his old man, hadn't it? Who the hell did little old pimply-faced Terry Grimes think he was— the son of a banker or a lawyer or some highfalutin politician? Did he really think that he *deserved* anything better than working in a sawmill?

He started the engine of his Dodge Dakota and cringed when he saw the fuel gauge. Three more days till payday, and the truck was already running on fumes. His bank account was as empty as his fuel tank, and Chevron had long ago jerked his credit card.

Hoping that by some miracle the fumes would get him home, he turned west on Columbia Avenue and went to Main Street, then turned right and headed south out of town. In the east a pumpkin moon rose against a sky full of stars.

Soon the engine coughed and died, as he'd known that it would. The power steering shut off, and Terry had to pull hard on the wheel to get the pickup safely onto the shoulder of the highway. He stomped the brake and halted, then snapped off the lights.

"No way this is happening," he muttered.

But it *was* happening. This was the kind of thing that happened to people like Terry Grimes. Educated people had good jobs, and they could afford to put gas in their tanks. They never endured the humiliation of hitchhiking home. Educated people led decent lives.

Ahead, the pumpkin moon was fading to platinum, and the silhouettes of tall Douglas firs loomed black against its face. Terry stepped out onto the asphalt, looked up the highway and down, but saw no sign of life. The only sounds were the snaps of the engine as it cooled and the croaks of tree frogs in the surrounding woods.

He figured that he was exactly halfway between the towns of Mist and Pittsburg, which meant that he faced at least a five-mile walk to a telephone, no matter which direction he chose. So, which way would it be? he asked himself—east or west?

He chose east, remembering that the cafe in Pittsburg had a pay phone that he could use to call his old man in Scappoose. Before he'd gone half a mile, headlights broke over a hill behind him, and he heard the roar of a big engine working through its gears. He stepped onto the shoulder and stuck his thumb out, hoping that the driver lived around here and that he would recognize him. The car thundered past, and his heart sank. But then the car slowed and geared down, its brake lights blinking until it came to a stop. The back-up light came on, and the car moved toward him in reverse.

It was an early-fifties Mercury coupe, a hot rod that appeared unfinished, painted primer gray and flecked with rust. The driver stepped out and waved at him over the roof. Terry recognized the rugged, heavy-browed face of a co-worker, Jerry Dragstead.

"Terry Grimes, I *thought* that was you," Dragstead said in his slow way. "Thought I saw your outfit 'bout half a mile back, sittin' by the road. What the hell did you do—run out of gas?"

Terry smiled sheepishly, confessed. Flat broke until payday, too. No telling how long that Dodge Dakota might sit at the side of the road. By the way, Jerry wasn't headed toward Pittsburg, was he?

"Don't see how I can avoid it," Dragstead replied, "since it's the next wide spot in this road. I can take you into Scappoose, if you want, 'cause that's where I'm goin' tonight. Gonna see a movie and get me one of them big drums of buttered popcorn they sell at the theater over there. Scappoose is where you live, ain't it?"

It was. Terry thanked him, called him a lifesaver.

"Better get your ass in the car, then," Dragstead said.

Terry slid into the passenger's seat, which was in bad need of repair. A stained blanket served as a seat cover. The interior of the car stank of cigarettes and mildew.

He got the fright of his life when something alive brushed along his calf and leaped onto his lap—a huge yellow cat with iridescent green eyes. Terry felt the pinpricks of its claws through his jeans.

"Don't pay any attention to old Shagnasty," Dragstead said, getting in behind the wheel. "He likes people." He gunned the engine and popped the clutch,
leaving a smear of rubber on the highway. As G-forces
pressed the heavy cat into Terry's chest, he heard Dragstead's laughter above the roar of the big V-8. "Yeah,
old Shagnasty likes people, all right—he thinks they're
delicious!"

IV

ON THE FINAL EVENING OF HIS LIFE, WADE BESWICK DE-
cided that serious drinking was in order. He left the head
shed and drove into southwest Portland. His destination
was Champ's, a dingy watering hole on Barbur Boulevard.

He sat in a booth opposite a big-screen TV, staring mo-
rosely at an infomercial for an appliance that looked like
a cross between a Dutch oven and a blender. The bar
crowd wasn't large, but it was noisy—mainly salesman-
types unwinding after a grueling day of selling refrigerators, Toyotas or laser printers on the endless commercial strip that straddled Barbur Boulevard. Wade felt
at home here in his cheap clothes, hunched alone in the
shadows, secure in the knowledge that no one knew him
or expected anything of him. Here he was just another
moribund drunk.

He watched a faggot-looking guy put the blender-
oven through its paces, but he heard neither the sales
pitch nor the rowdy bar noise around him. His mind was
elsewhere. Visions of unemployment danced in his head,
along with worries about criminal charges and lawyers'
fees and prison.

Would it really come down to that? he wondered—
serving hard time in Oregon State Prison? Could he re-

alistically hope that Tucker Bannon would decide that
firing was punishment enough for Wade, and decline to
press charges maybe for old time's sake if not through
Christian compassion?

Oh, yes—this was likely. *And I'll shit a turkey sand-
wich*, Wade thought.

He'd just taken the first sip of his third Jack Daniels
when he caught sight of a tall platinum blond, dressed
in a form-fitting business suit of gray flannel. She wore
a scarf of pink paisley and earrings with sparkling pink
stones. Sliding onto a barstool, she lit a cigarette and
surveyed the crowd through mirrored aviation sunglasses, showing no outward interest in anything or anyone around her. She ordered a drink.

This woman doesn't belong here, Wade said to himself. *She's something special.*

She took off the sunglasses, and her eyes met his.
Incredibly, her face brightened, and she didn't look
away. Wade wondered if he was imagining things,
knowing that he and Mel Gibson had little in common
beyond their respective rations of Y chromosomes. Still,
he couldn't discount the unfathomable factor of chemistry, which explained how lunchy little men with bald
spots so often managed to snag world-class chicks.
Chemistry sometimes played wonderful tricks.

The bartender delivered her drink, and the lady sipped
it, never taking her eyes off Wade. Then she slid off the
stool and walked smoothly toward his booth, her leather
shoulder bag bouncing on a slim hip. She set her glass
on the table next to his and asked if she could join him.

V

*Nunca tengas miedo de la luna,
mi niño, porque ella te cantará un arrullo.*

Nunca tengas miedo de las estrellas,
mi niño, porque ellas te enviarán un sueño . . .

Topper heard the words as clearly as if old Esmerelda were singing them into *his* ear, not Carter's—soft words, comforting words, an ancient Mexican lullaby. Countless times his *abuela* had banished his terrors with this sweet song, cradling his troubled head against her bosom after he'd awakened from some hellish dream.

Never be afraid of the moon, my boy,
Because she'll sing you a lullaby.
Never be afraid of the stars, my boy,
Because they'll send you a dream . . .

Topper lay over the ventilation duct in a small third-floor servants' bedroom at the rear of the house, his ear pressed to the grillwork. He'd left the light off, and the room was dark except for a shaft of cold moonlight slanting through the window. Directly below this room, on the second floor, lay Carter's bedroom.

A few minutes earlier he'd come in through the back door of the house and had paused in the mudroom to shed the dirty overshoes he'd worn while poisoning weeds on the edge of the yard. The mudroom was adjacent to the kitchen, where a hushed conversation was taking place.

It was Esmerelda and Pete Cochran, ladies and gentlemen, and they were talking about the little snotbag—old Carter-the-Farter. Remember him? Of course you do. Needless to say, they didn't realize that the Verminator was skulking nearby, scarfing up their every word. Pete was confiding in her, telling her that he was worried because Carter-the-Farter didn't seem like himself.

The kid's been manic, right?—hyper-good mood one minute, then down and depressed a few minutes later. Pete confided that he'd just been in Carter's room and had tried to talk to him, but the kid wouldn't do anything but blubber. Naturally, Pete thinks it has something to do with what happened two days ago, Carter leaving his bike up on the mountain, coming in late, passing up dinner and all that.

So what does my old abuela say? She offers to go up and see Carter-the-Farter herself, says that sometimes it takes an old grandmother to help a little boy get over his troubles. And Pete thanks her, tells her that he trusts her . . .

So Topper had bounded quickly up the rear stairs to the third floor, and had parked himself over the grillwork of the ventilation duct. He'd listened to Esmerelda's gentle questioning of the boy.

What was troubling him? she'd asked. Why did tears so often follow his smiles? Did he miss his old home in New York, his friends, his dog?

Did he miss his mother?—and here old Esmerelda's voice had come close to breaking. Carter had only whimpered softly.

Want to know what his trouble is, ladies and gentlemen? Listen to Dr. Verminator now, and you'll hear the definitive diagnosis. Whenever old Carter-the-Farter blinks his eyes, he sees the basement of the Mad Witch's cabin. He sees the jars full of cocks and eyes and fingers. He sees the Rat Choir doing its number, and he feels like he needs to tell someone about it. But he's scared— scared of the Verminator, naturally, as well he should be. He remembers that this is his and the Verminator's little secret, and that something horrendous will happen to him if he gives it up.

Isn't fear a wonderful thing, ladies and gentlemen? . . .

As he listened to the rest of the lullaby, Topper saw visions of another little boy, bruised and bloodied by a father who believed that God smiled on the beating of children. He relived that little boy's pain and terror as he had so often in the dead of night. In his chest he felt the seed of that little boy's rage, a seed that had germinated and grown like a noxious weed until finally bearing fruit of its own . . .

> *Nunca tengas miedo de la noche,*
> *mi niño, porque la oscuridad es tu amigo.*
> *Recuerda siempre que la Señora está cerca de ti.*
> *La Señora está cerca.*

A weird mix of emotion swirled in his chest. He loved his *abuela* as much as one human being could love another, for she'd never bailed on him, never failed to defend him in the face of his old man's abuse whenever she could. But he also resented the fact that she would sing this old lullaby to someone else.

> *Never be afraid of the night,*
> *my boy, because the darkness is your friend.*
> *Remember that the lady is near.*
> *The Lady is near.*

What really honked him off was the fact that Carter-the-Farter didn't deserve to hear that lullaby. Carter-the-Farter hadn't paid his dues.

The little snotbag has never gotten the sockful-of-sand treatment, ladies and gentlemen, so what the fuck does he have to snivel about? He's never known real terror, has he?—not the kind old Topper grew up with. Okay, so I showed him the Mad Witch's little hidey-hole, and I gave him a performance of the Rat Choir, both of which scared him. I'm sorry, but that just doesn't qual-

*ify—hear what I'm sayin'? His fear wasn't even pure
enough to give the Verminator a hard-on! He didn't
even . . .*

The Verminator's mind went blank a moment and became a deep, silent hole. Slowly the hole filled with
understanding and—*no!* Not just understanding, but *inspiration!* The hole became a boiling caldron of enlight-
enment. He understood now why the latest exhibition of
the Rat Choir hadn't produced the desired results.

*Ladies and gentlemen, I want you to put your hands
together and shout Amen! Get ready for the news, because the Verminator's going to give it to you with both
barrels . . .*

He rolled away from the grillwork, needing to hear
no more of Esmerelda's singing. He lay on his back and
stared into the shaft of cold moonlight, his mind labor-
ing, his heart thumping with excitement.

*When I took old Carter-the-Farter to the Mad Witch's
hidey-hole, I had the distinct feeling that I was about to
move into the next dimension, legs and germs—but
what-ho! . . . it was more than a feeling. It was a certainty! Yes, a fucked-for-sure certainty. I knew that when
I lit up the Rat Choir in front of Carter-the-Farter, the
taste of his fear would be strong enough to launch the
Verminator into a dimension where colors have voices
and shadows give you hand jobs. His fear was the key,
don't you see? . . .*

Just as fear had *always* been the key.

Unlike other red-blooded boys the world over, Topper
Bannon had never gotten his jollies over girls. He'd
never huddled in his room over a pirated issue of *Playboy* or *Hustler* and pounded his pud.

What gave Topper his jollies was the taste and feel
and smell of *fear*—sweet, gaseous fear induced by some
personally engineered outrage like the burning of live
rats. Fear radiating from someone like heat from a pot-

bellied stove, rising into the air and coalescing around
him like a sulfurous cloud. Wrapping around his cock
like an unseen hand. Whether it came from a boy or girl
mattered not a whit to him—all fear was fuckable, all
of it lovable and delicious. Fear had been his lover.

Until he reached the next dimension, that is.

*What I didn't understand, ladies and gentlemen, is
that I really DID reach the next dimension two days ago
in the Mad Witch's little hidey-hole. I really DID blast
on through to the other side, but I just didn't know it at
the time. Do you have any idea what in the fiddle-fuck
this means? . . .*

He took a deep breath and held it until his heartbeat
thundered in his temples and hammer strokes of light
thumped on his clenched eyelids.

*Put your thinking caps on, legs and genitals—all of
you. Now close your beady little eyes and think! Because
the Verminator has punched through to the next dimension, he's no longer horny for fear, right? But that
doesn't mean that he's no longer horny! God, no! Would
you look at this hard-on? I'm talkin' nine-inch spike
here! In this new dimension, fear doesn't get it for the
Verminator anymore. What gets it for the Verminator—
are you ready for this, legs and gens?—is—*

Ooooooooh, Topper wasn't sure if he should even
think this. But then, what the fuck did it matter? He sure
as hell wouldn't share his newfound inspiration with
anyone, least of all that beanie-weenie shrink whom the
school district forced him to see twice a week. The guy
was himself a Loony Tune, a believer in "positive
thoughts and desires."

*What gets it for the Verminator, ladies and gentlemen,
is . . .*

Go ahead and think it. Go ahead and say it.

. . . death.

Or should he say *life*?

Topper supposed it depended on how you looked at it.

VI

UP CLOSE, SHE WASN'T AS PRETTY AS SHE'D BEEN FROM a distance. A bit overpainted for Wade Beswick's taste— too much rouge on the cheeks, too much mascara. Plus, Wade wasn't keen on cinnamon-colored lipstick.

She'd said that her name was Stella.

"Know what?" Stella asked, resting her chin on the heel of her hand. "I'm tired of this place, aren't you? I'd love to see your sawmill."

"Are you serious? Tonight?"

"Of course. I've always wanted to see a sawmill, but I've never had anybody to show me one. Besides, it'd be nice to get out of here, don't you think—take a ride in the country, let the wind blow through our hair?"

Her voice was husky, a little rough. A smoker's voice. As a rule, women who smoked turned Wade off, but not this one. He couldn't remember when he'd wanted a woman as badly as he wanted Stella.

"I guess it could be arranged. I gotta tell you, though, I'm a skosh drunk. My driving is apt to be spotty."

"Well, *I'm* not drunk. And I'd be happy to drive as long as you do the navigating."

Wade thought a moment, his fingers playing with the fragment of a pretzel. He'd polished off four bowls of pretzels while telling Stella all about himself, his frustrations, his misplaced hopes. He'd also pounded down five Jack Daniels ditches. Without mentioning his recent dabbling in conspiracy and fraud, he'd confessed that his life and career had been a colossal waste, that he felt as if he were standing on the edge of a cliff with a strong wind at his back. He'd admitted that his marriage was a failure, that he'd tried to paw every woman who'd ever worked in his office. He'd told all this to a perfect stranger.

And Stella had been a good listener, the best he'd ever found.

"I gotta ask you sum'n." He struggled to keep her face in focus. "Why are you interested in a fat old troll like *me*?"

She reached across the table and took his hands in hers. "Sweetheart, let's not ask each other pointless questions. Let's just accept each other for what we are, give ourselves a night of warmth and go on from there. Is that too much to ask?"

It wasn't.

And Wade thought, *There it is—chemistry.*

They took his Explorer, Stella at the wheel, all the windows open. Wade noticed that she'd put on a pair of pink gloves to keep her hands warm. He let his head loll out the window, hoping the cold slipstream would sober him up. He meant to enjoy every minute of this night to the utmost, because God only knew when he'd see another night like it. Chances were that he'd find himself rotting in a cell before the year was out.

Stella drove as if she knew exactly where she was going, north on Highway 217 to the Sunset Highway, then west toward the ocean beaches. Wade pointed out the turnoff to Highway 47, but he got the feeling that Stella would have known where to turn whether he told her or not.

The highway was dark and lonely, the forest a black gulf beyond the shoulders of the road. Only rarely did they meet another pair of headlights. They listened to a Willie Nelson CD and sang along with Willie as the towns slipped by, most of them mere sprinklings of light.

They turned north onto Highway 49, having just
passed through the town of Mist. Buckthorn was only
minutes away now. Stella signaled right, slowed. Before
Wade could ask what the hell she was doing, she swung
the Explorer into an opening in the forest, an old logging
road.

"Precious, this road doesn't go anywhere," he said,
clutching the armrest. "And you better slow down, or
we're apt to tear a wheel off." He giggled nervously.

The Explorer bucked over potholes and ruts, its headlights jouncing through the trees and casting giant claws
of shadow. Stella hit the brake pedal hard. The sudden
lurch against the safety belt ignited fire pits of pain in
Wade's abdomen, where Pete Cochran's fists had landed
yesterday. He groaned and leaned back in his seat,
breathing carefully, praying for the pain to fade.

Someone jerked the passenger door open and clubbed
him above the left eye with what looked like a semi-
automatic pistol, causing an explosion of new pain.
Blood flowed in a warm sheet over his eye and down
his cheek. Rough hands unbuckled his safety belt and
hauled him out.

The door of the Explorer slammed shut, and the interior light went out. The night was opaque, like a damp
blanket thrown over his head. Someone pushed him forward, the man with the gun, presumably. Wade swung
around, trying to see who it was.

"S-Stella, where are you?" His own voice frightened
him, because it seemed weak and too high-pitched.
"Stella, are you okay?" He immediately knew how pa-
thetic and self-deluding this sounded, for clearly Stella
had engineered tonight's drama. She'd only pretended
to want him. Clearly she'd actually wanted something
else.

But *what*? What could a woman like Stella possibly

want from Wade Beswick, a man who had absolutely
nothing worth taking?

The rough hands prodded him forward, the muzzle of
the gun digging into the soft meat of his back and shoulders. A flashlight came on, and he saw Stella a few steps
ahead of him, stepping cautiously over the ruts in the
old logging road. She'd traded her pink stiletto heels for
a pair of white Nikes. Her hair glared like brushed aluminum in the cone of the flashlight.

She halted next to a Jeep Grand Cherokee that was
exactly like the one Tucker Bannon had bought for Peter
Cochran, leaned against it and lit a cigarette. She stared
at Wade with her heavily cosmeticized eyes, her face
hard with contempt. A mad thought crossed Wade's
mind—that Tucker or Pete had commissioned this outrage, possibly to exact vengeance over Wade's
conspiracy with the Conifer Group to steal the Mount
Olivet timberlands. Tucker might have hired these people to beat him, break his fingers or bust his kneecaps,
maybe even kill him.

Nothing would have surprised Wade anymore. Like
everyone else who lived in Buckthorn, he'd heard the
whispers about the horrors Tucker Bannon had perpetrated over the decades. Some of the old folks whispered
that Tucker had regularly beaten his children when they
were small, that he'd even murdered his own brother
thirty-odd years ago. Now Wade believed those whispers, swallowed them whole.

The man behind him forced him to his knees and tied
his hands behind his back with baling wire, causing
razor-bright pain. The man moved in front of him, went
to Stella and gave her a peck on the cheek.

"Another one bites the dust, eh, Lamp Chop?" he
said, waving his ugly pistol toward Wade. "Ain't a man
alive who can resist your charms, is there?"

"Gil, let's just do what we're supposed to do and get out of here," she said.

The man turned and faced Wade straight on. He was long and rangy, not over twenty-five, outfitted in baggy fatigue pants and glossy Doc Marten boots, Raiders ball cap, hunting knife in a scabbard on his belt.

"Shouldn't we at least let him fix his hair first? I can't do somebody with a piece of hair hanging off his bald spot like that. It seems—I don't know—sacrilegious, kind of."

"We don't have all night, Gil."

Gil went down to his haunches and beamed the flashlight into Wade's eyes. "How about it, dude—want me to fix that hair for you? Least I can do, seems to me."

He pushed the pistol into his belt and took a long-handled comb from his pocket, then went to work on Wade's hair, combing it forward, backward, from one side to the other. He patted it, poked at it, tried to make it stay in place. Wade endured, fought down sobs.

"There, there," Gil said, working with the comb. "I know what it's like to have shitty hair. Look at mine." He pulled off the Raider's cap, revealing yellowish gouts, like raw wool. "I've been dealing with this shit for years, man, but nothing works. I've even tried the skinhead look, but my skull's asymmetrical, and I don't look good bald. When I was a baby, my old lady left me sleeping too long on one side, so my head's kind of lopsided, you know? You gotta have a perfect head if you're gonna be bald, man—like Captain Jean Luc Picard on *Star Trek, the Next Generation.*"

Wade tried to look up into Gil's face, hoping to see some inkling of compassion, some sign of hope. Pain overwhelmed him—pain in his head, his wire-bound wrists, the bruises in his midsection. The worst pain was in his heart, the wounding by Stella, a woman he'd actually loved for a few dazzling hours.

"You know," Gil said, standing back and eyeing him with his arms crossed, "you would've done better by having your hair cut short and forgetting about trying to cover the bald spot. Bald guys look best with short hair—I'm talkin' *military* short, less than a quarter of an inch. You could've looked pretty good, especially if you'd gotten yourself into shape, lost some weight. Growing your hair long on the sides and sweeping it over the bald spot really sucks, man."

"Oh, for the love of God," Stella said, reaching into her shoulder bag. "This is getting ridiculous."

The last thing Wade Beswick saw was the stubby revolver in her hand and the muzzle flash that spat from the barrel. A .38-caliber slug shattered his brain before he could hear the roar.

VII

THEY STOOD A MOMENT OVER THE BODY, SHINING THE flashlight on it, watching it twitch and tremble. Beswick's broken head gave off steam in the chilly night air. Tree frogs grumped in the darkness around them.

Stella tucked her gun away, pulled out a monogrammed Mont Blanc pen and dropped it where she stood. "Todd wanted us to leave a calling card," she said to Gil Monahan.

Then she took out a Kleenex and bent down to Wade Beswick's body, dipped the tissue into a bloody chunk of cranial matter. She went to the driver's door of the Jeep Cherokee and wiped the tissue along the inner panel of the door, leaving a dark smear.

"Let's go," she said.

They drove into Buckthorn on Main Street and immediately cut over to Second in order to avoid driving past Tom Sawyer's Saloon, which appeared still to be open for business. Four blocks later they turned right onto Bannon Avenue and cruised slowly up the hill with the headlights off. Stella halted in front of an abandoned house where Gil had left a rented car earlier in the evening before stealing the Cherokee from Bannon House. He'd hidden the rental in the rear yard, so no one could see it from the street.

Before getting out, he blew Stella a kiss and told her that he would wait for her at this spot. He called her "Lamb Chop," told her that he would miss her.

Stella drove on slowly until reaching the front gate of Bannon House. She touched a button on a remote-control console, and the gate swung silently open. Taking care not to gun the engine, she drove slowly forward, leaving the gate open behind her. The strong yard lights in the front drive obviated turning on the headlights.

She touched another button on the console, which raised one of four garage doors. She parked the Cherokee in the garage and punched a switch on the wall, lowering the door again. Ducking out through a rear door of the garage, she trotted down the drive to the front gate, confident that no one at Bannon House had seen her come or go. She closed the gate behind her and moved toward the sound of an engine idling in the dark.

P
A
R
T

T
H
R
E
E

16

I

THE TELEPHONE JANGLED DANIEL KANTOR OUT OF A sound sleep.

"This is Nick Graybill," the caller growled. "We've got another one."

"Another what?"

"What the hell do you think? Another body, that's what."

Kantor rose on one elbow and squinted at the digital clock next to the telephone. 3:47 A.M. He could almost smell the Cigar's vile breath over the phone. "A Buckthorn killer–type body?"

"Yes, Kantor, a Buckthorn killer–type body. Think I'd call at a quarter to four in the morning to tell you about somebody's friggin' heart attack? I'm heading out to the scene now. I'll pick you up in five minutes."

Kantor gargled himself awake with Listerine, pulled on a sweatshirt and jeans, strapped on his nine-millimeter. He waited for Graybill on the front porch of the tiny duplex apartment that he'd rented on the edge of Paulsen, smoking a cigarette and watching a bank of fog crawl ashore from the Columbia River. Stars glittered overhead with icy ferocity.

The Cigar arrived in his cruiser with his flashers blipping like blue lasers. Kantor got in, and Graybill started briefing him immediately, talking as he drove. As usual, he wasted no time or words on pleasantries.

The killing had taken place less than a mile east of

Buckthorn just off Nehalem Road in a walnut orchard.
The deceased was apparently a mill worker named Terry
Grimes, whose pickup was parked on Nehalem Road
next to the orchard entrance. By outward appearances,
the condition of the body was the same as that of the
previous victims of the Buckthorn killer—naked, incin-
erated from the neck down, eyes gouged out, fingers and
penis amputated. The killer had nailed him to the ground
with eight-inch spikes.

Kantor visualized the victim, felt a reflux of acid from
his stomach into his gullet and wished that he'd brought
along a roll of Tums. He asked who'd discovered the
body.

"Rick Applegate, one of my night shift guys," Graybill answered. "Got a call from Mrs. Candice Bertinello,
lives east of town on Nehalem Avenue, just before it turns
into Nehalem Road. She got up to go to the can, looked
out the window and saw flames in the orchard. Called
nine-one-one. Applegate was there in ten minutes."

"Anybody else at the scene?"

"Couple of state troopers out of Hillsboro and a
Washington County deputy. I don't know if anybody's
called the crime-scene folks or the M.E. yet. You're the
pro from Dover, so I thought I'd leave all that stuff to
you."

Kantor took the radio handset off the hook, switched
to the Oregon State Police tactical frequency and radioed
the troopers in the walnut orchard, telling them to keep
everyone away from the body until he got there. Then
he took out his cellular phone and placed calls to the
homes of his "Scouts," Detectives Roberto Esparza of
the Portland Police Bureau and Ashley Tching of the
Tigard Police Department. He gave them detailed directions to the Grimes death scene and instructed them to
go there immediately.

Then he called the FBI and requested a real-time consultation with the Behavioral Science Unit and VICAP. He asked specifically for Dr. Ariel Sheplov.

II

CROWS GATHERED IN THE WALNUT ORCHARD AS THE eastern sky brightened from dirty gray to a mellow shade of peach. They flapped around in the trees, squawked at each other and taunted the grave-faced investigators, but never ventured too close to the atrocity on the ground.

"They smell cooked meat," Ashley Tching remarked to Kantor. "If we weren't here, they'd be having Terry Grimes for breakfast."

"Let 'em go to Denny's," Kantor said.

He couldn't stop staring at the bloodless face of Grimes's corpse, bathed in the harsh light of floodlamps on tripods around it. The flesh of the cheeks was chalky white and blistered along the underside of the jaw. The expression was totally neutral, the eye sockets black and empty, the muscles slack—the untroubled and beyond-caring mask of death. Deep creases around the corners of the mouth and eyes indicated ferocious grimacing, the kind that accompanied acute pain. The kid must have suffered abominably, Kantor thought.

He looked up and saw Bob Esparza walking toward him through the trees from the access road, the beam of his flashlight slicing through waist-high ground fog. "What've you got?" Kantor asked the young detective.

"Nothing earthshaking. We've got tire tracks from Grimes's truck that lead right up to the death scene. Then we've got tire tracks from the death scene to the truck, where it's sitting right now. I guess it means that the killer drove the truck back to Nehalem Road after doing the deed. Then he got out of the truck and went away, maybe in his own car.''

"He positioned his car in advance,'' Tching said. "We've seen this before, Bob, or weren't you paying attention that day?''

"Maybe he didn't have a car at all,'' Esparza replied. "He might've gone away on foot. I don't see any fresh tracks from another vehicle.''

"Oh, he's got a car or truck, all right,'' Tching said. "Can you picture this guy walking down the road loaded up with a gas can and all the tools he used on the victim? I'd say he parked his car on the pavement so he wouldn't leave any tracks, which is exactly what he's done at all the other scenes. We should canvass the area, see if anybody saw a vehicle parked anywhere along this road last night.''

"Sounds good,'' Kantor said. "Make it happen.''

He walked back toward the body, taking care with each step, searching the ground with a flashlight before putting his foot down in order not to displace or destroy any piece of undiscovered evidence. The fog wouldn't lift until midmorning, he knew, when the sun's rays started to penetrate the trees. Not until then could he and the other investigators "Sherlock'' the area, which meant dividing the crime scene into grids and doing an inch-by-inch search for clues.

Two men and a woman crouched near the body, all three wearing yellow waterproof jackets with "OSP'' on the backs—Oregon State Police. They were special death-scene technicians, whose job was to collect physical evidence and prepare it for transport to the crime lab and the medical examiner's office. A tall black woman in a down ski jacket hovered over them, occasionally giving advice or answering questions. A pair of FBI agents stood further away, wearing government-issue jackets of black nylon, one of them talking on a cellular phone.

The OSP team had taken pictures of the body and the surrounding scene, sampled the dirt and made plaster casts of the tire prints. At this moment they were preparing to transport the body itself. The tall black woman was Lucinda Johns, a deputy state medical examiner with whom Kantor had worked frequently before he took over the Buckthorn Task Force.

"You want to look for insects on the underside of the body, doc?" one of the techs asked.

She shook her head. "This thing hasn't cooled enough for infestation to occur, much less any egg-laying or larvae growth." She looked up and saw Kantor. "We're about ready to bag it and take it in, Lieutenant. Any last-minute requests?"

"Just the usual. I'd appreciate it if—"

"I know, I know—put a rush on it. Want to be there for the cut, or are you going to send one of your elves?" The "cut" was the medicolegal autopsy.

"I'll be there. I'll also want Tching and Esparza on hand. Plus the D.A., if you don't mind."

"Done. I'll call you and give you a time as soon as I know."

"Thanks, doc."

He approached the OSP team leader and told him to vacuum out the interior of the victim's pickup before Tching and Esparza dusted it for fingerprints. The killer had driven the vehicle from the murder scene back to the road, and he might have left trace evidence inside it—hair from his head or fibers from his carpet at home.

"No problem, Lieutenant."

"One more thing. Did you find any footprints in the vicinity of the body?"

"Nothing so far, sir, but it's still pretty dark. As you can see, there's a thick layer of twigs and leaves on the ground, which means we shouldn't get our hopes up. Your guy might've chosen this spot for that very reason—it's like walking on a padded carpet. If you leave any footprints, they don't last long."

"The son of a bitch thinks of everything," Kantor muttered.

"We found the victim's clothes piled neatly under that tree over there," the tech added, aiming his flashlight. "Want to take a look before we bag them?"

"I've already seen them," Kanter answered.

He watched as Dr. Johns carefully pulled the spikes from the charred hands and feet of the victim. She placed each spike into a plastic bag, then sealed the bag and marked it with a felt-tipped pen. Next, she inserted a hypodermic needle into the victim's neck and withdrew blood. A lab would reveal what chemicals, if any, the victim had ingested just prior to death.

"It'll show methamphetamine over sodium pentobarbital," Kantor said to the assistant M.E. as she packed the sample away. "Something to put him to sleep and wake him up again."

"Safe bet. This monster's got his drill down."

"Why mess with success?"

Johns and her assistant slipped the victim into a black body bag, and the OSP techs lugged it to the M.E.'s van on the edge of the orchard. Seasoned murder cop though he was, this was always a bad moment for Kantor, the bagging of the body. Seeing it happen made him feel as if he'd lost part of himself, made him think of widows and orphans and starving refugees. It always made him feel like crying.

That's me someday, said a voice in his head.

III

TUCKER BANNON STARED DOWN AT HIS SON-IN-LAW'S unconscious face and listened to his slow, labored breathing. The sun was long up and the children had gone off to school, but Pete Cochran hadn't stirred from his bed. And from the look of it, he wouldn't stir anytime soon.

Tucker grunted with satisfaction. The drugs had done their job—Tylox and Lorcet, three tablets of each. Both were powerful prescription painkillers that he'd hoarded over the past seven or eight years. He'd gotten the Tylox prescription after undergoing minor surgery to remove ingrown toenails, the Lorcet after the extraction of his few remaining natural teeth. He'd put the bottles aside and saved them, figuring that a man like himself might someday find a need for drugs like these—one that wasn't purely medical. And he'd been right, of course. The need had arisen when Todd Verduin called to request his help in ensuring that Peter Cochran's Jeep Cherokee could be taken from the garage and brought back without anyone noticing.

Last night before dinner, Tucker had pulverized the tablets and poured the powder into a small pill bottle, which he'd then hidden in his pocket. Later, he'd made a production of making Old Grampa Tuck's World-Famous Homemade Ice Cream, which he'd churned up in the same ancient hand-cranked ice-cream maker that he'd used when his own daughter, Sally, was a little girl.

Sarah and Tyler had been fascinated. While doing the chore, Tucker had told them a tall tale and had let each take a turn at the crank. After dinner, he'd served dessert with his own hands, setting a bowl of rich vanilla ice cream before each member of the family. He'd laced Pete's portion with the powdered drugs and had prayed that the chocolate syrup would cover the bitter taste, that the radical dosage would do no permanent harm.

The Lord had answered his prayer, as He nearly always did. Pete had cleaned his bowl and had even asked for seconds. Fifteen minutes after finishing his ice

cream, he'd started to yawn. By 8:00 he was in bed,
unable to keep his eyes open. He'd slept through the
night without stirring, never knowing that someone had
removed his Jeep from the garage just before midnight
and brought it back again a few hours later.

Now the question was when he would wake up.
Tucker glanced at his watch and saw that it was a few
minutes after nine, meaning that Pete had slept more
than thirteen hours.

Tucker's cellular phone bleeped, but the slumbering
Pete Cochran didn't flinch. The old man pulled the
phone out of his shirt pocket and answered it, watching
Pete's eyes for the slightest flutter. "Yes?"

"Tucker, this is Todd Verduin. The project we've
been discussing is complete, the one involving the
Lord's justice. We brought it in on schedule, just as I
promised. No snags, no foul-ups."

"What do you mean *we*? You haven't involved anyone else in this, have you?" Tucker suddenly got a
nervous feeling in his stomach, rather than the elation
that he'd expected to feel upon learning that Wade Beswick had gone to his reward.

"There's absolutely nothing to worry about, I can assure you. My associates are good as gold. Like myself.
Consummate professionals."

Tucker took a slow, deep breath to stave off the rage
that burned in his chest. "I'd hoped you would show
the good sense to operate alone on something this sensitive."

Verduin chuckled. "Believe me, Tucker, I handled it
in the best possible way—for *both* of us." In other
words, he felt a need to cover himself, to bring in someone to ensure that Tucker couldn't simply eliminate him
and be free of any connection to Wade Beswick's murder.

"I guess I don't have any choice but to trust you,"

Tucker said, trying to keep his tone from betraying his anger. "You'll want the other half of your payment, I suppose."

"Absolutely. And be assured that I haven't forgotten about our other project—the elusive Rosa Juanita. I'll talk to the plastic surgeon she consulted as soon as I've picked up the money. I can leave for Carmel today, in fact."

"That's good. I'm very anxious to find out where she is."

"And *who* she is, I would imagine."

"That too. The money is ready, so I'll expect to see you sometime this morning."

"I'll be there in an hour. Thanks, Tuck. Buh-bye."

Knowing that this piece of human garbage now thought himself his equal was almost too much for Tucker to bear. As he put away his cellular phone, he gritted his teeth and vowed that someday soon he would do himself the pleasure of putting a bullet through Todd Verduin's hundred-dollar haircut.

He heard a noise behind him and turned to find his wife in the doorway of the bedroom. Her stare went first to the inert figure of Peter Cochran in his bed, then to Tucker. Apprehension twitched in her face.

"What have you done to him?" she whispered.

"Now Dolly, there's nothing to get upset about. I've put him to sleep, that's all. I slipped a little something into his ice cream last night."

Dolly's face went white, and she put a hand to her mouth. "It's happening again, isn't it? You've started sinning again. I can see it in your eyes and hear it in your voice. Oh, Tucker . . ."

He didn't doubt that she could indeed see sin in his eyes and hear it in his voice. Having lived with this woman for nearly fifty years, he knew that she'd learned to read him like a book, exactly as he'd learned to read her. Sometimes he wondered whether people didn't live with each too long and get to know each other too well.

"You're working yourself up over nothing," he said. "I merely needed to make sure that Pete slept for awhile. Everything is fine. I expect that he'll start to . . ."

"Don't treat me like a child, Tucker. I know the things you've done in the past, and I know what you're capable of. I'd hoped that God had changed you, as I've always prayed He would. But I see that He hasn't yet answered my prayer."

"You don't know what you're talking about, woman. I've only . . ."

"You *kill*, Tucker. Don't try to pretend that you don't. I know that you killed your brother, Clarence. I know that—"

"Dolly, stop this!"

"No, I won't stop it. I'm your wife, Tucker, and I love you. I can't stand idly by and watch you mire yourself in the sin of murder."

Tucker took her by the arm and steered her through the door, pulling it closed behind him. He hustled her through the twisting, carpeted hallway to the master suite in the opposite corner of the house, taking care not to squeeze her arm too tightly. In half a century of marriage to this woman he'd never physically harmed her, and he didn't mean to start now.

Once they were safe in their own bedroom, he sat her down on the canopied bed and talked to her about the sin of killing. God had issued conflicting instructions on the matter, he explained. On one hand, God had said, "Thou shalt not kill," the fifth commandment, but on the other hand, He'd prescribed capital punishment for a slew of misdeeds. Smiting thy father or mother, cursing thy father or mother, bestiality and witchcraft were all capital offenses, as were many others, according to Exodus 21 and 22.

Biblical men of God were no strangers to shedding blood with their hands, Tucker explained with the patient tone of a kindly Sunday school teacher. Hadn't Moses himself killed an Egyptian who was mistreating a Hebrew slave? And hadn't Moses, upon coming down from Mount Sinai to find his people reveling in sin, commissioned the sons of Levi to go among the unfaithful and kill them with swords?

"Moses caused the death of over three thousand Jews that day," Tucker said, citing Exodus again, "but he was still a godly man. The Lord didn't turn His face away from him, and neither will He turn His face away from me."

"But those were special circumstances," Dolly protested. "You're not Moses, Tuck, and God hasn't commissioned you to punish anyone."

Tucker shook his head and shushed her, his red mole burying itself in a furrow. "I *am* a man of God," he said firmly. "You must believe that, Dolly." He smoothed her hair gently. "I'm like a prophet here in Buckthorn, as my father was before me. We Bannons are the chosen people here, favored by God above all others. He has given us much—this house, our timberlands, our business—and it's my responsibility as the head of this family to take care of what we have, so that we can pass it on to our heirs."

"And that includes killing people?"

"I'm simply telling you that I'll do whatever is necessary to protect what God has given us and to ensure that we have legitimate heirs. Yesterday I arranged for the killing of a vile, conniving man who'd betrayed me and tried to steal everything we have. I think God respects that, Dolly, don't you?"

"But why did you kill Clarence? He was such a gentle soul, a good man . . ." She was crying freely now, tears welling out of her eyes and spilling down her cheeks.

"He never in his life harmed anyone. All he wanted to do was laugh, to make others laugh."

"My brother was a libertine and a flake," Tucker protested. "We were as different from one another as two brothers could be. He—"

"Like Cain and Abel."

Tucker let the comment go. "Clarence had no respect for what our father had accomplished, and he was willing to borrow against everything we had in order to finance his own half-baked business schemes. If he'd gotten his way, everything we owned would've been mortgaged, and we could easily have lost it all."

"And for that you killed him?"

Tucker shook his head wearily. "Dolly, do we really have to go over all this again? You know very well what Clarence was—a drunkard, a fornicator. He could hardly utter a sentence without taking the Lord's name in vain. He even consorted with a lowly Mexican woman and produced a bastard child—"

"That lowly Mexican woman, as you call her, is our Esmerelda, and the bastard child is our Rosa, your own niece by blood."

"I *know* who they are. And I've done right by them, I think. I've done what any godly man would've done, under the circumstances. I gave them a home under this very roof, raised the girl as my own daughter . . ."

"You killed her father, your own brother."

"I killed him because—" He halted, choking.

A dark scene swam behind his eyes, one so clear that it could have happened last night and not thirty-four years ago. His brother's face stared up at him, spattered with blood, tearful and incredulous over the fact that things had actually come to this. Tucker had simultaneously loved and hated that face. Tucker fired his revolver again, and his brother's eyes went blank. The chipper roared as he fed his brother's body into it, the blades whining as they buzzed through flesh and bone, reducing the earthly remains of Clarence Bannon to fragments no bigger than puffs of popcorn. No one outside the family had ever guessed that the next rail carload of wood chips to the paper mill included the atomized remains of old Noah Bannon's second son, the cheerful one, the one who believed in progress and diversification. The townsfolk of Buckthorn had assumed that Clarence had simply run off to escape responsibility for his bastard child. At least this was what any of them had said *aloud*.

"I killed him because I had no choice," Tucker said, his voice hoarse. "And bear in mind that *you've* known about it all these years—"

"Only because Esmerelda confided in me. She followed you and Clarence to the mill that night, saw it all."

"—and that you share whatever guilt I bear, because you've kept quiet. It's called guilty knowledge, Dolly. The same goes for Esmerelda. She saw me do it, but she didn't report what she saw. I might add that she was quick to accept my offer of a job here. She obviously recognized a good thing when it presented itself—a home for herself and her child in a fine house. I gave her my solemn promise that her child would share in the Bannon estate, since she was a blood relation, the daughter of my brother. It's a promise I would've happily kept if Rosa hadn't run off."

Dolly glared at him. "Rosa went away for the same reason Sally did, and you know it—to be free of *you*, Tucker, and all that you've done to them. They knew that you killed your brother, and they knew that you killed—"

Tucker stood up suddenly, his anger raging like a furnace. It had hit him like a bomb blast. "That's enough, Dolly. None of this is doing us any good. I've tried to

be a good man, a good husband and father. If you understand nothing else, at least understand that.''

"What about Peter? Will he—?''

"Pete will be fine. I drugged him so he wouldn't go
traipsing off to that Vale woman's place like he did night
before last. I needed to make sure his Jeep stayed in the
garage.'' He smiled when he saw the confusion in his
wife's face, and his anger dissipated as rapidly as it
came.

"Does this have anything to do with the man who
came and took the Jeep last night?'' she asked.

"So you saw someone, did you? Well, you'll want to
keep that small tidbit to yourself. If anyone asks, you
don't know whether Pete's car left the garage last night.
Needless to say, you don't know that I rendered young
Pete unable to leave the house.''

"Now you want me to lie for you.''

"I only want what you've given me all these years,
dear Dolly—your silence and your understanding.'' He
bent to her, kissed her forehead with cold lips. "Did
anyone else see anything last night?—Esmerelda or the
children?''

"They were all in bed. I was up and about because I
couldn't sleep. My bursitis was acting up again.''

"If you'd like, I'd be happy to prepare something for
you,'' Tucker said with a wink. He touched her cheek
tenderly and kissed her again, then left the room, having
other business to mind.

IV

AT 10:35 A.M., DAN KANTOR ANSWERED HIS OFFICE TELE-
phone and heard the sweet voice of Dr. Ariel Sheplov
of the FBI's Behavioral Science Unit. She apologized
for taking so long to get back to him, but she'd been

in a beach house with her family on the Maryland shore when he'd called in the wee hours of the morning, her first vacation in years. Getting to a secure phone had taken hours. Her office had notified her of the latest killing, the details of which had been virtually identical to those of the Nockleby killing last fall.

She asked Kantor how he was holding up. As well as could be expected, he answered, considering that the killing of Terry Grimes had happened much sooner after the previous murder than anyone had expected. The Buckthorn killer had stepped up his schedule, and Kantor was afraid to even think about the implications. He asked Dr. Sheplov if he was authorized to panic.

"Yes, I'd say panic is in order," she replied. "Your maniac is having a crisis of self-control, Lieutenant. His urges have boiled over for some reason, possibly as a result of some stressful event or condition in his everyday life. His need to kill has overwhelmed his usual capacity to control himself for two or three years at a time. What it means is that he'll kill again, and probably soon. Past experience tells us that these animals need to do their thing ever more frequently."

"Terrific. Is there any percentage in trying to put together another psychological profile on him?"

"Not unless you've found something new in the physical evidence. To be blunt, Lieutenant, no forensic shrink can give you anything useful unless you come up with some new clue about what this guy is like. The evidence we now have allows only a general profile, and not a very good one at that. We can tell you that he's quite intelligent and resourceful, probably well educated, a stickler for detail—"

"All the stuff we already know."

"I'm afraid so. There's no way we can get more specific than that, considering the little we have to work with."

"Yeah. Well, I'll keep you posted. We've got people here from the FBI office in Portland, so you'll know everything as it happens."

"Fine. There is one bright spot in this black picture, Lieutenant, and you may already have spotted it."

"Lay it on me. At this moment I'm in dire need of bright spots."

"The killer's going to screw up. In fact, he may have done it already."

"Oh? How do you figure?"

"He's become impatient. As he devotes more and more attention to sating his appetites, he'll become less cautious, less exacting in his procedures."

"That's a bright spot? You're telling me that the next time he kills, he'll get careless and leave some nice clues lying around for me?"

"I suppose that's what I'm saying, yes."

"Well, forgive me for not turning a cartwheel, Doctor, but I'd just as soon not have another dead body on my hands."

"Into every life some rain must fall, Lieutenant."

Kantor chuckled in spite of himself. "I didn't mean to get sour on you. Finding mutilated bodies always makes me crabby, especially in the morning before I've had my Ovaltine."

"No need to apologize. By the way, how's our young Mr. Topper Bannon doing? I assume you've been keeping an eye on him."

"I'm in regular touch with Dennis Feldon, his therapist. It's still early in the game, but Feldon isn't what you'd call optimistic. He thinks Topper has built a wall around himself and that he's holding back his true feelings. Feldon senses that he says only what he thinks Feldon wants to hear. The next step might be medication, and Feldon's not too confident that even that will work."

Dr. Sheplov sighed audibly. "I was afraid of this. The kid might be beyond salvage. I can't overemphasize how important it is to keep an eye on him, Lieutenant. He's made of the stuff of monsters. For that matter—"

"You don't need to say it. You're convinced he's connected to the Buckthorn killings somehow, and I should be concentrating my investigative efforts on his environment, because whatever made Topper what he is probably did the same to the Buckthorn killer. That's what you think, right?"

"You're in fine form today, Lieutenant. Stay in touch, okay? And good luck."

Kantor went upstairs to the county commissioners' conference room, where Ashley Tching was preparing a detailed map of the crime scene. On the long oak conference table she'd laid out handwritten notes and sketches, Polaroid photographs of the body and the surrounding area, along with various rulers, compasses, felt markers and pencils. Her hands moved in easy, confident motions as she measured, marked and sketched on a flat expanse of poster paper, creating a picture of the crime scene that would enable investigators to visualize the movements of the killer and the victim. Noting the quality of her work, Kantor figured that if she ever decided to give up hunting killers, she could become an artist.

"I'll have this done by noon, Lieutenant," she said, barely glancing up. "By the way, Bob Esparza called in a few minutes ago, said he's got something important for you."

Kantor lit a cigarette and punched numbers on his cellular phone. Esparza answered on the second ring.

"It's me, Bob. What've you got?"

"I'm in Scappoose at Terry Grimes's place. I got a call a few minutes ago from a sheriff's deputy who'd just talked to a Chevron station operator here in town. He saw Grimes and another guy last night in his station, came in to buy five bucks' worth of gas. Said the guy was driving an old Mercury hot rod . . ."

"Hold it while I get something to write with." Kantor fished a pen and pad out of his corduroy sport coat. "Where's this Chevron station, and who's the guy who saw Grimes?" Esparza told him, and Kantor wrote it down, squinting from the sting of cigarette smoke in his eyes. "Stay at Grimes's place and keep on doing what you're doing," he told Esparza. "Tching and I will talk to the gas station man, then pick you up later."

"Right, Lieutenant."

"Oh, and Bob—" He remembered what Dr. Sheplov had said about the killer becoming careless. "Be extra thorough over there, okay? I have reason to think our man might be getting a little loose. We just may find something this time."

"Got it. See you later."

Kantor and Tching went down the back stairs of the courthouse to the parking lot, avoiding the throng of reporters in the vestibule of the sheriff's office. The first dribble of news about Terry Grimes's murder had attracted them like flies to yesterday's potato salad. Kantor knew that before nightfall the towns of Buckthorn and Paulsen would be wall to wall with humanity, as reporters streamed in from news outlets in every major American city, from major newspapers and tabloids, from wire services and television networks. Every one of them would want a piece of Dan Kantor, the man in charge of the Buckthorn Task Force. They would follow him wherever he went, always jostling for a chance to fire questions at him. They would demand to know what he was doing to catch the killer, and anything he said would sound bad, short of an announcement that he'd made an arrest. He could hear himself giving evasive answers, trying to sound responsive without really responding.

Kantor cringed: this wasn't the kind of press attention he'd envisioned for himself while pulling strings to get this job. Another killing wasn't supposed to happen on his watch.

The drive to Scappoose from Paulsen took twenty minutes. The owner of the service station told Kantor and Tching that Terry Grimes and another man had arrived around 7:00 the previous night and had bought five dollars' worth of gasoline, which they took away in a metal can. Grimes, who was a regular customer, had run out of gas between Buckthorn and Scappoose, and the other man had given him a lift to the station, they'd told him.

"Ever see this other man before?" Kantor asked.

"I might have, but I'm not really sure," the Chevron proprietor answered. "I got the notion that he worked with Terry over at the Buckthorn mill. Seemed like a local fella, the way he talked and everything. He even loaned Terry the money to pay for the gas, so I figured they was friends."

Kantor wrote this down. "Can you describe the car, maybe remember the license number?"

The proprietor took off his Chevron cap and scratched his scalp with a grease-blackened finger. Here's a man who knows cars, Kantor thought. "Well, I'd say she was either a 'fifty-one or 'fifty-two Mercury two-door, chopped roof, lowered suspension. Sounded like he was runnin' a small-block Chevy in her. Primer gray—probably ran out of money before he got her finished, like a lot of these fellas do. Right front quarter panel was getting rusty. Didn't pay any attention to the license number. Sorry."

"You've been very helpful," Kantor said, jotting the description of the car in his pad. "How about the guy himself? What did he look like?"

The proprietor put his cap back on his head and

scowled while trying to remember. "Big fella, over two hundred pounds if he weighed anything. Thick gray hair, combed straight back. Younger'n me—fifty, maybe fifty-five, I'd say. That's about all I can tell you about him, I guess. Didn't think too much about him at the time."

"You did great," Kantor said. "What you've told us really helps."

"There is one more thing," the proprietor said. "I seen a cat in the car, big ugly one. Yellow with dark stripes. Biggest, meanest-looking cat you ever seen."

Ashley Tching grabbed Kantor's arm. "My God," she breathed, "I think I know who this dude is."

"You do?" Kantor kept his pencil poised on his pad.

"It's got to be Jerome Dragstead. He works at the mill, drives an old Mercury and keeps cats. I specifically remember the big yellow one."

Kantor let his breath out.

Jerry Dragstead had been an object of the Buckthorn Task Force's attention from the very first, owing to his criminal record. Beginning in 1982, after the third killing, the Task Force supervisor had assigned officers to conduct full-time surveillance of Dragstead during the entire month of October, the only month in which the killer had struck. Dragstead had proved himself capable of killing more than two decades earlier. His victim had been a teenage boy, which had seemed nominally consistent with the victimology of the Buckthorn killer.

For the thirty-one days of seven consecutive Octobers, Dragstead had lived with cops watching his every move. They'd watched his house at night, followed him to and from the mill, to bowling alleys and movie theaters and restaurants. They'd called it the "Dragstead Detail."

During that seven-year period, the Buckthorn killer had struck three times—in 1983, 1986, and 1989, and the Dragstead Detail had verified that their man was home in bed when each of those killings occurred. After the 1989 killing, the then–Task Force supervisor had abolished the detail, as he probably should have done after the 1983 killing. Jerry Dragstead clearly was not the Buckthorn killer, despite what so many in the Task Force had wanted to believe.

After the Nockleby killing last October, Task Force investigators had interviewed Dragstead during their general canvass of Buckthorn and the immediate area around the town. By luck of the draw, Ashley Tching had been the one to knock on his door. She'd read the file on him and had known of the Task Force's earlier interest in him. During her visit to his house, she'd noted that he kept several cats and dogs. She'd seen the rusty Mercury in his yard.

Dan Kantor, too, had read the file on Dragstead.

"Call the Cigar and tell him to pick Dragstead up and hold him for questioning," he said to Tching. "Tell him to do no interrogating until we get there." In answer to her skeptical frown, he said, "I'm not saying Dragstead is the Buckthorn killer. But he spent time with the victim on the night he died, and that makes him a person of interest. Any problem with that?"

"Nope." She hurried over to Kantor's car to radio the sheriff's office, and Kantor finished his interview with the Chevron proprietor, who remembered nothing else about the man who'd accompanied Terry Grimes the previous night. Kantor and Tching thanked him and left.

By the time they arrived at Grimes's forty-foot double-wide on an old logging road west of town, the news media had arrived in force. At least twenty reporters were on station, replete with four television vans and satellite uplinks. Fortunately, the Oregon State Police had dispatched a detail to keep the crush of reporters behind a barricade of sawhorses that stretched across the front of Grimes's muddy lot.

"Good news, Lieutenant," Bob Esparza said, meeting Kantor and Tching at the front door of the mobile home. "We've got a footprint—out back by the bedroom window. There's a bunch of indentations around the house, apparently made by the killer as he cased the place. Looks like he took pains to obliterate them with a rake we found out back, but he missed one. The crime lab guys are making a plaster cast of it."

Kantor felt his pulse quicken. Maybe Dr. Sheplov had been right. Maybe the Buckthorn killer had become careless.

He ordered Ashley Tching to call a man named Tracy Livingston, who worked for the Nike Corporation in Beaverton. Livingston was the world's leading authority on shoe prints, especially those left by athletic-style sneakers. Law enforcement agencies around the country had used his services in tracking down felony suspects purely on the basis of prints found at the scenes of their crimes. Through microscopic analysis of tread patterns and wear marks, Livingston could ascertain the brand and model number of shoes, as well as the wholesale distribution points. Often as not he could discover the actual stores that had sold the shoes, which sometimes enabled investigators to learn the identity of the buyers through credit card records. In many cases he'd matched wear marks taken from plaster casts of the footprints with the actual shoes collected from suspects, as a fingerprint examiner would match latents to a suspect's fingerprints, thereby proving that the suspects had been at the scenes of the crimes.

One of the OSP investigators shouted something from the edge of Grimes's lot, where a clear-cut began. More footprints, he said. Kantor, Esparza and Tching hurried over to where the crime scene specialists had gathered to stare at shoe patterns in the mud.

"Get pictures and casts of these," Kantor said.

"Looks like our man circled around from the road and approached the trailer house from the rear. Anybody care to guess what size shoe he wears?"

"Looks like about the same size as mine, a ten," Esparza said. "I'm no expert, but I'd say these prints match the one up by the house."

"Livingston will be able to tell us for sure," Kantor said. He waved over one of the FBI special agents who'd shown up from the Portland office, a squat blond man named Bridenbaugh. "Could you get us some help analyzing these things?" he asked. "I understand that VI-CAP has experts on line who can look at a series of footprints and tell you how tall the guy is, how much he weighs, other good stuff like that."

"That's right," Bridenbaugh confirmed. "A bunch of scientists came up with a computer program that does exactly that, and it's damn reliable. Let me call Quantico and find out exactly what they need. They might want to send one of their own people to take the impressions."

Kantor breathed deeply and surveyed the scene around him. Grimes's dilapidated mobile home stood in the center of a muddy, unkempt lot, surrounded on three sides by a clear-cut, where ferns and a scrubby shrub called ninebark grew among the stumps and saplings. The front of the lot bordered an old logging road that junctioned with Highway 202 about two hundred yards south of here.

Dismal fucking place, Kantor thought, crushing a cigarette butt under his shoe. It irked him that hardworking Americans with full-time jobs couldn't afford better than this.

The footprints along the periphery suggested that someone had cased Grimes's mobile home before approaching it, sneaking through the low brush at the edge of the clear-cut. Kantor craned his neck in all directions but saw no other houses, no farmsteads or cabins. The likelihood that anyone had seen the intruder, other than Grimes himself, was small. Still: "Get a canvass going," he told Tching. "Hit every farmhouse and cabin on Highway 202 between Scappoose and Spitzenberg. We're looking for anything out of the ordinary—any strange vehicles or pedestrians, anyone seen entering this road during the past few days." Tching hustled off to relay the orders to the appropriate Task Force members.

Kantor's blood was pumping hard now. He approached the leader of the OSP crime scene unit and asked about tire tracks along the logging road and the driveway, whether they'd found any in addition to those of Grimes's pickup. The answer was no. But this didn't mean that another vehicle hadn't come or gone recently, for the tracks were a jumble. A dozen different cars could've come and gone, the team leader said. Kantor ordered him to check the dirt shoulders of the highway on either side of the turn-in to the logging road for footprints and tire tracks. The killer might have parked off the main road and walked into the clear-cut, thinking that the cops wouldn't scour the ground so far from Grimes's mobile home.

He turned to Esparza. "How about inside the house? Anything interesting?"

"No sign of forced entry or struggle. It almost looks like Grimes knew the guy and let him in. The place is a pigsty, lots of dirty dishes around, but there's a couple of fresh brewski cans on the coffee table in the living room. I'm guessing that the killer had a beer with Grimes before pumping him full of sodium pent."

"I want specimens off every dirty dish, drinking glass and beer can in the place, anything the killer might've touched with his lips," Kantor said. "He might be a secretor, and it would be nice to know his blood type."

A secretor was a person whose blood type was A, B,

or AB, and whose body secreted detectable antigens in body fluids like saliva and semen. A forensic scientist could analyze such fluids found at the scene of a crime and often determine a perpetrator's blood type, which enabled cops to disqualify any suspect whose blood type didn't match.

Esparza led Kantor and Tching through the front door of the Grimes home. Inside, the air smelled of mildew and dirty laundry. The living room was a clutter of unwashed dishes, food wrappers and empty beverage bottles. The furniture was cheap and worn, the carpet threadbare. Bed sheets hung at the windows in place of real drapes.

"Wow, how does anyone live like this?" Tching asked.

"People live in what they can afford," Kantor answered.

"I'm not talking socioeconomics here. I'm talking about basic housekeeping."

"The kid worked hard in a sawmill all day. He probably wasn't too keen on housecleaning by the time he got home at night."

Kantor saw magazines strewn around the room—*Off-Road, Field and Stream, Guns & Ammo*. He saw a crumpled bag that had held Dorito ranch-style chips, a half-empty jar of Planter's peanuts, beer cans, all evidence of a real human life, not an abstraction. The corpse he'd seen earlier in the walnut orchard hadn't really seemed like a person—corpses never do. But here in this humble mobile home Kantor could see, touch and smell the trappings of Terry Grimes's existence, the utensils with which he'd eaten his meals, the wrappers that had held his food, the couch where he'd lain and watched TV. The feeling of vacancy was overpowering, the absence of the human life that rightfully belonged here.

"We might as well get used to this place," Kantor said with a sigh. "We're going to toss it top to bottom, sift it up, down and sideways." He saw Tching and Esparza trade glances. "You both knew it had to happen," he added. "There's something here, a fingerprint or a hair or a thread, *something*. I can feel it in my bones. We're going to find it, kids. And it's going to give us this guy on a platter."

V

PETER COCHRAN AWOKE A FEW MINUTES BEFORE NOON on Wednesday, April 6, padded to the bathroom and stared at his own face in the mirror over the sink. *What's wrong with me*? he asked himself aloud.

His bloodshot eyes had blue pouches under them. His head throbbed and his mouth felt sawdust-dry. He'd slept almost sixteen hours straight—something he'd never done in his life. Until now.

He vaguely remembered stumbling off to bed last night after dessert, having suddenly become so sleepy that he couldn't keep his eyes open. He'd planned to call Nita after dinner, maybe talk her into driving to Hillsboro for a movie or a drink, but he'd simply been too tired. The moment his head hit his pillow, he'd blacked out.

He resolved to call a doctor in Hillsboro and make an appointment for a checkup. His first priority, though, was rejoining the world of the living, because sick or not, he had responsibilities to carry out. He showered, shaved and dressed in a sport jacket and casual slacks, his customary work attire these days. Feeling better but still wobbly, he made his way down the rear stairs, keeping a tight grip on the banister. Esmerelda met him in the kitchen and tried to force food on him, but the thought of eating made his gut lurch.

She informed him that the kids had gone off to school as they normally did, that Señora Bannon had gone to a meeting of the Ladies Circle at the church while Señor Bannon had gone to the mill on business. Everything was fine, she assured him, but Pete didn't feel assured. Something in Esmerelda's face wasn't right. She looked like someone who had recently received bad news. And Tucker was supposed to be ninety-percent retired, so why had he gone to the mill on a Wednesday morning when Wade Beswick was there to run the business for him?

Something wasn't quite up to snuff this fine day.

"What is it, Esmerelda?" he asked. "Has something happened I should know about?"

"It is not my place to discuss such matters with you, Señor Pete." She tried to turn away, but he caught her shoulder and gently pulled her around.

"Esmerelda, I need to know. Does it concern Sarah or Carter? Is it about—" He felt pinpricks down his back. "Topper? Is it about Topper? Has he done something bad? Has he? . . ."

Esmerelda looked wounded, and Pete immediately regretted having let his paranoia get loose. He knew that she loved Topper—he'd seen it in the way she mothered the boy and stood up for him whenever Tucker jumped him for this or that infraction. Pete started to apologize.

"The evil has returned," Esmerelda interrupted, whispering as though she feared ears in the walls. "*Ha matado a otra víctima.*"

"I don't understand. The *evil?*"

"It has taken another victim, a young man who worked at the sawmill. It is on the radio. The television, too."

"Are you talking about the Buckthorn killer?"

She crossed herself. "*Sí*. That is why Señor Bannon has gone to the mill, to tell all the workers. A sheriff's deputy came and gave him the news this morning, just as Señor Verduin was leaving."

Todd Verduin had been here? Pete sat down at the table, feeling unsteady. The hint of nausea he'd endured earlier ripened into an outright attack.

The Buckthorn killer, he'd learned from watching the taped TV report at Nita's house two nights ago, struck every second or third year, and because a killing had occurred only last fall, another wasn't due for at least a year and a half. He pointed this out to Esmerelda. Perhaps she'd misunderstood what the deputy told Tucker this morning.

"No, Señor Pete, I am not mistaken. You can turn on the radio or the television and hear for yourself."

Of course he could. Esmerelda hadn't misunderstood anything, he knew. The one who misunderstood things was Peter Cochran, a man who'd convinced himself that some good could come from breaking a promise to his dying wife. Sally had made him pledge countless times to keep their children away from their maternal grandparents, but good old Pete had decided that Father Knows Best. Better for the family, he'd decided, to bring them here, where Sarah and Carter could grow up in Tucker Bannon's house, like landed gentry. That was critical, wasn't it?—to spare his kids any inkling of life in the real world, where people toiled with their hands and sweated real sweat. No after-school jobs for these kids. God forbid they should ever scrimp and save for a new pair of high-tops or the latest Meat Puppets CD.

"I am sorry to be the one who tells you this," Esmerelda said, a tear sliding from her eye. "So very sorry, Señor Pete."

"Don't be sorry, Esmerelda. Someone had to tell me, and I'm glad it was you." He rose shakily from the table

and left for the sawmill, determined to face what was
left of the day head-on.

VI

AN OREGON STATE POLICE OFFICER STOPPED HIM AT THE
gate of Buckthorn Wood Products to confirm that he had
legitimate business here, then waved him in. He parked
between a television van and a Nehalem County Sheriff's cruiser that had expropriated his parking space.
Tucker's big Suburban stood in Wade Beswick's assigned slot, but Beswick's Explorer was nowhere in
sight.

He climbed the steps of the porch and walked through
the front door. Denise Ubaldo flagged him down as he
walked past her desk. She led him to a far corner of the
reception area, away from a somber gathering of strangers who waited there.

"Your father-in-law has closed the mill for the rest
of the day," she whispered, "in honor of Terry Grimes.
All the guys'll start heading home at one."

"Grimes. He's the one who was killed?" Pete tried
to picture the kid, but couldn't. He'd met all the employees of the mill, but he still couldn't put names to
faces for more than half a dozen of them.

Denise nodded, her brown eyes looking bloodshot, her
face drawn. "There's a couple of policemen in with
Tucker now. I don't know what they're talking about,
but I could guess. I imagine they'll want to talk to all
of us before too long. Every few minutes a reporter calls
and asks to speak to the person in charge, someone who
can talk about Terry. Now that you're here, that's you,
since Tucker's sort of retired, right?"

"Wrong. Tucker owns the place, he's in charge. Besides, I'm not good with reporters."

"Whatever you say, Mr. Cochran. But there's something else you should know. The sheriff came around
ten this morning and took Jerry Dragstead away—went
right out and pulled him off his straddle buggy. I assume
they took him to the courthouse in Paulsen."

Mention of Dragstead's name sent a chill down Pete's
spine. He remembered being followed two nights ago as
he walked home from Nita's house, and felt certain that
his follower had been Dragstead. He'd seen a big yellow
cat in the street, exactly like the one that had followed
Dragstead into Tom Sawyer's Saloon. Who else could
it have been?

"Was he under arrest?" Pete asked. "Did they put
him in handcuffs?"

"No, but they took him away in a police car. They
didn't say why they wanted him or when he would come
back."

"Who are *they*?" he asked, indicating the men who
sat in the reception area.

"Tucker's friends from the Mount of Olives Church.
The skinny red-headed man is Randy Roysden, the minister. They've come to pray with Tucker as soon as he's
free. It's what they do whenever a killing happens."

Pete saw that Pastor Randy Roysden was staring nails
at him. The pastor was a hawk-eyed man of fifty with a
brush haircut and a rusty mustache.

"This is nothing new for you, is it?" Pete said to
Denise. "You've seen all this happen before."

Four times, she replied, counting today. She'd been
with Buckthorn Wood Products for six years, having
started at the tender age of twenty. She ticked off the
names of the four young workers who'd lost their lives
during her tenure—Travis Langdon in 1989, Keith
McCurdy in 1991, Rich Nockleby last fall and Terry
Grimes today. But then she'd grown up in Buckthorn,
the daughter of a mill worker, and the murders were

among her earliest memories, one of life's ugly little realities that people simply lived with.

The horror of the thing now had Pete by the throat. He could barely talk. "Where's Beswick?" he managed.

"I don't know. It's strange—he never showed up this morning. After the sheriff's office called to tell us about Terry, I called Wade's house, thinking I should let him know there's been another killing. Nancy answered the phone—that's Wade's wife—"

"I know. Nice lady. I wonder what the hell she sees in him."

"She sounded really upset. She hasn't seen him since yesterday. He never even came home last night."

"Has he ever done anything like this in the past?"

"Not since I've been here. I've seen him come to work with a hangover and smelling bad—when he drinks, he goes to some bar in Portland, I'm told—but I can't remember him not showing up at all, not without calling in."

"There's probably nothing to worry about. I'm sure there's a good reason he's not here."

"Hey, I'm not worried—" She glanced at the floor. "I mean, you're right. He's probably got a good reason for not being here." Now she looked Pete in the eye. "Mr. Cochran, I want to thank you for what you did day before yesterday. I appreciate you saying what you said to Wade, about keeping his hands off Megan and me, about treating us with respect."

Pete shook his head. "Don't thank me, Denise. I behaved badly. I was lucky the sheriff didn't haul me off to jail."

"No, I need to thank you. Someone should've said these things a long time ago."

He smiled, then pushed through the door into his office. He started to remove his raincoat but saw something in the corner of his eye, movement, a face and body. He whirled to confront a tall, muscular woman standing behind the door, her hands coiled into fists. Pete gulped air and didn't let it out until he realized that she was Dr. Vonda Reuben.

"Vonda, you gave me a start," he said, trying to chuckle, failing. "Denise didn't tell me there was anyone waiting for me."

"That's because she doesn't know I'm here. Nobody does. I came in through a hole in the fence up by the boilers and sneaked in through the back door as soon as Wally MacKenzie opened up this morning."

"Are you saying you've been here four and a half hours—sitting in this office, all alone?"

"I needed to see you, and I expected you to show up before now. Some people come to work before noon, you know."

Pete put a hand on his desk to steady himself and sat down slowly. He took out a handkerchief and pressed it to his forehead, then to the back of his neck. He looked up at his guest. Her large face was hard as granite. She wore her customary baggy jeans, but had tucked her long, gray hair into a brimmed rain hat instead of letting it hang down her back.

"What's this all about, Vonda? Couldn't you've called, left a message or something?"

"I needed to talk to you face-to-face. It's not the kind of thing I can leave with your secretary."

"Look, you've caught me at a bad time. Maybe we can get together for lunch or something and . . ."

"To hell with that. This won't take long." She approached the desk and loomed over him, her fists on her hips. "Leave town," she said. "Take your kids and leave town today, now, the sooner the better. Buckthorn isn't a good place for you."

"What are you talking about?"

"You don't understand the Queen's English? I'll say

it again. Take your family and leave Buckthorn. It's what's best for you, believe me.''

Pete sat stunned, his mouth open. How many times in the past two weeks had he whispered the same advice to himself? He cleared his throat, got his voice under control. ''I'm afraid it's not that easy,'' he said. ''I've made a commitment to Tucker and this company. I can't just run out on him.''

''What's more important—your commitment to Tucker or the well-being of your children? Now listen to me, Peter Cochran, and listen carefully. The best thing you could do for your kids is drive into Paulsen, pick them up at school, hit the road and never look back. I'm telling you this because you seem like a nice man, and I like you. You and your kind don't belong here. Buckthorn is an ugly place, and if you stay, the ugliness will rub off on you. I've seen it happen. It's happened to me. Now *go*, damn it! Don't sit around thinking about it— just *go*!''

Pete shook his head. ''I can't. I wish I could, but I can't.''

''You mean you won't. If you really wanted to, you could walk out that door right now. I don't see any shackles around your ankles. I don't see anyone holding a gun on you.''

''What am I supposed to do? If I walked out that door, like you say I should, who do you think would hire me, with my work history? How do you suggest I feed my son and my daughter while I'm out there on the road?''

''I didn't come here to counsel you on a career change. I came to give you some advice that could save your family. There's evil in this town—you've probably felt it, if you're a normal, breathing human being. There's corruption and bigotry here. There's killing . . .''

Evil. Esmerelda had used the same word not half an hour ago.

". . . and if I were you, I'd be so worried about my kids that I'd never sleep nights."

Pete got to his feet. "What are you saying? Are you suggesting that Sarah and Carter are in physical danger?"

Vonda's face hardened. "I can only tell you this. The evil has changed, entered a new phase. No one can say who it'll strike next. Believe me, you and your kids don't want to be here to find out who it'll be."

She whirled and strode for the door of his office. Pulling it open, she turned back to him for a parting shot. "Trust me on this, Peter Cochran, and you'll thank me someday. Take your kids and go."

17

I

TUCKER BANNON FINISHED HIS INTERVIEWS WITH COPS and reporters, then met for prayer with Pastor Roysden and his delegation of coreligionists. He left for home without so much as poking his head into Pete's office to say hello, which gave Pete pause to wonder about the state of relations with his father-in-law. Denise Ubaldo went home soon afterward, leaving only Pete and Wally MacKenzie on the premises. Pete switched the telephones off, went back to his own desk and sat with his chin on his fists. The silence of the mill weighed on him, made him uneasy.

Shortly after 4:00, Wally opened Pete's door and leaned against the frame, a coffee mug in his hand. "You ought to go home," he said. "You look like you could use some rest."

"So do you," Pete replied. "I won't rat on you if you take off early."

"Nah. My little old house is pretty lonesome, now that Lucille's gone. I may as well stay and get some work done." Pete marveled that despite the lapsing of twenty years since their divorce, Wally still loved his Lucille.

"Let me get your opinion on something, Wally. Do you think that Vonda Reuben is—well, you know, a little . . ." He made a fluttery gesture with his hand.

"Vonda Reuben?" Wally stiffened. "What made you think of *her*?"

"She was here today. Sneaked in this morning right after you unlocked the doors, she said, and waited for me here in my office. She hid behind my door and almost gave me a stroke when I came in.''

Wally fidgeted, thought a moment. ''Vonda Reuben's a strange one, no doubt about that. She might be a tad crazy, I don't know.'' Talking about her seemed to make him uncomfortable. ''Some think she's got a screw loose, others think she's a witch of some kind. Wade's convinced she's a lesbian.''

''A witch? Why would anyone think that?''

Wally took off his glasses and rubbed his tired eyes. ''No good reason, except people like to believe weird things about those who seem out of the ordinary. Vonda lives alone, no man in her life. And she messes with herbs and potions, old folk remedies, stuff like that. The people of Buckthorn have always been a superstitious bunch, with all the talk about the Mad Witch and so forth, so I s'pose it's no surprise that they have their suspicions about Vonda.''

''The Mad Witch? What's that all about?''

Wally recounted the legend of the Mad Witch of Olivet, the recluse who'd lived on the mountain owned by Tucker Bannon's father, Noah. Back in 1934, the story went, she'd stood her ground against a logging crew sent to harvest the ancient stand of forest that grew there. Some no-brain logger had hit her in the head with an ax, and she'd died a few hours later. According to local lore, her ghost had harassed the logging crew and driven them off the mountain before they could fell a single tree.

''She supposedly appeared several times to Noah himself over the years,'' Wally went on, ''especially whenever he got it into his mind to start harvesting trees on that mountain. The old folks say she's the reason that no logging crew has been up there since the day she died. Every now and then somebody says he's seen her sneaking around in the woods, keeping an eye on whatever's happening at Bannon House. It's all just superstitious claptrap, you understand."

Pete fought an insane notion—*just superstitious claptrap*. He blinked, tried not to look unnerved.

"Uh—what does she look like, this Mad Witch of Olivet?" he asked.

"What does she look like?" Wally stared at him quizzically. "Well, I can't say I've seen her myself . . ." He gave a nervous giggle. "I hear tell she was a pretty woman in her day, light hair, nice figure. Folks who've seen her say she wears a long white dress. Why do you ask—have you seen her, too?" He giggled again to show that he was joking.

Pete relived the dream he'd had on his first night in Bannon House—standing on the second-floor landing of the rear stairs, staring out through a tall window into the night. Seeing a woman in the wood line, her long dress flowing in the breeze. The way she carried herself . . . so much like Sally . . .

Only a dream.

Which was more absurd? he wondered now—the notion that he'd seen his dead wife, or the notion that he'd caught a glimpse of the Mad Witch of Olivet?

"Pete—*Pete*, are you okay?" Wally approached the desk and stared down at Pete, his eyes round with concern.

"I'm okay. Gathering wool, I guess. I just need—" What did he need? He didn't know.

"You ought to go home and get some rest, buddy. Don't worry about locking up here. I'll take care of it."

"Thanks, Wally. I'll do that."

As he left the head shed, he thought about his kids, Sarah and Carter. By now they'd arrived home from school. If he wanted to, he could swoop them up with

a few packed bags and hit the road, as Vonda Reuben
had urged. Neither Tucker nor Dolly could stop him, he
knew. *Nobody* could stop him, if this was what he
wanted.

But how could he explain such a move to Sarah and
Carter, who had already suffered severe disruptions of
their lives, the loss of their mother, leaving the only
home they'd ever known? What could he tell them that
would make any sense to them? He couldn't admit that
he was afraid that the Buckthorn killer would get them,
because a father doesn't tell young children such things.
In truth he was more afraid of what Topper might do to
them—Topper, the kid who burned live rats while jack-
ing off, who saw a shrink twice a week because the
school district feared he was dangerous. Pete couldn't
see himself telling his children about *that*, either.

In the few weeks since arriving in Buckthorn, Sarah
and Carter had come to feel comfortable here, that much
was clear. They'd come to love their grandparents,
which troubled Pete in a visceral way. Already Bannon
House had become their home.

Both children still showed some symptoms of the
emotional wrenching they'd endured during the past six
months, especially Carter, whose behavior in recent days
had seemed downright manic. Pete tried to imagine
dragging his children away from their new home and
their grandparents, unable to explain why or even to tell
them where they were going. What would this do to
them? he wondered.

He got into his Cherokee, started it and drove through
the front gate of Buckthorn Wood Products. Instead of
proceeding straight on Main Street to Bannon Avenue,
which would have taken him back to the stately house
on the hill, he turned left on Nehalem, then right on
Front Street. He parked at the curb in front of the *Nehalem County Renegade* and walked to the front door.

He needed to see Nita.

He pushed against the glass door, found it locked. Darkness inside. He thought of pounding his fist on the glass, decided not to. He backed away, looked up to the second-floor windows of her apartment, saw darkness there, too.

Nita wasn't home.

II

THE PARKING LOT BEHIND THE NEHALEM COUNTY Courthouse was full of reporters' vehicles. The reporters themselves, together with sound and video technicians, had taken shelter from the drizzle in the vestibule of the sheriff's office, where they jostled and smoked while waiting for any announcement concerning the investigation of the latest Buckthorn killing.

Nita Vale circled the lot on her mountain bike, saw the congestion and decided that she knew a better way. She walked her bike up the front steps of the courthouse and locked it to the handrail just outside the front door. Her right foot still hurt. A glance at her watch told her that the building wouldn't close for another forty-five minutes, at 6:00 P.M., but even then the doors would be locked only to those outside. Like most other rural courthouses in Oregon, this one had no on-site security guards. At closing time the county commissioners' secretary simply closed up and went home.

The foyer provided no public access to the police department or the sheriff's office, which was why no reporters had laid siege here. Nita walked into the county commissioners' front office and greeted the receptionist, who smiled and said hi. Nita was a regular around the courthouse, always looking for some tidbit on local gov-

ernment to print in the *Renegade*. She asked to use the
bathroom, because the public john downstairs was full
of reporters, she said. The receptionist rolled her eyes,
knowing how it is, and waved her through the fold-up
door in the counter into a rear hallway.

Nita walked past the lavatory door and down a flight
of stairs, which she knew led to a dark corridor in the
basement. Signs on the doors announced the furnace
room, machine shop, custodial supplies, storage. Another door opened into a cramped, dingy coffee room
that served both the sheriff's office and the police department. Nita had been here before, most recently with
Dan Kantor, when she and he were still an item. She
knew that the coffee room had a telephone equipped
with an intercom. Luckily, the place was empty of
cops.

She picked up the phone and punched Kantor's ex-
tension number, half-expecting that he wouldn't answer.
He wasn't the kind of investigator who sat at his desk.
He had a crime scene to process, a suspect to interrogate.

But he *did* answer. "Kantor."

"Daniel, it's me—Nita. How're things?"

"Nita—uh . . ." He sounded discombobulated. Nita's
was undoubtedly the last voice he'd expected to hear.
"Where are you calling from? You're not in the building, are you?"

"Promise not to get mad? I'm in your coffee room.
Got a few minutes?"

"Jesus. How did you—? Never mind. Be there in a
sec."

Kantor walked into the coffee room, sat down at the
table with her. Shaking his head, he said, "I love small-
town departments. They don't stand on ceremony, and
they don't waste resources on extravagances like security." He lit a cigarette. "Care to tell me how you got
in?"

She told him, and he tried not to smile. He blew smoke over her head.

"So. To what do I owe this pleasure?" he asked.

"I wanted to see you, find out how you are. I haven't really felt good about the way you and I left things, you know? I felt like it was a little—abrupt."

"It was your show. I was just an innocent bystander."

"I know. I can see how you might've felt like I was—cold about it. I'm sorry, Daniel, I really am. After this latest killing, I started to worry about you. I know how committed you were to catching the guy before he got anyone else, and I—"

"Nita, let's not do this dance, okay?" The hopeful light she'd seen in his eyes flickered out. "We both know why you're here. You're either covering the Grimes killing for your paper, or you've decided not to abandon your book project after all and you're here collecting material."

Nita stifled a cough. The cigarette smoke was killing her. "Okay," she said. "If that's what you think, I guess I can't do anything about it. I won't waste any more of your time." She gathered herself to leave, but Kantor held up his hand.

"Don't go. I've just come back from Portland, where I watched Terry Grimes's autopsy, and autopsies always make me a little owly. Seeing you in Lycra is just what I need." They both smiled, and the light came back into his eyes. This was good—keep him hoping. "Let me buy you a cup of law-enforcement coffee. I could probably even rustle up a doughnut—you need some carbs to get you home, right? Dressed like that, I figure you rode your bike all the way up here from Buckthorn."

She accepted coffee but refused the doughnut. Kantor tamped out his cigarette.

"I believe in rewarding initiative," he said. "Go ahead and ask me about the Grimes killing, and I'll tell you whatever I'd tell any other reporter, except it'll be your exclusive because I've already said all I'm going to say to the press for the foreseeable future—*unless* I catch the killer, that is, in which case all bets are off.''

Nita took a pencil and pad from her fanny pack. "I didn't come here just to work the Grimes story," she said with as much sincerity as she could muster. "I really have been worried about you. But since you insist on being cynical . . ." She sat forward in her chair, all business now. "The word's out that you arrested Jerry Dragstead this morning. You don't really think he could be the killer, do you?"

"He's a person of interest, that's all. He was with the victim shortly before the crime happened."

"*With* the victim? What do you mean?"

Kantor explained what he'd learned from the service station operator in Scappoose. He'd spent much of the day grilling Dragstead, hoping that Dragstead might have seen, heard or intuited something helpful while he was in Grimes's company. So far, no soap. Dragstead would admit only that he gave Terry Grimes a lift to a service station and back to his pickup. He'd forcefully denied any connection with Grimes's death or even that he'd gone into Grimes's mobile home for a beer.

"So, do you plan to release him?"

"Maybe yes, maybe no. In any event, I can't keep him much longer unless I charge him. You know that."

"But Dragstead couldn't possibly be the killer. He was under tight surveillance when three consecutive killings took place. There's no way he could've . . ."

Again Kantor held his hand up. "Please, Nita—I know all about the old Dragstead Detail. They were watching Jerry when killings were going down back in 'eighty-three and 'eighty-six and 'eighty-nine, and they verified that he wasn't the guy. At least that's what they thought at the time."

"And there's reason to think different now?"

Kantor explained that one of his investigators, Bob Esparza, had pored over the record of the Dragstead Detail and had found some ambiguities. The cops who'd tailed Jerry Dragstead hadn't declared that he couldn't *possibly* have committed the killings, only that they had good reason to believe that he was home in bed when the killings occurred. They had followed him to his house, staked it out. They hadn't seen—

Kantor stopped himself. Nita saw in his face that he hadn't intended to tell her this much.

"If you want, we can go off the record," she said.

Kantor exhaled a long breath and rubbed his lips with a nicotine-stained finger. "Okay, off the record. I wouldn't do this for anyone else, you know."

Nita smiled her sweetest, saw his heart melt.

"Esparza says it's theoretically possible that Dragstead could've gotten out of his house without the detail knowing it. There's a lot of junk around his place, stacked firewood, old cars and stuff. Esparza's been over there scoping it out, and he thinks maybe Dragstead snuck out through the back and low-crawled to the tree line at the rear of his lot. Once he got back there, he could've gone his merry way and none of the cops would've known. He could've gotten back in the same way."

"Come on, Daniel. You don't really believe that."

"Hey, I check out every possibility, no matter how crazy it sounds."

Nita shook her head. "I feel sorry for you if Dragstead is all you've got. He has a history, yes, but you've got a drawer full of cops' statements saying he isn't the killer. If you ask me, that's a lot of baggage."

Kantor gazed at her a long moment, his hand darting toward his breast pocket for a cigarette, but halting. He decided not to have another just yet. "We're still off the record, right? Strictly for old time's sake?"

"Strictly for old time's sake."

"I've got more than Dragstead—which is why I'm sitting here calm and collected instead of bouncing off the walls. But it stays in this room, Nita. If it gets out and the killer gets wind of it, we're up Shit Creek without a trolling motor."

Nita felt her cheeks flush. She nodded.

Kantor's people had found footprints at the home of Terry Grimes, footprints that the killer had left. Even as he and Nita were speaking, a team of FBI technicians were getting soil samples and imprints in plaster casts. The technicians would take the samples and the casts back to Quantico, where another team of forensic anthropologists, orthopods and computer nerds would develop a physical profile of the killer, using a program created specifically for that purpose. Within days Kantor expected to know the height and weight of the Buckthorn killer, and maybe a great deal more. This was quite possibly the first major break in the history of the case, he ventured.

Nita gripped her pencil tightly, felt the point dig into her palm. The pain must have registered on her face, because Kantor asked if she was all right. Of course, she answered—the smoke in the room had made her woozy, that's all.

"That's it, then," Kantor said. "I've told you all I'm going to. I'd love to sit here and chat all evening, but I'm a busy man—places to go, people to see." He grinned and rose from the table. Nita rose with him.

"I'll leave the way I came," she said, moving toward the door that led to the rear stairs. "I don't want to run into the Cigar and have to explain what I'm doing here."

"Good thinking. By the way, I see you're walking a little stiffly. Foot still bothering you?"

She admitted that it was. Time to see a doctor, she supposed—a real doctor who would take X rays, prescribe pills, the whole deal. The herbal mixture given her by a naturopath friend just hadn't worked.

Kantor told her to take it easy. He started to say something else, perhaps suggest they get together for lunch sometime, a hopeful venture toward recapturing whatever they'd lost. But he held back. Nita was glad and pushed through the door toward the rear stairs before he could muster the courage.

18

I

THE GRAY-FLANNEL WOMAN HAD REGISTERED AS Stella LeHand at the spendy resort hotel in Monterey's Cannery Row and had paid cash for a room that fronted glistening Monterey Bay. She stood inside the glass door that separated the bedroom from the deck, her lips puckered around a short pipe full of cat. She inhaled deeply, held the acrid smoke in as long as she could bear it, and blew it out again, detonating stingers of light against her closed eyelids.

The high hit her immediately, a tingling flare that sharpened her senses and cleared her mind of all grayness. She opened her eyes and saw a pair of gulls jockeying for space atop a weathered piling that protruded from the water below, nipping at each other with their vicious beaks. Nasty birds, gulls—always feuding and fighting, always looking for an angle, totally ruthless with one another. A lot like the people Stella knew. A lot like herself.

The phone rang. Avis delivery for Mr. Verduin, a Mustang convertible.

"I'll tell him," Stella promised the clerk in her low, smoky voice. She'd rented the car with Verduin's Visa card, since rental car companies wouldn't take cash. "We'll pick up the keys at the desk," she added, and hung up the phone.

She went out to the deck and stood a moment in the fresh California sunshine, letting the drug take her on a carnival ride. The gulls stared back at her from their perch on the piling, and one of them meowed like a cat. Staggering away from the rail, Stella told herself that it was a small hallucination brought on by the dope, that it would pass. And it did.

She went inside to the mirror, straightened her expensive gray flannel suit, checked her makeup and her platinum hair. Not quite beautiful, she admitted to herself, but serviceable. Age had begun to coarsen her features, a fact that would have depressed her under any other circumstances. But not today, not with the cat racing through her pipes. In fact, the sagging lines of age would enhance her mission, make her more believable.

Everything was *sssmokin'*.

She drove the Seventeen-Mile Drive to Carmel with the top down, past dazzling ocean scenery, palatial homes and the ultra-exclusive Pebble Beach Country Club. Carmel was a quaint hive nestled in cypress and pine, bumper-to-bumper with tourists, a strutting ground for the rich. She found the address of Dr. Norman Jorganson on a shady street six blocks off the main drag and parked between a Mercedes and a Bentley.

Jorganson was a blond man of forty, lanky like a swimmer and tan like a movie star. Stella wondered if he'd been born with these looks or if he'd gotten them at the hands of a fellow cosmetic surgeon. Instead of a lab coat or a suit he wore a red golf shirt with an alligator embroidered on the front and Italian loafers with tassels. He seated her in his private office and asked how he could help.

"I'm tired of my face," Stella told him. "My life has begun to change for the better, and I love it—money, success, a relationship—everything I've hoped and worked for. But my face just doesn't seem to fit my new life, Doctor. I look in the mirror and I see the old me. I see a miserable failure who's becoming more wrinkled and saggy every day, and I want something different. I want a face that fits the *new* me."

"Actually, Ms. LeHand, you have a very nice face. I'm sure people have told you this."

"Oh, they have. And I appreciate your saying so."

"Aesthetic surgery isn't something to be undertaken lightly. Normally, I don't agree to take on anyone who I don't believe I can improve. In your case . . ."

"But I'm not necessarily looking to become *beautiful*, Doctor. I just want to be different than I am now, a little younger-looking, a little less *worn*. Is that so horrible?"

Jorganson smiled, having heard the plea before. He pulled a wheeled lamp next to Stella's chair, snapped it on and studied her face. He allowed that rhinoplasty might be of some efficacy, in order to remove the small bump on the bridge of her nose and create a more feminine contour. It would be an out-patient procedure, utilizing a mild sedative and a local anesthetic. He would make incisions inside her nostrils, through which he would chisel out the excess cartilage. Following the surgery, he would apply a splint made of plastic and tape in order to maintain the new shape until healing was complete. He'd done the procedure countless times, and he was optimistic that it would improve her appearance.

"But I want more than a nose job, Doctor," Stella said. "I want different cheekbones. I want to be rid of these crow's feet and these strings that are starting to show up under my jaw. I want younger-looking eyes. I want . . ."

Jorganson drew back, studied her face from this angle and that angle, frowning. "Ms. LeHand, I hope you know what you're asking. A total change of appearance invariably carries with it a profound emotional impact. It affects your sense of who you are. I'd need to be certain that you're strong enough emotionally to handle the enormity of it. Also I'd need to make sure that . . .''

"I'm not running from the law, Doctor. You won't find my picture on any wanted posters.'' They both laughed. "I just need to make a new start, that's all. Money isn't a problem for me, I can assure you of that.''

Jorganson still didn't seem convinced that radical cosmetic surgery would be good for her. Most cosmetic surgeons, he said, undertook such ambitious efforts only for those who had suffered extreme disfigurement through accident or disease.

Time to set the hook, Stella told herself. She mentioned her friend, Rosa Sandoval, who herself had been a patient of Dr. Jorganson seven years ago. Rosa had recommended Dr. Jorganson enthusiastically.

"She tells me that you gave her a totally new face. And I must say, you made her beautiful. I'm not asking you to do for me what you did for her, only that you give me a new start.''

"Seven years ago, you say? I can't say I remember the name.''

"Rosa said you would have before and after pictures of her in her file.''

"Yes, of course. I take photos of all my patients at every stage of their treatment and keep them for the record. It's always nice to have tangible evidence of what we're able to achieve in each case.''

Not to mention legal documentation if someone hates her new nose and tries to sue your dong off, Stella thought. "Would it be too much trouble,'' she asked, "to see those pictures? Rosa said that I would be amazed.''

Jorganson looked troubled. "The photos we take are confidential material, Ms. LeHand. I normally don't show them without written permission from the patients.''

"But Rosa *sent* me to you, Doctor. She wants me to see the kind of miracle you worked on her."

The surgeon thought a moment, weighing the potential liabilities. "I suppose it would be all right, just this once. What did you say her name was?"

"Rosa J. Sandoval. I believe she consulted you seven years ago."

Jorganson buzzed an assistant on the intercom and ordered Rosa Sandoval's file sent. Then he excused himself in order to check on other patients and return phone calls. A few minutes later he reappeared, holding two four-by-five glossies in one hand, a manila file folder in the other.

"Here she is—Ms. Rosa Juanita Sandoval, before and after. And you were correct, Ms. LeHand, the change in her appearance is dramatic. I've reviewed her file, and I must tell you that the procedures we used in her case were quite radical, not to mention time-consuming and costly. Moreover, you can see that she changed her hair color and began using tinted contact lenses."

Stella stared at the two photographs and wondered for a moment whether they showed the same woman. Jorganson wasn't exaggerating—the difference was astonishing. On the left was the swarthy Rosa Sandoval, a dark and handsome woman with intense brown eyes. On the right was someone Stella had never seen before, a woman whose golden-haired beauty was almost Nordic, whose eyes were a glacial blue.

She placed the pictures on Jorganson's desk, side by side. Then with easy matter-of-factness she stood and pulled a miniature Minox camera from her shoulder bag. Before Jorganson could protest, she hunched over the desk and shot six quick pictures of Rosa Sandoval's before and after photos.

"Thank you, Doctor," she said, glancing up at Jorganson, who stared at her with his mouth open. "You've been very helpful. I won't take up any more of your time."

Leaving the bewildered surgeon at his desk, Stella walked out into the spring sunshine, got into her rented Mustang, and drove back to Monterey. Before nightfall, she was sitting in a comfortable first-class seat on a flight to Portland.

II

DARKNESS CALLS AND SETTLES INTO BUCKTHORN LIKE an uninvited guest. Vengeance waits in the deep shadow at the rear of the ruined Allegro Theater, breathing the night, listening, watching. It leans against the wall and feels the bite of old bricks against its shoulder blades. It clutches a bundle to its chest, a grocery sack that contains a pair of Nike running shoes.

An occasional car or truck rolls past on Main Street, tires hissing over wet asphalt. The feeble street lights offer no threat. The threat, Vengeance knows, lies deep within itself, a long-suppressed hunger to throw caution to the wind and run amuck, to sate itself at long last without regard to the consequences.

It moves to the rear door of the old theater and muscles it open, squeezes through. Total darkness here, cold and humid. The stink of old wood and rot. Plenty of fuel around, probably enough to burn down the whole damn block—which wouldn't be much of a loss, since the only operating business on the block is Bertinello's Antiques, and who the hell would miss *that*? And who would miss Candy Bertinello, the dried-up old coyote who owns the place?

Vengeance feels its way through the backstage area of the abandoned theater into the auditorium, where it drops the paper grocery sack to the floor and flicks on a penlight. The beam plays across a high, dangerously concave ceiling, over peeling walls and the rows of devastated seats. The cinema screen looms near, a gray expanse of nothingness punctuated by rips and smears.

Vengeance crouches, opens the grocery sack and pulls out the shoes. It takes a quart-size plastic bottle from its backpack, twists off the cap, douses the shoes with gasoline. This done, it gropes around in the darkness for more fuel, which it piles over the gasoline-soaked shoes—moldering cardboard, pieces of crumbly carpet, wadded paper, upholstery stuffing. It rises, stands back and digs for matches.

A match flares, and Vengeance tosses it onto the pile, watches the fire take root with a soft *poof*! Flames dance and twist, causing Vengeance's spirit to soar, for fire can cause such exquisite pain. *Pain cleanses. Pain releases the soul from sin.*

Maybe this is the only hope for Buckthorn, Vengeance says to itself, watching the flames eat into the filthy carpet and begin to spread. If Buckthorn could burn to the ground—not merely the buildings but also the brutish folks who wallow here in their hopelessness—then maybe the town could become worthy of salvation. The agony of fire might enable Buckthorn to atone for having embraced the demon.

But alas, Vengeance knows that it can't burn the whole town. The best it can do is inflict the torment at which it has become so adept these past fifteen years. And even if the hunger overrides Vengeance's customary caution and causes it to make a mistake that brings its reign to an end, as nearly happened with the taking of Terry Grimes, even then, Vengeance will consider its life a grand success.

III

SATURDAY MORNING. ESMERELDA'S GOOD WAFFLES.
Strong coffee, strong sunlight.

Pete sat across the dining room table from Tucker,
who seemed uncharacteristically quiet this morning. The
kids had eaten breakfast already and had gone their separate ways, Carter to the third-floor playroom to watch
cartoons on TV, Sarah to her room, presumably to work
on this or that writing project. Dolly and Topper had yet
to appear.

It's time, Pete said to himself, *to tell Tucker that we're
leaving Buckthorn.*

But before he could speak, the front doorbell chimed.
A moment later Esmerelda entered the dining room and
addressed Tucker. *"Varios policía estan en la puerta,
Señor Bannon. Quieren hablar con el Señor Cochran."*

Tucker stared quizzically across the table at Pete, the
red mole over his eyebrow twitching. *"Los recibiremos
en el estudio,"* he said to Esmerelda. Then to Pete: "The
police are here to see you. I told Esmerelda to show
them into my study. Any idea what this is about?"

Pete didn't have a clue and said so.

In the study they found Sheriff Nick Graybill himself,
flush-faced and resplendent in his tight uniform, accompanied by two of his deputies and a skinny detective
from the Oregon State Police. Graybill and Tucker
shook hands, asked after each other's families. They
were obviously cronies.

The sheriff became abruptly serious. He approached
Pete and held up a Ziploc freezer bag, which contained
a Mont Blanc pen. "Mr. Cochran, do you recognize
this?"

Pete squinted at it, saw his own named engraved on

the gold-plated clip. He confessed that it belonged to
him. "My wife bought it for me in Switzerland three or
four years ago," he said. "I haven't seen it for a couple
of days, thought I'd misplaced it. How did you get it?"
He reached for the bag, but Graybill pulled it back.

"Mr. Cochran, would you mind telling us where you
were on the night of April fifth?"

Pete thought a moment, his gut tickling. "Right here,
I guess, all evening. I went to bed early, as I recall.
What's this about, anyway? How did you get my pen?"

The sheriff asked to see Pete's car. Tucker led them
out to the garage, buzzed the doors open. Inside stood
Tucker's Suburban, Pete's Cherokee and Dolly's Buick.
The OSP detective went immediately to the Cherokee,
opened its doors, and began scouring the interior with a
flashlight. A moment later he called to Graybill, motioned him over. They studied the inner panel of the
driver's door.

"Is that what I think it is?" Graybill asked the detective.

"If you think it's blood, I'd say you're right. The lab
will tell us for sure. I'll make casts of the tires."

Graybill approached Pete again, his thumbs hooked
into his gun belt. "Mr. Cochran, would you mind taking
a ride with us over to Paulsen? We'd like to talk to you
about the murder of Wade Beswick, find out exactly
what you know."

Pete's heart tried to climb into his throat. "The murder of . . ."

"Wade's dead?" Tucker asked.

"Couple of hikers found him late yesterday afternoon
on an old logging road south of town," Graybill explained. "He'd been shot, execution-style. The medical
examiner thinks he was killed late Tuesday or early
Wednesday. We found Mr. Cochran's pen at the scene."

"Wait just a damn minute," Pete said. "You can't

possibly think that I had anything to do with this.''

"Right now we don't know what to think, Mr. Cochran. That's why we want you to come up to the station with us.''

"Is he under arrest?'' Tucker asked.

"Not yet. We'll also want to interview everyone in your household, Tuck, including yourself, in order to get a clear picture of Mr. Cochran's comings and goings Tuesday night and Wednesday morning. We need to . . .''

"For Christ's sake!'' Pete shouted. "I *told* you where I was on Tuesday night. I was right here! Tell him, Tucker. I had dinner with the family and went to bed early. We had your homemade ice cream for dessert, remember? I was exhausted for some reason, couldn't keep my eyes open. I went straight to bed and didn't get up till almost noon the next day.''

Graybill caught Pete by the arm, held him. "There's no reason to get excited, Mr. Cochran . . .'' The two deputies quickly took positions on either side of him, and Pete saw that he did indeed have reason to get excited. He saw it in Graybill's eyes, in the eyes of the deputies. These people thought he was a murderer.

IV

TUCKER STOOD WITH HIS FAMILY IN THE FRONT DRIVE of Bannon House, one arm around Sarah, the other around Carter. The morning sun felt good on his shoulders, and the air was sweet with spring. The only flaw in an otherwise perfect morning was the pillar of dirty gray smoke that rose from the center of town. The old Allegro Theater had burned last night, and the flames had spread to Bertinello's Antiques. The Nehalem County Volunteer Fire Department had fought the fire through most of the night, but without success.

The six of them—Tucker, Dolly, Esmerelda, Topper, Sarah and Carter—watched the two sheriff's cars proceed slowly down the drive to the front gate, saw the gate swing open. A moment later the cars were gone, and with them, Peter Cochran. Things had begun to fall nicely into place.

Thank you, Lord.

He glanced at the kids, saw that their cheeks were wet with tears, which was only natural, he supposed. Seeing their father taken away by police was a traumatic thing, no question about it. But they would get over it. Tucker would give them a future so bright that the memory of their godless father would fade from their hearts like a dying sunset. They would take their place in this house as true Bannons, as worthy heirs to the lands and the fortune that the Lord had bestowed upon this noble family.

Tucker's cellular phone rang. It was Todd Verduin. He was on the Sunset Highway, about half an hour out of Buckthorn. He had something to show Tucker, something major: pictures of the new Rosa Juanita Sandoval.

"I'll be waiting," Tucker said, switching off the phone.

Thank you, Lord, at long last . . .

V

HE RECEIVED VERDUIN IN HIS DOWNSTAIRS STUDY. when he saw the photographs, his eyes widened and the mole on his brow buried itself in a wrinkle.

"You know this woman?" Verduin asked.

"Yes. I know her. And I know where she is."

"Then my work here is finished."

"No, Todd. Wait." He turned away from his desk

and wandered toward his gun cabinet, leaned against it. He stared out the window across the front lawn to the town below, where the pillar of gray smoke rose high into the sky. "I need your help. I'll make it worth your while."

"I hope you're not talking about getting more of the Lord's justice. That's not the kind of thing I want to make a habit of, Tucker."

"I'm talking about survival. This woman could bring ruination to me and my family."

"How?"

"She knows things about me—old things, old sins. I don't doubt she's capable of trying to blackmail me. Someday she'll expose me out of pure hatred, I'm certain. I can't live with that threat, Todd."

"I don't see how this is any of my business."

"Oh, but it *is* your business. You certainly don't want anything to happen to me, do you?"

"No, of course not. It's just that . . ."

"You see, I consider you my partner, Todd. What's good for me is good for you, and vice versa. If I continue to prosper, then so do you. But if I go down for any reason, well—I'm afraid the same happens to you. You understand what I'm saying, don't you, Todd?" Tucker watched Verduin's smooth face turn ashen.

"You want me to kill her, is that it?"

"As I said, I'll make it worth your while. *Partner.*"

19

I

THE HOLDING CELL IN THE NEHALEM COUNTY SHERIFF'S
Office was five feet by eight feet, a box of concrete
block amply littered with graffiti—Peter Cochran had
seen bigger closets. The furnishings included a stainless-
steel toilet basin, an overhead light bulb encased in
heavy wire, a cot and nothing else.

He sat on the cot, a blanket pulled tight around his
shoulders, staring at the toilet because he had nothing
else to look at. No magazines, no books, no radio or TV.
Claustrophobia occasionally overwhelmed him, and he
needed to bite his fist to keep from screaming. Mostly
he endured by screwing his eyes shut and envisioning
the faces of his children.

Until now he'd never seen the inside of a jail cell.
His criminal record consisted of a speeding citation on
the New Jersey Turnpike and assorted parking tickets.
The fact that he was a *murder* suspect seemed surreal,
a nightmare from which he struggled to wake but
couldn't.

He wondered what time it was, for the sheriff's deputies had relieved him of his watch, along with his wal-
let, his belt, his keys and his shoelaces before locking
him up. The cell had no windows except for a hinged
opening in the steel door that let his jailers look in from
time to time, probably to ensure that he hadn't figured
out a way to kill himself. Without windows or a clock,
Pete could only guess about how long he'd been here—

at least twenty-four hours, he was certain, which surely must be near the limit that the authorities could hold him without charging him.

Okay, this is it, he thought. *First chance I get, I'm asking for a fucking lawyer. No more Mr. Nice Guy.*

Until now he'd declined the offer of legal counsel, for he was an innocent man with nothing to hide. He'd felt certain that he could convince the cops that he couldn't possibly be Wade Beswick's killer. After all, cops were reasonable people, right? They cared about the truth and common sense, right?

Wrong. Sheriff Graybill and his people thought Peter Cochran was a killer, period. No matter that Pete had no felony record, that he was an educated man and a solid citizen, an upstanding member of the business community. Any moron could have seen that he had no reason to kill Wade Beswick or anyone else, but Sheriff Graybill apparently wasn't just any moron.

Upon Pete's arrival at the sheriff's office, the cops had interrogated him for six hours straight, working in shifts, Pete sitting in a metal folding chair in the middle of an office not much bigger than the holding cell, staring into the lens of a camcorder on a tripod, answering the same questions over and over again. His legs had cramped, his back had stiffened, and he'd gotten a headache that had threatened to split his skull. The smoke from Graybill's cigar had reddened his eyes, made them smart and itch. *What time did you finish dinner on Tuesday night? . . . When did you leave the house? . . . How did you manage to get your Cherokee out of the garage without anyone hearing you? . . . What did you do with the gun? . . . When did you first decide to kill Wade Beswick? . . .*

They'd taken a half-hour break for lunch and had resumed for a second six-hour marathon, followed by a half-hour break for dinner, then two or three more hours' worth of the same mindless questions. The "sweating" had ended only when the cops themselves became too tired to go on.

Though exhausted himself, Pete had spent a near-sleepless night on the smelly cot. Whenever he'd closed his eyes, his mind had ground through the impossibilities that the cops had presented him, beginning with the fact that his Mont Blanc pen had turned up at the scene of Wade Beswick's murder, ending with an investigator finding a smear of blood inside his Cherokee. Impossibilities, yes—because Pete hadn't gone out Tuesday night or early Wednesday morning. He'd been fast asleep in his bed, almost as if he'd been drugged. He hadn't gotten out of bed until almost noon on Wednesday.

Impossibilities.

But the cops *had* found his pen near Beswick's body. And they *had* found blood inside his truck. Forensic analysis of tire prints and the blood would soon prove that the Cherokee had been at the murder scene, he had little doubt of that.

The conclusions were inescapable. Someone had stolen his Mont Blanc and left it at the scene of Beswick's murder. Possibly that same someone had stolen the Cherokee from the garage in Bannon House, driven it to the murder scene, and driven it back to the garage again. Someone had taken pains to make Peter Cochran look like Wade Beswick's killer. But *who*?

Who on God's green earth would do such a thing?

II

DAN KANTOR KNOCKED AND SAUNTERED INTO THE CI-gar's private office without waiting for an invitation. He lit a Marlboro, turned a chair backward and straddled it.

"Nick, how about you and I duck out of here and get some lunch, talk a little shop? I'll buy."

"Quit strokin' me, Kantor," Graybill growled, engrossed in his paperwork. "I don't remember asking you to come in here."

"I'm not here to stroke you, Nick. I'm looking for an excuse to give you some free advice, one professional to another."

"Gosh, that *is* nice of you, Lieutenant—you being the hotshot homicide cop and me being a Podunk county mountie. But you're too late. I've already got a state detective helping me on the Beswick case, so I don't need you."

Kantor grinned, exhaled smoke. "All I want to do is save you some embarrassment by suggesting that you let Pete Cochran go. He's not your man."

"Is that right? And what makes you so friggin' sure?"

"Nick, the guy is Mr. Good Citizen. I saw the NCIC report on him a minute ago, and he's got no sheet. He's a daddy with two kids and an MBA, for Christ's sake. You can tell he's innocent by looking him in the face."

Graybill bit on his cigar, which had gone out an hour ago. Patiently he explained that last Tuesday, in the offices of the Buckthorn sawmill, Mr. Good Citizen had beaten up Wade Beswick and had threatened to kill him in front of ten witnesses. Graybill himself had taken the statements and had even talked Wade out of pressing charges.

He picked up a file folder from a pile on his desk and waved it in Kantor's face. In it, he said, was a preliminary report from the state crime lab in Portland, confirming that the tires on Mr. Good Citizen's Jeep matched tire prints found at the Beswick death scene. Within the next day or two, Graybill expected a forensic toxicology report verifying that the blood found in the Jeep matched

the victim's. He waved another folder, which held statements taken yesterday from everyone who lived at Bannon House, including the Cochran kids. No one had seen
Pete Cochran from the time he went to bed on Tuesday
night until noon the next day when he showed up for
work.

"So you think he snuck out of the house, drove to
wherever Beswick was and popped him, is that it?"
Kantor asked.

"Works for me. I figure he made a side trip to ditch
the gun and maybe his clothes, if they got bloody.
We've got the pen he dropped at the scene. One of your
OSP hotshots took a statement from Wally MacKenzie,
who works with Cochran over at the mill, saying that
Cochran looked haggard and stressed-out when he
showed up for work on Wednesday. Now tell me you
wouldn't look haggard and stressed-out if you'd gone
out in the dead of night, tied up your boss with baling
wire and blown his head off."

Kantor rose from his chair, approached the Cigar's
desk, his grin dissolving. "Listen to me, Nick, for your
own fucking good. A man doesn't grow to the ripe age
of thirty-six, never once stepping out of line, having
gone off to college and grad school, having fathered two
kids and become a big-time executive, then suddenly
decide to blow his boss's head off. I don't know what
planet you're from, but it doesn't work that way on this
one. If Cochran was capable of cold-blooded murder, he
would've showed some sign of it before now, but he
hasn't. He's never mugged anyone, never bought or sold
drugs, never even stolen a hubcap. The fact is, Nick, this
guy's got no sheet and he's got no motive. You already
know that, but you're sweating him anyway, and that's
being an asshole."

The Cigar sat silent as stone, anger ripening his round
face. "So what the hell do you suggest I do, hotshot?"

"I suggest you immediately release the innocent man you've got in your holding cell before he sues the County of Nehalem and ends up owning this building, your house and all your bowling trophies. Then I'd get busy and start trying to re-create Wade Beswick's last hours on earth, find out where he went, who he went with, who saw him. Check the phone records over the past month, find out who he's been talking to. Talk to his wife and relatives, his friends, his minister. That's the key to solving murders, Nick—the victimology. Get to know the victim, where he was and what he was doing, and you'll find your killer."

Kantor tamped out his cigarette in Graybill's ashtray and walked back toward the door.

"Seems to me that if you're so friggin' smart," Graybill said to his back, "the Buckthorn killer wouldn't still be out there walkin' around free. Maybe you should take your own friggin' advice, huh?"

"I'll get the Buckthorn killer, Nick," Kantor answered. "And I'm going to get him soon. You wait and see."

III

AT 11:15 A.M. ON SUNDAY, APRIL 10, SHERIFF NICK GRAY-bill handed Pete Cochran a shoe box that contained his personal effects and told him to count his money before signing the release slip. Pete did so, found nothing missing, signed his name and said thanks.

"Wait a damn minute," the sheriff said. "I'm not through with you yet."

Pete took a deep breath. "Yes, Sheriff?"

Graybill pointed the mangled end of his cigar at him. "I want you to know that you haven't fooled anybody here, Mr. Cochran. I'm not sure why I'm letting you go like I am, because I've sent people to the slam with less than I've got on you.''

I'll bet you have, Pete thought, grinding his teeth.

Graybill put his cigar back in his mouth. ''Don't plan any long trips out of town. In fact, plan on making yourself real available to me until further notice, you understand?''

Pete nodded. He doubted whether Graybill had authority to restrict his movements without formally charging him, but he said nothing. He wanted only to get out of this hellhole and back to his kids. He went to the pay phone in the vestibule, meaning to call Tucker and ask for a ride home. Fierce sunlight poured through the glass doors that led to the parking lot, a golden blessing after the stifling holding cell. While digging in his pocket for a quarter, he saw media people loitering beyond the doors, their boom microphones at the ready, their portable cameras close at hand.

''They're covering the Buckthorn killer story,'' said someone behind him, and Pete turned to confront a lanky, dark-complected man with a hooked nose and closely cropped graying hair. ''You can bet your ass, though, that they'd be interested in *you*.'' He handed Pete the front page of the Sunday *Portland Oregonian*'s Metro section, which contained a prominent headline:

Mill official held in slaying of Buckthorn business leader

''Good God,'' Pete whispered, his eyes racing down the columns of the story. It was a lean recounting of his altercation with the deceased several days ago, the subsequent investigation and his detainment. An ex-executive of Patriot Mutual, the story called him. Recently moved from New York, a widower. Sheriff Nick Graybill had stated for the record that Peter Cochran wasn't actually the prime suspect, not yet—only a "person of extreme interest."

"They didn't leave out much, did they?" Pete said to the stranger. The guy wore a corduroy sport coat over neatly pressed khakis and penny loafers. Pete felt that he'd seen him somewhere before, maybe even met him.

"Only the fact that you didn't do it." The man put out his hand. "Lieutenant Dan Kantor, State Police."

Pete grabbed Kantor's hand with both of his. "You've made my day, Lieutenant. I'd just about given up on cops. You don't know how good it feels to find one who doesn't think I'm a cold-blooded killer." He now recognized Kantor from the TV documentary that Nita Vale had screened for him Monday evening—this was the head of the Buckthorn Task Force.

"Call me Dan," Kantor said. "I work homicide myself, though I'm not on the Beswick case."

"You're after the Buckthorn killer, right?"

"Right. Anyway, I read the file on you, saw your NCIC readout. It seems pretty obvious that you're not the killing type."

"NCIC?"

"National Crime Information Center. It's an on-line reference system run by the FBI. If you'd committed a felony during your adult life, NCIC would have known about it, and so would we."

Pete grinned sheepishly. "I appreciate your faith in me, but I wish Graybill shared it."

Faith wasn't a factor, Kantor replied. It was simply a matter of knowing a little about human behavior. He explained that a person almost never became a killer overnight. People who killed nearly always had criminal backgrounds and patterns of violence in their lives. They usually had records of chemical abuse and dependency. Pete's past was clean of any such indications.

"I'm headed into Buckthorn on business," Kantor

added, "and I'd be happy to give you a lift. I imagine you're anxious to get home, take a shower."

"You have no idea." Pete hadn't bathed or shaved since yesterday. His beard felt like an emery board, and he suspected that he smelled like a goat. "If I never see this place again, it'll be too soon."

They used a side door to evade the reporters. Once outside, Pete appreciated for the first time that spring had arrived. Azaleas and rhododendrons bloomed in bright gobs of color along the stone walls of the courthouse. Asian plum trees stood proud along the curb, clothed in pink blossoms. The day was sweet with the perfume of flowers and the music of newly migrated songbirds. Pete inhaled deeply, grateful for air untainted by cigarette smoke and Lysol.

Kantor had parked his car on Paulsen's Main Street, half a block from the courthouse, rather than use the media-infested parking lot of the courthouse. The two men chatted as they walked, like old friends. Within minutes they were on Highway 49, speeding south toward Buckthorn. Pete cracked his window to let the soft air wash across his face.

"Sheriff Graybill told me not to leave town," he said. "It made me feel like I was in an old western movie— still do, in fact. The reality of this thing hasn't quite sunk in yet—Wade getting killed, me being the prime suspect."

"Graybill's not in any danger of being invited to join Mensa," Kantor replied, chuckling. "On the other hand, put yourself in his shoes. From where he stands, you look like a damn-good suspect. Your pen was found at the scene, your Jeep's tire prints match those found at the scene, ten or twelve witnesses heard you threaten Beswick the day before he died—at first blush it looks pretty bad for you."

Pete's mood sunk abruptly. "I know how it looks.

I've tried to make some sense of it, but I can't.''

"Well, you'd best try harder. The only reason Graybill hasn't charged you is that he hasn't found a weapon and he doesn't have any witnesses. *Yet*. He may come back at you, unless you or somebody else explains the pen and the Jeep.''

"What's to explain? It's pretty obvious that someone has set me up.''

"Any idea who?''

"Hey, I haven't been in town a month yet. I've made an enemy or two in my time, but never this fast, and never anyone who'd do something like *this*.''

"Can you think of anyone who might want to kill Beswick?''

"I'll tell you what I told Graybill. Wade Beswick was a cretinous fool. Lots of people hated the guy—almost everyone I've met so far, in fact. But I never heard anyone say they wished he was dead.''

Minutes later the outskirts of Buckthorn materialized through gaps in the trees ahead. They passed the entrance to Royal Chinook Park, then crossed a bridge over the creek of the same name. Now they were in the town proper, if Buckthorn could still be called a town. The ruined hulk of St. Agnus Roman Catholic Church loomed on their left, its tall steeple ragged with flaking paint, the yard choked with weeds. On all sides were abandoned buildings and houses, lifeless husks that were once homes to living families and businesses. Buckthorn seemed more dead than alive.

"This place is sick,'' Pete said suddenly. "Look at the buildings, the decay—it's *sick*. People get killed here—the Buckthorn killings and now Wade, God knows who else. I even found out that one of our employees did time when he was young for chopping a kid's head off with a shovel, because the kid and his buddy had tied two cats together in order to make them fight. Can you believe that?''

"Oh, I can believe it. Jerry Dragstead, right?"

"You know about it."

"Yeah, I know about it. And you're right—this town *is* sick. I can't wait for the day I put Buckthorn behind me for good."

They drove the next few blocks in silence. Then Pete said, "A friend of mine—her name is Nita Vale . . ." He saw Kantor's face brighten. ". . . she suggested that I ask you something."

"Nita's a friend of yours?"

"She's—" Pete wanted to say that she was more than a friend but wondered how it would sound, if it was even true. "She's one of the few people around here I feel comfortable with. You're acquainted with her, I take it."

Kantor smiled faintly. "Oh yeah. I used to feel comfortable with her, too."

"As I was saying, I'm concerned about my late wife's brother."

"Topper? I know all about him."

"I understand that he's seeing a therapist because he's had mental problems of some kind—problems with rats and lewd behavior and fire. You've taken an interest in him, I hear."

"I've taken an interest in him because he's a weirdo, and no weirdo escapes my attention these days. I'm sure you can understand why."

Pete nodded. "I saw the news special you did. Nita played me a tape of it."

"Then you probably heard me say that the Buckthorn killer is a psychosexual maniac, which explains why my ears pricked up when I got wind of Topper. I don't know if he's a budding serial killer, but he's got the earmarks, and that made me nervous. Anyway, I sent his psychological tests and his shrink's notes to the FBI's Behavioral Science Unit, which specializes in working up profiles of serial killers. They've concluded that Topper suffers from antisocial personality disorder. I can't tell you any more than that, I'm afraid.''

Pete rubbed his tired eyes. ''Dan, I need to know whether Topper is dangerous to forms of life higher than rats. I need to know if there's any chance he might hurt my kids.''

Kantor started to answer, but held back. ''I'm not sure I should get into this any deeper with you. Most of it is privileged information. I've probably told you too much already.''

''For Christ's sake, Dan—Topper and I are family. My wife was his big sister, and I live under the same roof with the kid. I've got a right to know if he's dangerous.''

They turned onto Bannon Avenue and proceeded up the shady hill toward the barred gate of Bannon House. Still Kantor said nothing, but only stared silently at the road ahead.

''Look, Dan—do you have kids?''

''Two daughters, fourteen and twelve. They live with my ex-wife.''

''Then I'll talk to you as one father to another. Is Topper capable of hurting a child? Are my kids safe living in the same house with him? I need to know, just like you would if they were your kids.''

Kantor wheeled into the drive of Bannon House and halted the car before the steel-barred gate. He leaned his head against the headrest. ''You can't repeat any of this. And remember that I'm no shrink. All I can tell you is what the shrinks have told me, okay?''

Pete nodded.

Kantor related what the FBI's Dr. Ariel Sheplov had said after reviewing Topper's test results and paperwork, using her exact words. *The kid might be beyond salvage . . . He's made of the stuff of monsters . . .* Sheplov had spurred Kantor to arrange an intervention. Thus, he'd engineered the deal among the D.A., the school board and the Bannons to get Topper into therapy in return for not charging him with lewdness and related crimes. But Dr. Dennis Feldon, Topper's therapist, wasn't happy with the results thus far. The boy had built a wall around himself, had started telling Feldon what he thought sounded good. Medication might be the next step, but neither Sheplov nor Feldon was optimistic about that, either.

Pete's stomach did a slow flop. He sat quietly and stared through the gate at Bannon House, which stood clean and solid above the tatters of Buckthorn. "I appreciate this, Dan."

"Like I said, I'm no shrink. But if they were my kids, I wouldn't let Topper anywhere near them. And I certainly wouldn't stay under the same roof with him. Even if he wasn't dangerous, it can't be healthy for children to spend time with the likes of him."

"I hear you." Pete shook the cop's hand. "Thanks for the ride."

Kantor drove off, and Pete punched a four-number code into the security console on the gate post. The bars parted with a clank, and he walked up the drive, his face hard with the knowledge of what he must do.

IV

HE FOUND TUCKER AND DOLLY ON THE REAR PORCH, where they sat in white wicker chairs, sipping cups of hot chocolate. Dolly wore a shawl, Tucker a heavy Pendleton shirt and his trademark bolo tie. Sarah, Carter and Topper frolicked in the yard with a large black and tan dog, a Bernese mountain dog, one that almost looked like . . .

Pete wondered if he was hallucinating.

It *was* Gerard. The kids were roughhousing with Gerard, tossing a Frisbee for him to fetch, laughing, cavorting. Sarah, Carter and Gerard, just like old times, happier times. And Topper bounded around the yard after them like an overgrown grade-schooler, his screeching laughter grating on Pete's ears.

"Kids! Kids!" Tucker shouted from the porch. "Look who's back!"

When they saw their father, Carter and Sarah made a beeline for the porch, Gerard galumphing hard on their heels, Topper hanging back. They threw their arms around Pete's neck and planted loud kisses on his face. Gerard leaped up repeatedly and nearly knocked him down. Pete couldn't remember when he'd last experienced so intense a rush of pure joy.

Had he been in jail? Carter wanted to know. Had he taken a lie detector test, and had he gotten to know any other criminals? Pete winced at his son's use of *other criminals*, then laughed about it. Sarah asked whether he was home to stay, her eyes betraying a hint of grown-up fear. She asked how the police could have been so stupid as to suspect him of murder. Pete gave short, reassuring answers to each question and tried to appear more confident than he felt.

More hugs, more kisses. Sarah and Carter told him how much they'd missed him, and hearing this gave Pete a warm glow in his chest.

"Dad, isn't it a miracle about Gerard?" a breathless Sarah exclaimed, pulling the big dog to her. "The Lord sent him to us, just like I prayed He would. It was a blessing, Dad. I knew He'd do it if I had enough faith, and I prayed extra-hard in church this morning—"

So Tucker and Dolly had taken the kids to church.
Again.

"And I prayed, too!" Carter shouted, not to be out-
done. "I gave my heart to Jesus, and Jesus sent Gerard
to us. Isn't it awesome, Dad?"

Pete exchanged an icy glance with Tucker, who sat in
his wicker chair with a cup of hot chocolate warming
his palms, looking smug. Pete had mentioned to his in-
laws more than once that he and Sally had never been
religious, that they'd tried to inculcate the children with
humanist values and beliefs. But Tucker and Dolly
clearly couldn't have cared less about his beliefs.

"Kids, I don't think it was Jesus who sent Gerard to
us," Pete said. "I think it was probably Grampa Tuck.
I think he called the Dischmanns back in Scarsdale and
arranged to have him sent in order to surprise us. I hope
you thanked him."

"But it was Jesus who touched his heart and made
him change his mind about not liking dogs," Sarah insisted. She glanced at Dolly for support, who only
smiled and sipped her hot chocolate. "He even built a
kennel for Gerard beside the guest cottage. See?" She
pointed excitedly at a large chain-link cage with a spacious doghouse at one end. "Only Jesus can change the
way a person feels overnight, Dad. I *know* this as much
as I know I'm standing here talking to you."

Pete forced a smile. "We'll talk about it later, okay?
You and your brother just have fun for now."

Sarah and Carter bounded away with Gerard, and Pete
watched them go, his throat aching. Gerard's arrival had
done wonders for them, but now they believed in Jesus
and the power of prayer, having been manipulated by
their grandparents. Had their mother's ashes not lain in
an urn, she would be turning in her grave.

"Tucker, can I talk with you privately?" he asked.

"You bet. How about right after lunch?"

"How about right *now*? In your study."

Once they were alone behind the closed doors of the old man's study, Pete wasted no words. "We're leaving, Tucker. I don't want my son and daughter to spend another night under this roof. We'll be out before nightfall."

Tucker scratched the red mole above his eyebrow. "My gosh, Pete, you're not angry about my sending for the dog, are you? I thought it would be a nice surprise, not only for the kids, but for you, too. I had no way of knowing that you'd be in jail when he got here. I—"

"For God's sake, Tuck, this isn't about Gerard." Pete collapsed into a chair, so tired he could hardly stand. The near-sleepless night in jail had caught up with him. "I suppose I owe you some sort of explanation. I hardly know where to begin, but I may as well start with Topper. To be frank with you, I'm afraid for Sarah and Carter, what he might do to them. I don't want them to be . . ."

"Topper has had some problems, yes, as I've told you before. But those are under control now. He's undergoing therapy, and I've taken a strong hand with him, like any good father would do. Topper's fine, Pete. You have absolutely nothing to be afraid of."

"I've got information to the contrary, Tucker. In any event, it's not a matter that's open to discussion. I'm not taking any chances when it comes to the safety of my children."

Tucker removed his rimless glasses and polished them vigorously with a handkerchief. "And where do you plan to go, Pete?"

"I suppose we'll rent an apartment in Portland for the time being, and I'll start laying a plan of attack. I'll get a job and we'll find a small house in a decent neighborhood. It'll be tough at first, but we'll get by."

Tucker picked up the Sunday issue of the *Portland*

Oregonian and tossed it across the desk to Pete. "Have you seen the front page of the Metro section? There's a story about you and the murder of Wade Beswick. It falls just short of calling you the leading suspect." He put his glasses on again, magnifying his gray stare. "The *Oregonian* goes to more than a million people around the region, Pete. If you'd had a TV set in your jail cell, you'd know that four of the five Portland stations ran news items about you and Wade on their news shows last night. No telling how many people now know about your connection with this ugly, brutal thing—hundreds of thousands, I'd say. The question I have is: Who the dickens is apt to give you a job when you're the prime suspect in the murder of your former boss? Hmmh?"

Pete cringed. This question had eaten at him since Lieutenant Kantor showed him the newspaper in the vestibule of the sheriff's office. "I suppose we could go somewhere else, another city," he answered. "Maybe we'll go back to New York."

"Well, I hope you're not planning to take the Cherokee. The title and registration are in my name, you see. If you and the kids disappear and that vehicle is gone, I'll swear out a warrant on you, Pete. Then you can deal with a charge of auto theft as well as murder. All this should look great on your résumé, don't you think?"

Pete started to say something, but held back. No doubt of it now: Tucker meant to keep him here, like an animal in a cage if need be—anything to keep Sarah and Carter in the family. Fuck the Cherokee. He and the kids could rent a car or even call a cab from Portland. When push came to shove, all they really needed was transportation to the airport.

Tucker's flinty eyes scanned him from top to bottom, appraising him, taking his measure. "I should probably tell you, Pete, that Sheriff Graybill called me this morning after you'd been released. He told me that you're to keep yourself available to his department until the investigation of Wade's murder is over. I'm supposed to call him if I have reason to believe that you've absconded. If that happens, he plans to put out an all-points bulletin on you, which would go to every law enforcement agency in the country. Do you have any idea what that means?''

"I think I do. I . . ."

"It means that no matter where you go, you'll have cops hanging all over you, asking you questions, dogging your every move. I imagine this would make life unpleasant for you and the kids, and that it would make job-hunting a little—uh—awkward, to say the least. Wouldn't you agree?''

Pete's mind whirled with suspicions. That Tucker had somehow engineered all this ugliness seemed weirdly feasible. Pete didn't doubt that the old man would do absolutely anything to ensure that Sarah and Carter never left Bannon House, including frame him for murder. But did this mean . . .?

"Concerning my son," Tucker went on, "I can assure you that he's no danger to Sarah and Carter, or to anyone else for that matter. You saw him a few minutes ago, playing and laughing with them. He loves those kids, and he would never harm them. Oh, he's a little off center, I'll give you that, and he's had his problems in the past, but he's fine now. You have my personal guarantee on that.''

Wonderful, Pete thought.

"I really wish you'd reconsider your decision to leave," Tucker added. "Now that Wade's gone, I need you more than ever at the mill. I've even decided to make you the top dog, promote you to mill manager. You've got a lot to learn about the business, but you're a bright guy. I think you're exactly what the business needs.''

Pete stared at Tucker for a full fifteen seconds, his jaw hanging. "You're unbelievable, do you know that? One minute you're threatening to call the cops on me if I take your Jeep, and the next minute you're promoting me. How can you possibly think I could stay on here after all that's happened?''

"You'll stay because you're tough and you're smart, and because in your heart you know it's right for the kids. You can't simply walk away from all this, Pete. Oh, Buckthorn Wood Products doesn't look like much, to be sure—but there's wealth here, and that's important to a man like you, a businessman. You can't turn your back on a chance to get your piece of it, anymore than you can stop eating or breathing. You need it for Sarah and Carter, and you need it for yourself. When you get over this nonsensical fear of a seventeen-year-old boy, you'll come to the same conclusion.''

Pete couldn't deny that he'd failed to think through his intention to leave Bannon House immediately. The realities of finding a job and setting up a home were daunting under the best of circumstances, but doubly so in view of his being a murder suspect. He had precious little savings. The monthly rental income from the house in Rye wouldn't go far toward the maintenance of two children and a dog, much less pay for good schools and colleges. He needed time to think, he told himself. He could still leave, but not quite so soon. He needed to prepare.

"All right,'' he said, his voice hoarse, "you win for now. But only under the following conditions.''

"Pete, do you really think you're in any position to impose conditions?''

"Either you agree to them, or my kids and I are out

the door. I'll take Sarah and Carter away and you'll never see them again.''

"All right, I'm listening.''

"First, you guarantee that Topper will never be left alone with my kids. You make sure that Dolly or Esmerelda or you yourself are available at all times to supervise whenever they're together.''

Tucker made a pained face. "Pete, I can't say yes to that. Sarah and Carter are curious, independent kids. They like to explore, go off on their own. I can't guarantee that they'll . . .''

"The second condition is that you and Dolly stop proselytizing them. No more taking them to church, no more praying together, no more religious activity of any kind.''

Tucker let out a long, slow breath. His huge hands coiled into fists, then relaxed. "All right. Anything else?''

"You stop trying to steal them from me. No more expensive gifts without my permission. No more spoiling them.''

"Pete, we're not trying to steal your children from you. We're only trying to make them feel loved. We're their *grandparents*, and we're trying to make up for lost time.''

"You've heard the conditions. Either you agree to them and promise to live by them, or we're gone. What's it going to be?''

The old man's square jaw rippled as he clenched his teeth. Pete saw what Sally must have seen in her father, felt what she must have felt—a hatred of this tyrant who pulled strings and manipulated everyone around him. Small wonder that Sally had run away and had refused to look back.

"All right,'' Tucker said finally. "I'll agree to your conditions.''

"Good. Now there's just one more thing I want." Pete strode to the huge, glass-enclosed gun cabinet that occupied most of one wall. His eyes wandered over the collection of weaponry until alighting on an item that looked serviceable. He tugged at one of the door handles of the cabinet and found it locked. "Open it," he said to Tucker.

"A gun? You want me to give you a gun?"

"Open the cabinet, Tucker."

The old man pulled a key ring from his pocket and sorted through the keys with his thick fingers until finding the right one. He unlocked the cabinet and stood aside. Pete reached in and took the pistol he wanted.

"That's a Smith and Wesson Model 39," Tucker said with a wry smile. "You'll want ammo and an extra magazine, I assume." He went to a drawer and returned with the magazine and a box of cartridges. Pete could see in his face that he regarded this as a victory of some sort—he'd driven Pete to arm himself. This after turning the kids into born-again Christians. "If it's a combat piece you need, I've got others that are more capable. You might consider that Colt there, or this Glock . . ."

"I like this one," Pete said. The gun felt oddly comfortable in his hand, heavy and all-business. The feel of it took him back many years, to a sunny Midwestern afternoon when his father taught him to shoot the old service .45 that he'd brought back from the Korean War. This Smith and Wesson was of similar design, and Pete needed no instruction on how the slide and safety worked.

"If you plan to carry it outside the house, you'll need a concealed-weapons permit," Tucker said. "It's not hard to get one in Oregon—for most folks. For *you*, though—well, it might be tough. You see, the county sheriff issues the permits, and Nick Graybill might look at you funny when you hand him an application, your being a murder suspect and all.''

Pete stuck the gun into his belt. "I don't need a permit. Nice of you to care, though."

"Pete, I've already told you that you have nothing to fear from Topper. Now and then he does something or says something that makes the average person—wait a minute." He took off his glasses again, stared at Pete and smiled. "It's not Topper, is it? It's *me*. You're scared of *me*."

"I'm not scared of anything," Pete lied, patting the butt of the pistol. "Not anymore."

In truth he was scared of damn-near everything, starting with the Buckthorn killer. He was scared of Topper and Sheriff Nick Graybill and Jerry Dragstead, who'd followed him in the dead of night for some unfathomable reason. He was scared of whoever had tried to frame him for the murder of Wade Beswick, and yes, he was scared of Tucker. He was even vaguely scared of the Mad Witch of Olivet.

He knew that the gun couldn't possibly protect against all that he feared, but he meant to keep it within reach until he and his children had put Buckthorn behind them for good.

20

I

AT THE CLOSE OF THE 11:00 A.M. SERVICE AT THE MOUNT of Olives Gospel Church, Pastor Randy Roysden blessed his drab little flock and nodded to an usher in the rear, who started to pull the bell rope. Three blocks away on the east side of Buckthorn, Dan Kantor parked in front of Jerry Dragstead's humble clapboard bungalow and stood a moment in the cool sunlight of noon, listening to the peal of the church bell. Overhead, a V-formation of Canadian geese flapped northward, honking loudly.

Kantor watched the geese until they disappeared over the tops of the surrounding forest, then dragged his mind back to the matter at hand. On the day following Terry Grimes's murder, he'd ordered Dragstead detained and had interrogated him thoroughly over a twenty-four-hour period. But when Dragstead insisted on getting a court-appointed lawyer in accordance with his Miranda rights, Kantor had released him, having no real evidence that justified holding him any longer.

After days of foot-dragging, the state district court had finally issued a search warrant for Dragstead's house. Dragstead had suffered several fruitless searches years ago when the Buckthorn Task Force first considered him a viable suspect, and the current judge had steadfastly refused to issue another warrant. But the D.A. had eventually persuaded him that the cops had a reasonable expectation of finding a particular pair of shoes in

Dragstead's possession—Nike cross trainers, size 11-D, which a civilian shoe expert had determined to have made the prints around the late Terry Grimes's mobile home. Dragstead's shoe size was 11-D. The warrant also covered human body parts (eyes, severed penises and fingers), implements of torture, steel spikes, sodium pentobarbital and hypodermic needles suitable for administering the drug, even though past searches of Dragstead's residence had never turned up such items.

Esparza and Tching came out the front door as Kantor approached, having arrived shortly after dawn with a team of Task Force detectives to execute the warrant. Kantor lit a cigarette as they came near.

"Give me the good news," he said. "Tell me you found a shrine in the basement with pickled sex organs on the altar."

"No shrine, Lieutenant," Esparza replied, smiling sadly. "No pickled sex organs, no bulletin board with eyeballs pinned to it, no Tupperware bowls full of severed fingers. If he's got a shrine, it's somewhere else."

"I'll settle for the shoes then. That's all I really wanted anyway. To hell with hypodermic needles and body parts."

Tching shook her black mane and sighed. "Sorry, Lieutenant. There's nothing more incriminating here than a pack of unlicensed cats and dogs. If you'd like, we can arrest him for *that*."

Kantor spat on the ground, his mood suddenly foul. As he neared the front door, an odor hit him hard—used cat litter. "Where's our boy?" he asked, steeling himself to go inside.

"Living room, watching the Celtics and Rockets," Esparza replied.

"Find any sex literature, pornography, stuff like that?"

"Half a dozen old *Playboys, a Hustler* or two."

"*Playboy? Hustler?* This guy's supposed to be a closet gay, isn't he? What's he doing with girlie mags?"

Esparza shrugged and Kantor grunted, flicked his cigarette onto the lawn and went in. He caught glimpses of cats darting around corners, hiding from yet another stranger in their home. The room was disheveled as a result of the cops' search, but otherwise clean. A wood stove crouched in a corner, tongues of fire dancing behind the glass screen. Poster-size photos of big-eyed pets covered the walls, testifying to Dragstead's love of animals—cocker spaniel puppies, a pair of collies, a picnic basket full of kittens, at least a dozen others.

Dragstead himself sprawled in a recliner and stared at a TV set, a huge yellow cat in his lap. Dressed in gray work pants and sweatshirt, his silvered hair slicked back, he could have been an aging carnival roadie, one of the guys who pounds tent pegs with a sledge hammer. He hadn't shaved this morning, and whiskers peppered his jaw like iron filings. On each side of the chair lay a large dog, one that looked part-German shepherd and another that looked part-rottweiler.

"Hello, Jerry," Kantor said, settling onto the sofa. "Who's winning?"

"Rockets by ten in the third," Dragstead answered. The shepherd-mix stared suspiciously at Kantor, a low rumble rising in his throat. "Don't worry about Nitro," Dragstead said. "He don't bite. Not lately anyway."

"How about the other one?"

"Stink? Hell no. Stink don't hardly walk unless it's to get to his food bowl. He's old and tired, same as me."

Kantor glanced around at the pictures on the walls, at the innocent eyes staring down from every angle. "Jerry, you and I need to talk. We can do it here, or we can do it at the station in Paulsen—your call."

Dragstead picked up the remote control and snapped off the TV. "Let's do it here."

"Good. I just got off the horn with the state crime lab in Portland. Remember those samples of cat hair we found at the scene of Terry Grimes's murder? They match the sample we took from your pal last week." He nodded at the cat curled in Dragstead's lap.

"I already told you that Shagnasty sat on Terry while we was drivin' back and forth from the gas station to his truck. It don't surprise me that Terry had his hair on him. This old cat's a fuckin' hair factory." Dragstead stroked Shagnasty's neck and waved his hand, releasing a flurry of wispy cat hair into the air.

"That's not all, Jerry. We took plaster casts of some footprints around Grimes's trailer house, and I sent them to an expert in Beaverton. He got back to me last night, told me that the shoes were Nike cross-trainers, size 11-D. That just happens to be your size, doesn't it?"

"Lots of guys have my size of shoe," Dragstead answered, cool as ice. He shook an unfiltered cigarette out of a pack, lit it and spat a shred of tobacco off his tongue. "I know what you're doin' here. You're tryin' to rattle me into sayin' something you can use to nail me. You want me to be this killer so bad you can taste it."

"Not true, Jerry. I'm here to help, that's all. If you're doing these horrible things, then you're hurting. I want to help you make the hurt stop, that's all. And I don't want you to harm anyone else. It's what you want, too, I think."

Dragstead looked up. "You must think I'm one stupid son of a bitch. You're not lookin' to help me. You're lookin' to help *yourself*. You hang these killings on me and you're hot shit, the cop who took down the Buckthorn killer, isn't that right? It's gotta be worth some money, like maybe you write a book or something, sell a million copies. Or maybe you sell the story to *Inside Edition* and become a fuckin' celebrity."

Kantor cringed, cleared his throat. "I don't think you're stupid. A man couldn't get away with doing these things for as long as you have and be stupid."

Staring into Dragstead's face, Kantor tried for the umpteenth time in the past five days to make himself believe that this brute was smart enough to stalk, torture and kill nine young men over nearly two decades without leaving a single useful clue. Again he failed. Clinging to hope, he said, "Tell me, Jerry—do you read any magazines?"

"Magazines? Every now and then I pick up a *Hot Rod* up to the drug store in Paulsen. Sometimes I buy me a *Playboy* or something. Is that some kind of crime?"

Hot Rod. Playboy. Not *Scientific American* or *Psychology Today* or even *National Geographic*, the kind smart people read. Kantor glanced around the room, looking for books, for works of art other than sappy puppy and kitty pictures. But there weren't any. A man as smart as the Buckthorn killer surely needed more than this. Such a man needed good things to read, good art to look at, other smart people to converse with.

"You belong to any organizations, discussion groups, anything like that?"

"Oh yeah, I forgot to mention that I'm president of the fuckin' Rotarians."

"I was thinking that you might need someone to talk with from time to time—you know, trade ideas, share your insights."

"Lieutenant, I'm an ex-con. Thirty years ago I killed a kid, and I put another one in a home for dimwits. You think the Kiwanis is gonna ask me to join them for lunch? You think anyone around here would want me in his fuckin' discussion group?"

"How about friends? Got any friends?"

"Like I said when you questioned me last week, I only got one—Scotty Dunn—and he's layin' in a hospital bed over in Portland on account of Wade Beswick put him there. Him and me used to fix up our cars, help each other keep them running. I'm waitin' for you assholes to say I killed Beswick, 'cause of what he did to Scotty. I s'pose that's next, ain't it? Good old Jerry Dragstead, everybody's favorite suspect."

Kantor got to his feet, wandered around the room. He went to the window that faced the rear of the property. The backyard was a clutter of cannibalized auto bodies, ruined transmissions and rusting engine blocks. A rickety shed sheltered several cords of split firewood. Esparza, Tching and two other detectives walked slowly along the tangled wood line that abutted the yard, their heads down as they poked through the weeds, searching. Two of Dragstead's mongrels followed them, their tails wagging, thinking this was a game.

Kantor could see that what Esparza had suggested last week could indeed be true: Under cover of night, Dragstead could have crawled through the weeds of his backyard to the woods and escaped the surveillance of the cops who'd tailed him during those seven successive Octobers, back when the Dragstead Detail was in effect. The cops had probably sat in cars at either end of the block, watching the house from two different angles. They would've gotten drowsy, like all cops on details like this. They could've missed things, especially in the dark. They wouldn't have expected their man to low-crawl out the back.

Yes, Dragstead could have eluded his tail and gone out to torture and kill Brad Scheider in '83, Joshua Rittich in '86, and Travis Langdon in '89. But Kantor wondered whether he could have crawled to the wood line while lugging along a can of gasoline, not to mention his tools of torture, including steel spikes and something

like a sledge hammer to pound them with. He supposed
that Dragstead could have stashed the gas and the tools
somewhere far from his house, maybe in the trunk of a
car he'd prepositioned in a dark alley on the other side
of town. After all, he would have needed transportation,
and he couldn't have taken his regular car from the
driveway without the cops noticing. And he would have
needed to perform all the preliminary surveillance of his
victims before the month of October started, before surveillance by the Dragstead Detail got under way.

Kantor turned from the window, feeling queasy. Dragstead *could* have done all this, yes. But *had* he? Were
those 11-D's really his?

"Want to know something, Jerry? My shoe expert in
Beaverton is tracking down the distributor and the re-
tailer of the shoes you wore when you killed Grimes.
We'll find out where and when you bought them, get
the sales clerk to identify you. I've got FBI scientists
working on the footprints you left in Grimes's yard, and
they'll soon be able to give me your height and weight,
the length of your stride, the whole nine yards. I'll put
you into those shoes, Jerry, and when I do, your story
ends."

Dragstead set Shagnasty on the floor and got to his
feet. *This guy could break me in two*, Kantor thought,
his gun hand twitching.

"I want you out of here," Dragstead said with real
menace. "If you had anything on me, we wouldn't be
havin' this conversation. I'd be sittin' in a cell, and
you'd be throwin' your press conference or talkin' to
your agent. If you've got anything more to say, say it
to my fuckin' lawyer."

Kantor forced a grin. "You got it, Jerry. But don't
think you've seen the last of me." He walked slowly
toward the door, halted when he came to it. "You know,
I really don't need the spikes or the body parts or the

tools you used to torture those boys. All I really need is to put you into the shoes. Think about that, Jerry. And think about doing some good for yourself, about being a man and facing up to this thing.''

''Fuck you, Kantor. You're a piece of shit, know that? Someday, somebody's gonna give you what you got coming. Now get out of my house.''

Kantor saw homicide in the big man's eyes, still alive and searing thirty years after it took the life of one teenager and maimed another. He moved through the door into the sunlight, glad to be out of Dragstead's sight.

II

CLOUDS OVER BUCKTHORN, LIKE DRIPPING VEILS. THE drizzle befitted a Monday morning, which this was— April 11, 1994.

The Verminator hunkered in the weeds behind the Allegro Theater, which three days earlier had burned to a mound of blackened bricks and sticks, along with Bertinello's Antiques next door. Only within the past twenty-four hours had the mound stopped smoking and steaming, but no one had yet begun the task of hauling the wreckage away. The Verminator doubted that anyone ever would.

He crouched next to the old corn popper until the school bus was safely out of sight, feeling generally good about things.

I know what you're thinking, ladies and gentlemen— when the old man finds out that the Verminator skipped school again, he'll be honked off like a Russian bear, probably try to put his size-eleven up the Verminator's ass, might even start swinging a sockful of sand. But guess what—I don't give a rusty fuck! I don't give a fuck about school, and I don't give a fuck about the old man. The Verminator has moved into a new dimension, folks, and the old dimension doesn't matter anymore. All that matters is . . .

He scrunched his eyes tight and fought down a rush of sexual excitement. He tried to think rationally, not as the Verminator but as Topper Bannon. It wasn't easy. A new craving had possessed him, dominating his sleep, his daydreams, his hopes and schemes. It clung to his mind like a gigantic, slimy leech, sucking the humanity out of him while injecting him with visions beyond anything he'd ever experienced.

He knew that his life would change beyond all recognition if he ever gave into the craving. The cops would hunt him down, and if they didn't kill him outright, they would clap him into an institution for the remainder of his natural life. Society didn't cotton to dudes who butchered little kids and burned them to death, that was certain.

So, ladies and gentlemen, I say, What the hell? If it happens, it happens. You can't stop progress, right? The Verminator can't go on killing weeds and rats forever, now can he? No fucking way. And he sure as hell can't start trying to act like a normal, red-blooded American boy—not at the ripe old age of seventeen. Hell, I've never had a date with a girl, never mind kissing or fucking one. It's way too late for that shit! I wouldn't know where to begin . . .

He trotted north on Second Street to the intersection with Bannon Avenue, where the Mount of Olives Gospel Church stood naked and white. He caught sight of the Reverend Randy Roysden in the churchyard, his hair stiff as a scrub brush, his mustache redder than a brick. The pastor stood before the marquee, busy with the placement of new plastic letters onto the white background, the title of next week's sermon: "You Can Light Up the World."

When he saw Topper, Roysden paused in his work, straightened and smiled in his wrinkled, middle-aged way. Topper smiled back, thinking, *I can read your face, Randy. I know what you want, you fuckin' queer. Maybe you've got everyone else in town fooled, but you don't fool me!*

He left Roysden behind, though he could feel the pastor's gaze on his back as he trotted up the hill toward Bannon House. Passing by the main gate, he continued on to the stone stairway that led upward through a tangle of ferns and ninebark to the rear of the Bannon estate. He reached the door of the gardener's shed and dug for his key, glancing at the great house once or twice as he freed the lock, fearful of seeing his father's face framed in a rear window, watching. He pushed through the door into the welcoming gloom and leaned against the door, barely breathing.

If he saw me, I'll soon know. If he saw me, he'll be here within the next thirty seconds. The old son of a bitch doesn't fuck around. A minute came and went, two minutes, three. The Verminator was home free, and he breathed easy.

We need to make preparations, folks. Gotta make sure everything is ready to go when the big moment comes . . .

He filled a plastic gallon can with gasoline from a five-gallon can. A gallon should be plenty, he told himself, and not too heavy to carry on his bike. He strapped the can to the cargo carrier over the bike's rear wheel. Then he went to a wall rack, took down his trusty .410-gauge shotgun, slung it onto one shoulder and slid a box of shells into the pocket of his breaker. From the workbench where he mixed his weed-fighting poisons he took his Coleman flashlight, snapped it on to verify that it had good batteries, and pocketed it. He pulled a large

plastic sack from a dispenser, folded it, pushed it in next
to the flashlight.

Finally, he took from a drawer a long K-Bar hunting
knife with a wicked, black blade. He tested the edge
against his thumb, found it sharp enough to draw blood.
Sucking the wound, he pushed the knife back into its
scabbard, strapped it on and stood still a moment, sa-
voring the weight of the thing on his hip. He'd ordered
the knife out of a men's adventure magazine a few
months back, not really knowing why he wanted it but
liking the lethal look of it, perhaps even unconsciously
foreseeing the need that he would soon have for it.

He pedaled up Mount Olivet on the familiar trail to a
fog-shrouded stand of buckthorn, leaned his bike against
a hemlock and stood still a moment, listening to occasional splats of water dripping from tree branches. Then
he set off through the green gloom, lugging the shotgun,
the gasoline, the flashlight, the ammo.

Minutes later the cabin of the Mad Witch appeared
before him like a dark dream, nestled in tongues of mist,
a shadowed place mounded with vines and moss. The
air smelled of oldness. Topper halted and stared at the
cabin as he always did, his eyes probing the maws of
its windows, the cave beyond its door. A skittering
sound reached his ears, low against the hush of the forest—rats, no doubt. This was, after all, Rat City.

He felt no fear. Rather, he felt a sense of having come
home.

*No sense waiting around—right, ladies and gentle-
men? We've got a show to do here . . .*

He set down the gasoline can and leaned the shotgun
across it. Squatting low, he crept into the tunnel of
blackberries that grew against the south wall of the cabin
and beamed his flashlight on the first of the wire cage-
traps that he'd baited two days ago. A pair of rats chittered and scratched inside it, terrified of the light. Topper

dragged the trap into the clearing, then went back in to check the others. More rats, big and glossy and oily-eyed, whiskers twitching. One by one he dragged the traps out to the daylight, with five rats clawing at the wire.

Ladies and gentlemen, I want you to give it up for the Rat Choir—that's it, a great big Buckthorn welcome. Let's hear it now ... that's it! ... What have we got here?—two females and three males, it looks like. As all of you out there in Imagination Land know, this is a big day for these little guys. Not so very long ago, the Verminator would've lit 'em up and made 'em sing for you, and all that delicious pain and terror would've made my cock do the bossa nova. But hey, those days are gone, chums—it's like a whole new age for the Verminator. And a whole new day for the Vermin, too ...

He flipped the latch of the first cage and shouted *Shoo!*, causing the first pair of rats to dash for freedom.

You see, we're going to start having a new kind of guest on the show—no more rats, no more mice or squirrels or moles or groundhogs ...

He flipped the latches on the other cages, swung the doors open. Shouted *Shoo! Shoo!* The rats skittered away into the thicket, whipping up swirls in the ground fog.

Isn't that exciting, folks? Doesn't it almost make you blow a 'gasm just thinking about it? I'm talkin' about having a whole new kind of guest on "Adventures with the Verminator"—like a dog, maybe, a big ugly Bernice something-or-other, named Gerard! And then I'm talkin'—Here the Verminator paused to collect himself, because the very idea was so rich, so full of sex. *I'm talkin' about a real live boy, and I won't mention any names, but his initials are Carter-the-Farter. That's right! I'm not shitting you—the Verminator plans to have Carter-the-Farter on the show real soon. And after*

*that, Carter-the-Farter's sister, Sarah-the-Slug. We're
gonna have 'em on the show, and we're gonna make
'em sing for you, yes sir! Is that fuckin' awesome, or
what?*

Something silenced him, movement in the brush.
Something bigger than a rat, no doubt about that. He
stood rock-still, breathless, his heart pounding. He felt
eyes watching him. His flesh crawled.

He scanned the area around him, expecting the Mad
Witch of Olivet to jump out of the brush at him at any
moment, her killing claws spread wide. He could almost
feel her cold, dead mouth on his neck, the bite of her
teeth on his skin.

*Now wait just a fuckin' second, ladies and gentlemen.
The Mad Witch isn't someone to be scared of. If she'd
wanted to kill me, she could've done it a million times.
Hell, she can get into the house, can't she? Hasn't the
Verminator woken up in the dead of night to find her
standing over his bed? No, there's nothing to be scared
of here, because the fact is, the Verminator and the Mad
Witch are made of the same thing. It's like we're brother
and sister, y'know? Or maybe mother and son. We've
got the same heart . . .*

He took the plastic bag from his pocket, shook it out,
and slid the shotgun into it, then tossed in the box of
shells. He picked up the gasoline. Flicked on his flashlight. Walked into the cabin, dank and black. Down into
the root cellar, where the air reeked of something fungal,
down into the holy of holies. The beam of the flashlight
played over the Mad Witch's altar and the Kerr jars,
their contents floating in murk—fingers, eyes, penises.

The Verminator rested the shotgun in a corner of the
room, the plastic bag protecting it from moisture dripping down the walls. He placed the gasoline can next to
it. He stood up straight and breathed deeply, feeling
dizzy with anticipation.

Simple as that, friends and neighbors. Everything's set up and ready. Stay tuned, okay? I can guaran-fucking-tee that our next show's going to be a lollapa-looza!

III

A FEW MINUTES BEFORE NOON ON THE FOLLOWING Wednesday, Nita Vale lugged the final bundle of the latest edition of the *Nehalem County Renegade* into the ThriftyKwik in Paulsen and hastily arranged the papers in the display rack. Her rounds completed for another week, she drove back to Buckthorn as fast as her wheezing old VW would carry her. Foregoing her usual stop at Vonda Reuben's house on publication day, she went straight home to her building, the former Komack's Mercantile Emporium on Front Street. She saw Pete Cochran's green Grand Cherokee parked next to the loading dock, Pete sitting behind the wheel. He waved to her, and her heart leapt.

She got out of the VW and ran to him despite the ache in her injured right foot. They came together at the rear door, fell into each other's arms and kissed hungrily in the chilly shade of the alley. Nita fumbled with the key and finally got the door open, already peeling her clothes. They scrambled up the stairs to her bedroom and made furious love on top of the bedspread.

"My God," she said when it was over, leaning back against a pillow, "I don't know about you, but I needed that." She buried her fingers in Pete's hair and gazed into his lean, haggard face. "I needed it so much it almost scares me."

"Me, too," he whispered, nuzzling her ear. "Like I needed it yesterday and the day before. Like tomorrow and the day after." He smiled, which was good to see.

Nita loved his smile, just as Sally had. She understood
fully what Sally had seen in him.

The previous week hadn't been kind to Peter Cochran.
Stress and worry had deepened the lines around his
mouth and eyes. He'd started carrying a gun, which
made Nita uneasy.

The trouble had begun nine days earlier with Wade
Beswick's near-braining of Scotty Dunn and had
reached a crescendo with Pete's arrest on suspicion of
killing Beswick. During a long night in jail he'd reached
the unavoidable conclusion that someone had tried to
frame him, probably the same person who'd committed
the murder—someone who'd had the opportunity to
steal his monogrammed pen and "borrow" his Jeep long
enough to drive to the murder scene and leave damning
tire prints. As if all this weren't stressful enough, Dan
Kantor had verified Pete's fear that Topper Bannon was
a budding psychosexual maniac who might be a danger
to Sarah and Carter.

For the past three days, since Monday, Pete had visited Nita during the noon hour, and each time they'd
ended up here in her bed. Afterward they'd eaten light
lunches and talked, and Pete had returned to his office
at the Buckthorn sawmill. He'd phoned her in the afternoon, again in the evening—more stolen moments of
refuge, the beginnings of a routine, Nita supposed. In a
mere three days, each had become a major feature of the
other's life.

"I'll rustle up some lunch," she said, swinging off
the bed. "I don't want to send you away on an empty
stomach."

Pete bounced out of bed behind her, caught her before
she could take a robe from the closet. He gathered her
naked body close to his. "What do you say we go crazy
and have lunch at Chubby Chuck's? Wally MacKenzie

says they make great milkshakes. A walk in the fresh air will do us good.''

''Fresh air in Buckthorn? You're forgetting about all the smoke your sawmill belches out.'' She pinched his ass.

''It's not *my* mill, dear heart. It's Tucker Bannon's mill.''

''But now that Wade's dead, you're the honcho, the cheese, the big dog.''

''Not true. The place runs itself. I've put Wally MacKenzie in charge of all the consequential decisions. I'm just a figurehead.''

They took what started out to be a quick shower, but things got out of hand when they agreed to soap each other's backs. Pete entered her from behind, Nita pressing her face against the tiled wall of the shower stall and mewing like a kitten with every thrust. Afterward they toweled each other off, giggling like teenagers.

While drying her yellow hair with a blow-dryer, Nita asked whether lunch at Chubby Chuck's was wise. The place would be full of guys from the mill. Rumors were sure to fly, and Tucker Bannon would shortly learn that his spanking-new mill manager was squiring around one of the town's environmentalist-vampire-lesbians.

''This may come as a shock, but I don't care,'' Pete replied. ''What's he going to do—fire me?'' He mimed playing violin music. ''Anyway, as soon as I get my ducks in a row, I'm taking my kids out of here. We'll disappear so fast it'll make Tucker's head spin.''

Chubby Chuck's on Main Street was an unrecon-structed small-town greasy spoon. Cigarette-scarred counter, swiveling stools, ceiling fans. A sign on the wall said, *This ain't Burger King. You're gettin' it MY way.* Nita and Pete sat at a corner table in the rear, the only one that was vacant. Noisy mill workers sat at the other tables, and Nita caught a swarm of disapproving glances.

The owner herself waited on them—Charlene Nielson, a severe woman of fifty who'd inherited the cafe from her father, the original Chubby Chuck. Nita ordered a small salad with plain oil and vinegar on the side, while Pete ordered something called a Double Chubby Chucker, which was half a pound of beef on a huge sesame bun with melted cheese. He also ordered a strawberry milkshake, which arrived in a tall metal cup that was almost too cold to touch.

The crowd started to trickle out as Pete and Nita ate, for the official lunch hour was winding down. Watching them go, Nita felt sorry for anyone who lived according to a heartless clock—report to work at eight, eat lunch at twelve, go home at five, do it all again the next day. She felt sorry for their calloused and blistered hands, their aching arms and backs, their sawdust-scarred lungs. But at the same time she was angry at them because of their blindness. Hard though their lives were, almost to a man they hated and reviled anyone who dared to suggest that they deserved something better. *What kind of creature chooses this existence?* she asked herself. *What kind of creature chooses darkness over light?*

Pete misread the tension in her face. "What I said earlier—about taking my kids out of Buckthorn—I didn't mean to imply that I'd leave you behind. What we've had—*have*—is very important to me, Nita. I hope you know that I couldn't just give you up."

Nita's anger subsided for the moment. "Pete, I don't have any right to expect anything from you. My God, we've only known each other for ten days. Besides, if you asked me to come away with you today, I'd have to say no. I can't leave the *Renegade*, not after all I've invested in it. It's become part of me."

"So I don't have a right to expect anything from you, either. Is that what you're saying?"

She winced. She didn't want to hurt him, because she *did* care for him. She cared for him more than she'd ever dreamed she could care for a man.

"What I'm saying, Pete, is that we need to let nature take its course. We can't just . . ."

The last group of hard-hatted mill workers rose noisily from a nearby table and made for the front counter to pay their checks, their work boots clopping and scraping. Each threw a look toward the table in the rear, a silent jeer. Nita's anger coiled again. Could she ever explain *this* to Pete? Could she ever make him understand how much Buckthorn needed the *Renegade*, how much a captive people needed to hear a strong, clear voice of dissent? Her work in Buckthorn was far from finished.

"It's okay," Pete said, putting his hand over hers. "You're right. We should let nature take its course. I don't want to smother you, but I sure as hell don't want to lose you, either."

"And I don't want to lose you, Pete." This was the truth, or as much of it as she dared let out.

"I've got to tell you something, Nita. Since my wife—since Sally died—I've lived for my kids, tried to put them first . . ." He looked away, swallowed. Days earlier he'd told her about the circumstances that had led to his coming to Buckthorn. He'd told her about the loss of Sally's life insurance policy, about accepting a job driving a delivery truck in Long Island. "The fact is, I've been lying to myself, Nita. When Tucker offered me a job here, I took it as much for *me* as for the kids. We needed money, and this was a way to get it. I felt I could guarantee the kids' future, but I also wanted to get back into the business world. I saw the job as a way to get another shot at being somebody special—not some grubby truck driver, but an *executive*, a *businessman*."

Nita squeezed his hand.

"I've discovered something important," Pete went on. "What I've been chasing all these years is illusory. Ever since I was a little kid I've wanted to be a shaker and a mover—a *quality person*. I thought I'd made it at Patriot Mutual, that I'd achieved what I'd always wanted, but what I had there wasn't quality, Nita. And *I* wasn't quality, either. In fact—"

Nita pulled his hand to her lips and kissed it. She shook her head to show him that this wasn't necessary, but he forged on.

"I've got to say this. You're the only good thing that's happened to me since I can't remember when. You've reminded me what it's like to be a real human being, what's it's like to live—"

"Pete, don't. I'm not what you think I am."

"Yes, you *are*. And you're exactly what I need. You're kind and thoughtful. You're sensitive and smart and . . ."

Nita pulled her hand away. "Peter, I'm *not* Sally."

He stared at her for a long moment, his mouth forming an O. "God, is that what's been happening here? Have I been trying to turn you into . . .?" He shook his head. "Nita, I'm not trying to make you into her. If I've given you that impression . . ."

"I sensed it from the minute we met, Pete—when you first saw me, you saw Sally. And it still happens. You know it does. To be honest, I feel honored and flattered, because I know how good she was, how decent and beautiful and . . ." Her eyes started to tear, and she blinked. "You can't expect me to take up where she left off. I may look like her and remind you of her, but I can't *be* her, okay?"

Pete stared at the plastic tablecloth. "I'm so sorry."

They quietly finished their meal, and Peter walked her

back to the *Renegade*. He kissed her as they stood in the alley next to his Grand Cherokee, a warm spring breeze fanning her hair.

"Nita, those things I said back in the restaurant—I've always had a problem with my mouth. Once I set it in motion, I forget where the off-button is. Please forgive me."

"There's nothing to forgive, Pete."

"I suppose everyone comes to a moment when he knows he can't hold onto the past any longer—for me, that moment is now. I loved my wife more than anything else in the world, but she's gone. I finally *feel* it, Nita, and I can accept it. I can start moving forward again. I have you to thank for that."

"I'm thankful to you, too. Maybe someday I can tell you why."

He held her close a long moment. "I've made a decision," he said. "You may think this is crazy, and it probably is, but I've got to find out who tried to frame me for Wade's murder."

"And how do you propose to do that?"

He grinned. "I was hoping you'd give me some ideas. You're the investigative reporter."

"Are you serious?" She untangled herself from his arms.

"I'm trapped, Nita. I can't do any serious job hunting while I'm a murder suspect, and I don't have the money to take care of the kids if I don't have a job. The rental income from the house in New York isn't enough. And it's a lead-pipe cinch I can't wait for the cops to nail the real killer. They think they've already got him—*me*."

"Pete, I don't like the sound of this. What if the killer feels threatened and gets scared? He might come after you."

"Then it would be him and me, wouldn't it?—one on one. We'd resolve this thing one way or another." He patted the pistol in the pocket of his jacket.

"Pete, you're not Judge Dredd. This guy has already killed, and it's reasonable to assume that if he's pushed, he'll do it again. Seems to me we should leave the police work to the professionals."

"Under ordinary circumstances I'd agree with you, but these aren't ordinary circumstances. My kids are living in the same house with a seventeen-year-old who's becoming a certifiable psychopath. I need to get them out of there, and I need to do it soon."

Nita sighed. "And where do you plan to start your investigation?"

"I don't know yet. I guess I'll sit down and do some hard thinking, come up with a plan. Look, I was serious when I said I hoped you'd help me."

"I was never much of an investigative reporter. I worked the Metro beat in Portland, and the news mostly hit me over the head—robberies, murders, rapes, not the kind of stuff you had to dig for. Besides, it was a long time ago."

"Well, if you come up with any ideas, I'd like to hear them. I can't sit on my hands any longer. I need to *do* something."

Before leaving, he asked if he could see her tomorrow, and she said yes, same time, same station. Pete had insisted that they meet during the daylight hours on weekdays, when Sarah and Carter were safe in school; this arrangement meant that for the foreseeable future Pete and Nita would have no dinners out in the evening, see no movies, take no weekend excursions to the coast. He wouldn't leave his kids at Bannon House when Topper was around, even though he'd exacted Tucker's promise to ensure continuous adult supervision. Nita understood his misgivings, his mistrust of Tucker Bannon.

After he left, she limped up to her apartment and readied herself for cycling, slipping into Lycra togs, helmet and riding shoes. She then left Buckthorn on her Trek mountain bike, pedaling south on Highway 49 toward Birkenfeld. Three miles down the road she came to an intersection and took the left fork toward the town of Mist.

The cool air was delicious in her lungs. The country-side was alive with the green smells of spring, and the afternoon sunlight warmed her shoulders like liniment. She felt free and strong. If not for excursions like this, she doubted that she could endure the gray dilapidation of Buckthorn or its landscape of fear, failure and hope-lessness.

On any given afternoon, Nita could easily ride the thirty-odd miles to Scappoose and back without raising a sweat. Though the route was hilly and curvy, the grades weren't long or steep. And she was a strong cy-clist. Sometimes she cut south at Pittsburg and rode down Highway 37 to Buxton. On other occasions she rode north to the village of Mayger on the south shore of the Columbia, where she would linger on a high ridge and watch container ships ply the river to and from Port-land. She'd explored scores of side roads and trails throughout this little corner of Oregon, some winding across the logging-scarred faces of mountains, others to hidden valleys and ravines. She knew all the shortcuts, the alternative routes. She knew this country so well that she could even make long trips at night without getting lost.

A short distance out of Buckthorn, she caught sight of a low, black car in her helmet mirror—a Camaro or Trans Am, she thought, less than a quarter-mile behind. Daggers of sunlight glinted off its polished sheet metal. She felt a nibble of anxiety, because she'd seen this car or one like it around Buckthorn over the past few days. She'd gotten the feeling that its driver was interested in her—only a feeling, because she hadn't actually seen

him up close. Like many women she had a sixth sense
about these things. *He's looking at me, staring at me*, a
voice had whispered inside her head. *I can feel his gaze
crawling over my skin.*

On Monday afternoon she'd stepped out her front
door to collect her mail and had seen the car parked on
Columbia Avenue near the abandoned Buckthorn City
Bank building, facing Front Street. Again the voice had
whispered, but she'd ignored it. On Tuesday she'd
glanced out her living room window and had seen the
car cruise slowly past the *Renegade*, its smoky windows
reflecting the façade of the building like mirrors.

Despite her gathering apprehension, she'd dismissed
the notion that she was under surveillance or that someone might actually intend some evil toward her. Nita
Vale simply didn't think of herself as the victim type.
But today the notion wasn't so easy to dismiss, because
the car had slowed to maintain its distance behind her.

She glanced at her speedometer, and her gut tightened: the car was pacing her at exactly twenty-six miles
per hour.

IV

STELLA LEHAND GRIPPED THE WHEEL OF THE TRANS AM
with both hands, eyes glued to the cyclist on the road
ahead. A bead of sweat crawled out of her hairline and
slid down her forehead into a painted eyebrow. She
glanced into her rearview mirror, saw a 1971 Datsun
station wagon driven by Gil Monahan and hoped for the
umpteenth time that she could trust him to do this thing
right. The sad truth was that the guy was an unredeem-
able fuck-stick. She wished that she didn't need him.

For that matter, she wished that she didn't need to kill
this woman, Nita Vale. Doing that fat fuck Beswick had

been one thing, but this was something else.

Stella had surveilled Nita Vale thoroughly for the past four days, noting her comings and goings, whom she associated with, how she spent her time. Having discovered that Nita was a cycling freak, Stella had hatched the scheme to run her down on the road, make it look like a hit-and-run. After all, the woman rode her bike at all hours of the day and night, regardless of the weather, so an accident was far from unthinkable. On Monday, for example, she'd taken off on a midnight ride that lasted damn-near four hours, despite a chilly drizzle. Yesterday she'd ridden to Hillsboro before turning back, also in the rain. Surely nobody would be surprised if she turned up dead at the side of a lonely road. The cops would assume that some joy-riding high-school dude had lost control of his car and fled in panic without reporting the mishap.

Within the past ten days Stella had proved to herself that she would do just about anything if the money was right, including cold-blooded murder. But this didn't mean that she had no heart, no sense of justice. Wade Beswick had been a self-consumed Judas, an intolerable waste of oxygen. Nita Vale, on the other hand, was merely weird, having gone to extremes to change her identity and start a new life. Certainly no sin in Stella's book, for she herself had set records in weirdness.

Unfortunately Stella had no real choice in the matter—not if she wanted to put her own life on track. Tucker Bannon was the man with the checkbook, and she couldn't afford to let him become disenchanted with Todd Verduin. Not yet, anyway.

She picked up the hand-held VHF radio from the seat beside her, keyed it and used her baby-doll voice: "Glen Campbell, this is Platinum on channel 16."

The radio crackled. *"Platinum, this is Glen Campbell, go."* Gil's voice was metallic and hard to read over the droning of the stolen Datsun. He'd chosen his call sign because he admired no one in the world as much as Glen Campbell, the Man with Perfect Hair.

"Our baby sister is a couple blocks ahead of me," Stella reported, using code to mislead anyone who overheard the conversation on another VHF radio. "The coast is clear. If you want to surprise her, I say do it now."

"Roger that, *Platinum*. This is Glen Campbell—over and out."

Over and out. The guy was *such* a fuck-stick.

Stella pulled onto the shoulder of the road and slowed almost to zero. The Datsun went around her, Gil giving her a thumbs up and grinning stupidly from ear to ear.

V

NITA HEARD THE ROAR OF THE CAR BEHIND HER, SAW the junky yellow station wagon and the billowing cloud of oil-smoke spewing out its rear. The low black car had pulled off the road to let the station wagon go around it.

Her stomach knotted in terror, for things were perfectly clear now. The driver of the black car was the Stalker, while the driver of the station wagon was the Mangler. They were a team, and they meant to turn Nita into roadkill.

The station wagon veered to the right, its wheels edging onto the shoulder of the road, kicking up clods and gravel, its engine whining. Nita caught a glimpse of the driver's face, his mouth agape in a frenzied *yeowww!*, as if this was an innocent roller-coaster ride.

Nita pedaled furiously, but she knew that she had no hope of outrunning an internal combustion engine. Her only chance was to do the unexpected, catch the bastard off guard. She braved another look back, saw that the station wagon was less than two hundred yards away and coming on strong, doing at least sixty. To her right was a shallow ditch, not sufficient protection if she swerved into it, because the Mangler would simply plow in after her. A barbed-wire fence ran along the ditch, enclosing a pasture where half a dozen horses grazed. She knew that she could never get over that fence quickly enough to save herself.

Working on instinct and adrenaline, she steered toward the centerline of the road, knowing that she had only a few seconds before the Mangler caught her. The Mangler was close now, and when Nita stole a backward glance, she saw bugs on his windshield, rust on his grille. He'd pulled the car back toward the centerline, keeping her in his sights. Nita swerved suddenly to her left, like a jackrabbit, causing him to miss. The old station wagon blew by her so closely that the slipstream tugged at her hair and breaker. Exhaust fumes stung her eyes.

The Mangler hit the brakes. His tires shrieked on the asphalt as the station wagon spun out of control. The rear of the car whipped around so that the Mangler faced Nita again, and she saw terror contort his face.

A young man, she thought . . . *Now he's as scared as I am.* . . . It was a sweet thought.

The station wagon doughnutted around again, its front wheels coming to rest in the right-hand ditch, stalled. Pumping hard, Nita steered around the car and headed east, her tires humming over the pavement, the wind fresh against her cheeks. She remembered that around the next curve was a gate to an unpaved road that led into the hills, to meadows where local stockmen pastured cattle in the spring. She hoped to reach the gate and ride cross-country up the hillside, where neither the Mangler nor the Stalker could follow in their cars.

She heard a sharp pop in her left ear, and then a second and a third. Something hissed close by her cheek. Bullets pinged on the asphalt ahead of her, gouging out small craters. She glanced behind and saw the driver of the station wagon standing on the road, a stumpy machine pistol in his hands. He fired again, bright knots of flame exploding from the muzzle. Nita heard the crack of bullets as they broke the sound barrier only inches over her head.

Panic flared. She pedaled harder than she'd ever pedaled in her life, weaving from side to side to make herself a more difficult target. Rounding the curve to the left, she saw the wooden gate that led to the pastures. It was closed, and she prayed it wasn't locked. She skidded to a halt, pounded the latch, and the gate swung open, causing her to shriek with relief. She headed up the hill on the gravel road, her leg muscles screaming.

Behind her on the highway, the Mangler jammed a fresh magazine into his weapon and jumped back into the station wagon. The starter wound, and the old engine roared to life again.

VI

GIL MONAHAN WHEELED OFF THE HIGHWAY ONTO THE gravel road. Stella followed in the Trans Am.

The unpaved road twisted northward around a hillside heavily skirted with blackberries. Because the ground was damp from last night's rain, the Datsun raised no dust, and Stella could see the cyclist several hundred yards ahead. *We'll get her now*, she thought, following Gil into a tight right-hand turn. *No way can she outrun us*.

But then Nita Vale swerved off the right shoulder of the road and headed uphill through an opening in a bunker-

line of blackberries, jouncing over rocks and clumps of
brush, her legs pumping like pistons. Gil stomped his
brake pedal and skidded to a halt. Stella drew alongside
and jumped out of her car, clutching a short .38 revolver
in her fist. Gil had already taken aim with his Uzi, bracing his elbows against the windshield of the station
wagon.

"Would you look at that bitch ride a bike!" he
shouted. "She's like a cyborg, man. She's like some
kind of fucking machine. Ever see anybody go up a hill
like that?"

"For Christ's sake, don't let her get away!" Stella
shouted.

"If they find her full of bullet holes, they're gonna
know this wasn't any hit-and-run, Lamb Chop."

"Let's just get it done, God damn it!"

Gil fired a short burst that crackled through the ravine
like a string of firecrackers. The rounds kicked up
chunks of mud and grass around Nita Vale, but she rode
on untouched, climbing higher up the hill toward a stand
of Douglas firs on the summit. Gil fired another burst,
then another—more chunks of mud and bark, but no
blood, no chunks of flesh and bone.

"Son of a bitch!" he spat, repositioning himself for
another try. "These fucking things are meant for close-in
work, not long-range stuff like this." He let fly a continuous burst, the weapon bucking in his hands until running out of ammo, the spent cartridges tinkling like
metal rain on the hood of the car. But Nita crawled ever
higher up the steep hillside, zigging and zagging.

"For the love of God," Stella huffed, bracing her revolver on the hood of the Datsun. "We can't let her get
away. We've come so *close*! . . ." She popped off six
precisely aimed rounds, but the snub-nose .38 was even
less accurate than the Uzi at long range. Nita Vale disappeared into the gloom of the trees, and Stella knew

that pursuing her further would be useless—for now, at least.

VII

LATE THAT AFTERNOON, SHERIFF NICK GRAYBILL AND an Oregon State Police detective walked unannounced into Peter Cochran's office at Buckthorn Wood Products, despite a loud protest from Denise Ubaldo at the front desk.

"Sorry to barge in like this, Mr. Cochran," Graybill said, sneering, "but I need to ask you some questions, and I don't have time for ceremony." He dropped a police artist's sketch onto the blotter in front of Pete. "Know this woman?"

The sketch showed a woman of indeterminate age with huge, overly made-up eyes and heavily shaded cheeks. Short hair, maybe blond or gray—no way to tell, since the sketch was in pencil. Bangs cut razor-straight across her forehead.

Pete studied the picture. The crudely drawn facial features didn't ring any bells, but the *hair* was familiar. The gray-flannel woman had worn hair like this, a wig, most likely. Hair this radical didn't occur in nature.

"Who is she?" he asked, his skin crawling.

"I was hoping you'd tell me," Graybill said around his cigar. "She was with Wade Beswick at a bar in Portland on the night he got killed, place called Champ's. Ever been there?"

Pete shook his head.

"The bar hostess gave us a description of this lady, said they left the place together around midnight. I suppose you don't know anything about that, either."

"I wish I could help you, Sheriff, but I don't know this woman."

The Cigar harrumphed and threw a disbelieving glance at the OSP detective, who seemed content to let Graybill think he was running the show. "Then I don't guess you and this lady set up poor old Wade, so you could get him alone out in the woods and cap him through the forehead. That a safe assumption?"

Pete bit his tongue to keep it under control. He picked up the sketch, eyed it again. "Like I said, I don't know her, but I may have seen her before—or someone who looks like her. It was last fall after my wife died . . ."

He told of his encounters with the gray-flannel woman in those excruciating days immediately following Sally's death, first at his house in Rye on the occasion of the remembrance gathering; then early the next week, when the woman had sneaked into the offices of Walker, Schwinden and Cohea to hide in the closet. Graybill listened intently, glowering with suspicion, while the OSP detective wrote it all down in a small notebook.

"You say she was tall, and that she wore gray flannel, like a suit or something?" Graybill asked.

Pete confirmed this.

"And you have no idea who she is?"

"I don't even know if it's the same woman. This sketch isn't exactly gallery quality. I thought the hair looked familiar, that's all."

The two cops stared at each other, then at Pete. The Cigar finally spoke, tapping a fat finger on the sketch. "This woman wore gray flannel that night at Champ's," he said. "I've got statements from three different people who were there—she wore a gray flannel suit, a pink scarf and earrings with pink stones. What do you think about *that*, Mr. Cochran?"

"What am I supposed to think? I've never had any involvement with her. I figured she was a common thief."

"You're telling me this woman attends a party at your house in New York—"

"It wasn't a party. It was like a wake for my wife."

"Whatever—and she turns up in your wife's office the following week in Manhattan, jumps out of a closet at you?"

"It sounds ludicrous, I know."

"It sounds a hell of alot worse than that. It sounds like a guilty man pulling lies out of his ass."

"Give me some credit, for Christ's sake." Pete was on his feet now. "If I was going to concoct a story, I could do a hell of alot better than *this*."

"So you don't think it's the same woman—the white hair, the gray-flannel suit? You think it's a goddamn coincidence that a woman who looks like this was in your house last fall, then in your wife's office, then with Wade Beswick in a bar the night he died?"

Pete put his hand over his eyes. The situation had become absurd, almost comical. He could have laughed, could have cried. "Sheriff, maybe it *is* the same woman—I don't know. Maybe she killed Wade, maybe she didn't. The point is, I don't have any connection with her beyond what I just told you. I didn't arrange to have her lure Wade into the woods. I had no reason to kill him."

"No matter that you threatened to do just that the day before he died—in front of witnesses, yet."

Pete looked away, sighed, and willed himself to say no more. For once he meant to keep his mouth from getting him into even deeper trouble.

"Listen, Cochran," said the Cigar, "you're not fooling anybody. I've got your tire prints at the scene of Wade's murder and his blood inside your Cherokee. I've got the fancy Swiss-made pen you dropped. Now I've got the woman with the white hair and your admission that you know her . . ."

"I *don't* know her, damn it! How many times do I have to tell you?"

"You just admitted that she was at your house in New York, and later in your wife's office. Sounds to me like you know more about her than you're willing to let on."

That was it—Pete had had it. He thrust out his hands to the Cigar, offering his wrists for the cuffs. "Let's quit fucking around. Take me in, if you're so sure I'm guilty. Charge me, give me the rubber hose. Give me an excuse to sue your fat ass off." They glared at each other for a full ten seconds.

Graybill took his cigar out of his mouth, pointed the chewed-up end at Pete. "I'll find this woman and sweat the truth out of her. And when I do, I'll be back for you." He turned on his heel and headed out the door, the OSP detective following close behind.

Pete dropped into the chair behind his desk and tried to reconnect his nerve endings. He wondered how close he'd come to goading Graybill into hauling him in for another sweating—too close, he feared.

He glanced around his office, at the paintings on the walls—Seurat's *Bathers*, in particular, the one Sally had so loved—then at his diplomas and awards, all neatly framed, as his life had once been neatly framed, bordered and respectable, safe behind glass. He stared at the picture of Sally on his desk, the pictures of his kids, their faces full of smiles and their eyes full of simple trust—trusting that no harm could ever reach them because they were among the golden, the children of *quality* people. The world existed for *them*, their smiles said, a myth that Pete himself had perpetrated.

But harm *had* reached them, and thus far Pete had been powerless against it. He'd even compounded it. He'd brought his children here, right into the center of the evil that Sally herself had managed to escape.

Pete's eyes smarted, but he wouldn't let himself cry.
Not this time.

The intercom beeped, and Denise Ubaldo said,
"Nita's on line two for you, Pete. She doesn't sound
like herself."

He picked up the phone, heard the tremulousness in
Nita's voice. What was wrong? he asked. Had something
happened? He felt a nibbling of panic.

"Peter, I need you," she said. "I need to have you
with me *now*."

VIII

THEY HUDDLED IN THE LIVING ROOM OF HER SECOND-
floor apartment, his arms around her. She told him what
had happened only an hour ago on the lonely highway
between Birkenfeld and Mist. She described the platinum-
haired woman in the gray suit, the low black car and the
young man with the automatic assault weapon who'd
tried to run her down. She recounted her ride up the
steep hillside into the forest and her escape via back
roads and trails into Buckthorn. She tried to describe the
horror of being shot at, of missing death by inches, but
words failed her. She shuddered in Pete's arms.

He asked whether she'd seen either of her assailants
before, and she shook her head. She'd seen only the low
black car, a Camaro or a Trans Am, lurking around town
for the past few days. Until this afternoon, she hadn't
seen the driver.

Pete visualized the platinum blond in her gray suit—
Nita hadn't gotten close enough to determine the fabric,
but Pete was certain that it must have been flannel. A
very conservative dresser, this woman—anything but
chic. The last time he'd seen her, which had been in
Sally's office in Manhattan, she'd worn white Nike

sneakers with her somber executive duds. Sheriff Nick Graybill had been right, Pete knew now: This was the woman who'd crashed the remembrance gathering for Sally in Rye, who'd knocked him down after bolting out of a closet, the woman who'd lured Wade Beswick to his murder. How could she *not* be the same woman? How many people dressed in gray flannel year-round, wore platinum-blond wigs, and orbited the life of Peter Cochran for what seemed to be the sole purpose of wreaking havoc?

He held Nita close, wanting to make her feel protected, but also needing her warmth. He kissed her, massaged her shoulders, reassured her that she was safe with him. The cool weight of the pistol in his coat pocket was a comfort.

Nita drew away suddenly and went to the kitchen to make coffee. Pete warned her to stay back from the windows, to close the blinds, but she seemed curiously unconcerned. So Pete closed the blinds himself and switched on a lamp, for the afternoon had darkened with rain clouds. Nita sat in an armchair and thumbed through a magazine, the latest issue of *Cycling*.

"We've got to call the police," Pete said. "We should've done it long before now." He picked up the cordless phone from the coffee table.

"No. Not the police."

"What? Why not? Someone has just tried to kill you, for God's sake."

"Calling Nick Graybill won't do any good—he's totally consumed with the Beswick murder. He won't have time for me."

"He's not the only cop in the county. I'll talk to Dan Kantor. I'm sure he'll—"

"Pete, no! I don't want Dan to know about this. I don't want any cops, okay?"

Pete turned and stared at her. She appeared almost

smug, as if she'd just learned some delicious secret. It was Sally's look, one that Pete had seen ten thousand times. A look that said, *I'll get my way—we both know it, so you may as well get used to it.*

Pete sat down slowly on the sofa across from her, something twisting inside him. The *look* seemed almost studied, as if she'd practiced and rehearsed it in order to get it right: a certain tilt of the head, the squared shoulders, the way she bit her lower lip. And for the first time he noticed actual genetic shadings of the Bannon family—the pronounced jawline, the slope of the eyebrows, despite the widely spaced eyes and the severe Latin cheekbones.

Logic said, *She would've needed to know Sally in order to mimic her like this.* Or maybe Bannon blood actually flowed in her veins.

Pete swallowed hard and decided to leave this alone for now. "The woman in the black car—I've seen her," he said. Nita's magazine fell into her lap, and she stared back at him. "In New York, right after Sally died, she came to our house, crashed the remembrance gathering. And later . . ."

He told the rest of it, the incident in Sally's Manhattan office, the visit this afternoon from Graybill and the news that on the night he died, Wade Beswick had left a bar in the company of a platinum blonde in gray flannel. Could anyone doubt that this woman had killed Beswick, or at least had a hand in his killing? Pete couldn't. And now the woman and an accomplice had just tried to kill Nita, a fresh horror.

"Don't you see? Someone wants *both* you and Beswick dead," he said. "We need to tell the cops, Nita, because it's valuable data. It might get them off my back and lead them to the real killers before they take another crack at killing you."

"It's not that simple." Nita stood up and limped to a

shaded window, parted the Venetian blinds and looked
out.

"Sweetheart, it *is* that simple. All you need to do is
tell the police about what happened to you this afternoon. I'll grant that Graybill's no mental giant, but
there's a state cop on the Beswick case, and I doubt he's
a total idiot. If he's got half a brain, he'll conclude that
someone hired the platinum blonde to kill both Beswick
and you. Since I'm not on your enemies list, I'll be in
the clear, and the cops will be on the right track for a
change, looking for someone who wants both you and
Wade out of the way."

"Pete, I *know* who wants me dead, but I could never
tell the police about him."

"You *know* . . . ?" Nita's expression stopped him,
having become hard and cold as granite. This wasn't a
look he'd ever seen in Sally's face. It frightened him.
"Nita, you've got to tell . . ."

"I'll deal with it in my own way, like I always have
before. Now please go. I'll talk to you tomorrow."

"I can't just go. I can't leave you alone like this.
What if . . . ?"

"*Go*, Pete. Your kids are probably home from school,
and they need you. I'll be all right, I promise."

So much like Sally, he thought, his pulse racing, *so
sure of herself, charging ahead like a freight train, and
yet . . .*

Before he knew what had happened, she'd shepherded
him down the stairs and out the door.

IX

AS HE NEARED THE ACCESS ROAD TO BUCKTHORN WOOD
Products, a whistle sounded from the roof of the boiler
plant, signaling quitting time. Five o'clock. Nita

had been right—his kids had come home from school two hours ago, and he hadn't been there to meet them. He scolded himself and vowed never again to let this happen, not while they still lived in Bannon House.

He turned into the parking lot of the mill and nosed into the space reserved for the mill manager—himself, now that Wade was gone. He planned to put in a quick appearance at the head shed and go home immediately, leaving Wally MacKenzie and Denise Ubaldo to close up shop. But before he could slide out from behind the wheel of the Cherokee, a silver BMW pulled into the slot next to him. A man got out, light-haired and immaculate in a well-cut business suit.

"You're Peter Cochran, aren't you? I'm Paul Garson." The man approached, held out his hand. "You may have heard my name in connection with the Conifer Group in Portland."

Pete shook his hand, thinking, *The Conifer Group— my God!*

Garson was a few years younger than himself, a gaunt figure with worried eyes behind horn-rimmed glasses. He appeared as if he hadn't slept well lately. "Sorry to accost you like this, but can we talk privately? It's very important. I've been waiting over an hour."

Pete chuckled. "But you just drove up . . ."

"I was parked over there in the mill workers' section, watching for you. Your parking space was empty, so I figured you'd gone out. I didn't want to meet you inside, and I couldn't call on the phone. You see . . ." Garson fidgeted, wiped one hand with the other. "I don't want our conversation to end up on tape, if you know what I mean."

"On tape? I don't understand."

Garson smiled, but without humor. "Come on, Mr. Cochran. You know your phones are bugged. You guys probably tape everything that goes on in your shop, right?"

The *Conifer Group*. Pete figured that Garson had come to demand repayment of the two-point-five million that Buckthorn Wood Products had borrowed to upgrade its production line. Or maybe he'd come to start formal foreclosure proceedings.

"I'm not aware of any recording equipment in our offices," Pete said. "Anyway, I'm pressed for time at the moment. I was about to head home and . . ."

Garson grabbed his arm, a desperate gesture. "Please, Mr. Cochran. This won't take long."

Pete swatted the man's hand away. "Look, Mr. Garson, I've had a hard day, and it's starting to rain. I suggest we get together with our lawyers during regular business hours. Why don't you call me tomorrow, and we'll . . ."

"God damn it, I've come to make a deal! I'm here to tell you that my partners and I will do anything you and Tucker want—we just don't want to end up like Wade Beswick."

"Like *Wade* . . . ?" Pete saw raw fear in Garson's face, saw it tug the corners of his mouth. The man looked close to a breakdown. "What the hell are you talking about?"

"Don't act dumb. We both know why Beswick is dead. He turned on his master, bit the hand that fed him. Tucker Bannon isn't the kind of man to let something like that go unpunished, is he?"

"You're out of your mind."

"Be that as it may, I'm authorized to tell you that we'll pay anything within reason to put an end to this matter. We'll simply pretend that none of it ever happened, all right? Just tell me what you people want."

By now a noisy traffic jam had developed near the front gate—gunning engines, honking horns, whining fan belts. The mill workers were anxious to park their butts on barstools and wrap their hands around cold cans of beer. On the shore of the millpond loomed the head rig building, a dinosaurian hulk of corroding metal, its blades silent for the night. Straddle buggies stood abandoned in the lumberyard. Higher on the hill the boiler rumbled and belched smoke, as it would through most of the dark hours, powering the floodlights that kept the complex as bright as noon, even at midnight. An aged watchman and a boiler man were the only night-shift workers at Buckthorn Wood Products these days.

Pete nodded toward the head rig. "Let's go up there and talk. It's about as private as you can get."

"Fine." Garson followed along, although he looked hesitant. *He's scared of me*, Pete thought. *He probably thinks I'm going to feed him to the head rig, saw him into four by sixes*. He smiled, despite the sick feeling in his gut.

They took shelter from the rain inside the head rig building, at the base of an elevated walkway next to the great saw with its oily, toothy blades. The dark interior stank of damp sawdust and fresh sap. Now Pete wished they hadn't come here. The place gave him the creeps.

Garson presented an offer—the Conifer Group would write off the two-point-five million it had lent Buckthorn Wood Products and hand over an additional one-point-five million as a gesture of "goodwill," if Tucker and Pete would assure them that the police would never find out about the conspiracy with Wade Beswick to defraud Tucker of the Mount Olivet timberlands. The principals of the Conifer Group would pledge never to divulge their knowledge that Tucker had arranged Wade Beswick's death. A kind of equilibrium, Garson called it, chuckling nervously—a balance of terror. Mutually assured destruction. Life goes on, nobody goes to jail. Nobody gets killed.

Pete stared incredulously at Garson, who looked so thin and pale that he might fade into the mist if he were to step out the door. "Tell me something," Pete said above the growl of the nearby boiler. "Why should I believe any of this? Why would *anybody* believe it?"

"Because I'm a reliable witness," Garson said flippantly. He knew firsthand about the fraud attempt, he explained, because he'd been in on it from the beginning. He'd been the one whom Beswick had initially approached. He'd listened to the man's proposal and had taken it to the Conifer Group partners. He'd signed off on it with his vote and had functioned as the partners' go-between with Wade. He'd been present when Tucker's hireling, Todd Verduin, had delivered audio cassettes of a private meeting that Wade had attended with the Conifer Group in its Portland offices. The tapes were the smoking gun, the incontrovertible evidence of an attempt at fraud.

"Todd Verduin brought you the cassettes?"

Garson nodded. "He's some kind of surveillance expert, been working for your father-in-law a long time. Apparently he bugged our offices—we have no idea how. We hired our own private investigator to check him out. His reputation for integrity is—how should I say this?—somewhat less than sterling."

Pete remembered that Todd Verduin drove a black Trans Am. Verduin had given him a ride home in the car, having possibly saved him from God-only-knew what kind of harm at the hands of Jerry Dragstead, who'd followed him from Nita's place in the black of night. A seed of suspicion took root in the cellar of Pete's mind, but for the moment that's all it was—a seed.

"I don't know why I'm telling *you* all this," Garson went on, "as if you're pure as the driven snow. You're up to your ass in guilty knowledge, just like I am."

"I swear to you, this is the first I've ever heard about any deal that Wade cooked up with you or anyone else. I did know about the loan, but only because I stumbled

across it in the company's financial records. Wade never
bothered to tell me about it.''

"Of course he didn't tell you about it. He was counting on us to foreclose before you could get your hands
on the company's finances. What he didn't know was
that Tucker had hired Verduin to bug the offices of his
own company—that's the kind of stuff Verduin does for
his clients, bugging offices and phones, putting in hidden
cameras. Tucker no doubt overheard a phone conversation between Wade and me—candid talk about our plan,
gory details.'' Garson pinched the ridge of his nose between his eyes and massaged it. "Jesus Christ, we
should've known better. How could we have been so
fucking careless?"

What a guy, Pete thought. *Tortured by guilt not for
having committed a serious crime, but for having gotten
caught. He should work for an insurance company.* "I
don't understand why Tucker sent you the tapes," Pete
said. "Why not simply go to the cops?"

"It was his cute way of telling us to eat shit, to forget
about ever getting our two-point-five million back, never
mind the Mount Olivet timberlands. And we would've
let it go at that, except for what you guys did to Wade."

"Now wait just a damn minute—"

"Hey, look at it from our point of view. We don't
have any way of knowing just how far Tucker's sense
of justice might push him, and we figured it was time
to reach an understanding. For all we know, he plans to
kill *all* of us."

Pete vigorously denied any involvement in Beswick's
murder, news stories to the contrary notwithstanding.
And much to his own amazement, he found himself de-
fending Tucker Bannon, insisting that his father-in-law
was no murderer. Conniving and overbearing, yes, perhaps even ruthless in his own way—but certainly not a
murderer.

"Okay, so you're not in the mood to talk about a deal," Garson said, peeking through a crack in the scarred wooden door to make certain that no one was outside. "I can relate to that. You don't know me from Adam. I could be a cop, or I could be wearing a wire, right?"

Pete hadn't thought of this, but it seemed plausible. A *wire*. How could things have come to this—when Peter Cochran of all people needed to worry that the police might be taping his conversations?

"Just remember that we're not exactly defenseless, Mr. Cochran. If anything unfortunate happens to one of the Conifer Group partners, the rest of us will go en masse to the police. We'll tell everything we know and try to bargain down our sentences to avoid jail time. You and your father-in-law will go to prison for murdering Wade Beswick." Garson grinned crookedly and offered Pete a business card. "On the other hand, if you and Tucker come to your senses, call me, and we'll get together. Being mature businessmen, I'm sure we can reach an accommodation."

"This is crazy," Pete said, taking the card. Garson pushed through the door and walked back across the muddy parking lot, a stick figure stepping awkwardly over ruts left by logging trucks. Pete watched him get into his BMW and motor away.

The rain intensified. Gauzy clouds dropped low over the town, darkening the evening prematurely. Pete drove home like a robot, eyes glazed over, headlights on and wipers swishing, his mind cluttered with fears and suspicions.

Could Tucker actually have arranged the murder of Wade Beswick, or maybe even pulled the trigger himself? Pete couldn't quite dismiss the notion, despite what he'd told Garson. Only four days ago he'd almost concluded that the old man had framed him for Beswick's

murder in order to get custody of Sarah and Carter. If
Tucker was capable of framing his own son-in-law for
murder, then he might also be capable of doing the actual deed.

Pete's mind raced on. Todd Verduin—now *there* was
a piece of work—drove a black Trans Am. One of Nita's
would-be killers, the platinum blond in gray flannel, had
also driven a low, black car—possibly a Camaro or a
Trans Am, Nita had said. Someone with a vivid imagination might conclude that the gray-flannel woman had
driven Verduin's car this afternoon while chasing Nita,
which would mean that the gray-flannel woman had a
link to Tucker, who was Verduin's client. If she had
indeed participated in the killing of Wade Beswick,
which appeared to be the case, had she done so because
Tucker had hired her?

As Paul Garson had pointed out, Tucker certainly had
reason to want Wade Beswick dead: Wade had con-
spired to steal the bulk of the Bannon family's fortune.
Garson had been right in suggesting that Tucker wasn't
the kind to let this magnitude of transgression go unpunished.

Pete remembered something else: Verduin had visited
him in his office—on the day Wade died—ostensibly to
introduce himself formally and to offer his services as a
security guy. Reconstructing the meeting in his mind,
Pete remembered that Verduin had directed his attention
to the Seurat print on the wall, something about the penciled print number. Had this been a distraction that enabled the private detective to steal his Mont Blanc pen
in order to plant it at the scene of Wade's murder?

Other questions gnawed at him as he approached the
front gate of Bannon House. Most vexing was the question of how Nita figured into the puzzle. Why would
Tucker want her dead? And why hadn't she let Pete call
the police to report the attempt on her life?

He remembered the last thing she'd said before pushing him out the door this afternoon: *I'll deal with it in my own way, like I always have before.*

X

TUCKER SCARCELY FELT THE RAIN ON HIS FACE AS HE strode toward the gardener's shed at the rear of Bannon House, a sockful of sand swinging from his fist. He scarcely noticed the spatters of rain on the lenses of his glasses. For that matter he was aware of little beyond the heat of righteous, God-given anger boiling up from the depths of his soul.

"I'm ready to do Thy will, Lord," he breathed. "I'll be your weapon, your staff. Use me to smite the evil that has arisen before me."

A light burned in the gardener's shed, meaning that the boy was there, hunched over his poisons and traps, in all likelihood. The *Verminator*, he called himself.

Tucker chastised himself for not having seen the evil in this Verminator nonsense long before now. Letting a boy immerse himself in killing wasn't healthy, even if mice and bugs and weeds were his only victims. Tucker wished that he'd forced him to take up good wholesome activities at church and school, encouraged him to play football and basketball, taken him fishing and hunting, instead of letting him hole up here in this stinking shed, breathing toxic fumes and hoarding the carcasses of gophers and moles. "I should've seen this coming, Lord . . ."

He tried the door, found it locked. He didn't call out to the boy, didn't even knock, but stepped back and launched a heavy boot at the latch. The door gave way with a crash and a shower of splinters.

Topper jumped up from his workbench, his eyes

round as silver dollars. Tucker watched the color drain
from his broad face as he beheld the wrath of God
having come to beat the Devil out of him.

"I just got off the phone with Andrea Dorn, the superintendent of schools," Tucker said. "She informed
me that you've played hooky for three days running."

"Dad, I—"

"Shut your accursed mouth!" Tucker advanced several steps, expecting Topper to back away, to begin cow-
ering, but the boy stood his ground. "That's not all she
told me," he went on. "She'd just spoken with your
therapist, and he'd informed her that you've been un-
cooperative and dishonest with him. You've been telling
him what you think he wants to hear, and today you
didn't even bother to show up for your therapy session."
Tucker whipped the heavy sock into an open palm, but
Topper didn't flinch.

*What is this, Lord? Has the Evil One made him
brave? Does he really think he can stand against Thy
wrath?*

"Dr. Feldon doesn't help me anymore, Dad. He's a
waste of time."

"A waste of *time*? Is that what you think?" Tucker
made a production of removing his glasses, folding
them, slipping them into a pocket of his Pendleton shirt.
"You're not qualified to say what's a waste of time and
what isn't. Apparently you're not even bright enough to
understand that Dr. Feldon is the only thing standing
between you and a locked cell in some institution for
the criminally insane. That's what they want to do, you
know—put you in an institution. Dr. Feldon says you've
got something called *dissociative disorder*, which means
that you let yourself become this Verminator character
in order to escape responsibility for the evil things you
do. Your sick, half-breed brain tells you that it's not *you*
who's bad—it's the Verminator. You've been *dissoci-*

ating—understand?'' He unbuttoned his cuffs and started to roll up his sleeves.

"What are you going to do?" Topper asked.

"What I always do when you need a lesson in God's goodness. Only it'll be different this time, because you probably won't be able to walk for a week, maybe a month depending on how far He lets me go. Or maybe you'll never walk again, which might turn out to be a blessing. The Lord might make a cripple out of you just to keep you from doing the Devil's mischief. If that's what happens, we'll all raise up our voices to the Lord and give thanks unto Him.'' He grinned through clenched dentures.

"No," Topper replied, stiffening to his full height. "Not this time. I won't let you hurt me anymore, Dad."

Tucker finished rolling his sleeves. "Is that so? Think you're man enough to stand against me?"

The boy stared back at him, his eyes as opaque as nuggets of coal. Tucker felt a twinge of uncertainty, the first time his faith had ever faltered. Was the rage that boiled inside him really God's, he wondered, or was it his own—a foul, man-made thing that stank of human passions and delusions? Had God actually given him this yearning to inflict pain and injury on the boy, or was this simple brutishness?

Help me, Lord. Give me the strength not to doubt Thee.

"Hey, can you believe this shit, ladies and gentlemen? Old Hairy Ears actually thinks he's going to give the Verminator another thumping. You've got to hand it to him, he's got stones, doesn't he? Let's hear it for old Hairy Ears—come on, now. Give it up for old Hairy Ears and his stones . . ."

Tucker's mouth went dry. Before his very eyes the boy became something hellish, a grinning caricature of himself that capered and mugged before an unseen studio audience, acknowledging laughter and applause that happened only inside his head.

". . . but the funny thing is, ladies and gentlemen, he doesn't understand what's been going on here. He doesn't realize that a new administration has come to power. He thinks the Verminator will fold up like a cheap pup tent and let him pound away with his sockful of sand, just like all those other times. *Wrong*-O! . . ." He made a harsh, wrong-answer buzz from deep in his throat. "This time it's gonna be different—right, ladies and gentlemen? This time the Verminator's gonna protect himself . . ."

Tucker's rage took him finally. He drew back his arm to strike, seeing not the boy he'd raised from infancy, but an absurdity, an affront to God and all who worshipped Him. "*A worthless person, a wicked man!*" he shouted, quoting his favorite book of the Old Testament, Proverbs. "*Talks with a perverse mouth; He winks with his eyes, He shuffles his feet, He points with his fingers . . .*" He swung hard at Topper, meaning to lay the sockful of sand square on the boy's face, but Topper dodged away. The blow found nothing but air.

"Whoa!—that was close, ladies and gentlemen!"

Tucker lost his balance but caught it again, then rounded on Topper for another try. Now he wanted more than merely to thrash the evil out of the kid. He wanted to punish and maim, to beat him to a flinching pulp. "*Perversity is in his heart,*" he shouted, swinging. "*He devises evil continually. He sows discord . . .*"

This time Topper blocked the blow with his forearm and lashed out with his other fist, catching Tucker flatly in the teeth. Sparks erupted behind the old man's eyes, and suddenly his mouth was full of blood. He knew that the blow had fractured his upper dentures. Somehow he managed to catch himself on the edge of the workbench and break his fall to the floor. He scrambled to his feet, spitting blood, trying to focus on the shifting shape of Topper as he posed and strutted before his invisible audience.

"And the Verminator scores a hard right to old Hairy Ears' jaw, ladies and gentlemen, and the old boy goes down like a sack of shit! What a counterpunch! What footwork! My-oh-myyyy."

Tucker's breath came in wet hisses now, speckling his chin with blood. Strong though he was, and still in good shape, the weight of age dragged on him. His arthritic knees sang with pain. His arm throbbed where he'd bruised it while falling against the workbench.

He growled more from Proverbs, his words thick around broken teeth. *"Therefore his calamity shall come suddenly. Suddenly he shall be broken without remedy . . ."*

He managed to catch Topper on the side of the head with the sock, and it was a good, hard blow. He expected the boy to go down, but no—Topper staggered, swaggered, and snatched up a metal bucket from a corner of the shed. Tucker managed to fend off the first roundhouse swing, but the second landed on the top of his head, causing another explosion of stars. A second blow came, and Tucker couldn't fend it off, couldn't even see where it came from.

"Lord God, protect Thy servant . . ."

"And the Verminator scores another blow with the pail, folks, and another and *another*! Would you look at this?—old Hairy Ears is bleeding from the top of his not-so-hairy head!"

Tucker went hard to the floor. He was a mass of pain now, a jerking, uncoordinated puppet. He tried to regain his feet, but the blows kept coming, landing on his head, his shoulders, his arms, each igniting a new knot of pain.

"And the Verminator scores again! And *again*! And *again*! And . . ."

One blow caught Tucker in the temple, but it produced no stars, only murky lumps of gray and brown that flowered behind his eyes like swabs of dirty cotton. He no longer heard Topper's screeching or saw the bare lightbulb swinging on its cord overhead. For a moment he wondered if he'd plunged down the chute of death, if the next face he saw would be the Lord's. But alas, he awoke suddenly on the unforgiving cement floor of the gardener's shed, not to the singing of heaven's angels but to the soft whimpering of a woman.

The face he saw belonged not to the Lord, but to Dolly. Her cheeks were wet with tears. Tucker found himself lying with his head in her lap, felt her soft hands cradle him.

"Where's Topper?" he asked, struggling to sit up. He could barely talk around broken dentures and lacerated gums. His head throbbed with every heartbeat. "What has . . . what has he . . . ?"

"He's gone," she said. "He ran away, up the mountain."

"How long ago?"

"Only a few minutes. Esmerelda has gone after him. We heard the racket and ran out here. He was . . ." She whimpered, struggled to keep control of herself. "He was beating you. You were here on the floor, and he . . ."

"I know, I know." He levered himself up onto his elbows, took inventory of his aching body. "I don't think I'm hurt bad—for an old man, that is." Which wasn't quite true. His head felt as if it might explode, and he had double vision.

"I thought you were—dead," Dolly said.

"Well, I'm not. What about the kids? Did they see any of this? Are they outside?"

"They're in their rooms. Peter had just come home, and I've asked him to keep them there."

"Good, that's good. Now help me back to the house. I need to find my spare teeth. And I need to think."

"I should take you to the emergency room in Hills-boro, make sure you're all right."

"No need of that—I'll be fine."

She helped him into the house, got him to their bed-room, where she began cleaning his cuts and bruises, applying antiseptic and bandages. She informed him that he was developing a pair of spectacular shiners.

"Black eyes are the least of my worries," he told her. "The important thing is to find that boy, get him back here."

"He'll come back on his own. It isn't like him to stay away."

"That's exactly the problem, Dolly—he's not him-self. Something has gotten into him, turned him into someone I don't even recognize. You should've seen him a while ago, doing his TV-show thing, except it's no longer make-believe for him. It's *real*. I could sense that he really believed that he was this—this *Verminator* fellow, someone completely unlike our Topper. I tried to beat it out of him, but he's too big now. And too strong."

Dolly's face tightened. "Then what should we do about him? If he's become dangerous, we can't simply let things lie. *Can* we? Tucker, we have the children to think of."

Tucker lay back on the bed and stared at the ceiling. "Yes, the children." Real *Bannon* children, with pure *Bannon* blood in their veins. Not poor mixed-breeds like Topper. "We need to pray about it, ask the Lord's guid-ance. We've come so close to making this family what the Lord has always wanted it to be, and I won't let . . ." He was about to say that he wouldn't let Topper keep them from achieving their destiny, even if more blood must flow—Topper's, mixing with the blood of those

others who'd threatened the well-being of the Bannon
family. But Tucker didn't say this.

Sometimes it's best for a man to keep his own counsel.

XI

*PETER, FIND THE CHILDREN AND TAKE THEM TO THEIR
rooms . . . !*

Gramma Dolly had given the order the very moment
Pete had set foot through the door, using a tone that had
reminded him of his own mother's, back when he was
a small boy in a western suburb of Chicago, a place
where tornadoes occasionally touched down and demol-
ished whole neighborhoods. Blinking, he'd seen a scribble of lightning across a black sky, heard his mother's
voice against the keening wind: *Peter, take your sister
to the basement—Now! Don't argue with me! . . .*

So he'd obeyed, as he'd obeyed his own mother so
many years ago, asking no questions, demanding no ex-
planations. This was no tornado, but it might've been
something worse. *Much* worse. He'd hustled Sarah and
Carter from the third-floor playroom to their respective
rooms on the second floor, while Dolly and Esmerelda
had dashed out the rear door of the house to tend to
some unknown emergency.

The kids had looked at him as if he was crazy. They'd
asked what was wrong, and he'd assured them that nothing was wrong. That everything was fine. But something
was dreadfully wrong, he knew. Pete's imagination had
spun out of control: *We don't worry about tornadoes
here in Buckthorn—we worry about cold-blooded
killers . . .*

Moments after closing Sarah and Carter in their
rooms, he'd caught a glimpse of Tucker and Dolly on

the rear stairs, Tucker's head draped with a bloody towel, Dolly propping him up. *It's all right*, the old woman had said, waving away Pete's offer to help. *Don't worry about us—we'll be fine*. They'd disappeared into their bedroom, and that's where they'd stayed. Only the occasional flush of a toilet provided any reminder of their presence in the house. As for Esmerelda and Topper, they were simply gone, Esmerelda having left a half-prepared pan of lasagna in the kitchen, probably intended to be tonight's dinner.

An unnerving silence fell over Bannon House, reminding Pete of a museum after hours. With the kids safely ensconced in their rooms, he reconnoitered the first floor of the mansion, his hand on the pistol in his sport coat pocket. He tiptoed from room to room, peeking around corners, searching for any clue as to what had caused the recent uproar, finding none. He glanced over the sumptuous furnishings, the Oriental carpets, the curved brass chandeliers, the antique hutches and vases and knickknacks, occasionally running a fingertip over a porcelain urn or a brocade tapestry, thinking, *Sally touched this. She grew up in these rooms.*

But the touch of old household fixtures produced no sense of closeness to her, no inkling of her presence, and that was hardly a surprise. Sally had hated this house, her parents, the whole town. She'd run away from Buckthorn and had never looked back, except—

Pete remembered the letters from Rosa Juanita Sandoval, whose surname was the same as Esmerelda's. The letters represented the sole surviving artifact of Buckthorn in Sally's life, the one thing she'd taken with her. A *relationship*. Pete wondered whether the time had come to find out what was in those letters.

Six o'clock came and went, and Esmerelda still hadn't shown up, so Pete invaded the kitchen and prepared food for himself and the kids—ham sandwiches and yester-

day's left-over stew warmed in the microwave. He called
Sarah and Carter down from their rooms and set the
simple fare before them in the breakfast nook, hovering
nearby with the reassuring weight in his pocket. Naturally, both children were curious about why Esmerelda
hadn't served dinner as she normally did, and why
Grampa Tuck, Gramma Dolly and Topper weren't eating
tonight. Rather than tell a bald-faced lie, Pete speculated
that Tuck and Dolly didn't feel well—this sometimes
happened to older folks, he said. As for Topper and Esmerelda, he supposed they'd gone out. He said nothing
about the troubling glimpses he had gotten of Tucker
and Dolly on the stairs.

Afterward, they retired to the third-floor playroom to
watch TV, Gerard curling on the floor at one end of the
sofa and snoring loudly. Pete kept an ear cocked for
sounds elsewhere in the house, the slamming of a door,
footfalls on the stairs, anything to indicate the return of
Esmerelda or Topper. But he heard nothing. Before he
knew it, the kids were nodding off and the eleven
o'clock news was on, with coverage of Kurt Cobain's
suicide and how Hillary Clinton made $100,000 in the
futures market.

News of the outside world seemed trivial, his private
worries having swollen to occupy every cubic inch of
his consciousness. His father-in-law was a murderer, in
all likelihood. His brother-in-law was a teenage journey-
man psychosexual maniac. Someone had tried to kill the
new woman in his life, and Pete himself was a suspect
in the murder of Wade Beswick. With woes like these,
he couldn't work up much sympathy for a smacked-out,
self-obsessed rock star or much interest in the first lady's
way with pork bellies.

While the kids dozed on the playroom sofa, he lugged
the mattress from Carter's room into his own and outfitted it with sheets and pillows. He then shook them

awake and informed them that they would sleep in his room tonight—Sarah would use Carter's mattress, while Carter would share his dad's bed. It would be like a camping trip, he told them, or a slumber party. It would be fun.

"*Fun?*" Sarah whined. "This is your idea of *fun*? Why can't we just like sleep in our own rooms?"

"This is *so* weird," Carter chimed in.

"It's not weird, and it *will* be fun," Pete insisted. "Trust me."

"Daddy, there's nothing to be afraid of here," Sarah said, planting her fists on her hips. "You don't have to stand guard over us, okay? We'll be perfectly safe in our own rooms. The Lord will watch over us, just like He always does."

Pete shook his head, forced a smile. "I know you think this is crazy, but humor me. It's important that we stay together tonight." And tomorrow night, too, he thought. And all the nights after that.

"It's about Topper, isn't it?" Carter said, his eyes wide and blue. "You're worried about him, aren't you? You think he's bad."

"What makes you think that, bud?" Pete asked. The boy looked away, and Pete thought, *He knows something. Or he's seen something.*

After the customary washing of faces and brushing of teeth, the children retired to their new beds, and Pete, too, lay down to sleep, but his anxieties wouldn't let him. Whenever he closed his eyes he saw faces—that of the gray-flannel woman, her gaze hard and homicidal, her teeth bared in a tight grin. Or Paul Garson's, his lips trembling as he negotiated for his life. Or Todd Verduin's, vulpine and smooth, almost childlike. He saw Vonda Reuben, Nick Graybill, even Jerry Dragstead . . .

It was the image of Jerry Dragstead that jolted him

awake, the beginnings of a nightmare. *Jerry Dragstead.
And a big yellow cat . . .*

He sat up in bed and checked the shaving kit he'd
shoved under the bed, felt inside it for the pistol. The
cool metal felt good to the touch, and he took courage
from it. Then he heard sounds downstairs, indefinite
whumps and thumps of people moving around on
carpeted floors, faraway footfalls on the stairs, the
squeak of a hinge. A dropped shoe, maybe, or a closing
door. He had no way of knowing whether he'd heard
Esmerelda or Topper. Or both. Someone had come
home.

He slept finally, but not for long. A sad melody
nudged him awake, sung in a contralto that floated on
the dark like a fallen leaf in the wind.

> *Nunca tengas miedo de la luna,
> mi niño, porque ella te cantará un arrullo. . . .*

Pete's hair stood on end. The voice was unmistakable,
but also impossible—it belonged to Sally. He knew almost no Spanish, but he could have sung along, so often
had he heard this song.

> *Nunca tengas miedo de las estrellas,
> mi niño, porque ellas te enviarán un sueño . . .*

She'd sung it to Sarah and Carter when each was
small—a mere lullaby, she'd said. On rare occasions
she'd even sung it to Pete, once when he'd suffered
acutely over failure to land a particularly desirable job,
one that had seemed well suited to his skills and experience. He'd been unable to sleep after getting the rejection letter, and she'd sung to him, soothing him, helping
him endure the sting of defeat.

Nunca tengas miedo de la noche,
mi niño, porque la oscuridad es tu amigo.
Recuerda siempre que la Señora está cerca de ti.
La Señora está cerca.

"Dad, do you hear that?" Carter asked, turning over in bed to face him. "It's Mom's song. It sounds like . . . almost like . . ."

Pete shushed him and swung out of bed. The luminous dial on his watch said 3:15. The rain had stopped, and a fulgent moon glared through rips in the clouds, brightening the bedroom. Gerard snored next to the window, a reassuring sound. Pete shrugged into his bathrobe.

Where was he going? Carter wanted to know, and Pete shushed him again. What could he say?—that he meant to hunt down the ghost and tell her how sorry he was for breaking her trust, then beg her forgiveness? His throat became tight. He told himself that he didn't believe in ghosts, not even Sally's, no matter what his ears told him.

"Only down the hall," he managed, crouching to fetch the pistol from under the bed. Keeping it hidden from his son, he slipped it into the pocket of the bathrobe. "Lock the door behind me, and don't let anyone in until I come back. Understand?"

By now Sarah too was awake, and she scrambled from the mattress on the floor into the bed with her brother. Pete gave her a thumbs-up as he slipped out the door, thinking how pale she looked, wondering whether the moonlight was responsible or whether she was that terrified. Her thirteenth birthday was only weeks away, but in this light—wearing her calico nightdress—she looked like a small child. *My little Sluggo . . .*

The floor in the hallway creaked under Pete's weight, as floors in old houses do, but the singing went on, drawing him deeper into the hallway on his left. Carefully

planting one bare foot in front of the other, he made his
way past the main staircase toward the front wing of the
house, where the Bannons had their rooms. Master suite
straight ahead, Topper's room off to the right.

The hallway was almost black, for Pete had decided
not to switch on a light lest he warn the intruder, whoever she was. He needed to find her, maybe capture her.
He needed to *see* her.

Keeping close to the left-hand wall, he felt his way
past the door of the bedroom where Sarah had slept before tonight, past the bathroom she'd used. He turned
right at the sewing room, heading past the door that led
to the master suite, where Tucker and Dolly slept. A
mere dozen steps from Topper's door now, he knew the
location of the singer—Topper's room. A soft light in-
fused this branch of the hall, from a window beyond the
open door, a mixture of moonlight and the glow of ex-
terior security lamps.

> *Nunca tengas miedo de la luna,*
> *mi niño, porque ella te cantará un arrullo . . .*

Pete's hand tightened on the pistol, but he kept it in
the pocket of his robe. As he neared the door, he felt a
cool lick of air, and he discovered that he was sweating
like a butcher. But he heard something, too—a low
whimper, a desolate sob. Two more steps took him
nearly to the door. He pressed his back against the left
wall of the hallway before inching forward, far enough
now to glimpse the interior of Topper's room.

He leaned around the doorjamb, sweat burning one
eye. What he saw jolted him. A young woman with short
blond hair sat on the edge of Topper's bed, singing to
the boy as he lay naked on tangled sheets. Topper wept
as she sang the lullaby, his sobs wracking him, con-
vulsing him, shaking the bed. The woman wore a long,

diaphanous dress of gray or white, possibly the same dress she'd worn when Pete first saw her in the wood line behind the house. Her back was to him, so he couldn't see her face. But he could see the way she held herself, so straight and square-shouldered, ever the paragon of good posture.

It was Sally.

But *not* Sally.

It *couldn't* be Sally, he screamed silently, no matter that she sang with Sally's voice. Sally was dead and gone, and even if the dead *could* come back, Sally wouldn't, because coming back would violate everything she stood for. A hater of superstition and a militant disbeliever in all things that go bump in the night, she would never deign to show up as a ghost and prove that she'd been wrong about these things.

So who was this woman? The Mad Witch of Olivet? The thought caused another jolt of ice down Pete's spine.

The voice was Sally's, no doubt about that.

He felt himself lean forward into the room, his body fighting itself, part of him craving a final close encounter with the woman he'd so loved, a chance to tell her how sorry he was for breaking his promise. For fucking things up so badly for himself and the children. He craved one last kiss, one last embrace. But another part of him recoiled in dread from this thing that might not be Sally, that *couldn't* be Sally.

"Mommy!" cried a little boy in the dark—and Pete nearly jumped out of his skin. "Mommy! . . ." Something brushed by him, a wiry body, and he realized that Carter had followed him through the hallway. His hand flew out instinctively, grabbing the boy before he could go more than a step into Topper's bedroom. The woman shot to her feet, whirling around and fanning the dress she wore. She flew to the window and plunged through it, escaping over the tiled roof that covered the northern porch. Pete heard the thumping of her feet over tiles, but then Topper started to scream at the top of his lungs— a screeching, inhuman sound that set Pete's teeth on edge. With Carter flailing in his arms, Pete retreated back toward his room, where he spent the next hour trying to calm him.

21

I

THE FOLLOWING MORNING, A THURSDAY, PETE ROUSED Sarah and Carter, fed them instant Cream of Wheat with sliced bananas, and took stock of the situation. Neither child seemed especially upset over last night's unnerving goings-on, which amazed him and restored his faith in their resilience. Both seemed resigned to attending school as usual, for which Pete was glad. School, he figured, was the best place for them these days, the *safest* place. Topper wouldn't dare try to harm them there. So he escorted them to the front gate of Bannon House and waited with them until they were safely aboard the bus.

He then drove to work, though he had no intention of trying to accomplish anything in his new capacity of sawmill manager. He wanted to get out of Bannon House and avoid a face-to-face confrontation with Tucker, because he feared that he might not be able to control his hatred of the old reptile. Too, he needed to speak with Denise Ubaldo.

"Denise," he said, leaning over the receptionist's desk, "can I see you in my office?"

"Certainly."

After she closed the door behind her, Pete said, "You speak and read Spanish, right?"

"Of course. It's my first language."

"How would you like to do a little personal work for me? My wife left some letters when she died, quite a lot of them actually, written in Spanish. I'd like to know what's in them. I'll pay you, naturally."

"I'd be happy to translate them for you, and there's no need to pay me. Do you have them with you?"

"They're in storage, but I'll pick them up and bring them to you today. I really appreciate this, Denise."

"It will be my pleasure, Pete. I'm glad you asked."

II

DAN KANTOR SHOWED HIS BADGE TO THE VETERINAR-ian, Dr. Gary Corliss, and thanked him for seeing him on such short notice. He explained why he was here in Hillsboro: Pursuant to an ongoing criminal investigation, the Oregon State Police had undertaken to check out every recorded loss of sodium pentobarbital that had occurred in northwestern Oregon since 1981. State pharmaceuticals regulators had supplied a long list of doctors' offices, medical clinics, hospitals and veterinary facilities that had reported losses since that time, and the OSP had begun a routine inquiry into every one. Kantor did not reveal that the investigation concerned the Buckthorn killer. Neither did he reveal that he was personally acquainted with one of Dr. Corliss's regular clients—Jerry Dragstead.

"I'll be happy to help any way I can," Corliss said. He was a husky man in his mid-forties, thick-necked and light-skinned. He looked like he'd played linebacker in high school.

"It says here you reported a loss in 1988," Kantor said, consulting papers inside a manila folder. "Can you tell me exactly what happened?"

Corliss explained that he'd just opened a practice in downtown Hillsboro, a small clinic only a few blocks from his present location. Like other vets, he kept an inventory of sodium pent for use as an anesthetic and a euthanizing agent—for putting animals to death, in other words. In the summer of 1988, a fire had destroyed his inventory of the drug, not a big fire—just a volunteer assistant getting careless with a Bunsen burner in the lab area. So it hadn't really been a matter of failing to account for the drug. His inventory of sodium pent had simply gone up in smoke.

Kantor nodded, jotted notes in a small spiral pad. Any chance, he asked, that the fire could have been intended to obscure a theft? Corliss laughed and said no. The volunteer assistant had been an upstanding member of the community who couldn't have had any use for sodium pent outside the clinic.

Kantor scanned an NCIC printout and noted that Corliss himself was a solid citizen with no convictions for drug possession or trafficking, no felony beefs of any kind. He jotted more notes

"One more question," he said. "You have a client named Jerry Dragstead."

"That's right. Lives up in Buckthorn, owns a whole passel of dogs and cats."

"Have you ever euthanized a pet for him?"

"Oh sure, half a dozen times, at least. He owns so many animals, it seems like he's always in here with a thirteen- or fourteen-year-old dog who can't walk anymore. I don't mean to imply that Jerry doesn't take good care of his animals—he does."

"Has he ever asked to be present during the procedure?"

"Always. He holds the animal's head while I put the needle in and cries like a baby."

"So he knows about sodium pentobarbital, does he?"

"Well, yes. I suppose he does."

"Does he know where you keep it?"

"That I couldn't tell you, Lieutenant, but I doubt it."

"Thank you, Doctor. I appreciate your time." He turned to leave, but something caught his eye, a poster that showed an evergreen tree emitting oxygen molecules into a bright blue sky. The caption said, *Save your breath . . . Save a tree*. The lower margin of the poster was gone, and with it whatever logo had been there, in order to accommodate the mat and frame.

Kantor squinted at the poster and tried to remember where he'd seen one like it.

"That was given to me by an old girlfriend years and years ago," Corliss explained, having noticed Kantor's interest in it. "It's getting old and tattered, but it's still a nice piece of art, so I keep it around."

"Yeah, it *is* a nice piece of art. Thanks again, Doctor. No need to show me out."

While driving back to the Nehalem County Sheriff's Office in Paulsen, Kantor talked by cell phone to Detective Ashley Tching. He told her that he'd checked out the first three outfits on his missing-sodium-pent list but had drawn blanks. Only a dozen left, which he would save until later. He asked how the other investigators had fared with their lists, and learned that none had done any better than he.

He'd just walked through the door when Dr. Ariel Sheplov called from VICAP to pass on the preliminary results of tests conducted by the FBI's forensic anthropology team on the footprints around Terry Grimes's mobile home.

"Are you ready for this, Lieutenant? The team analyzed the soil for moisture content and density, then went to work with a computer model—essentially the same one that paleoanthropologists have used to identify dinosaurs from their fossilized footprints. They constructed a physical profile of the man who left the prints, and here's the kicker: the guy is much lighter than a man who normally wears an 11-D shoe—*much* lighter.

And his stride is considerably shorter than average.''

"Lighter? You mean in weight?"

"Exactly. Based on the modeling, they don't think he could weigh more than one-forty, maybe less. There are some other anomalies, but they're still working on those. We'll have more for you soon."

"Thanks, Ariel. You people are gems. I'll be waiting with bated breath to find out what else you come up with."

He hung up and saw Roberto Esparza standing in his doorway, immaculately dressed and groomed as always. "What've you got, Bob? Something good, I hope."

"Remember a couple weeks back, when you and Ashley and I were talking about the victimology in the Buckthorn cases? It prompted me to start reanalyzing everything we know about the victims, starting with the first one." He walked to Kantor's desk and laid a photo down, a glossy black and white of a young man named Kelly Franklin, who had breathed his last on October 30, 1976. "I starting calling members of his family, his mom, his old friends, just to find out what they remembered about him in the days immediately before he got killed. Some of them are still in town, others have moved. Anyway, I found out—" He paused and looked over his shoulder to make sure they were alone. "—I found out that our boy Kelly was quite the cocksman. He'd been making the rounds of women all over the county, *married* women, among them someone named Lucille MacKenzie. At the time she was married to an accountant at Buckthorn Wood Products, a guy named Wally MacKenzie."

"And?"

"A few months before he was killed, Kelly got caught with Mrs. MacKenzie in the backseat of a car by none other than Wally himself. The MacKenzies were divorced soon afterward. Anyway, there was scuttlebutt about the possibility that Kelly met his end at the hands of a jealous hubby.''

"Does this Wally MacKenzie have an alibi for the night of Franklin's death?''

"Says he was in Portland at a meeting of the North-west Timber Operators Council. Apparently it checked out, because there's nothing more about it in the investigative record. On top of that, he's got no sheet.''

Kantor lit a cigarette and blew out a cloud of smoke. "So he's alibied for Franklin's murder, and we've got nothing to tie him to any of the others. Sounds like a dead end to me.''

Maybe not, Esparza replied, smiling. Just for the hell of it, he'd visited MacKenzie in his home on the out-skirts of Buckthorn. The guy had been cordial, willing to answer questions. Esparza couldn't help but notice the extensive collection of antique logging and milling equipment in and around the house, most of it restored to exhibition quality—old double-handled whipsaws, circular mills, blocks and tackle, other stuff that Esparza couldn't begin to identify. This was MacKenzie's hobby, it seemed, collecting and restoring old machinery and tools. Of particular interest were the spikes affixed to the wall of MacKenzie's den, arranged in an interesting pattern of concentric circles. All were identical—eight inches long, three-eighths of an inch in diameter, three-quarter-inch caps. They'd come from an old water flume on the mountain behind the Buckthorn mill, MacKenzie had explained.

Kantor took a long drag from his cigarette and thought a moment. His heart rate sped a little. "You're telling me that the spikes are like the ones the Buckthorn killer uses,'' he said. "You're telling me that after eighteen years of looking, finding not one other spike like these, you walk into MacKenzie's den and find them in a collection on his wall.''

"Like I said, Lieutenant, he's an enthusiast."

"You figure he has any other hobbies, any other collections?"

"You're thinking like body parts, right? We probably won't know till we look, will we?"

"No, I guess not. What does this guy look like?"

"Small and wiry, thick glasses. Wears his hair like the old Beatles, when they first came over from the UK. He's not over five-seven, probably doesn't weigh much more than a hundred and forty."

Kantor took a deep breath. "Find Tching and meet me upstairs in the conference room, five minutes. I've got to call the D.A. and talk to him about another search warrant."

III

NOON. PATCHY CLOUDS. ON-AGAIN-OFF-AGAIN SHOWERS, occasional dazzling sunlight. Steam rose from Buckthorn's ruined streets whenever the sun shone.

Pete parked the Grand Cherokee on Front Street at the main entrance of the *Nehalem County Renegade*, rather than at the rear, since he no longer cared who saw him coming and going. He pushed through the glass door and headed for the newsroom, where he found Nita pecking at a computer keyboard, already at work on next week's issue.

She smiled when she saw him, waved him to a chair. "I hope you're not mad at me for the way I acted yesterday," she said, "though you have every right to be. I didn't mean to act so mysterious about calling the police."

"I'm not mad," he assured her, bending to kiss her cheek. "I've been worried about you, though. Have any shady characters been hanging around?"

"You're the first. I have a feeling that the people who tried to do me in yesterday won't try it here in town. They want me somewhere out in the wilds, where there won't be any witnesses."

"I hope you're right." He sat in the chair next to her desk and pulled a business card from his pocket. "Remember what I said yesterday about finding out who tried to set me up? I think this guy represents my starting point. I'm going to find him and ask him some pointed questions. Want to come along?"

Nita took the card from him and read it. "Todd Verduin, Security, Surveillance and Investigations. What does this mean—he's a private detective or something?"

Pete explained who Todd Verduin was, then told her about yesterday's visit from Paul Garson, a partner in the Conifer Group. He related what Garson had alleged concerning Wade Beswick's involvement in a plan to defraud Tucker of the Mount Olivet timberlands. The Conifer Group partners had offered not only to write off the two-point-five million they'd lent Buckthorn Wood Products but also to pay Tucker an extra one-point-five million to keep quiet about it. And to let them *live*.

"So why do you want to talk to this Verduin character?" Nita asked. "He sounds like the sort it's best to stay away from."

"I'm sure he is. In fact, I'm reasonably sure that he stole my pen, the one that the cops found at the scene of Beswick's murder."

"In other words, *he's* the guy who's framing you. Good God, you've got plenty of reason to stay away from him, Pete—*far* away."

"I'm through being the patsy, Nita. From now on, I'm taking an active role in the protection of my interests. If necessary, I'll grab this prick by the lapels and shake some answers out of him. If he's bugged our offices and phones like Garson seems to think he has, he must have some tapes lying around that could prove interesting.''

Nita rolled her eyes, as though this was the craziest idea she'd ever heard. "What if he kills you, Pete? Where will that leave your kids—and *me?* If Verduin's half as bad as you suspect he is, killing you won't be any big deal to him.''

Pete allowed that this was true. But he had no intention of letting Verduin or anyone else kill him, and he said so.

Nita folded her hands and stared at them for a long moment. In this light, in this pose, she no longer looked so much like Sally. She seemed to have lost her radiance, which Pete found strangely reassuring. She was human after all, not an iron woman. Yesterday's ordeal with the gray-flannel woman had affected her. "All right,'' she said finally, "I'll go with you—but only because I'm afraid to let you go alone. I still think this is a very bad idea.''

An hour later they were in northwest Portland, an old quarter full of venerable Victorian houses and expensive boutiques. The traffic was horrible, as bad as Pete had seen anywhere, but he felt strangely exhilarated. It was good to be in a city again, where humanity flowed like a river, where the noise of commerce filled the air. Nita guided him directly to the address on the business card, an apartment building on NW Everett Street.

"He must work out of his apartment,'' she said, looking at the building, which was four stories tall and constructed of white brick. The corner units had quaint balconies of white-painted wrought iron. A sign in front introduced it as the Everett Arms. "I wonder how he gets away with it—this place isn't zoned for offices, I'll bet.''

"He must do okay,'' Pete said. "I'm sure this isn't a cheap neighborhood.''

Through some miracle a parking spot opened up half a block east on Everett, and Pete nosed the Cherokee into it. The sun peeked out from behind a gray cloud as he and Nita walked toward the Everett Arms.

"Have your gun?" she asked in a low voice.

Pete nodded and patted the breast pocket of his sport coat to reassure her, though his stomach was in knots. He wondered if he could actually use the thing against another human being.

As they approached the lobby of the Everett Arms, a middle-aged black woman came out, pushing a double stroller with a set of year-old twins in it. Pete helped her with the heavy glass door, then motioned Nita through. At that moment the elevator doors opened on the far end of the lobby, and he saw the gray-flannel woman get off and stop before a wall of marble to check her appearance in its polished surface. Pete's heart skipped a beat. He grabbed Nita and pulled her back outside, hurried her down the walk.

"Don't look back," he whispered, rounding the corner to the left. "Just walk."

"Pete, you're hurting my arm! What are you doing?"

"It's your friend and mine, the platinum blond. She just got off the elevator. I don't think she's seen us— yet."

They crossed 20th Avenue, heading west, walking as fast as they could without breaking into a run, the pistol bouncing against Pete's rib cage. Nita halted suddenly, nearly pulling him off balance. "Why are we running from her?" she asked. "So what if she sees us? She certainly won't try to kill me on a busy city street. Or you either. I say we go back and confront her."

Pete thought a minute, then shrugged. Maybe Nita was right. So they turned around and headed toward the Everett Arms again, only to see the gray-flannel woman's back, her buttocks swinging as she hurried down the walk in the opposite direction. Seconds later she rounded the far corner and disappeared.

"What now?" Nita asked.

"We do what we came to do—find Verduin."

They went back to the lobby of the Everett Arms and approached the front desk, where a doorman sat in full brass and braid, a college-age kid with shoulder-length hair and an acne-scarred face. Pete handed him one of his own business cards.

"We're here to see Mr. Todd Verduin," Pete said.

"Sorry," the doorman said, handing back Pete's card. "You just missed him. I can take a message if you'd like, or you can use the phone to access his voice mail."

"I happen to know he's in," Pete said. "I also know that he's not going to be pleased if you don't send us up. Now I suggest you buzz him."

"And I told you, he's not here. He walked out not more than two minutes ago. Hell, you almost ran into him the first time you came to the door."

"I don't understand. We would've seen him."

"But you *did* see him, man. He walked right by you." The kid grinned, obviously enjoying the confusion in Pete's face. "Look, I'm in big trouble if I tell you this, because I don't think I'm supposed to know. But the chick in the gray outfit—remember her—big hair, all white and shiny? That's Todd Verduin, man."

Nita and Pete stared first at the doorman, then at each other, their mouths open. "You mean—" Pete now knew why Todd Verduin had looked familiar that day in his office. He'd seen him before. In New York. First in Rye during the memorial gathering for Sally, then in Sally's office some four days later. Not as Todd Verduin, private investigator, but as the gray-flannel woman.

"He thinks he has everybody fooled, y'know," the doorman went on, "but he kind of blew his cover one

day. Came to the desk in drag and left a note for somebody, signed his real name. I checked the signature
against the one on his mailbox card, and *voila!*—it was
the same, y'know? The guy makes an excellent babe,
right?—except when you get down the basics, y'know,
like what's under the dress and everything.''

"Come on, Pete," Nita said, taking his arm. "Let's
get out of here."

"Like, you won't let on to anybody I told you this,
okay? I mean, I could get into some deep shit over it,
hear what I'm sayin'?''

"Don't worry," Pete said. "We won't say a word to
anyone.''

During the drive back to Buckthorn, Pete and Nita
discussed the meaning of what they'd just learned, that
Todd Verduin and the gray-flannel woman were the
same person. For starters, Pete said, it meant that Verduin had bugged the Cochrans' house in Rye, probably
so Tucker could keep track of his grandchildren's lives
as well as Pete's prospects of landing a job. That was
why the gray-flannel woman had gone upstairs during
the memorial gathering—not to snoop or pilfer, but to
plant bugs in the phones, the walls, God only knew
where else.

But why, he wondered, had he—or she—turned up
the following week in Sally's office? When Sally was a
week dead? When someone else was about to occupy
her office?

Nita offered that Verduin had come to retrieve listening devices that he'd planted while Sally was alive.
Maybe he'd come to look for something else among
Sally's effects, a memento that Tucker wanted or a document. Something in Nita's tone suggested to Pete that
she knew more about this than she let on.

Which got Pete to thinking about other issues, like
why Tucker wanted Nita dead. Verduin and an accom-

plice had tried to kill her on a lonely country road—not because they had anything against her personally, but because Tucker had hired it done. *Why?* he asked Nita. What had she ever done to Tucker that made him hate her so?

"You don't know for sure that Tucker was behind it," she answered lamely. "It could've been someone else."

"Bullshit. It was Tucker. Just like it was Tucker who hired Verduin to kill Wade. With Wade it's no mystery—he stabbed Tucker in the back and tried to steal fifty million dollars' worth of standing timber from him. But *you*. Why *you*, Nita?"

She turned away from him, kept her eyes on the sights speeding past the passenger's window.

"Does it have anything to do with your son?"

"My *son*?" She stared at him now, her cheeks coloring. "What in the hell are you talking about?"

"Come on, Nita—give me some credit. Topper Bannon is your son, isn't he? For some reason you gave him up to Tucker and Dolly, and they raised him as their own. But something went wrong, didn't it? You and Tucker had a falling-out, some misunderstanding . . ."

"Shut up! You don't know what you're talking about."

"Don't I? Then suppose you enlighten me. Start by telling me why you sneaked into Topper's room last night and sang him a lullaby in Spanish, the same one my wife sang to our kids. Your voice sounded just like Sally's, probably because you and she learned it together when you were babies. You and she probably sang it together a million times."

"No! You're wrong, Pete!"

"I'm *not* wrong! You sang that song to Topper the way a mother sings to her child—I heard the love in

your voice, the sadness, the hurt. I'm not deaf, Nita, and
I'm not blind. I *saw* you."

"It wasn't me!"

"Don't lie to me, God damn it. I know what I saw.
The way you hold yourself, your mannerisms, the way
you wear your hair—it's all Sally. You even make love
the way she did, which means the two of you must've
traded some very deep and personal secrets over the
years. I figure you and she grew up together, maybe in
the same house. You must've been so close that you
acted alike, talked alike, and after a while even started
to *look* alike. It happens to people who are close, even
if they're not related by blood. Christ almighty, is it any
wonder I was drawn to you? You have so much of Sally
in you, or maybe it's the other way around—I don't
know—maybe she had you in *her*."

Nita put her hands over her face and sobbed. "Please,
don't say any more. I don't want to hear any more of
this . . ."

They drove on in silence for a long while. Pete exited
the Sunset Highway and drove into Hillsboro to a rental
storage facility. He parked the Cherokee, let himself into
a storage bay and returned with a leather valise, which
he stowed in the cargo compartment. They set off again
en route to Buckthorn.

"Care to talk now?" he asked Nita, whose eyes were
red from crying.

"What's there to talk about? You seem to know
everything already."

"Not true. All I really have are suspicions and theories. What I need from you is the truth."

"Why do you need it from me? You've done pretty
well on your own."

"I was hoping that you and I owed each other something—the truth, if nothing else. I was hoping that you
felt something for me like what I feel for you."

Nita chuckled, and it sounded bitter. "Whatever you feel for me, Pete, is what you felt for Sally. I've said it before, and I'll say it again—you see her in me, and that's what you love. As for the truth—I can't give it to you. It's too ugly, even for me."

Pete said nothing more until stopping in front of the *Renegade*. "I don't want this to be the end for us. What we've had is too good, Nita. I've needed it, and I still do."

Her eyes filled with tears again, and he saw the depth of the hurt she suffered. He wanted to pull her to him, but he didn't, because he didn't know how she would respond.

"You don't need *me*," she said, her voice pinching. "You need Sally . . ." She slid out of the Cherokee, slammed the door hard and ran into the building. Pete sat a long moment, gazing into the fading afternoon, feeling a vacancy in his chest, as if someone had just ripped his heart out.

22

I

TUCKER BANNON GULPED FOUR ASPIRIN TO SILENCE THE squealing pain in his arthritic knees, then stared at his own face in the bathroom mirror. He really didn't look that bad for a man of sixty-seven, he told himself—aside from the spectacular purple and yellow rings around both eyes, that is. And the archipelago of scabbed-over contusions across his forehead and scalp. And the fact that his spare dentures made him look comically toothy.

The boy worked me over fairly well with that old water bucket, but I'm still standing straight, Lord. It'll take a lot more than that to put this old logger down.

It was Friday morning, not yet 8:00. He'd woken to the stirring of the children at the other end of the house, the sounds of Sarah and Carter readying themselves for school. He'd heard them thump downstairs for breakfast, heard their young voices as they called their dog, Gerard. Now he watched from his bedroom window as they walked down the drive with their father and Gerard to the front gate, where they waited for the bus. He watched the bus take them off to school.

Tucker's heart swelled with love, and with pride. For Sarah and Carter were his flesh and blood. They would carry on the Bannon family tradition when he and Dolly had gone, inheriting the business, the house and land, the obligations of community leadership. *Not* that Tucker planned to leave this world anytime soon—he had too much work to do. He needed to train these children in the way of the Lord and teach them His wisdom. He needed to impart the strength of his own father, Noah Bannon, and imprint on them his own tough-minded morality. And most important, he needed to take steps to protect them against the designs of the Evil One.

This was his first priority.

Climbing the rear stairs, he glanced out the tall vertical window in the stairwell at the gardener's shed. To his surprise, he saw that Topper had repaired the door. A light was on inside, meaning that the boy was there—doing what, Tucker didn't want to guess. Playing hooky and not even bothering to hide it, that much was apparent. *He's getting pretty cocky, isn't he, Lord?*

Tucker could no longer avoid an ugly truth: Topper had become dangerous—dangerous to his own father and perhaps even to his young cousins, Sarah and Carter. With his own eyes Tucker had witnessed the hellish transformation that the boy had undergone two days ago in the gardener's shed.

There's only one way to deal with this, Lord. I've heard your voice, and I'm ready to do it.

But first things first. Tucker went to the "quiet room," let himself in with a key from a large ring on his belt, and closed the door behind him. He sat at the main console and put on a pair of headphones, taking care not to rip open the scabs on his scalp. The flip of a switch started a tape rolling, one that contained recordings of telephone conversations and goings-on in the head shed over the past few days. He'd fallen behind in his routine surveillance. It was time to catch up.

Virtually everything he heard was inconsequential—no conspiracies by company officers to defraud him, no whispered plans to steal inventory for building a deck or a patio, not even much taking of the Lord's name in vain. He was about to forego the rest of the audiotape and start checking the closed-circuit TV tapes when

something caught his ear on the track that corresponded
to the hidden mike in Pete Cochran's private office.

It was Peter's voice, talking low, interspersed with
Denise Ubaldo's.

"You speak and read Spanish, right?"

"Of course. It's my first language."

*"How would you like to do a little personal work for
me? My wife left some letters when she died, quite a lot
of them actually, written in Spanish. I'd like to know
what's in them. I'll pay you, naturally."*

"I'd be happy to translate them for you . . ."

Scarcely believing his good fortune, Tucker switched
the machine to reverse and replayed the section of tape,
verifying what he heard. Pete was talking about the letters from Rosa Sandoval to his daughter, letters written
in Spanish. Over the years, Rosa had sent photocopies
to Tucker, letting him know that she was in possession
of the gruesome truth about him, that she'd undertaken
to document it, and that she could go to the police anytime and effectively end his life. But the Lord had delivered her into his hands, and now the letters, too.

"They're in storage," Pete said, *"but I'll pick them
up and bring them to you today. I really appreciate this,
Denise."*

"It will be my pleasure, Pete. I'm glad you asked."

Tucker checked the date on the tape counter, verifying
that the conversation had occurred yesterday. He didn't
have much time. He shut down the machine and dialed
Todd Verduin's emergency number.

II

FOR ESMERELDA SANDOVAL THE PAST FORTY-EIGHT
hours had been *infierno en la tierra*, hell on earth.

It had started Wednesday with the pitched battle between Topper and Señor Bannon in the gardener's shed, provoked no doubt by the old man—he'd brought with him a sock stuffed with sand, his preferred weapon for beating the boy. This time Topper hadn't curled up in a fetal ball and accepted the beating, as he had throughout all of his earlier life. This time he'd fought back like a young lion and probably would have killed Señor Bannon if Esmerelda and Señora Bannon hadn't intervened. He'd fled into the forest of Mount Olivet and had stayed away until the wee hours of the morning.

Esmerelda had searched for him throughout the night, tramping the damp trails on the mountainside and crying out his name until her voice became so hoarse that she could barely speak. Many times she'd tripped over fallen logs or slipped on mossy ground. Her face showed the scratches of fir needles and rough bark. She'd searched until she could barely move, until her aging muscles screamed for rest.

Returning to Bannon House, she'd found that Topper had come back. Relieved, she'd collapsed into bed and had slept the sleep of the dead, only to dream of a screaming woman—a woman whose voice she knew. The woman was her lost daughter, Rosa, having come home to sing a lullaby to her poor, sick son. It *had* been only a dream, hadn't it? she'd asked herself upon waking. *Sí, un mero sueño.* What else could it have been?

Esmerelda had spent much of yesterday in rest and recuperation. Only today had she managed to undertake her customary routine of housework and meals, having fed Sarah and Carter their breakfast before sending them off to school. Señor Bannon had spent most of the morning in the "quiet room" on the third floor, and this afternoon had retired to his first-floor study. The Señora had whiled away the day in the music room, playing hymns on her electric organ. Topper had skipped school again to hole up in the gardener's shed. Esmerelda had

taken lunch on a tray to him, but he'd refused it, refused
even to open the door for her. She feared that something
terrible had happened to his mind, that the many years
of stress and abuse at his father's hands had twisted his
reason. She yearned to hold him and sing to him as she'd
done so often when he was a little boy, believing that
the old Mexican lullaby would again soothe his mind
and give him rest. But he wouldn't let her near him, and
this hurt.

Around three o'clock she began preparing the evening
meal, a nice roasted chicken with a shrimp cocktail ap-
petizer, one of Topper's favorites. She happened to
glance through the kitchen window into the rear yard
and saw Topper emerge from the gardener's shed, wearing a canvass backpack and carrying a length of heavy
rope. He walked straight to the kennel that Tucker had
built for Sarah and Carter's big dog. The dog saw him
coming and jumped up on the door, bracing his huge
paws against the chain-link, his tail wagging wildly.
Topper pulled the door open, grabbed the animal by the
collar and looped the rope around its neck. Cinching the
noose tight, he pulled the dog out of the kennel and set
out across the yard toward the wood line.

Panic took Esmerelda's breath away. She thought immediately of the horrible things that Topper had done to
rats and mice over the years, sick things that no sane
person could hope to understand. Topper was taking Gerard into the forest in order to commit some unspeakable
sin.

She flew out of the kitchen toward Señor Bannon's
study, the muscles in her legs still burning from her ordeal in the forest two days earlier. She didn't care about
the pain now. The double oak doors of the study stood
open, and Señor Bannon sat in his great leather chair
with a shotgun across his lap, his chin resting on his
chest. She heard him snore, saw his head move slightly

with every breath. Afternoon sunlight slanted in through the window, spotlighting him as if he were the star of a one-man play.

Esmerelda approached his desk, saw an open box of shells on the blotter. He'd been loading the gun when he fell asleep. She reached out to shake him but jerked her hand back. She realized that if she told him what she'd just seen Topper do, he would go after the boy not with a sockful of sand but with the shotgun.

Now she hated Tucker Bannon with every fiber, not for the pain he'd caused her, but for what he'd done to Topper, for what he'd done to Rosa when she was a child, and for what he'd done to his own daughter. It was a delicious hatred, sweet and pure. And Esmerelda hated herself for tasting it.

She was about to back away when she noticed a folder on the blotter next to the shotgun shells. The typed name on the cover caught her and held her. *Rosa Juanita Sandoval*, it said. Carefully she reached for the folder, keeping her hand well clear of the Señor's hand. She picked it up, opened it, saw a report written by the man who came often to confer with Señor Bannon, the private detective named Verduin. Esmerelda flipped a page over and saw two color photographs clipped to the report, one of Rosa in her late twenties, and the other of . . .

"¡Oh Dios mi! ¿Puede ser éste? . . ."

Nita Vale. A plastic surgeon in Carmel, California, said the report, had transformed Rosa Sandoval into Nita Vale, the young blond woman who'd bought the *Nehalem County Renegade*, the strange young woman who'd caused so much whispering in Buckthorn over the years with her scorching editorial attacks on Tucker Bannon. Esmerelda placed the folder back on the desk and fled the study, her hands shaking.

She went back to the kitchen and stood a moment next to the telephone. From the music room at the far end of

the house came the sound of the Señora's electric organ,
"Just a Closer Walk with Thee," played badly. Esmerelda hardly heard it. She snatched up the phone, punched
the buttons. She needed help, and she knew only one
person who could give it, the one person in town she
could count on—Dr. Vonda Reuben.

III

*IT'S GOTTA HAPPEN SOON, GOTTA HAPPEN SOON, GOTTA HAPPEN
soon . . .*

The craving had become a rhythmic thing, a pounding
thing. It made him quiver and shake. It dominated him
like an addiction, even though he hadn't yet tasted the
drug.

Gerard gave him no trouble, except when Topper tried
to coax him into the fruit cellar of the Mad Witch's
cabin. The big dog wanted no part of the ladder, and
Topper ended up hog-tying him and pushing up him
over the edge of the trapdoor opening. Talk about yelp-
ing and whimpering!—Topper wondered if the pooch
had broken something when he hit the cellar floor. No
matter. Gerard's hours upon this earth were numbered.
What did a broken bone or two matter at this late stage?

*Are you ready for this, ladies and gents? This is really
gonna knock the bung out of your pickle barrel.* He
looked at his watch. *The time is now two fifty-five. In
exactly twenty minutes school will be out at Nehalem
County Elementary and Middle School, home of the
Paulsen Polecats. The kids will get on the school buses
and go home to their stinky little mommies and grubby
little daddies. Except for two of them, and I think you
know who they are . . .*

He stepped out the door of the Mad Witch's cabin.
The sky had cleared to a bracing blue, what he could

see of it through the tall cedars and firs. The air was tart with the smell of a rain-soaked forest. He strode through the thicket to the trail that led down the face of Mount Olivet to Bannon House. Through an opening in the brush he could see the town below, Buckthorn, a clutter of low buildings and low lives. To the north lay Paulsen, hidden by hills. He halted and pulled out the cell phone that he'd swiped from his parents' room this morning and punched the number of the school office.

"Hello," he said, deepening his voice to sound as old as possible, "this is Peter Cochran of Buckthorn Wood Products over in Buckthorn. How're you today? Good. Say, we have a minor family emergency here, and I need to talk to my daughter, Sarah Cochran. She's in the seventh grade. I wonder if you could call her out of class for me. It'll only take a minute, I promise. Yes, I'll hold."

The office staff at Nehalem County Elementary and Middle School was most cooperative. Scarcely five minutes later Sarah came on the line, sounding breathless.

"Daddy, what's wrong?"

"Nothing's wrong, Sluggo—" Topper had overheard Pete call his daughter this nickname, then quickly apologize for doing so. Apparently it was an old nickname that she hated. "I want you to listen and listen good, okay? Don't say anything, especially if the office staff can hear you—just say uh-huh and huh-uh, got that?"

He heard an anxious breath, almost a whimper. Finally: "Uh-huh."

"I guess you know this isn't your old man, right? Do you know who this is?"

"Uh-huh."

"Good, good. You recognize my voice, eh? That's cool, way cool. So you know there's nothing to be scared of, right?"

"Uh-huh."

"Okay, now listen to me, Sluggo, and don't say anything . . ."

He told her that he had Gerard. He told her that Gerard needed her and Carter. Something weird was about to happen, and Gerard could be in danger. So here's what he wanted them to do: They should ride the school bus home to Buckthorn as usual, but they should get off at Second Street and Columbia behind the old Allegro Theater, what was left of it. They should wait there for him, and he would pick them up soon in his dad's Suburban. He would take them immediately to Gerard, and everybody would be like totally blissed-out.

"Got that, Sluggo? Just hang there behind the theater and don't talk to anyone about this. Okay?"

Another deep breath, an expression of delicious fear. "Uh-huh."

"Okay, I'm gonna hang up now. You be cool—okay, Sluggo? If you say anything about this to anyone, I'll know about it, and I promise that you'll never see your precious Bernice mountain dog again, except for his burned-out carcass, maybe." This brought an actual whimper. "Be cool, I said. Don't start blubbering or anything. Just keep it together, right? You with me, Sluggo?"

"Uh-huh."

"Okay. I'll see you soon. Gotta go." He hit the off button and punched the number of Buckthorn Wood Products.

"Hi, this is Alex Davis over at Nehalem Elementary and Middle. I'm running our spring soccer program this year, which you may have read about in the paper. Anyway, I wonder if you'd relay a message to Mr. Cochran for me. It seems his two kids, Sarah and Carter, didn't transfer to this school until after our sign-up deadline, but they've expressed an interest in playing this year.

So I figured, Oh, what the heck, it's not their fault they missed the deadline, so I went ahead and signed them up. We're having our orientation meeting after school this afternoon, which means they'll miss their regular bus. But we've arranged a special bus to take the soccer kids home when the meeting's over. They'll be a few hours late, and I just wanted to let Mr. Cochran know, so he wouldn't worry.''

Denise Ubaldo thanked him and promised to relay the message to Peter Cochran.

"Thank *you*," Topper said. "You have a nice evening." He punched the off button and stood a minute, mugging before his imaginary studio audience. *Pretty fuckin' crafty—right, folks? The Verminator doesn't need a bunch of hysterical people pounding the bushes for a couple of missing kids, now, does he? Hellll, no! Isn't it amazing what you can do by simply reaching out and touching someone?*

He started down the trail, chuckling under his breath. Already he had a hard-on so big that it hurt to walk.

IV

DENISE UBALDO GAVE PETE THE MESSAGE FROM SOME-one named Alex Davis at the school in Paulsen and informed him that she'd already called Esmerelda to tell her not to expect the kids to come at the regular time. Esmerelda had sounded almost relieved, she said.

"Thank you, Denise." Pete sipped from his fifth cup of coffee since noon and thought, *I don't blame her. Like me, she probably assumes that school is the safest place for them.*

Denise paused at the door of his office. "Pete, are you busy after work tonight?"

"I guess not. Why?"

"I've translated a good portion of Rosa Sandoval's letters to Sally. There are things I think you should know—sooner, not later. I've put off discussing this with you all day, because I don't think this is the right place. Could you come by my house after work?"

"I don't see a problem with that. Where do you live?"

"Over on Columbia Avenue, almost at Third. As you know, I usually walk to work, it's so close, but today I brought my car. I have the letters locked in the trunk. I didn't want to leave them in my house all day."

"I see," Pete said, looking uneasy. "In that case I'll follow you home at quitting time. Maybe we should leave a little early and beat the jam-up at the front gate."

"Good. That sounds good, Pete." She turned quickly and went out, leaving her new boss with a fresh case of nerves.

V

DETECTIVES ASHLEY TCHING AND BOB ESPARZA BURST into Dan Kantor's smoke-filled cubicle, their faces bright with excitement. They reminded him of a pair of rambunctious schoolkids. Tching waved a blue-backed legal document in his face.

"The district court came through for us," she said. "This is a search warrant for Wally MacKenzie's house. The D.A.'s office just sent it over."

"I'll be damned," Kantor replied, taking the warrant from her. "Signed, sealed and freshly peeled. Nice."

"So when do we do it?" Esparza wanted to know. He shoved a fresh stick of Juicy Fruit into his mouth and chewed with enthusiasm. "Tomorrow morning, crack of dawn?"

"That'll be fine," Kantor said. "I'll call the OSP

Crime Lab and lay on our best Sherlocks. If there's anything there, they'll find it."

"Any word from VICAP on the shoes or the footprints?" Tching asked.

"Not since yesterday. All we know is that the guy who made those prints is a real shrimp, not over one-forty."

"That fits MacKenzie," Esparza said. "But we don't know his shoe size yet, so we probably shouldn't jump to conclusions."

"Hey, we need a lot more than his shoe size, my friend. We need the actual shoes in order to put him at the scene of the Grimes homicide. And it wouldn't hurt to find an altar with severed fingers and dicks all over it."

"At least we can finally rule out Jerry Dragstead," Tching said.

"Not so fast. When it comes right down to it, we still don't know beyond a shadow of a doubt that it was the killer who left those prints around Grimes's house. We can be pretty sure, but that's not good enough, as you both know. Let's not forget that Dragstead's the only guy we've got who's ever killed anyone for the record."

Tching shook her head, looked doubtful. "Lieutenant, the guy's about a hundred ants short of a picnic. He's just not smart enough to do crimes like these and get away with them for eighteen years. I'm sorry, but that's the unexpurgated truth. We've been wasting our time with him."

Kantor grinned at her and exhaled smoke. "Humor me. Let's not rule him out, all right?"

Esparza put in his two cents' worth, occasionally snapping his gum as he talked. "My gut says it's MacKenzie. I know, I know—" He held up both palms, a defensive gesture. "We really don't have anything on him. But here's what I think . . ."

He laid out his theory. Back in 1976, Wally Mac-
Kenzie surprised his pretty wife, Lucy, in flagrante with
Kelly Franklin. Their marriage ended, but MacKenzie
still loved her madly, never stopped loving her. He
seethed over his loss for months afterward and finally
decided to take revenge on young Kelly Franklin. He
cut the guy's dick off, snipped off his fingers, gouged
out his eyes and let him bleed until he died—there, that
should teach him a lesson. Weirdly enough, MacKenzie
discovered that he liked doing this, that it gave him *una
experiencia sexual asombrosa*—an awesome sexy rush.
As psychosexual killers often do, he made his ritual
more elaborate with subsequent victims, using sodium
pentobarbital to make them cooperative and burning
them to death after mutilating them. Knowing that his
new hobby could land him in a padded cell for the rest
of his life, he became extra-careful. He plotted and
schemed, laid detailed plans, came up with a step-by-
step checklist that kept him from making mistakes. He
was a methodical guy, an *accountant*, for Christ's sake,
and he believed in doing things by the numbers. He took
his victims from the work force at the sawmill where he
himself worked, which meant he had plenty of time to
scope out their movements and habits. The only mistake
he ever made was assuming that a detective named Esparza wouldn't someday saunter into his den and ask
about the spikes on the wall.

"... like I say, it's just my gut," Esparza concluded,
snapping his gum. "But so far, my gut's never been
wrong."

"Like you yourself said, let's not jump to conclusions," Kantor reminded him. "Let's execute the search
warrant and see what we come up with. In the meantime,
maintain strict secrecy in this matter, especially with the
Cigar and his people. I don't want him blabbing any of
this at the bowling alley and tipping MacKenzie off."

"That may be a moot point," Tching said. "Bob here already paid MacKenzie a call and asked him about the spikes. If he's smart enough to be the Buckthorn killer, he probably knows enough to get rid of anything around the house that might be incriminating."

"Let's hope he's too cautious to make any sudden moves," Kantor said, knocking his desktop with his knuckles.

Esparza laughed. "That's not wood, Lieutenant. It's cheap wood-grained veneer over metal. It's a *cop* desk."

"It's the thought that counts, smart ass. Now you two get out of here and let me finish my paperwork."

An hour later the sheriff's office shift changed, leaving the place quiet. Nine-one-one calls went to the Washington County dispatcher in Beaverton, "Wacka," so there were no on-site dispatchers here in the Nehalem County Sheriff's Office. After the secretaries went home, Kantor was virtually alone in the station, except for the patrol officers who occasionally came by.

He busied himself filling out his "murder book," the investigative record that would become part of the Buckthorn Task Force's permanent file. This would be the raw material of his own best-seller, he'd decided—the one he would write when the killer was behind bars. It would be a far better book than Nita Vale's, if she ever actually finished it. Why? Because only an investigator on the case could tell the story with authentic pain and agony. Kantor envisioned his book becoming the biggest thing since Bugliosi's *Helter Skelter*, which was the definitive account of the Charlie Manson case. He tried to estimate how many millions Bugliosi had made on that book, then gave up. Kantor himself would settle for three or four.

The gamble he'd taken in seeking this job was close to paying off after all, he was certain. Very soon he would find the killer. He could feel it in his bones.

Something was about to resolve itself—the tangle of contradictions that had plagued him, the dead ends and blind alleys—into a coherent theory of who had committed these crimes and why.

He tapped the desk with his knuckles again, not caring that it wasn't real wood. The killer would go to prison, maybe to the gurney for a lethal injection, and the world would be rid of him at long last. The good people of northwestern Oregon would breathe easy again. Dan Kantor would write his book and get rich. He would set up fat trust funds for his daughters, take them to the Mediterranean every summer, and eventually send them to expensive colleges. He might even do something nice for his ex, like buy her a white Lexus, which she'd always wanted. As for himself, his tastes were simple. All he really needed was a presentable condo in some warm clime, a small sailboat . . .

The phone rang, startling him, and he snatched it up. It was Dr. Ariel Sheplov of the FBI's VICAP. They traded pleasantries, Kantor remarking that she must be working late. He listened to her talk about the most recent findings of the forensic paleoanthropology team concerning the shoe prints taken from Terry Grimes's property. He jotted things on his spiral pad, circled things he'd written earlier, the blood draining from his face.

"I see. Yeah. You're sure there's no mistake about this? Okay. Thanks, Doctor."

He hung up the phone and collected himself. He needed a cup of coffee. Badly.

The previous shift hadn't bothered to brew a new pot, so Kantor went to the soda machine, plugged money into it and pulled out a Diet Pepsi. He took a long gulp and groped in his shirt pocket for his smokes, his mind absorbed with what Dr. Sheplov had just told him. He almost didn't hear the sounds behind him, the opening of a door, the soft movement of fabric over skin, the tiny squeak of a rubber sole against tile. The sounds failed to register in his consciousness until it was too late. He was about to turn around, an instinctive motion, when something thudded into his back. He felt his breath go, but not through his mouth or nose. He heard wet sounds and looked down, saw the long blade of a hunting knife sticking out through his shirt. The air in his left lung hissed and whistled as it escaped through the hole in his chest.

VI

TOPPER PARKED HIS FATHER'S SUBURBAN AT THE mouth of the stone stairway that climbed from Bannon Avenue to the rear of the estate. He glanced in both directions and saw no one, no life of any kind, no foot traffic, no cars or trucks. Bannon Avenue was a parade of silent, crumbling houses forsaken to weeds and rot. He pulled Sarah and Carter out of the cargo bed and shoved them toward the stairs, motioned them to start climbing. Controlling them was easy, for he'd handcuffed them together with cuffs he'd ordered from a mail-order outfit that advertised in gun magazines. He'd also taped their mouths shut with silvery duct tape, wrapping it several times around their heads so they couldn't peel it away with their free hands.

The Verminator is nothing if not careful, folks.

They climbed the lichen-covered stairs, helping themselves along by pulling on the cast-iron railings on either side. Foliage grew thick along both flanks—azalea and devil's club, deer brush and ninebark, sword fern and shield fern, lace fern and licorice fern. Topper knew them all by name, knew the weeds from the good guys.

They skirted the rear of the grounds of Bannon House,

staying well inside the wood line, until coming to the trail that ascended through a virgin forest to the summit of Mount Olivet. Topper pointed into the glade and said, "That's where we're going, beeny-weenies. Let's not dawdle now. Move it out, move it out, move it out."

Carter whimpered and whined like a puppy, for he knew what lay near the summit of the mountain, well off the trail and hidden from the sane world. Topper looked at Sarah and saw her glaring at him with blue fire in her eyes. She was a tough one, and Topper knew that he dared not let his guard down.

I'll save her for last, make her watch what happens to old Gerard and Carter-the-Farter. Doing her will be the ultimate rush!

Deep into the hike, he heard voices on the trail ahead. He pulled Sarah and Carter off the trail and forced them into a crouch behind a tall clump of deer brush. "Quiet now, beeny-weenies," he whispered. "If you make any noise, your trusty old Bernice mountain dog is gonna die. But if you stay nice and quiet, the Verminator's gonna let him live, and someday we'll all laugh about this over Long Island iced teas. We gotta deal or what?" They nodded, their eyes desperate.

The voices came closer. Women's voices. Topper recognized that of his *abuela*, speaking Spanish. The other woman he didn't recognize.

Pushing the children's heads down, he craned to peer through the branches of the deer brush and saw the two women pass by, walking down the Mount Olivet trail toward Bannon House. He recognized Vonda Reuben, the quack herb doctor who lived on Nehalem Avenue— tall and muscular, her gray ponytail swishing from side to side as she walked.

"I was certain that we'd find him at the old cabin," his *abuela* was saying in rapid Spanish. "He wasn't on the summit—where else could he be?"

"This mountain has a thousand places to hide," Vonda Reuben said, speaking Spanish like a native. "The important thing now is to take care of the children. You must be there when they return from school . . ."

Topper stifled a giggle. *When they return from school—from soccer orientation—right, ladies and gentlemen? Sorry about that!*

"But my Theodore is just a child, Doctor. He needs me, as well. We *must* find him . . ."

After waiting another five minutes, Topper rousted the kids and set them on the trail again. By the time they reached the stone cabin, the forest gloom had deepened into dusk. Shadows sprawled black across the mossy walls of the cabin, and the darkness within seemed thick, almost velvety. The air was rich with the stink of fungus and rot.

Topper halted his prisoners and stood a moment at the edge of the clearing, watching, listening to the rustle of needles, the odd creak of a great hemlock trunk, the plop of moisture falling from a high branch—forest sounds. The women had been there, he knew, but had they gone inside?

I'm betting they didn't. Hell, they didn't have old Gerard with them on the trail, did they? That means he's still in the cellar. We're home free, folks.

Pushing the children forward, he said, "Let's get this show on the road—what d'ya say?" They held back, fearful of the old cabin, which didn't surprise him. The place still scared *him*, but he'd never let fear deter him. He didn't let it deter him now. "*Move!*" he commanded, giving each a hard shove.

And they moved toward the door, which yawned like open jaws.

It's gotta happen soon, gotta happen soon, gotta happen soon . . .

VII

PETER COCHRAN GOT UP FROM THE KITCHEN TABLE AND went to the sink, worried that he might become physically sick. For more than an hour he'd listened to Denise Ubaldo's interpretation of Rosa Sandoval's letters to Sally, beginning with the very first, sent in 1978 to a dormitory at the University of Illinois, where Sally was a freshman. The story that had emerged from the yellowing, neatly inked pages was one of enduring love and unquenchable hatred, rambunctious youth and stentorian abuse by a man who called himself a father. It was a story of escape and retribution, of memories both painful and precious.

And it was more.

A letter dated June 6, 1982, had begun:

Querida Sally,

¡Felicitaciones! ¡Ahora eres un profesional! ¡Como te envidio . . . !

"Congratulations! You're now a college graduate! How I envy you . . ."

The joyful, light-hearted tone set the reader up for the horror that followed.

Hay algo que me viene molestando desde hace mucho tiempo, Sally. No puedo posponer contartelo por mas tiempo.
Cuando yo era joven, mi mamá, Esmerelda, me contó que tu padre mató a su hermano, quien era mi papa. . . .

"Something has bothered me for a long time, Sally. I can no longer put off telling you. When I was a young girl, my mother, Esmerelda, told me that your father killed his brother, who was *my* father. . . ."

Rosa elaborated, telling the story as her mother had told it to her.

Pete turned on a faucet and splashed water on his face. Denise Ubaldo asked if he needed a drink, and he nodded—something strong, please. She took a bottle of Johnny Walker Red from a cupboard and poured a generous slug into a tumbler, handed it to him, then poured one for herself. Pete knocked the Scotch back and breathed deeply, grateful for the fire in his throat. Denise sipped hers, poured him another.

"I wouldn't have taken you for a Scotch drinker," Pete said, saluting her with his tumbler.

"I keep it around for its medicinal value," she replied, and they both chuckled.

"So old Tucker Bannon killed his own brother," Pete said as if he didn't quite believe it. "I suppose I shouldn't be surprised. It's not like I haven't had reason to think he's capable of such a thing."

Denise didn't ask him what he meant by this. "Everyone around here has heard the rumor," she said. "It's like a local fairy tale that nobody really believes. Tucker had a brother named Clarence, and they apparently never got along. Clarence was the kind of man who liked to take chances with the family's money, and you can imagine how that went down with Tucker. One day Clarence just disappeared—I suppose it must've been at least thirty years ago, well before my time. Some people said he got sick of things in Buckthorn and split for a happier place. Others say Tucker did him in. At any rate, it's only a rumor."

"Esmerelda thought it was more than that. She confided it to her own daughter."

"I'm certain that she wanted Rosa to know that her father hadn't abandoned them."

"I can understand that—I guess." He thought not of

Rosa, but Nita Vale, still living with the brutal knowl-
edge of what had happened to her father, still hating
Tucker Bannon for it. He thought of Sally, dying with
that knowledge in her head. *Tucker killed his brother.*
He killed Wade Beswick. And now he's trying to kill
Nita . . . Where would it end?

They went back to the table, and Pete felt a little better, a little stronger. The kitchen was close and warm,
as spotless as an operating room. A crucifix hung over
the door that led to a porch.

Denise Ubaldo's small house stood well back from
the street in a neighborhood that was mostly tumbledown and derelict. She kept her yard mowed, her rhododendrons trimmed, her roses nicely pared. From
where he sat, Pete could gaze through the window over
her sink and see blood-red roses against a cloudless evening sky. Stars had begun to pop out.

"Are you ready to go on?" Denise asked.

"Ready as I'll ever be."

She glanced at the notes she'd made since undertaking
the translation yesterday. "We've gotten up to 1986, and
now we find a reference to something that happened
when the girls were sixteen . . ."

Pete pictured the cousins at sixteen. Pretty girls, no
doubt, in full bloom sexually, one a Nordic blond, the
other a Latin brunette. Still prankish and playful, especially in each other's company, one always egging the
other on. In her letters, Rosa had referred to stunts they'd
pulled as children, some of them dangerous. They'd often crawled out of the second-story windows onto the
roof of Bannon House to spy on other family members
through bedroom windows, night or day, rain or shine.
They'd discovered an old coal chute in the basement,
which had fallen into disuse since the installation of a
fuel-oil furnace many years before their births; it provided access to a trapdoor outside the foundation,

TAINTED BLOOD   481

which—after they'd figured out how to pick the lock—
enabled them to sneak out at night, to come and go
without their parents' knowledge.

These were among the happier memories. Less happy
were allusions to the switchings that Tucker Bannon often gave Rosa, always stripping her naked and hauling
her across his lap . . .

Withhold not correction from a child . . .

Tucker had always quoted a Bible verse to justify his
depravity, and it had become a dark joke to the girls.
Several times Rosa had alluded to it in her letters, bits
of cruel humor.

"Rosa had become involved with a young man who
worked at the sawmill," Denise went on. "His name
was Kelly Franklin. It isn't really clear from the letter,
but I think that he must have been a few years older
than the girls . . ."

Kelly Franklin. Pete wondered why that name
sounded familiar.

In her letter, Rosa referred to the fact that her mother,
Esmerelda, had never liked Kelly, a fact that had served
only to heighten Rosa's interest in him. Kelly, it seemed,
was as interested in Sally as Rosa—hearing this gave
Pete a pang. The young man must have been a smooth
talker, because he persuaded the girls to join him in a
ménage à trois.

Denise's voice became thin at this point, and her
brown eyes watered. She sipped her Scotch.

"It's okay," Pete said, taking her hand in his. "We
can get through this."

"They went to the guest cottage behind Bannon
House to party. Apparently Kelly brought some weed,
some marijuana . . ."

"I know what it is, Denise."

"They drank wine, smoked weed, and listened to
Kelly's boom box—Rosa mentioned that the music was

from Three Dog Night, which must've been a popular
band back in those days. I was only two years old at the
time . . .''

"A very popular band. Go on."

"They all three began having sex together, there in
the bed of the guest cottage. For Sally, I think it was
the first time . . ."

Pete felt another pang, though he'd known perfectly
well that he hadn't been his wife's first lover, just as she
hadn't been his first. All the same, he would have preferred not to know the gory details of her first outing.

"This is where it gets bad," Denise said, her large
face paling. Her hand went cold in Pete's. "Sally's father, Tucker, surprised them, barged in on them. I don't
know how he happened to discover what was going
on . . ." She pulled her hand away, picked up one of
Rosa's letters and scanned it. She didn't translate literally, but interpreted. "He was in a fit of rage. He
must've hit Kelly Franklin in the head with something
hard and heavy—it doesn't really say. All I can tell you,
Pete, is that he killed the boy. He killed him and . . .''

Pete could see that she was struggling not to cry, not
to choke on the enormity of what she was saying. He
discovered that he was holding his breath.

". . . cut off his penis and his fingers. Then he cut out
his eyes. It was like a ritual, I think. Something religious.
The penis had gone where it shouldn't go, and the fingers had touched things . . ." Denise drained the last of
her Scotch and grimaced. "And the eyes had seen what
they shouldn't see. So it was a kind of justice, I suppose,
justicia de Dios, maybe—at least this is what Rosa says
in the letter. Tucker actually thought he was performing
God's justice. She says that she has seen all this happen
in her dreams, over and over again . . ."

Denise bent forward to the tabletop and cried silently,
her tears falling into her hands. Pete sat and stared

through the window at the stars. He now knew where he'd heard the name Kelly Franklin. It was the name of the first victim of the Buckthorn killer.

VIII

TOPPER BEAMED A FLASHLIGHT OVER THE FACES OF Sarah and Carter as they huddled in a muddy corner of the Mad Witch's cellar, their faces grimy, their eyes glistening with terror. He'd handcuffed them back to back, so they couldn't wrap their arms around each other.

"So tell me, ladies and gentlemen, have you been enjoying the show so far? Did you like the opening monologue?" He placed the flashlight back on the shelf that held Kerr jars full of awful, naughty things, so that the beam hit him like a stage light. "I don't see much enthusiasm here, and that's not making me happy."

He crouched down to them, first to Carter. He pulled off the duct tape that covered the boy's mouth. It hurt, but the boy didn't cry. Neither did Sarah cry out when Topper pulled the tape off her face.

"Now they can both talk and cheer—Sarah-the-Slug and Carter-the-Farter. Isn't this just bitchin'? I mean, is this a great country or what?"

"P-please don't do anything to us," Sarah begged, tears slipping down her cheeks. "We just want to go home. You said we could go home if we cooperated with you. *Please*, Topper—"

"Oh, I lied through my overbite. Sorry about that. Anyway, letting you go wouldn't be any fun, now would it? You'd miss the best show we've ever had here on *Adventures with the Verminator*. You think it's been awesome so far, wait till you see *this*." He started to peel off his clothes, accompanying himself by whistling the *William Tell Overture*. First his Starter jacket, then his knee-length black sweatshirt. Then his Nike cross trainers, his baggy jeans, and finally his flowered boxer shorts. He mugged naked in front of them, strutting and high-stepping, his penis rigid in the dank air of the cellar.

"Oh God, p-please! . . ." Sarah murmured, not looking at him.

"No sense praying, Sluggo. You know, I've been going to church almost from the day I was born, and I can tell you from bitter experience that prayer changes nothing. God doesn't answer prayer, Sluggo—He only laughs at it. Prayer is as big a waste of time as psychotherapy."

He went to the furry mound in the opposite corner of the cellar and dragged it into the center where the light shone. "You know this guy, don't you—the old Gerard-Burger, the trusty Bernice mountain dog . . ."

"It's *Bernese* mountain dog, you miserable cretin!" Sarah shouted at him. "And if you hurt him, I swear I'll kill you!"

"Hey, that's what I like—*spunk*. Spunk burns real well. I've seen it with rats, as has my man, Carter-the-Farter. Rats are among the spunkiest of the vermin, and I'm here to tell you they *burn*, man. They burn big-time! Isn't that right, Carter-the-Farter? You've seen it happen right here in this room."

Carter turned his face away, his shoulders shaking as he wept.

Topper ran a length of heavy rope through the knots around Gerard's front and rear paws, then put an end of the rope across an overhead timber. He hoisted on the rope with his full weight. The big dog cried out in pain.

"God damn you!" Sarah screamed. "You're hurting him! Put him down, you fucking bastard!"

"Heyyyy, listen to the little Christian's language—

pretty impressive, isn't it, ladies and gentlemen? And I thought she'd swallowed all that born-again crap.''

"What *are* you? What in the fuck *are* you, man? Put him down!''

Gerard was now wholly off the floor, his dark fur matted with mud and dripping. He caught sight of Sarah and Carter, gave a pitiful whine.

"Jesus, Mary and Joseph, this dog is heavy," Topper muttered, tying the rope to another timber. "He must weigh over a hundred pounds, I swear to God." Gerard's weight caused the ceiling to sag and creak, to issue tiny streams of dust as he swung slowly back and forth, rotating first one direction, then the other.

"You fucking *animal*!" Sarah screamed, her tears flowing hot. "What has Gerard ever done to you?"

"It's not a question of what he's done to me, it's what he's going to do *for* me. You see, little missy, I'm going to douse the old Gerard-Burger with gasoline—I've got some in that can over there, and if you sniff real hard, I'll bet you can smell it. Then I'm going to flick my Bic, and doo-woppity-wop-wop—the old Gerard-Burger will go up in flames. And you know what? He'll sing like Plácido Domingo, I'll bet you that. Granted it may sound like Plácido Domingo on *fire* . . ." He paused to acknowledge laughter from the imaginary studio audience.

"You're sick!" Sarah screamed. "You're going to a prison for sick, ugly perverts!"

"Not beyond the realm of possibility, little missy. But back to the matter at hand. The old Gerard-Burger'll be the warm-up act, the one that gets the Verminator right up close to the edge." He wagged his stiff penis back and forth. "At the very moment he crosses over into that great beyond, the Verminator's gonna *verminate*! That's right, folks—right-cheer on this stage . . ." He did an Ed Sullivan impression. ". . . the Verminator's gonna fuck the departing spirit of this big ugly dog. And when that's done . . ." He turned slowly to cast his eyes on the children. ". . . it'll be Carter-the-Farter's turn. Of course, we'll want to cut a few things off him first, which is why we brought our trusty K-Bar hunting knife."

Sarah shrieked, her voice cracking. She struggled against the handcuffs, causing her brother to cry out in pain.

"And then it'll be your turn, little missy. Hear me? First you're gonna watch your beloved Gerard-Burger go up in smoke, then you're gonna watch your scrawny little brother do his patented Carter-the-Farter fire dance. And finally . . ." Topper took a deep breath, his eyes glazing. "I'll truss you up like Gerard here, and I'll cover you in sweet-smelling gasoline—you'll get it in your eyes and nose, probably make you hack and wheeze—and I'll take a few pieces of you to save for later, maybe put them in one of those jars there, with somebody's cock and eyes and whatnot. Then I'll set you off like a fucking Buddhist monk, and that's gonna put the Verminator right into the next dimension!"

Drained of all energy, Sarah could only croak. She let her head loll against the muddy wall of the cellar. Topper found the can of gasoline he'd stashed earlier, then rummaged through the plastic bag to find the K-Bar.

"Watch this now, you guys. It's gonna be awesome." He took the screw off the can. He started to douse Gerard, who panted heavily and whined. The big dog tried to lick his hand. "Hey, that's a good boy," Topper whispered. "You'll be just fine . . ."

Topper heard something and froze, the gasoline spilling onto his bare foot. A creaking or a cracking, he thought, like someone picking his way through the wreckage upstairs. Had he imagined it? He heard it again, told himself it was a rat or a raccoon. Lots of vermin up there, lots of garbage for them to tunnel

through. He'd heard such sounds before, and had sometimes expected the Mad Witch herself to burst in on him.
But nothing had ever happened. No one had ever come.

Hearing the sounds, Sarah screamed, dredging up
strength from somewhere deep—a piercing little-girl's
scream that seared Topper's eardrums. Carter added his
own shrill cry for help, hoping that someone had come
to rescue them. Topper dropped the gasoline can,
glanced once at the trapdoor.

Nobody's coming, for crying out loud.

He rummaged through the plastic sack for his lighter,
found it, took it out. Turning back toward the gasoline-
soaked dog, he held the lighter high and thrust his hips
forward. For a harrowing moment he wondered if flicking the lighter would cause an explosion. *Here we go,
folks. The Verminator's gonna verminate!* . . .

He didn't see the powerful form move smoothly down
the stairs behind him, didn't hear the heavy tree limb
whistle toward his head. The instant the wood struck his
skull, Topper Bannon's world went black, and the lighter
fell to the muddy floor.

IX

VONDA REUBEN FINALLY GOT THE CHILDREN TO STOP
screaming.

While searching the pockets of Topper's trousers for
the key to the handcuffs, she assured them that they were
safe, that she would let nothing harm them or their dog.
She found the key and freed them. Though neither Sarah
nor Carter had ever met her, they hugged her so tightly
that she almost couldn't breathe.

She lowered Gerard to the floor and worried away the
ropes on his paws. Sarah was overjoyed to find that he
could still walk, though he was stiff and rickety. He

licked all their faces, even Vonda's, and she let him,
though she wasn't an ardent dog lover.

Leaving Topper where he lay, they climbed the ladder
and picked their way through the wreckage of the stone
cabin. Spears of moonlight angled through the tall trees,
showing them the way to the trail. From then on, the
going was easy.

X

"... SO ALL HER LIFE, ROSA ENVIED AND ADMIRED
Sally," Denise Ubaldo explained, her eyes focused on
the letter in front of her, "because Tucker never beat
Sally, never told her she was a willful, weak-blooded
half-breed. Rosa came to believe that she herself was
truly bad, while Sally was good. As it says here, *'Más
que cualquier cosa en este mundo, quería llegar a ser
tú.'* It means, 'More than anything in the world, I wanted
to become you.' "

And this, Pete said to himself, explained why Rosa
Juanita Sandoval reinvented herself as Nita Vale. She'd
hated the person she'd been as a child, the object of
Tucker's abuse and humiliation, a dark half-breed with
tainted blood in her veins. She'd admired her cousin, the
blond and blue-eyed Sally, who had mustered the gump-
tion to break away from Buckthorn and start a new life.
So Rosa decided to go her cousin one better. She started
a new life as a new person. She underwent plastic surgery and changed the color of her hair and eyes. She
remade herself in her cousin's image, or as close to it
as she could get. And then she returned to Buckthorn to
do battle with Tucker.

Pete wondered how she knew about Sally's favorite
way of making love. Had she observed it during the
ménage à trois with Kelly Franklin, or had Sally con-

fided in her, possibly by letter after marrying Pete? He supposed it didn't matter.

Denise paused to wipe tears away, then continued. "In this letter she refers to a promise that she made years before to Sally—that she would never reveal to anyone that Tucker killed Kelly Franklin. They knew that a murder trial would require Sally to testify about what she saw on the night it happened, which would mean that the ugliness of Buckthorn would become part of her life again and part of her new family's life as well. Sally couldn't bear the thought of this happening, her husband and children finding out about all these horrible things. So she'd forced Rosa to promise never to tell anyone."

"Sally was good at forcing people to promise things."

"And Rosa has kept it all these years, as far as I can tell."

Pete's eyes started to burn, so he shut them. He took a deep breath. Some people, he thought, are better at keeping promises than others.

When he opened his eyes again, he saw something that startled him. A huge yellow cat sat on a hanging planter on Denise's rear porch, visible through the glass pane of the backdoor. He thought of Jerry Dragstead and the monstrous feline that followed him everywhere. But this couldn't be the same animal. *Could* it?

"Denise, do you own a cat?"

"No. I'm allergic to them. And dogs too. If I get near one, I swell up and break out in hives."

Pete rose from the kitchen table and walked into the living room, glancing out the picture window toward the street. He felt inside his sport coat for the Smith and Wesson but didn't take it out.

He thought of his kids and winced. They'd come home from school again to find him gone. But he comforted himself with the knowledge that Esmerelda had

been there for them. By now she would have given them
dinner and started them on their homework.

Movement caught his eye on the street beyond Denise
Ubaldo's white picket fence. A low, black car glided by
with its lights off and halted in front of a deserted bungalow a few doors away. The interior light went on
briefly and a man got out, but Pete couldn't see him
clearly, thanks to the blossoming rhododendrons that
bordered Denise's yard.

"Verduin," he said aloud, his pulse banging in his
ears. Of *course*. A low, black car like the one that had
chased Nita two days ago, like Verduin's Trans Am.
Tucker Bannon clearly had reason to want Nita dead,
and he'd already commissioned Verduin to kill her. If
he knew that Nita and Pete had become lovers, he probably wanted Pete dead, too, because lovers whisper secrets to each other, don't they? And Nita had plenty of
secrets to whisper.

"Denise, we've got to get out of here!" he shouted.
He heard her chair scrape across the linoleum, saw her
appear in the doorway, a massive woman in a bright
print dress. Her face was pale, her eyes huge.

"Is something wrong?" she asked. "Have you—?"

She took a step forward, but a loud crash stopped her
cold, a shattering of glass and wood. Someone had
kicked the rear door in. Pete heard the thud of heavy
boots and saw a dark shape in the kitchen behind her, a
man clothed in camouflage. A string of sharp pops filled
the air, a blast from an automatic weapon. Denise's left
eye blew out, along with a gout of brain tissue. Blood
erupted from her nose and mouth, and she jiggled forward in a crazy dance as more bullets stitched her back.
She went down in a heap on the living room carpet.

Pete whirled away, his hand stuck in the breast pocket
of his sport coat, still clutching the Smith and Wesson.
He lunged into the rear hallway toward a bedroom,

vaguely aware that bullets were splintering the woodwork around him. He burst into a dark bedroom and
immediately sprawled headlong over a bed, rolled across
it and found himself wedged tightly against the wall. He
heard another loud crash as the living room door gave
way, more footfalls and men's voices.

"Did you get him?"

"Negative. He's in the bedroom. He ain't goin' anywhere."

"See any letters?"

"Affirmative, spread all over the kitchen table. If you
want to get 'em, I'll take care of the asshole."

"Jesus, Gil—cut the affirmative-negative shit, okay?
We're not in the fucking Green Berets."

Pete struggled to free the pistol from his sport coat,
but the hammer had caught in the lining. A shadow filled
a portion of the doorway, and he realized just how incompetent he was in the field of deadly combat. He
couldn't even get his fucking gun out. The man in camouflage leaned into the room and—

Everything went black as if the power had failed.
From the other end of the house came a loud crash, the
pop of a silenced firearm, more loud crashes.

"What happened to the fuckin' lights, Hot Toddy . . .?"

Pandemonium. Muzzle flashes, splintering woodwork.
Pete wriggled away from the bed and scooted on his
hands and knees to the window, a rectangle only slightly
brighter than the surrounding black. He pulled his sport
coat over his head and bulled through it, shattering the
panes and the frame, ripping away the screen. A staccato
blast of bullets followed him, along with loud cursing.
Stunned and bloodied by broken glass, he staggered to
his feet and ran toward the rear of the house, nearly
garroting himself on a clothesline. He fought through
rose bushes and azaleas, thorns tearing at him and ig-

niting strings of pain. As he was about to plunge into
the alley, someone reached out from behind a bush and
grabbed him by the arm. He flailed in panic, punched
and kicked, even tried to bite.

"Mr. Cochran, it's okay. It's me, Jerry Dragstead."

Dragstead! Pete fought to free himself, fought to get
his gun out, but Dragstead's grip was like a vise. The
big man expertly whirled him around and put him in a
painful hammer lock, then pushed him into the alley.

"Don't talk, just run, Mr. Cochran. Follow me, turn
when I do, and duck when I do."

Headlights came on behind them—the Trans Am.
Verduin and his accomplice had correctly surmised
Pete's escape route. Dragstead forced Pete into the yard
of a derelict house, where the weeds grew man-high.
They clambered through an obstacle course of abandoned washing machines, refrigerators and kitchen
ranges to a rear porch that sagged under the weight of
English ivy. They hid on their bellies behind a stack of
rotting mattresses.

"Keep your mouth shut and they won't find us, Mr.
Cochran," Dragstead whispered. "They don't have time
to do a real good job lookin' for us. I figure someone
heard the ruckus and called the cops by now. A deputy's
apt to be here in a minute or two."

Pete bit his lower lip and screwed his eyes shut. He
heard the Trans Am whisper past, its tires squelching
through mud. In his head he saw Denise Ubaldo lying
dead in her own blood, and grief sliced through him like
a knife. He'd known her only three weeks, but he'd liked
her. She'd been a good woman with a kind heart, and
her loss pained him. He felt tears welling through his
clenched eyelids.

Dragstead jerked him to his feet again. They hurried
back the way they had come, passing by the rear of
Denise Ubaldo's house, which stood black and lifeless

in the moonlight. They came to Third Street and turned right, walking only a block to Nehalem Avenue.

"My place," Dragstead said, pointing to a house with a yellow porch light. "You'll be safe in there, 'cause Todd Verduin don't know where I live. Could you use a beer or somethin'?"

This is unreal, Pete told himself as Dragstead led him up the front walk to the door. *I'm having some sort of episode. I'm not walking into Jerry Dragstead's house . . . !*

XI

THE CHILDREN WERE MISSING—SARAH, CARTER AND Topper—and the Bannons were beside themselves. Tucker had called the principal of Nehalem County Elementary and Middle School at her home and found out that no soccer orientation meeting had occurred after school today. For that matter, the school had no faculty member named Alex Davis.

"What this means is that the children have been missing for almost six hours," he fumed to Dolly and Esmerelda in his study. "We've got to assume that they've been kidnapped. We have no choice but to call the sheriff." He picked up the telephone and started to dial.

"I know where Topper is," Esmerelda said.

Tucker put the phone down and stared, his eyes nested in purple pouches, his face bruised from the beating Topper had given him two days earlier. "Do you intend to tell us or stand there like a silly Mexican statue all night?"

Over an hour ago she'd received a call from Vonda Reuben, notifying her that Sarah, Carter and their dog were safe with her. Vonda had taken them to her house on Nehalem Avenue and planned to keep them there

until their father came for them. Bannon House wasn't
safe for them—not while Topper was around. Sarah had
told Vonda about Topper's call to the school and what
he'd done to the children at the stone cabin. But Esmerelda didn't tell the Bannons this.

"He is in a stone cabin near the top of the mountain,"
she replied. "It is a very old place."

"I'm familiar with the place," Tucker said. "It's been
abandoned for years. How do you know he's there?"

Esmerelda said nothing.

"I asked you a question, woman! Answer me, or by
God Almighty, I'll beat it out of you."

"I-I know someone who's seen him. I'm told that he
tried to harm the children, Sarah and Carter, but they
are safe now. It is Theodore who needs help. He's been
hurt—"

"Oh merciful God!" Dolly exclaimed, wringing and
twisting a handkerchief in her hands. "You say they're
safe? Praise God! Where are they, Esmerelda? You must
tell us where they are."

"I cannot do that, Señora."

"You knew they were safe all this time, and you
didn't tell us? You put us through—"

A door slammed at the rear of the house. Someone
had returned home. Tucker picked up the shotgun that
had lain across his desk and rested it in the crook of his
arm. Dolly clutched at his arm as he started to go. "No,
Tuck. You must not do this. He's our son, after all—
our only son."

"I know very well what he is, Dolly. He is an abom-
ination in the sight of the Lord. He's a danger to us all,
especially the children. We can no longer take the risk
of letting him hurt someone, least of all Sarah or Carter.
They are the future of this family. The destiny of the
Bannon line lies with them." He pushed away her hands
and headed for the door.

"No, Tucker!" Dolly snatched a brass poker from its stand on the hearth and swung it at her husband's head. It struck with a thud, and he fell to his knees, clutching his head with both hands.

"Esmerelda, keep him here in this room!" Dolly screamed. "I'll find Topper and take him somewhere safe." She rushed from the room, her feet pounding on the carpet.

"Señora!" Esmerelda shouted after her. "Be careful! The boy is not himself!" She bent to tend Tucker Bannon's injury, saw that he was bleeding through a new gash in his scalp. He shoved her away and scrabbled around with his hands, feeling for his shotgun on the carpet.

"Get away from me, woman! I have work to do."

"No, Señor Bannon. You are hurt. You must let me help you."

"Get away, I said!" He shoved her hard against the brick mantel of the fireplace. "I'm coming to do your bidding, Lord. I've heard your voice, just as I've always heard it in the past."

He found the shotgun and pulled himself to a standing position. Esmerelda watched in horror as he straightened to his full height, his shoulders square, his eyes afire with holy zeal.

"Take now thy son, thine only son whom thou lovest, and offer him upon the mountain for a burnt offering," he intoned, quoting Genesis the way he remembered it. *"And Abraham rose up, and took his son Isaac, and went unto the place God had told him . . ."*

Esmerelda moved to stop him, but an explosion erupted somewhere in the house—a gunshot. It rattled the glass in Tucker's gun cabinet and reverberated through the empty rooms, leaving behind a deathly silence. Tucker turned and stared at her, blood streaming down his face from the gash in his scalp. For a horrific moment she thought that he would shoot her. But oddly, he only smiled.

"*And Abraham took the wood of the burnt offering, and laid it upon Isaac his son; and he took the fire in his hand, and a knife . . .*" He cocked the shotgun and moved smoothly into the hallway.

Esmerelda stumbled after him, barely able to keep on her feet. Her shoulder ached from the collision with the brick mantel, and her fat legs still throbbed from the ordeal she'd endured two days earlier and again today, searching for Topper on the mountain. She followed Tucker into the pantry, saw him stand a moment in the doorway of the kitchen, dark against the white tiles.

A groan came out of his mouth, low and rumbling, as if he'd seen something that no man should see. He walked unsteadily into the kitchen. Esmerelda edged up to the door, looked in, and fought to keep her stomach from emptying. Señora Bannon lay on the white-tile floor, her chest a mass of mangled flesh, a lake of blood beneath her. Her face was gray and vacant, her eyes open wide in wonderment.

Topper sat on the countertop opposite, naked as the day of his birth, his skin scoured raw by nettles, needles and thorns. Blood ran down his neck and chest from an ugly laceration on the side of his head, undoubtedly from the blow that Vonda had dealt him as he was about to burn the Cochrans' dog. On the counter next to him lay his .410 gauge shotgun, the one that Tucker had given him to shoot gophers and crows with.

Tucker fell silent now and stood a long time over Dolly, the woman who had shared his bed for nearly half a century. He muttered something, sniffled and coughed. He raised his eyes to Topper.

The kid smiled at him, and Esmerelda thought, *That's*

a good smile, not an evil one. She crossed herself and kissed the crucifix around her neck.

Tucker leveled his Ithaca twelve-gauge at the boy's face. *"To every thing there is a season, and a time to every purpose under heaven . . . A time to kill, and a time to heal . . ."* His voice was strong and certain, the voice of a Christian man who knows his duty.

"It's okay, Dad," Topper said. "I'm back now. I've gone over the top, and I'm back. I'm not the Verminator anymore. It's okay . . ."

Tucker blew his head off.

XII

TOTAL SURREALISM, PETE THOUGHT, SITTING IN JERRY Dragstead's living room with dozens of wet-eyed puppies and kittens staring down from the walls, a giant yellow cat named Shagnasty sleeping in his lap, and a large dog named Nitro watching his every move. *This isn't happening. This is a scene from a French gangster movie.*

Except that it wasn't. Denise Ubaldo was really dead. And Tucker Bannon wanted Pete dead, too, just as he wanted Nita Vale dead. As he'd wanted Wade Beswick dead.

Pete sipped from the bottle of Miller Lite that Dragstead had presented him. Dragstead smoked a Camel while he explained how he'd happened to be at Denise Ubaldo's house tonight.

"I followed you over there because I was hopin' to get a chance to thank you for what you did for Scotty Dunn," he said, blowing smoke out through his nose. "That's the only reason—same reason I followed you home from your girlfriend's place a couple weeks back. I just wanted to thank you, man."

"*Thank* me? For what? I didn't do anything for Scotty."

"Yeah, you did. You planted a couple of hard ones on Wade Beswick, that sorry sack of shit, for what he did to Scotty. And you told him to be nice to the ladies around the office, show 'em a little fuckin' respect. I wanted to thank you for that. Shows me there's finally somebody around here with enough balls to do what's right for people. I admire men who care about something besides makin' an almighty buck, okay?"

"That's all you wanted to do—*thank* me? Why couldn't you've made an appointment to see me or called me on the phone? Jesus Christ, you almost gave me a heart attack when you followed me that night."

"I didn't want people to see me and think I was suckin' up to the new man. That's not my way. I like to thank a man face-to-face, eyeball to eyeball. Anyways, I'll say it now, better late than never. Thanks for what you did."

So what had Dragstead done, exactly, back at Denise's just now?

The big man grinned with his bad teeth. He'd "staked out" the house from the porch of an abandoned home across the street, intending to flag Pete down when he left. But then two men had arrived and approached the place with machine guns drawn. Dragstead couldn't stand by and watch a murder go down, so he sneaked into Denise's back porch and pulled the breaker switch at what seemed a strategic moment. Taking advantage of the ensuing confusion, he'd dashed into the kitchen and coldcocked one of the assailants with a hard right "upside the head." He'd run outside again after glancing out the dining room and seeing Pete flee across the backyard. Caught him just before he got to the alley.

"I guess you know the rest," Dragstead said, swallowing half a bottle of beer in a gulp. "I wanted to make sure you got away from them cocksuckers, and I knew I could show you a few tricks, since I know the lay of the land around here. I'm just sorry I couldn't do nothin' to help Denise. I saw her on the floor, the moon shining through the window, just lightin' her up like nobody's business. I don't guess there's any chance that she might . . ." His words trailed off and he stared at Pete, waiting. Pete shook his head sadly. "That's what I was afraid of."

Pete leaned back on the sofa, drew a deep breath and let it out. "Jerry, I want to thank you for what you did for me tonight. You could've gotten killed. Christ, if I could've gotten my gun out of my coat, I probably would've shot you myself. Why did you do it?"

"Tried to do what's right, that's all. Same as you."

"Same as me."

"Yeah." Dragstead swallowed the rest of his beer, went to the kitchen, and came back with fresh ones both for himself and Pete. As if it were that simple, Pete thought, accepting the bottle—doing what's right. He wondered if in all his life he'd ever consciously tried to do what was purely *right*, not what was merely legal or acceptable or fashionable.

An idea flashed in his brain, and he immediately rejected it. It was crazy and desperate. It couldn't work. And yet, why not grab his problem and spear it to the quick? Tucker had framed him, tried to lure his children away, tried to kill him. Why not take this war home to the enemy, to Tucker himself? He knew that he couldn't simply wait for the old man to make his next move. Pete needed to take the initiative.

"Tell me, Jerry—how would you like to help me catch Wade Beswick's killer, as well as the Buckthorn killer?"

Dragstead swallowed wrong and spit beer down the front of his work shirt. He coughed loudly and looked at Pete with disbelieving eyes. "You're sayin' you know who the Buckthorn killer is?"

"I do. I'd like to get him talking about his crimes, get him to open up to me, and record it on tape. Trouble is, he won't open up unless he thinks he's going to kill me, so I've got to let him get the drop on me, as they say."

"Who is it? I'd like to know, 'cause I've spent most of my adult life tryin' to prove it ain't me."

"It's Tucker Bannon."

"Tucker Bannon. I'll be fucked. You sure about this?"

Pete told him about what Rosa had written to his wife in her letters. He told him about his own talk with Paul Garson. About the attempt on Nita's life.

"Wow," Dragstead said. "I had no idea, man—big, rich dude like him, got the world by the balls. Why would he want to do things like that to people?"

Pete couldn't hazard a guess. A sickness, maybe, the worst kind imaginable. Or pure evil, who knows? As for the men who'd killed Denise, they worked for Bannon. They had killed Beswick and had framed Pete. With some luck and some deft maneuvering, Pete figured he could get Tuck to talk about these things and tape it without his knowledge. But it would happen only if Tucker assumed that Pete wouldn't live to repeat what he'd heard.

"We need to set things up so you're the cavalry, Jerry, so you can come riding to the rescue at the last minute. Are you up for it?"

"Count me in. I'll do whatever you want."

Pete took out his pistol and handed it to him. "Ever use one of these?"

Dragstead hadn't, but how hard could it be? He'd seen plenty of cop shows on TV. He knew enough to squeeze the trigger, not jerk it.

Pete endured a sick moment of misgiving, but he couldn't turn back now. "You'll be fine. Before we do anything, we need to go over to the head shed and pick up a couple of cell phones. I'll explain as we go."

"You got it."

"But first I want to use your phone, okay?"

"Be my guest."

Pete called Bannon House to check on the kids, hoping that Esmerelda would answer. She did, after the fourth or fifth ring, but she didn't sound like herself. In a low voice, as if fearful of being overheard, she told Pete what had happened at Bannon House tonight and on Mount Olivet earlier. She told him where he could find Sarah and Carter, assured him that they were fine. And she begged him not to come back to Bannon House, for God only knew what might happen if he did.

Pete stood for a long moment by the telephone, feeling faint. He leaned against the wall and tried to think. "Esmerelda, I want you to do something for me. I want you to leave that place. But before you do, go to my room, to my closet, and find something for me—I think it's on the top shelf, over to the left. It's a camcorder, a Sony camcorder—know what it is?"

Of course she knew. Did he want anything else?

"Just the camcorder. Bring it to Vonda Reuben's house as soon as you can. Can you do that for me?"

Of course she could, though she couldn't imagine why anyone would need such a thing at a time like this. Pete thanked her and warned her to be careful and not to let Tucker know she was leaving.

XIII

THEY DROVE ACROSS TOWN TO THE SAWMILL OFFICE, where Pete picked up a pair of cell phones—his own and the one that had belonged to Wade Beswick. Then Dragstead drove them to Vonda Reuben's house and office, which was just down the street from his own.

"I'll wait in the car," Dragstead said. "Dr. Reuben don't like me much."

"To hell with that," Pete said, getting out of the old Mercury street rod. "You're with me. If she doesn't like you, that's her problem."

Pete's reunion with his kids and the dog was loud, joyful and short. Tears flowed freely, even from Vonda's normally cold, dry eyes. A few minutes later Esmerelda Sandoval arrived from Bannon House, carrying the camcorder Pete had asked for. She and Vonda hugged each other and shed fresh tears.

"Listen everybody, I have some sad news," Pete said. "Denise Ubaldo is dead." Vonda sat down suddenly in a chair, a hand pressed tight over her mouth. Pete told the rest of it as briefly as he could, hugging his children close as he did so. He also recounted how Jerry Dragstead had saved his life.

"What's important is that we're all safe now," he added. "There's just one more thing that needs doing, though." He and Dragstead traded glances. "Jerry and I'll make sure it gets done, and we'll come back here when we're finished. Until then, I want you all to stay here and take care of each other, okay?" He took a deep breath, looked at Vonda. "I'd like to talk with you alone a minute, if you don't mind."

They went from the living room to one of her examination rooms, which was hardly bigger than a closet. Pete suddenly hugged her and sobbed deeply against her shoulder. He apologized for blubbering. He thanked her for saving the only things that made his life worth living—his kids. He confessed that he should have listened to her when she admonished him almost two weeks earlier to take them and flee Buckthorn.

Patting his head, Vonda told him it was all right to cry. Men shouldn't be afraid to do it, she said—a few more tears and a little less testosterone might make the world a more livable place. She advised him to let it all out, and he did. In a surprisingly short time the torrent ended, and Pete felt strong again, as if he'd just shed a tremendous weight.

"Tell me one thing," he said. "Why did you go back up the mountain to that old cabin?" Vonda smiled, shrugged. She'd just had a hunch, she told him. A very *good* one. Pete hugged her again.

Pete took out his cell phone and dialed Nita Vale's number but got her answering machine. This worried him. He left a message that warned her to be on guard and told her that she could reach him through Vonda Reuben. He then looked up Wally MacKenzie's home number in Nehalem County's slim phone book and dialed it.

"Hello." A TV commercial blared in the background, someone singing about how she liked what Toyota did for her.

"Wally, it's me, Pete Cochran. We've got trouble, and I need your help."

"Pete . . . you don't sound . . . what kind of trouble?"

"I can't get into it over the phone. But I need you to meet me in ten minutes at the mill. Got that?"

"Ten minutes—at the mill? Jesus, what's this all about, buddy? Can't it wait till . . . ?"

"It can't wait, Wally. Just be in front of the head shed ten minutes from now. And Wally—have you ever operated a camcorder?"

"A camcorder? Well—yeah, I guess so. I rented one and shot a bunch of footage at my nephew's wedding last summer."

"Good, good. I'm hanging up now. I'll see you soon. And Wally—don't tell anyone where you're going."

XIV

THROUGH THE WINDOW OF HIS STUDY TUCKER BANNON
saw the rotating beacons of emergency vehicles in the
town below, red and blue blobs of light sweeping over
streets and alleys. At least three police cruisers, he figured. A couple of ambulances. East side of town, right
about where Denise Ubaldo lived, unless he missed his
guess.

These were good signs.

Then he saw Todd Verduin's black car move up the
drive and halt at the front of the house. He'd forgotten
that he'd given the detective the digital access code
needed to get through the front gate. *Don't let me forget
to change it, Lord.* Verduin and another man got out of
the car, walked into the portico and rang the bell.

Tucker rose from his leather chair and made his way
to the foyer. He pulled the door open and saw Verduin's
delicate mouth drop open in shock.

"What's the matter, Todd? Never see a couple of
shiners before?" He turned and headed back toward his
study without bidding his visitors to follow. They followed anyway.

"I've got the letters you wanted, Tucker," Verduin
said. "There's over a hundred here—I assume that's all
of them."

"Good. You also managed to silence Ms. Ubaldo and
Mr. Cochran, I assume."

"One out of two—the fat woman, Ubaldo."

Tucker walked through the double doors of his study
and turned around suddenly, his face hard with anger.
"You mean that Pete is still alive? Is that what you're
telling me?"

Verduin's cohort spoke for the first time. "It's not

like we didn't give it our best shot. There was some other asshole there, and he cut the power to the place, and . . .''

"Shut up, Gil,'' Verduin said. "Don't worry, Tucker. Cochran won't do anything stupid. After all, you've got his kids, right? He wouldn't do anything that might put them in danger, now would he?"

"That's the problem, Todd. I don't have Sarah and Carter here. I don't even know where they are. They've been missing since school let out this afternoon.''

"This *does* present a problem."

"I say we get paid for what we've done so far," Monahan put in.

"Shut up, Gil."

"What you've done so far doesn't amount to a teaspoon of dirt," Tucker growled. "You haven't managed to kill either Nita Vale or Peter Cochran. Why would you deserve any payment until you've finished the job?"

"Killing people is very tricky work, Tucker," Verduin said, "not to mention dirty and distasteful. It's also dangerous. Things can and do go wrong. I've got a nasty bruise on the side of my head, courtesy of somebody who wants Pete Cochran to stay alive.''

"Quit your bellyaching! Killing is like any other kind of work. You put your back into it, use your head, and it gets done.''

"Tucker, the killing stops now unless you agree to give me half of everything you have—the house, the mill, your timberlands, any cash you have on hand.''

"You must be insane.''

"No, merely realistic. Unless Nita Vale and Pete Cochran die, you're going down in flames. I don't know what's in these letters, but it must be serious shit, or you wouldn't need to put your own flesh and blood in the ground to keep it from getting out. And now Pete knows what's in them, too, doesn't he? That's why he's got to

go, too—right? Let's face it, Tucker-my-man, you need
my help. And my help is going to cost half of everything
you have.''

"You don't know what you're saying. The Lord will
never let you . . .''

The telephone rang, and Tucker stared at it, wondering what he might say if someone asked for Dolly or
Esmerelda. Or Pete. It rang again, and he picked it up.

"Hello.''

"Tucker, this is Pete. Can you talk?''

"Pete. Yes. Yes, I'm alone here.''

*"Alone with two dead bodies, you mean—Dolly's and
Topper's.''*

"How did you know that?''

*"Never mind. You and I need to have a meeting, Tuck.
We need to reason together, nose to nose like gentlemen.
What you tried to do to me tonight—it was unneces-
sary.''*

"I don't know what you mean.''

*"Of course you do. You know exactly what I mean.
You've always been right about me, Tuck—I'm a businessman at heart. And being a businessman, I'm always
willing to talk about a deal. I figure that each of us has
something the other needs, and being good businessmen,
there's no reason we shouldn't reach an agreement that
accommodates both of us. Now let's get together and
talk. What do you say?''*

Tucker looked up into the delicate face of Todd Verduin. This would be his last chance, he knew, to set his
world right. "Yes, all right. We'll meet. Where and
when?''

*"The mill. The parking lot, where there's lots of space
all around us. Come alone, Tucker. Don't bring your
thugs with you, or I'll go straight to the police and tell
them everything I know.''*

"Very well. I can be there in ten minutes. And we'll talk."

"Ten minutes, good. I'll see you then."

Tucker hung up the phone. "Once again the Lord has delivered my enemy into my hands," he said to Verduin. "That was Pete, and he wants to have a meeting. As for the cost of your help, I've decided that half of all I have is a reasonable price."

"Good," Verduin said. "Now let's get our ducks in a row for this meeting, shall we?"

XV

NITA VALE CLIMBED THE STAIRS TO HER APARTMENT, still wincing every time she put weight on her left foot. In the darkness of her living room the blinking red light on her answering machine stood out like a lighthouse on a lonely shore. She listened to the message from Pete Cochran and immediately dialed Vonda Reuben's number.

"Hello, this is Vonda Reuben."

"Vonda, it's Nita. Is Pete there? What's going on?"

"Brace yourself, girl. Are you sitting down?" Vonda gave her a quick replay of today's events—the near tragedy in the cellar of the stone cabin on Mount Olivet, the killing of Dolly and Topper Bannon, the killing of Denise Ubaldo, the attempt on Pete's life. Nita sat down slowly, listening to the words, picturing the faces of the dead.

Dolly. Denise. And little Theodore, her own son.

Something crashed in her heart. A mental wire gave way. Reality as she'd known it unraveled.

"Remember when I told you that I had a theory about who the Buckthorn killer was?" Vonda asked.

"Yes. I remember. You wouldn't tell me."

"I thought it was too crazy, but after talking to Pete tonight, I know I was right. It's Tucker. It's your uncle, Nita. Oh yes, I know who you really are, have for some time. It's okay, girl. You're still you, as far as I'm concerned."

"I-I don't quite know what to say."

"Don't say anything. Just get your ass over to my place where you'll be safe. Pete's afraid that this Verduin character will come after you in your apartment, and so am I."

"Where is he? Pete, I mean. Can I talk to him?"

"He's gone to the mill to have a meeting with Tucker. It sounds crazy, I know, but he's convinced that . . ."

Nita hung up the phone and fought the urge to heave on her carpet.

XVI

DETECTIVE ASHLEY TCHING STOOD IN THE CORRIDOR OF the Nehalem County Sheriff's Office and watched the state medical examiner's team take Dan Kantor's body up the steps to the waiting van. Stark floodlights blinded her as TV cameramen jostled for footage, as reporters shouted questions to anyone who looked like law enforcement.

Fighting down a sob, Tching approached the OSP detective who'd driven in from Portland to investigate the case, a heavyset man with a short, silvering beard and longish gray hair. Tching introduced herself, told him she'd worked with Kantor on the Buckthorn killer case. The man gave her his condolences. He too had known Kantor, liked him, admired him.

"How did it happen?" Tching wanted to know.

"Best we can tell, the assailant came in through the basement corridor, probably got into one of the county offices upstairs and hid until everyone went home. Came down here and caught the lieutenant from behind as he was taking a soda out of the machine.''

''He couldn't have gained entry in any other way?''

''Not too likely. The main entrance to the S.O. is locked after the normal business day, and there's a video camera above the door. We've played the tape and there was nothing on it but deputies coming and going. They're all clean, of course.''

''Of course. What it boils down to is that the Honorable Sheriff Nick Graybill never paid any attention to security in this building. He never bothered to lock a damn door that provided access to his department through the offices of civilian agencies...'' Anger pinched off her voice, but she recovered quickly.

''Seems to me you hit the nail squarely on the head, Detective.'' The OSP detective turned away, and Tching ducked into the cubicle that had been Kantor's. Bob Esparza sat in Kantor's chair. When they saw each other, they both cried silently—no hugs, no pats on the back. Just silent tears.

''You make anything of this?'' Tching asked after catching her breath.

''I don't know. Maybe.'' Esparza took a Kleenex from the box on Kantor's desk and blew his nose. ''I saw a bloody footprint in the break room, leading out through the utility corridor. It looked an awful lot like the ones we found around Terry Grimes's place.''

''Bob, a quarter of the population of Oregon wear shoes like that.''

''I know, I know. But listen to this...'' He referred to notes Kantor had made in his ''murder book'' just before his death and earlier in the little spiral pad he'd always used. Kantor had received a call from Dr. Sheplov at VICAP, and she'd given him an update on the

investigation of the killer's footprints by the forensic paleoanthropology team.

"It's hard to make this out," Esparza said, squinting
at the notes. "His handwriting was awful, but it looks
to me like he wrote the word 'lump' and circled it. Is
that the way you read it?"

Tching examined the writing and agreed. *Lump*. So
what did it mean? she wondered aloud. She noticed that
on the following line Kantor had jotted, *"See Corliss,
little book."*

"This probably indicates his little spiral pad," she
said, picking it up and opening it. "Who do you suppose
this Corliss is?"

Esparza thought the name sounded familiar. His face
brightened. "Wait a minute—that name was on the list
the state health folks sent over, the one with all the reports about missing sodium pentobarbital."

"Right. Here it is—Dr. Gary Corliss, a veterinarian
in Hillsboro. It was a routine interview, except—except—Bob, look at this."

In the margin of the interview notes Kantor had written, *"Volunteer assistant, 1988."* He'd circled the
phrase in a different color of ink, maybe after talking to
VICAP, Esparza ventured. And below it he'd written,
"Call—who?"

"I take this to mean that he wanted to find out who
this volunteer assistant was," Tching said. "Something
he'd heard from VICAP made it important to know."

"You're a genius, Detective. Listen to this." He par-
aphrased Kantor's notes on the interview with Corliss.
"There was a fire in Corliss's clinic in 1988 which
caused the loss of some sodium pent. A volunteer assistant had gotten careless with a Bunsen burner. Corliss
said that the person was a solid citizen who certainly
wouldn't've used the fire to cover a theft."

"But something the Lieutenant heard from VICAP

made him want to find out who this person was.''

"And it has something to do with the word *lump*.''
Esparza spun around and pawed through the rack of telephone directories behind Kantor's desk until finding the
one for suburban Washington County. He fanned it open
to the C's in the white pages and quickly found Corliss's
home number. "You want to call him or should I?''

"I'll do it,'' Tching said, picking up the phone.

XVII

VENGEANCE CROUCHES IN THE WEEDS BEHIND ARM-
strong's International Harvester, keeping to the shadows
of ruined bulldozer tires stacked in black columns along
the property line. After a few moments of cautious reconnaissance it climbs into the driver's cab of a junked-
out Diamond-T logging truck, a vantage from which it
can watch the gate of the neighboring sawmill without
being seen. Beyond the gate lies the mill itself, a massive
assemblage of cutting machines and corroding metal, a
man-made monster that eats forests.

Ah, man. What a piece of work. And the *creatures*
he builds . . .

Killing Dan Kantor was easier than Vengeance had
anticipated, but the killing brought no joy or satisfaction.
Kantor had simply ventured too close to the truth, and
Vengeance couldn't allow him any closer. Killing him
hadn't solved the problem for the long term, of course,
for his underlings would carry on in his stead. But it had
bought precious time. Time to bring this whole sorry
mess to conclusion. Time to arrange one final plunge
into a luxurious bath of pain and fire.

Thus, tonight's prey was special. Tonight Vengeance
would take the one human being it had always intended

to be its last, the one who had given meaning to everything that Vengeance had ever done.

XVIII

PETE WAITED AT THE EDGE OF THE MILLPOND, THE HEAD rig building looming at his back. Yard lights illuminated the area around him, but he felt certain that someone approaching from the main gate could not pick him out amid the clutter of the buildings. Minutes ago he'd sent the watchman and the boiler operator home, assuring them that they would receive pay for a full shift.

Jerry Dragstead had taken his position in the nearby pole deck shed, where on workdays an operator maneuvered newly arrived logs into the pond with a huge contraption that resembled a crane. Wally MacKenzie had positioned himself inside the head rig building with the camcorder, his mission to aim the lens through a ventilation opening atop a ladder that ascended the near wall. From this spot he could get footage of anything that happened in the area of the millpond.

The camcorder had a detachable microphone and a twenty-foot cord. Pete had positioned the mike at the top of the door frame directly below Wally, hoping that it would pick up his and Tucker's conversation. The trick was to lure Tucker as close as possible to the door without making him suspicious. Pete would call MacKenzie on his cell phone the moment he saw activity at the front gate, thus giving him time to get the camcorder ready before Tucker arrived. When the time came to signal his rescue, Pete would simply yell for Jerry.

His preparations complete, Pete waited, his eyes sweeping the area of the front gate and the head shed. Bugs hovered and hummed over the millpond, while others besieged the yard lights. The boiler rumbled low on the hillside behind him, while water sprinklers hissed on its roof, killing stray coals that swarmed from the chimney like angry fireflies. Pete listened to the sounds of the mill and wondered if he would be alive an hour from now.

"Hello, Pete."

He spun around and saw Tucker Bannon standing not five feet away, his head spotted with bandages that shone white in the glare of the yard lights. He looked as if he wore makeup to play the part of a zombie in a cheap horror movie, his eye sockets blackened to look corpse-like, his shirt crusty with blood. In his hand he held a clubby pistol that he pointed squarely at Pete's chest.

Pete tried to talk, but only stammered. He wondered how the old man could have sneaked up on him, how he'd gotten in. He thought of MacKenzie and Dragstead in their respective hiding places, watching Tucker approach but being unable to send a warning.

"In case you're wondering, there's a hole in the fence up by the boiler," Tucker said, showing his dentures. "I used it instead of the main gate. I suppose I should've replaced that section of fence years ago, eh?"

"Tucker, it doesn't seem right, your holding a gun on me. I thought we came to talk about an agreement, a way to work things out."

"I'm afraid that's not possible, son. It seems we've been overtaken by events."

"Overtaken by . . . ?" Pete suddenly felt dizzy. He touched his forehead, swayed on his feet. "Tucker, I need to sit down. I'm not feeling well . . ." He staggered toward the head rig building, half-expecting a bullet to rip into his back. *I need to get him closer to the door . . . !* He leaned against the corrugated-metal wall and felt the chill through his sport coat. "I'm sorry. So much has happened tonight. I'll be okay now—I think."

"You'll be more than okay, Pete. If you confess your sins and give your heart to Jesus, you'll slumber in His arms tonight." Tucker came closer, his eyes glittering. "I'll give you that opportunity. I figure it's the least I can do. After all, you did all right by my Sally, until you lost your job, that is. You were a good husband, a good father. You deserve a shot at heaven."

Pete tried to swallow but couldn't work up any spit. Was the camcorder getting this? he wondered. "Why do you need to kill me, Tuck? I told you that I'm willing to reach an accommodation with you, and I meant that. We're businessmen, aren't we? We should be talking about business, not about killing."

"I have nothing to discuss with you, Pete. Now, if I were you, I'd go to the Lord in prayer. I don't have all night, and it's getting cold out here."

"Won't you at least listen to my proposition? You owe me that much, Tucker. For God's sake, what can it hurt to listen?"

"Make it quick."

"I'll keep my mouth shut about what you and Verduin did to Wade, in return for which you tell the sheriff that I was home with you and the family on the night he got killed—that'll get me off the hook. Then I'll go to the Conifer Group and negotiate some hush money— hell, they've already approached me about it—a little something to guarantee our silence about the scam that Beswick tried to engineer. I estimate that they'd be willing to part with, say, a million and a half. We'll . . ."

"You *know* about what Beswick tried to do?"

"Of course. He tried to steal Mount Olivet from you. That's why you had him killed, isn't it?"

Tucker's lower lip trembled. "I had him killed because he was an ungrateful fool, and he dared to tamper with something that has belonged to the Bannon family for over sixty years.''

"I can understand that.'' Pete's mouth was so dry that he would have given a hundred-dollar bill for a drink of water. "As for the other things, killing Denise, trying to kill Nita Vale, the Buckthorn killings—I'll keep my mouth shut about all that. All I ask in return is to run this mill, just like I'm doing now. I'm not asking for a raise or anything like that.''

"What are you talking about, you miserable fool?''

"I-I'm just saying that I can live with whatever you've had to do in the past. Look, I'm no angel myself, Tucker. I understand what it's like to be a human being. If you've had to kill people in order to keep what you've got, so be it. I don't pass judgment on people just because . . .''

"You think I'm the Buckthorn killer, don't you? You learned from one of Rosa's letters that I killed that little lecher, Kelly Franklin, and now you think I killed all the others. That's it, isn't it?''

Pete was close to panic. "What else was I supposed to think? I mean, you killed him, cut off his—cut certain things off him, and . . .''

"I cut off his penis because it had defiled a pure Bannon woman. I cut out his eyes because he'd shamed her with them. I cut off his fingers because of the evil he'd committed with them. I did these things, Pete, *not* because I wanted to. *Not* because I'm some sort of depraved monster. I did them because the Lord God in heaven commanded me to do them! But I didn't kill the others—they were Satan's work, or the work of his demon, the Mad Witch of Olivet.''

Pete watched Tucker's face quiver as his emotion built. The gun started to tremble in his hand, and Pete feared that it might go off. *Okay, it's over*, he said to himself. *We've either got it on tape, or we don't.*

"Jerry!" Pete yelled at the top of his lungs. "*Now*, Jerry! It's gone far enough!"

He saw Dragstead bolt out of the pole deck shed and run toward the head rig at full gallop, holding his pistol in both hands, aiming it at Tucker.

"Drop the gun, Mr. Bannon!" Dragstead shouted. "Drop it right now, and nobody gets hurt!"

Tucker no longer seemed excited. "Oh, Pete—did you really think I'd fall for this? Is your regard for me *that* low?"

"I said *drop* it, Mr. Bannon! Do something stupid and I swear to God, you're a dead man, you perverted fuck! Drop it *now*!"

Pete forced his mouth to work. "I think he means it, Tucker. You'd better drop the gun."

Tucker glanced toward heaven. "Lord, why do you put these aggravations in my path?" He whirled and popped off three rounds at Dragstead, only one of which found its mark. It entered Dragstead's mouth and exited the back of his head, taking a fist-sized chunk of his skull. He went down, convulsed briefly and lay still.

The door of the head rig building opened, and Wally MacKenzie emerged into the glare of the yard lights, hands on his head, looking miserable and defeated. Todd Verduin walked behind him, carrying Pete's camcorder and holding what appeared to be an Uzi submachine pistol. Yet another man followed Verduin, young and rangy, similarly armed. He wore camouflage fatigue trousers, a black sweatshirt and a ski mask.

Verduin shoved MacKenzie against the wall next to Pete. "We found this sorry specimen on a ladder next to that vent." He pointed to where MacKenzie had perched with the camcorder. "He was taping your conversation with Mr. Cochran here. I doubt he got anything good—the light's inadequate, and you've got all that background noise from the boiler. Still, just to be on the

safe side . . ." He took the videocassette out of the recorder and slid it into the pocket of his jacket.

Tucker smiled malevolently at Pete. "This little stunt
wasn't worthy of you, son. I expected something better,
something more creative. You didn't really expect me
to show up without doing a thorough reconnaissance,
did you? And I hired professionals. The least you
could've done is get competent help." He threw a dis-
paraging glance at MacKenzie, another over his shoulder
at Dragstead's body.

"What're you planning to do with us?" MacKenzie
asked.

"Honestly, Wally—don't be thick. I'm going to kill
you, along with your coconspirator, here. God hasn't
really given me any choice in the matter, you see. I'm
going to feed you to the chipper and then run a log or
two through it to obscure all the bloody debris—no
sense making the millmen suspicious, is there? By this
time tomorrow your pieces will be at the Boise Cascade
paper mill, floating in some vat."

MacKenzie groaned and hung his head.

"Come on," Tucker said, waving his pistol. "I want
the two of you to drag your fallen comrade around to
the chipper. You may as well make yourself useful in
your final minutes of . . ."

Suddenly a sharp hiss filled the air, the sound of escaping steam. It came from the power plant next to the
boiler, the site of a great steam engine that drove the
head rig, the resaws and edgers and planers. The ground
shook as gears engaged, as the steam piston started to
chug.

"Someone has started up the power," Tucker said.
He approached Pete and thrust his face close. "You sent
the boiler man home, didn't you? And the watchman?"

Pete nodded, thinking, *Christ, he was three steps
ahead of me all the way.*

"Never mind all this," Tucker shouted to his minions. "Let's get that body around to the chipper."

"But what about whoever's up there?" worried Verduin's pal in camouflage. "What if he sees us and . . . ?"

"Shut up, Gil!" Verduin said. "We'll deal with him later." He grabbed MacKenzie roughly by the shirt and pulled him toward the corner of the building but stopped in his tracks when the head rig started up with an ascending whine. The conveyer engaged with a sharp clank of metal against metal, ready to start its roll into the black opening at the edge of the millpond. The debarker rumbled to life, its wicked knives swiping the air in search of a log to peel.

"He's in there, whoever he is," Tucker shouted above the din, pointing his pistol at the entrance to the head rig building. "That's where the operator console is located."

Gil swung into action. "I'll find the son of a bitch! Give me two fuckin' minutes, man!" He strode toward the door, his Uzi out in front of him. He jerked the door open and plunged inside. Five seconds later he backed out through the door again, staggering, his hands empty of the machine pistol, a logger's ax embedded deep into the base of his neck. He turned toward Verduin, his face slack with disbelief, then tumbled as if he were a marionette and someone had cut his strings.

Tucker stared openmouthed at the dying Gil Monahan, and Pete seized the opportunity. He grabbed the old man's gun hand. "Wally, run!" he shouted, but MacKenzie didn't run. Rather, MacKenzie tackled Verduin from the side, and both rolled to the ground, flailing and fighting. Tucker was strong, Pete found out. And Tucker intended to die before giving up the gun. He stomped Pete's feet with his heavy logger's boots, launching bolts of pain up Pete's legs. Taking an awful chance, Pete let go of Tucker's gun hand and planted a hard right on his chin, snapping his head to one side. But Tucker recovered and fought on, so Pete kneed him hard in the groin and hit him in the jaw again, this time with everything he had. Tucker went down, his gun flying off and splashing in the millpond. As he scrabbled to recover his feet, Pete kicked him in the face, then kicked him in the gut. Now the old man stayed down, wheezing and gasping.

Things didn't go as well for Wally MacKenzie, feisty though he was. Verduin managed to throw him off and scramble away, then turned with the Uzi and fired a quick burst, catching MacKenzie in the arm and the lower body. He leveled the weapon at Pete and would have squeezed the trigger if someone hadn't grabbed him from behind and pulled a hunting knife across his throat. Verduin immediately let go of the Uzi and clutched his neck with both hands, his eyes bulging, blood geysering through his fingers. He sank to his knees, then to his haunches. He sat for thirty seconds or so before death took him.

Nita Vale stood over the body with a hunting knife in her fist, her long white dress grimy with the filth of the sawmill and spotted with blood both old and new. Her hair shone gold in the glare of the floodlights. Her eyes glistened. *She's beautiful*, Pete thought, choking back emotion. *A vision.* In this light she looked enough like Sally to make him cry.

He saw that she'd dropped what appeared to be a cycling pack near the door of the head rig building. As she walked over to pick it up, he noticed that she still limped slightly, and that she wore dark cycling tights beneath the dress. She also wore white Nike sneakers that appeared much too large for her feet. After picking up the bag, she walked over to him, stared for a moment into his eyes. She reached up to touch his face.

He wanted to ask her so many questions, but his heart was too full, and he knew that if he spoke, he would blubber like a little kid. His rationality hung by a thread. *How had she known to come here? And why had she dressed like this? Where had she learned to kill so smoothly . . . ?*

Her arm snaked over his shoulder, and he felt her breath on his face. She leaned into him, her lips parted, her breasts pressing against his chest. Lost in her eyes, he scarcely felt the needle sink into his neck.

XIX

REALITY DIMMED BUT NEVER WINKED COMPLETELY out. His body became a lead weight that he lacked the strength to support, so he simply sank to the ground like a pearl dropped into a jug of molasses. Whenever he could muster the strength to move his eyeballs, he watched her—this dream-thing with the cool hands and the golden hair. This Nita, this Rosa, this *Sally*.

He watched her work, watched her fill the hypodermic needle with some drug from a small bottle, the same one she'd injected into *him*, he would've bet. Watched her go to Tucker Bannon's side as he struggled to recover his senses and get to his feet. Watched her plunge the needle into his neck.

She peeled his clothes until he was naked, his body as white as the underbelly of a fish. The drug had made him docile, pliable, and he seemed not to care. She stretched him out on the ground, face up, and she sang to him—Sally's lullaby, the one in Spanish. Pete could barely hear her voice over the rumble of the mill.

Nunca tengas miedo de la luna,
mi niño, porque ella te cantará un arrullo. . . .

She took from her cycling pack a heavy hammer and a handful of spikes. Somewhere deep in the subbasement of Pete's mind a Klaxon sounded. Revulsion roiled. Understanding of her intentions filtered to him through the drug fog, and he struggled to rouse his leaden body in a desperate effort to stop her. He failed, managing only to scrabble forward a few feet on his hands and knees before falling to his chest. He watched in horror as she nailed Tucker Bannon to the ground beside the millpond, as bugs swarmed over the water, as pale stars peered through the yellow mist of the yard lights. The clanking of the hammer on the spikes reminded him of the noisy radiator pipes in the dormitory room he'd lived in during his freshman year at the University of Illinois.

Another injection now, some other drug, Pete supposed—something to drag the victim back to consciousness and full appreciation of the ordeal ahead. Nita—or was she the Mad Witch of Olivet?—sang the lullaby over and over as Tucker came awake. From her pack she took a small array of utensils and laid them on the ground near one of Tucker's bleeding hands. Pete saw them clearly: an electric carving knife, barbecue tongs, pruning shears, an X-Acto knife.

He tried to call to her, but his speech came out like mush. He raised a hand, tried to signal her, but could only flail. His greatest horror was knowing how powerless he was in the face of this evil, that he had absolutely no way to stop it.

With Tucker awake and wailing loudly, Nita—the Mad Witch—went on with her work, first using the pruning shears to take off his fingers. Straddling his head and holding it tight between her knees, she removed his eyes with barbecue tongs, slicing away clinging vessels and nerves with the X-Acto knife. Finally, she used the battery-powered carving knife to slice off his penis.

Pete tried not to watch but couldn't stop himself. Disciplined worker that she was, the Mad Witch collected the body parts and took them to the edge of the mill-pond, stood still a moment and scattered them across the water. Then she stood over Tucker and surveyed her handiwork thus far. The old man had ceased his wailing. His breath now came in short, sharp huffs. He'd gone into shock, Pete knew. Soon he would die. Singing the lullaby again, the Mad Witch pulled up the spikes from his wrists and feet, tossing them aside. She dragged him toward the maw of the head rig, where the conveyer led to the knives of the debarker.

"Nita, *no!*" The drug was wearing off. Pete could speak and move with some coordination, maybe even stand. "No! Please don't do this!"

Showing incredible strength, the Mad Witch hoisted the white, bloodied form of Tucker Bannon onto the conveyer, positioning him in the trough so that the rollers would carry him into the debarker. She then marched through the door of the head rig building, disappearing from Pete's view. There wasn't any doubt about what she intended to do.

He thought briefly of trying to lift Tucker off the conveyer, but he knew it would be hopeless. Nita would start the contraption before he could get the old man free, and he himself might become caught in it. His best bet was to catch her and try to reason with her, maybe hold her back.

Right—reason with the woman who'd just nailed her uncle to the ground and mutilated him. Restrain the Mad Witch of Olivet. Bargain with the Buckthorn killer.

He chased her through the door, staggering against the jamb and bruising his shoulder. A sign tacked to the inside surface said: REMEMBER—SAFETY FIRST! Beneath the sign hung an outdated calendar with a photo of a woman wearing a sailor's cap and nothing else. The interior of the building was a labyrinthine tangle of gears,

belts, conduit, pipes and railings. The smell of wet sawdust stung his nose and made his eyes water. Spears of
light thrust inward from the powerful floods outside, admitted by cracks in the corroded metal walls.

Pete saw Nita ahead on the walkway, just visible in
her white dress, making her way parallel to the conveyer
that led from the debarker to the head rig. She climbed
a wobbly set of stairs to a cage surrounded in chicken
wire—the control console. Pete almost screamed with
fright as the head rig itself started to whine, its oily teeth
blurring almost to invisibility as the RPMs mounted. She
hadn't wasted any time.

Pete wondered how she'd learn to run this equipment,
then decided he didn't care. She'd probably sneaked in
at night to study the controls with a flashlight. Or years
ago—back when she was a rowdy teen—Tucker himself
might have brought her here, and maybe Sally, too, just
to show his girls how a sawmill worked. He might have
let them sit in the console and showed them how to
control the powerful servos that guided and maneuvered
the logs through the debarker and the head rig. What did
it matter? Nita knew how to operate the equipment. And
Tucker was on his way to the debarker.

The conveyer started to roll. Pete stopped dead in his
tracks, wondering now whether to go forward or backward, whether he should try to overpower Nita or attempt to pull Tucker off the conveyer. He glanced
rearward at a rectangle of yellow light, the opening
through which logs came on the conveyer from the millpond. The air was alive with the grinding of gears and
the shriek of pressurized steam. Servos clanked and
boomed. He saw the fishy-white form of Tucker moving
toward him, prone on the conveyer.

The debarker engaged, its knives whirring as they rotated on their heavy steel drums. Tucker was only ten
feet away, his arms waving now as he tried to pull him-

self out of the conveyer trough. Somehow over the din of the machinery Pete heard him scream.

Pete staggered against the safety rail, felt it give, and barely caught hold of a steel brace to keep from tumbling into the debarker. *Take a bad step or lean wrong, and this mill will eat you,* Wade Beswick had warned. Pete swung one leg over the rail, keeping hold of the brace, and reached downward, trying to ascertain whether he could reach Tucker from here. He saw that he couldn't. So he swung the other leg over and started inching toward the yellow mouth of the conveyer line.

Six feet away stood a vertical bundle of pipes, all dark with age, that joined a similar but horizontal bundle that ran overhead. By the time he reached them, Tucker was nearly directly below. Pete wrapped one arm around the pipes and screamed, for they were near to scalding. Still holding on, he let himself slide down toward the conveyer and just managed to grab the old man's mutilated hand as he moved past him. He gripped the hand with all his might, stopping Tucker's progress toward the fanning knives of the debarker. Tucker screamed, for he'd halted while the conveyer rollers themselves continued to rotate and abrade his bare flesh.

"Help me, Tucker!" Pete shouted, his voice breaking. "You've got to help me! I can't do it alone!" He felt his grip on the hot pipes begin to loosen. If he fell, he and Tucker Bannon would go through the debarker together. "Get out of there, Tucker. Fight it! Pull yourself out!"

"Perversity is in his heart," Tucker wailed, quoting the Bible, his empty eye sockets gaping. *"He devises evil continually. He sows discord . . ."*

Pete knew now that he himself would fall. His left arm, the one encircling the bundle of hot steel pipes, had begun to give. The pain screeched in his head.

"Therefore his calamity shall come suddenly; Sud-

denly he shall be broken without remedy . . .''

And Pete fell. But a strong hand caught him from above and pulled him back. Tucker's bloody hand slipped from his, and Pete heard the old man enter the debarker. The screams were unbearable, though short-lived.

Suddenly Pete was back on the walkway. All around him were people with flashlights, scurrying, hurrying.

''In there—she's in there, at the control console,'' someone shouted.

Uniforms, badges. The cops had come. And a young detective named Roberto Esparza had saved Peter Cochran's life.

23

I

TWO DAYS LATER, ON SUNDAY, APRIL 17, PETE RECEIVED two visitors in his hospital room at Good Samaritan in northwest Portland—Detectives Ashley Tching and Roberto Esparza. They asked how he was and he assured them that he was fine—second-degree burns on his left arm and chest, a few nasty bruises and contusions, but nothing serious. He planned to leave the hospital tomorrow, Tuesday at the latest.

"How about your kids—need any help with them while you're laid up?" Tching asked. Pete thanked her for asking, told her that Vonda Reuben had booked Sarah and Carter into a hotel in downtown Portland and had offered to care for them until he was out of the hospital.

"We thought you might want to know," Esparza said, "that Nita Vale, also known as Rosa Juanita Sandoval, has confessed to all the Buckthorn killings except for the first one, as well as the killing of Daniel Kantor, Todd Verduin and Tucker Bannon. She did all this in the presence of her lawyer, for the record—signed, sealed and peeled, as Lieutenant Kantor might've said. She plans to plead guilty, but the D.A. says he'll believe it when he sees it. By the way, we'll also need a statement from you, but it can wait. I know you've got a lot on your mind right now."

"I appreciate that," Pete said.

"You might also be interested to know that Wally

MacKenzie is on the mend. He's out of surgery, and the doctor's pretty sure he'll have full use of his legs again," Esparza went on. "We talked to him a minute ago, and he told us he'll sign a statement swearing that he heard Tucker Bannon say he hired Verduin to kill Wade Beswick. So you're officially no longer a suspect in the Beswick case."

Pete let out a long sigh, grinned feebly. "Thanks again for what you did last night, Detective. If you hadn't come along when you did, I'd be in twenty or thirty small pieces, right along with Tucker."

"That's what we're here for—to serve and protect." Esparza and Tching traded amused glances.

Pete held up yesterday's *Oregonian*, which had bold headlines screaming across the entire front page:

POLICE APPREHEND BUCKTHORN KILLER!

Task Force Supervisor is among the killer's last victims

"I just learned about Dan Kantor. I'm very sorry. I only met him once, but he seemed like a decent man."

"One of the best," Tching replied, glancing down.

"Something puzzles me, though," Pete said. "I read this thing from top to bottom, and nowhere does it say just how you people happened to show up at the Buckthorn sawmill last night with a squad of troopers. There's some vague reference to an anonymous tip, but that doesn't tell me much."

"We didn't want to talk about it with the media," Tching answered, "because it involved evidence in an ongoing murder investigation. Since Nita Vale has confessed, though, I guess it's okay to tell you."

She explained that Dan Kantor had received a call on

Friday from the FBI concerning the scientific evaluation of footprints found at Terry Grimes's house. The scientists had earlier determined that a small man had left the prints, even though the shoe was an 11-D, a size associated with a large man. In last night's call, Kantor learned that according to the computer simulation that the scientists had developed from the prints, the man also walked with a *limp*.

"At first, when we looked at his notes, we thought he'd written *lump*," Tching said. "His handwriting was unbelievably bad. At any rate, this information spurred Dan to check back with someone he'd interviewed yesterday morning, a veterinarian in Hillsboro who'd reported a loss of sodium pentobarbital back in 1988. Dan had learned that—"

"Sodium *what*?"

Tching explained what the drug was, as well as its significance to the case. Then she explained about the fire that had happened in the vet's office, attributable to a careless volunteer assistant, resulting in the destruction of a large quantity of sodium pent. According to Kantor's notes, he'd intended to call the vet back and get the name of that volunteer assistant, which hadn't seemed important at the time of the interview, but which became important after he talked to the FBI. Tragically, Kantor hadn't lived to carry out his intentions.

"So we made the call for him," Tching said. "The vet told us the name of that volunteer assistant back in 1988—none other than Nita Vale, the brand-new owner and publisher of the *Nehalem County Renegade* in Buckthorn. The doctor also told us that Dan had admired a poster that hung in his back room—something about trees emitting oxygen, saving your breath, I'm not quite sure. The poster had been a gift from Nita. It was a print published by the Earth Insurrection, of which she's an active member."

"Yes, she is," Pete said, remembering that the same poster hung in Nita's newsroom. *Save your breath . . . Save a tree.* "So the Lieutenant had seen the poster on Nita's wall, and after talking to the FBI he remembered that she walked with a limp because she'd hurt her foot while running."

"He also remembered that she had a shrine, like many psychosexual killers do."

"A *shrine*? I don't understand."

"A repository of information about their victims, a place where they can go to relive the murders. Sometimes it's nothing more than a scrapbook. Other times it's an actual chapel in the basement or the attic, where the killer goes to commune with whatever sick god he thinks he's appeasing. The lieutenant made a reference to it in his notes."

"In Nita's case, it was her 'death room,' " Esparza put in, "the place where she collected all the pictures and notes concerning the killings. You've probably seen it."

Pete nodded. He was feeling sick again.

"Of course, she also had the cellar in the stone cabin on Mount Olivet, where she kept the pickled body parts," Esparza added. "The shrinks at VICAP say it could've been her way of memorializing her first lover, the father of her child. Nita herself stated that after Tucker Bannon killed and mutilated Kelly Franklin, she collected his eyes, his sex organ and his fingers—they were all of him she had left. She thought it was important to save them. Why? It's hard for a normal person to understand."

Tching supplied another tidbit. Nita revealed in her statement that she used her bicycle not only to surveil her victims before killing them, but also to escape the crime scenes. After drugging the victims with sodium pent, she used the victims' own pickups or cars to transport them *and* her bike to the scenes. After doing her bloody work, she simply pedaled away on her bike, which explained why the cops never found the tire prints of a second vehicle at any of the scenes.

"I'd appreciate it if you'd keep what we've just told you to yourself," Tching said. "If Nita decides not to plead guilty, this stuff will be important to the prosecution, and we wouldn't want it to get out prematurely."

"I understand. Thank you again, Detectives. Let me know when you want my statement."

After they'd gone, Pete lay back on his pillow and stared at the blossoming Pacific dogwoods outside his second-floor window. A long time later, he picked up the telephone and called his kids.

Epilogue

THE COCHRANS DIDN'T RETURN TO RYE, NEW YORK. Much as Pete had loved Sally, he couldn't live in the house he'd shared with her—not now. Not after Buckthorn. So he put it up for sale, asking somewhat less than he'd asked earlier, and sold it quickly.

Though Buckthorn had changed him more than he could know, he was still a businessman at heart. He found a job in Portland with a small but growing corporation that operated bento shops throughout the metro area. As chief financial officer he played a pivotal role in the company's expansion into Seattle and Northern California. He found a comfortable house in Lake Oswego, a prosperous suburb of Portland, and bought it. The place had a large fenced yard suitable for Gerard, a deck shaded by tall Douglas firs, and a Jacuzzi. Life became even-textured, almost serene. A year after the debacle in Buckthorn, the kids' psychologist pronounced them no longer in need of regular counseling.

Inasmuch as Tucker Bannon had named Sarah and Carter in his will, they inherited the entire Bannon estate, which was in probate for two years. The estimated value, inclusive of the Mount Olivet timberlands, was more than $60 million. As their trustee, Pete faced decisions on how to dispose of the property. On one hand, he wanted to keep the mill in operation for the sake of the people whose livelihoods depended upon it. On the other, he felt a need to preserve Mount Olivet in its pristine condition, since so few other stands of old-growth timber remained anywhere in Oregon. The final decision would wait until Sarah and Carter both reached their majority, so that they could enter into it as educated, enlightened adults.

In the meantime, Pete named Wally MacKenzie the new mill manager, and empowered him to undertake a vigorous program of modernization. The Conifer Group was most eager to finance the program at low interest. The goal was to turn the Buckthorn mill into a state-of-the-art manufacturer of specialty building materials and to retain its workers to operate new machines and make new products. Wally threw himself wholeheartedly into the project and proved himself a resourceful, energetic executive. Scotty Dunn recovered from his injuries and became one of Wally's shift supervisors.

Pete made certain that the Bannon estate provided amply for Esmerelda Sandoval, who moved into a neat little bungalow in Hillsboro. Occasionally he drove out from Portland to visit her, and they talked for hours. Sometimes she visited the Cochrans in Lake Oswego and cooked for them, because this was what she loved.

One warm summer night, after the kids were in bed, she and Pete sat together on his deck and listened to the breeze stir the firs. She reminisced about the days when Sally and Rosa were little girls, about the games they played. She remembered that they'd found a long white dress somewhere, probably a castoff pulled from some neighbor's garbage can. They'd taken turns wearing it. Whichever girl wore it was the Mad Witch, and the other would hide from her—a variation of hide-and-seek. Rosa had never really stopped playing that game, Esmerelda said. And neither had she stopped visiting the Mad Witch's cabin.

At least once a month Vonda Reuben blew into town

and took Pete out for microbrewed ale. During one such session, Pete confided that he still suffered guilt for breaking his promise to Sally. Sometimes the guilt even roused him out of a deep sleep.

"You don't have anything to feel guilty about, Peter Cochran," Vonda assured him. "Look, Sally wasn't exactly honest with you, either. She held back some very important information about her past and her family. If she'd leveled with you in the beginning, you never would've let Tuck and Dolly Bannon in the door, would you?"

Hearing this helped, and Pete starting sleeping well again.

Nita Vale was serving a life sentence without possibility of parole, and Vonda, ever the faithful friend, visited her regularly, something Pete could not bring himself to do. Vonda was also collaborating with the physicians who were studying her friend in an effort to learn what makes serial killers tick.

"She opens up to me because I'm the only one she has," Vonda told Pete one evening over a beer, more than two years after Nita's conviction. "For that matter, she's the only one *I* have—except for you, of course. Anyway, the researchers videotape our sessions. They give me questions to ask before I go in."

"Does Nita know about this?" Pete asked.

"Oh yeah. Actually she's glad about it. She figures, what the hell?—if she can do something for science, then maybe her life hasn't been a total waste."

"So what makes her tick?" Pete asked. "What makes someone do the things she did?"

The big woman thought a moment, rubbing a thick finger along the rim of her beer mug. Then she started to talk, her voice low and cautious. A tear spilled down her nose. She told a story about a little girl cursed with

tainted blood in her veins—*Bannon* blood. The little girl
hadn't asked to be a Bannon, hadn't asked for the abuse
that Tucker Bannon had heaped upon her. The little girl
hadn't asked for the cravings that led her to trap and
torture mice and squirrels, a sin of her childhood that
she confessed to Vonda on videotape. The taint had
made her a monster, just as it had made Tucker a monster, and Topper too.

"I'm not saying that it's all hereditary," Vonda
quickly added, seeing Pete's stricken expression. "You
see, I'm not using the word *blood* in the wholly biological sense. I'm talking about anger and an unquenchable
hunger for revenge. You've got to remember that Tucker
abused her mercilessly when she was young, made her
feel like dirt. Life under his thumb was hell for a little
girl he deemed a burden sent from God. Later, Rosa
found out that he'd killed her father. Then he killed the
boy she loved, mutilating him before her very eyes, and
stole her baby boy from her. How could she *not* have
hated him?"

The tentacles of Rosa-Nita's hatred eventually reached
beyond Tucker Bannon to embrace his mill and his
workers, his town, the people of Buckthorn. Rosa-Nita
came to see herself as a dark angel whose mission was
not only to torment Tucker—as she'd done by sending
him copies of her damning letters to Sally—but also to
exact vengeance from him and the town that clung to
him. So she'd started luring young mill workers with
her feminine charms, sticking needles into them when
they least expected it, and doing to them what Tucker
Bannon had done to the father of her child. She'd become *Vengeance*.

And she'd loved it. Painful as this was for her to admit
it to Vonda, her only friend, she'd loved inflicting pain
and death. This was the taint of Bannon blood, the love
of torture and killing. Unlike most serial killers, Nita had

imposed a rigid discipline upon her murderous routine, one that had kept her from making mistakes and leaving clues that might lead to capture. Only when she decided to break the discipline did she make a mistake—leaving footprints around a victim's home while casing it. Learning of the mistake caused a fissure in the dam that held back her cravings, and when the dam broke, she set upon the task of killing Tucker Bannon without regard for the consequences, not caring whether she was caught, whether she lived or died. Killing Tucker was the one crime that Rosa-Nita didn't regret.

After hearing this Pete had sat silent a long moment, the blood draining from his face. He'd excused himself and gone to the men's room of the pub, spent nearly an hour locked in a toilet stall. He and Vonda never again talked about such things.

Occasionally he nearly convinced himself that visiting Nita was something he needed to do, but he always backed away from it. A part of him felt that he *owed* her for the short time they shared as lovers, but another part yearned to forget that he'd ever made love to a thing that craved inflicting pain and death. Still, questions burned inside him that he desperately wanted to ask her, questions about Rosa-Nita's childhood alongside his Sally's. Had *Sally* ever trapped and tortured small animals? Had *Sally* ever shown any inclination to . . .

No, no. Pete knew that he couldn't bear asking such questions. He also knew that he might not be able to stomach the answers. If tainted blood flowed in his children's veins, Pete Cochran didn't want to know about it.